Futuristic Romance

Love in another time, another place.

"A shining new star has arrived in the futuristic galaxy!"
—*Affaire de Coeur*

TREASURES OF THE HEART

"I came to apologize," Lancer said before she had a chance to order him out.

Thena lifted her chin in defiance and stared him straight in the eye. "Apologize? For what?"

"For being such a boor," he said in soft tones. "When I said your virtue was safe with me, I didn't mean to imply you weren't desirable, because you certainly are."

He moved close enough to inhale her fresh scent. "I simply meant I was brought up to respect a lady, and I would never impose myself on you. See, I brought you a gift, in apology."

He held up the wristcom and watched as her face relaxed.

She reached out to stroke it with her forefinger. "It's beautiful," she said in a hushed voice.

He gently captured her right hand and clasped the bracelet on her arm. Raising her hand to his lips, he kissed the inside of her wrist. Looking deep into her eyes, he asked, "Am I forgiven?"

"Yes, I...yes. How can I ever thank you?"

"Golden Prophecies is the ideal story for those who like their romances with a little myth and magic."
—Anne Avery, bestselling author of *All's Fair*

Golden Prophecies

Pam McCutcheon

LOVE SPELL **NEW YORK CITY**

LOVE SPELL®

February 1995

Published by

Dorchester Publishing Co., Inc.
276 Fifth Avenue
New York, NY 10001

Cover art by John Ennis

The name "Love Spell" and its logo are trademarks of Dorchester Publishing Co., Inc.

Printed in the United States of America.

*For Laura Hayden, Deb Stover, Karen Fox, and Paula Gill—
the wonderful Wyrd Sisters, who believed in me even when
I didn't.*

Golden Prophecies

Prologue

I'd rather be knee-deep in Denebian slime. Lancer Morgan closed his ears and his mind to his father's persuasive voice and stared out the study window. The cold, overcast view, typical of Washington, DC, in March, reflected his mood exactly, and he didn't want the warmth and comfort of the luxurious room to seduce him. The last thing he needed was to relax around this cagey old campaigner.

When the rhetoric paused behind him Lancer crossed his arms and tightened his lips. "I'm not interested."

"You haven't even heard my proposition yet," said Hudson Morgan.

Lancer turned to face him with reluctance. "I don't need to. Damn it, Dad, you know I'm not interested in joining the 'family business.' I'm a holofilm producer. I *like* being a holofilm producer, and I'm not going to enter politics just to meet your image of what a Morgan should be."

"Please, son, just hear me out before you decide."

"If this is just another one of your schemes . . ."

"I promise you it isn't. Please, just listen to my proposition, and if you're still not interested, I'll drop the subject and never mention it again."

"All right. Let's hear it." After all, he could always walk out if he didn't like what his father had to say.

Hudson leaned on one corner of the desk and tapped the disk lying on it. "This is a copy of a report from a scout miner who is also one of our agents. He was prospecting out of his sector on our instructions and found a world of humans no one knew existed."

Intrigued, Lancer relaxed enough to perch on the other corner of the desk. "Humans? That's not very likely. Unless—"

"Right. They're descendants of the *Odyssey*, the colony ship lost over two hundred years ago."

"That's incredible. Why haven't I seen this on the newsvids?"

Hudson leaned forward with a confidential air. "The scout reported directly to me. I've been keeping it quiet until we can investigate. If what he discovered is true, it could have a monumental impact on the entire United Planets Republic."

Lancer grinned. "Okay, you've got me interested. Just what *did* he discover?"

"The inhabitants appear to have some sort of ability that allows them to foretell the future."

"Oh? What kind of joy juice has this scout been swilling?"

Hudson sighed. "I know it's hard to believe, but this man is one of our best agents, and he isn't likely to be taken in by a hoax."

His father wasn't the type to be taken in either, but the whole idea was bizarre. "Does he have any proof?"

"Yes, well, proof of a sort—a prediction, given to him by one of the inhabitants."

"Come on, Dad. Give. What was it?"

Hudson hesitated. "Basically, it implied interstellar war is imminent, though it can be averted."

"Implied?"

"Yes, the wording is a bit obscure, but that's how the agent and I both interpreted it."

"Perhaps it was deliberately obscure, so you could interpret it however you want." Lancer shrugged. "Besides, it's obvious to anyone with half a brain that the *United* Planets aren't exactly united anymore."

"I'd agree with you, but these people have been isolated for over two centuries. How could they possibly know what's going on in the Republic?"

"Perhaps your agent *wasn't* the first one to discover the planet."

"I thought that too, but he has ways of confirming there's been no other spacecraft in the area for over fifty years."

Lancer mulled it over, absently twirling the disk

in circles on the desk. "For the sake of argument, let's say this . . . precognition is legit. How does it work?"

"He said they use a small indigenous animal in their ceremony that looks like a cross between a monkey and a cat—the colonists call them moncats. The moncats seem to have something to do with the predictions, but our agent didn't stick around to learn any more—he quite rightly returned immediately to report."

"So why are you keeping it so hush-hush?"

"Think about it: The potential ramifications are staggering."

Lancer nodded slowly. His father was right. "Yes, I see what you mean. If this got out, you'd have corporations vying for predictions so they could get an edge on their competition. Hell, the crime contingent would be ecstatic, gambling would be a joke, and even ordinary citizens would want to use their abilities to . . . find out who their spouse should be or . . . what Aunt Mazie was really doing in the shed with the gardener."

Hudson smiled grimly. "I'm glad you understand. We need to investigate this thoroughly before we release it to the public, if ever."

Uh-oh, here it came. "So that's what you want me to do? Investigate this planet?"

"Precisely. I need someone to determine how this talent operates and what the impact might be on the Republic."

Lancer crossed his arms in a defensive posture. Hudson was beginning to get to him. "Why me?

You're the Defense Minister—why don't you just send the agent out again?"

"We can't send a scout miner back to the same area. It would be too out of character. Besides, I want to keep this strictly confidential. I can't risk the word getting out—I need someone I can trust completely."

Lancer frowned. "Then why not Alexander or Darian? They're better suited for this than I am."

"Your brothers are too much in the public eye—"

"And I'm not?"

"Yes, of course you are, but for a different reason. As you pointed out, everyone in the family but you is in politics. If they were to make a trip now, when war is imminent, there'd be too much unwelcome speculation."

"Granted, but—"

"On the other hand, you've just finished your current holofilm, and it's well known you prefer to take solo vacations. It's also common knowledge that relations between us are strained, so few people are likely to make the connection, including your brothers."

Well, at least this time *he* was in the know and his brothers were left out. Lancer grimaced. Lord, what a petty thought. When would he ever outgrow this childish need for his father's approval? Lancer had finally reached a point in his career where he was gaining respect, and all his father saw was that it wasn't politics. Maybe this time . . .

"All right," Lancer conceded. "Maybe I am the logical person to go. But why should I?"

A look of pain crossed his father's face. "I'd hoped you'd do it as a favor to me."

Lancer raised an incredulous eyebrow and Hudson took a different tack. "As I see it, these prophecies could play a pivotal part in the coming months. I hate to think what might happen if the rebels gain control of the oracles. They wouldn't hesitate to use them for their own ends, and to hell with the rest of the Republic. It could destroy civilization as we know it."

Hudson's gaze turned intense. "We've *got* to control these abilities before they do—before they even *hear* about them. Don't you see—"

The melodious tones of the intercom interrupted him. Hudson frowned and pressed a stud on his desk. "Yes? What is it?"

Alexander's voice came over the speaker. "The Treasury Minister is holding on line one."

Hudson grimaced and slanted an apologetic look at Lancer.

Lancer held up his hands in resignation. "I know the drill. You need privacy, so I'll just go—"

"Please, son. This shouldn't take long. Could you wait in the next room for a few more minutes—think about it before you give me your decision?"

"All right," Lancer agreed grudgingly. "I'll think about it—but then my decision's final."

Without waiting for a reply Lancer strode into the adjoining room and shut the soundproofed door firmly.

As the ambience of the light, airy room penetrated his awareness, Lancer stilled and let the memories wash over him. This had been his mother's sitting room—and young Lancer's only refuge from the demanding pressures of being the youngest scion of the Morgan family.

Lancer lowered himself reverently to his mother's favorite armchair, remembering. She'd always been on his side, always stood up for him against his father and brothers. She was the only one who'd understood his zest for life and his abhorrence of being sacrificed for the sake of political expediency.

A wave of loving sadness filled Lancer as he stared at her portrait over the fireplace. She'd been so beautiful, so vibrant and alive . . . and had died so young. He missed her.

"What should I do, Mother?" he murmured.

He knew what her answer would have been. She'd always challenged him to look beneath the surface, beyond his emotions, at the larger consequences of his actions. Memory supplied her exact words. *Think about it rationally, dear. What are the pros and cons? What would you gain by doing as your father asks—and what would you lose?*

Her advice was as good today as it had been then. What *would* he gain? Maybe a little of his father's respect for a change. And, admittedly, the satisfaction of knowing he was able to help the Republic in its hour of need. Lancer was as patriotic as the next man; he just didn't like having it shoved down his throat all the time.

Okay, so what would he lose? He'd be one step closer to giving in, to becoming a clone of his father just like his brothers, that was what. If that happened, Lancer would lose his self-respect—and if a man didn't have that, he had nothing.

Damn it, he couldn't be the only choice for this mission. There had to be someone else. Lancer cast about in his mind for other candidates, but none measured up. Much as he hated to admit it, he *was* the obvious choice. And, if his father was to be believed, that meant the fate of the universe was in Lancer's hands.

So, it was his self-respect against the fate of the universe. Gee, tough choice.

Ah hell, he wouldn't necessarily lose his self-respect by accepting this mission. After all, he didn't have to agree to do any more of them. In fact, he'd make damned sure this was the last.

Lancer had to chuckle. It looked like he'd just talked himself into doing as his father asked. He hated the thought of having so much riding on his shoulders, but trust good old Dad to come up with the one argument Lancer couldn't refuse.

Hudson opened the adjoining door and entered, looking apprehensive. "Son—"

Lancer didn't wait to hear any more. He turned to his father in a mixture of anger and wry humor, saying, "Okay, damn it, I'll do it—but only to save the universe. Is that understood?"

Hudson relaxed visibly and smiled. "Yes, son, it's understood."

With his decision made, Lancer was eager to get on with it before he changed his mind. "Good. Now that *that's* settled, what do I tell the natives on this planet?"

Hudson hesitated, obviously debating whether to comment on Lancer's abrupt change of heart. Luckily for Hudson, he chose to ignore it. "Just mention what the Republic has to offer—"

Lancer held up his hands. "Whoa, I'm no diplomat."

"Don't worry. I don't want you to sell them on the Republic. Just mention what we have to offer; then show a film I'll give you. Professional diplomats will follow up later." Hudson paused. "It would probably be best if you use your holofilms as a cover. And I'd also like you to see if you can find out what happened to take the colony ship so far off course. Just remember, your main purpose is to ascertain the validity of their claims."

Lancer nodded. "Okay, I can do that. I might even get a good holofilm out of this—hoax or not." He ran through his upcoming projects in his mind. There was nothing really pressing, nothing that couldn't be delayed. "How long do you think this will take?"

"It takes about two weeks to get to their planet, so I'd estimate you'll be able to accomplish what you need in six to eight weeks."

"Okay, you've got a deal." Lancer stood and shook his father's hand. "By the way, what's the name of this planet?"

"Appropriately enough, they've named it Delphi."

"Delphi, huh? I wonder what cryptic mutterings their oracle will have for me?"

Chapter One

The longer Thena waited outside the Dodona Cavern Council Chamber for the others to join her, the more her curiosity grew. The man from Earth, the Terran, had been left alone inside. She couldn't help but wonder—just what did a Terran look like?

She eyed the small gap in the heavy curtains screening the doorway. There was one way to find out. Should she? It wasn't exactly proper, but just a peek wouldn't hurt.

She peered through the opening at the Terran. He was wandering around the room, touching everything in sight—the smooth redstone walls, the dark morlawood table, the colorful tapestries, even the bioluminescent lightmoss that ringed the room in clay planters.

From this angle she could only see his back. He was shorter than the average Delphian, only half

18

a head taller than herself. He was, however, very well-proportioned; his curious one-piece garment hugged his broad shoulders and narrow hips, appearing to be molded to his body.

At last he turned toward her, and she got a good look at his face. He appeared to be in his early thirties, just a few years older than she was. His tanned face was sharply defined, with a straight nose, a square chin, and dark brown eyes under short, wavy black hair. All in all, she was a bit surprised. He looked so . . . provincial, not at all like the representative of a technologically advanced society. Would he be able to help her with her problem?

Thena's moncat stirred restlessly on her right shoulder and she reached up and gave it an absent pat. "The man looks quite ordinary, Seri. Why is everyone so excited about him?"

"What did you expect?" asked Nevan, who had silently come up behind her. "Two heads and cloven hooves?"

Thena and Seri both started and the moncat tightened her prehensile tail around Thena's neck. Embarrassed at being caught snooping, Thena forcibly composed herself and turned a bland face to the tall blond man.

"Of course not, Nevan. I just expected him to look different—more exotic."

"My dear, you're the highest-ranking pythia on Delphi. There's no need for you to skulk behind the drapes. Why didn't you go in to meet him?"

Thena stiffened. He had no right to censure her,

even if he was her Councilman and Observer. "I was waiting for you and Father. Would you have me meet a strange man unchaperoned?"

Before Nevan could make another of his gently chiding remarks she added, "Never mind, here comes Father now."

As always when she saw her father, Ketori, Thena marveled at how perfectly he looked the role of the Council Captain. He towered over her, his long gray hair and matching gray eyes giving him a look of distinction. His clothing too was gray, the thigh-length chiton and loose trousers enlivened only by the two gold status bands on his sash.

Ketori inspected her, clearly looking for faults. Thena had been determined not to miss meeting the Terran, so she had taken special pains with her appearance. She'd put on her best white chiton and brushed her hair until it shone, catching it up in a polished morlawood comb above her right ear to leave her shoulder free for Seri.

Ketori gave her a grudging nod. He never let up, never let her forget she was the Golden Pythia. Just once, she wished he would greet her as his daughter—not some ideal image into which he was molding her. He seemed to forget he only held his position by virtue of being *her* closest male relative. If she weren't the Golden Pythia, he would be nothing.

A lifetime of obedience kept her silent. Someday she'd find the life-mate who would take Ketori's place as Council Captain. But not yet. First she had to find a solution to her dilemma or no one would mate with her.

Typically, Ketori was spare with his praise. "I'm glad to see you're both so prompt. Remember, this man could help us immeasurably. Don't do anything to jeopardize that."

Nevan frowned. "Why do we need his help?"

Thena remained silent, not wanting to get involved in this minor power struggle. Ketori reprimanded Nevan with a look, and Nevan's defiant gaze fell before his Council Captain. Apparently satisfied with the Councilman's capitulation, Ketori parted the curtains so they could precede him into the Council Chamber.

The Terran turned from his inspection of a tapestry and gave them an engaging smile that crinkled the corners of his eyes and provided a glimpse of perfect white teeth. Thena revised her earlier assessment; maybe this man wasn't so rustic after all.

The stranger shook hands with Ketori and Nevan. "Hello. I'm Lancer Morgan. I'm very honored to meet you."

He then turned to Thena. When she didn't offer her hand he hesitated, then grinned and gently took it anyway.

She let him keep it for a moment, curious to see what he wanted with it. His roguish smile widened as he looked deep into her eyes and brought her hand to his lips.

The kiss, soft and warmly caressing, appeared innocent enough, but it had an odd effect on her, sending a tingle zinging along her nerves from the tips of her fingers straight down to her toes.

"How charming," he said in what Thena was sure was a well-practiced, seductive tone. "If all the Delphian women are as lovely as you, I fear I shall lose my heart forever."

Well practiced, yes. But still, it worked. This was totally outside her experience. *Now* what was she supposed to do?

To add to her confusion, Seri began purring softly. Ketori and Nevan were well aware that the empathic moncat was an accurate reflection of Thena's emotions, but she'd never had problems controlling her emotions around Seri before. Thena had to stop this *now*. Nevan began to frown, and she gently tugged her hand out of the stranger's grasp.

Lancer appeared to suffer the removal of her hand with aplomb and shifted his gaze to Seri, who sat on Thena's shoulder. "Ah, this must be a moncat." Gesturing toward the animal, he said, "May I?"

Few people were brave enough to touch a moncat, even with a pythia's consent—and pythias seldom granted it. But Seri seemed to have no objections, and Thena was curious to see what they would make of each other. She nodded her permission.

Stepping closer to Thena, Lancer raised his hand slowly to the moncat. Rather than bristling at the familiarity, Seri grasped his forefinger in one small paw, brought it to her nose, and sniffed it delicately. Lancer chuckled at the solemn look on Seri's furry little face.

22

Thena found the man's nearness no less disturbing than his kiss. Oh, she'd been close to men before, but never one who was so near her own height. Their breath mingled as he brought his face closer to study the moncat, and Thena became acutely aware that his face was just inches from her own.

How ridiculous! She was acting like a novice, an adolescent pythia unable to control her emotions. *Was this a symptom of*—Thena cut off the thought. No, of course not. It was a perfectly normal reaction to a very attractive man.

Thena licked her lips nervously and Lancer's gaze shifted to their unconsciously moist invitation, giving her a slow, seductive smile as intimate as a kiss. Thena tensed, uncomfortable with his overly familiar behavior. Seri, ever sensitive to the slightest nuance of Thena's emotions, glared at Lancer and emitted a short, sharp hiss of reproof.

Lancer backed off hastily. At his surprised look, Thena gave him an amused smile, hiding her relief. "Moncats sense the emotions of those around them," she explained, soothing Seri's russet fur. "You must have done something to offend her." *Or me*, she added silently, knowing he would understand the unspoken implication.

The Terran gave them both a look of renewed respect and grinned.

Ketori, who had observed the scene dispassionately up to this point, suddenly seemed to become impatient. "Moncats are useful creatures, but hardly the reason you're here. Please, take a seat."

Thankful for the interruption, Thena complied.

Ketori sat at the head of the table with Nevan to his left. Thena started to sit to Ketori's right, and Lancer moved to hold the chair for her. Thena seated herself gracefully, trying to look as though she was quite accustomed to the courtesy, and murmured her thanks.

Nevan frowned again when Lancer sat next to her instead of at the end of the table as expected. Was Nevan jealous? He had no right to be. She knew he wanted to be her life-mate, but she had no intention of exchanging one domineering Council Captain for another.

"What is it you want of us?" Ketori asked Lancer.

Lancer leaned forward. "I'm here for two reasons. First, a few months ago a scout miner returned from a survey of this sector to report the discovery of your colony. Since the original colony and its ship were believed to have perished over two hundred years ago, the United Planets Republic is very interested in discovering what happened. They're also anxious to restore your status and provide you with all the help and assistance the original colonists would have received."

"We seem to have done quite well without your assistance so far," Nevan pointed out.

"That's true. You've done remarkably well, but please don't be too hasty in refusing our aid. The Republic has vast resources that can help you in ways you cannot imagine."

Ketori nodded. "We'd like to hear more, but such a momentous discussion requires the concurrence of the full Council. Can you wait until they're all present so you can explain it in depth to all of us?"

Thena tried to hide her disappointment. She'd seldom been allowed to sit in on Council sessions. Now how would she find out what she needed to know?

"Yes, of course," Lancer said. "When would it be convenient to talk to them?"

"The other three Council members are scattered over the continent. Normally it would take at least two months to call them all together. However, we have an annual meeting at the summer solstice, which is coming up in two weeks. They'll all be here then."

Lancer rubbed his hands together. "Excellent. Now that we've taken care of my official reason for coming to Delphi, I'd like to discuss my personal reasons. You see, I'm a holofilm producer."

"What's a holofilm?" asked Nevan abruptly.

Thena glanced at him in surprise. He wasn't usually this rude.

Lancer hesitated. "It would be easier to show you than to try to explain it. May I?"

Obtaining Ketori's consent, Lancer retrieved a box from behind the drapes and opened it. Pulling out a peculiar instrument made of black metal, he set it on the far end of the table, then made minute adjustments to several round knobs.

"Watch the space in front of you," he directed.

Lancer flipped a switch and an image appeared suddenly above the table, startling them. Thena gazed in wonder at the scene before her. The entire image was only about two hand spans high. The man depicted there was wearing an unusual archaic costume and was declaiming to an invisible audience, " . . . whether 'tis nobler in the mind to suffer the slings and arrows of outrageous fortune—"

"Why, I recognize that speech," said Thena. "It's Hamlet's soliloquy, isn't it?"

Lancer fiddled with some buttons and the sound reduced to a whisper. "That's right. I'm glad to see some aspects of Terran culture have survived here."

"Not much, I'm afraid," said Ketori. "We lost most of our technology quite early. One of the few things that survived were the books our ancestors brought with them. They're our greatest treasures, and we still perform Shakespeare's plays, among others, several times a year."

Nevan scowled. "But *we* don't perform with our backs to the audience."

Lancer smiled at him. "Ah, but that's not all of it. Please, get up and walk around it—view it from all sides."

The three Delphians followed his advice, and Thena was surprised to find they could see all sides of the little man in the image.

Seri was interested too; Thena felt the moncat's natural inquisitiveness intensify until Seri couldn't stand it any longer. Seri leapt softly onto the table, then crept up to sniff the image. Rising to her hind legs, she reached out to touch it. When her paw passed through the man with no resistance, she hissed and backed up quickly, then leapt to

Thena's shoulder and turned an accusing look on Lancer.

He laughed. "This is a holofilm. Some are used as educational tools or as a factual record of past events, but most, including mine, are produced strictly for entertainment—just like the plays you perform."

He turned off the machine and they seated themselves.

"It's all very interesting," said Ketori. "But I'm afraid you'll find no one on Delphi who could operate your machine or afford to purchase it."

"Oh, I'm not selling it! When the news of your lost colony is released the rest of the galaxy will be clamoring for information about you, so I'd like to make a holofilm about Delphi to tell your story."

This was all moving so fast, and with so many new concepts being thrown at them, Thena was having a hard time taking it all in. Ketori looked uncertain too.

Lancer added, "Of course, you'll be compensated for your cooperation in whatever manner of payment you choose."

To Thena's surprise, Ketori began to look interested. "We may want to reacquire some of the technology we lost," he conceded. "But I doubt payment for our story will purchase all we would need."

Lancer grinned. "You'd be surprise how much people will pay for entertainment. And I can guarantee that as soon as the word gets out that your colony has been found, you'll be inundated with merchants who'll want to trade with you."

"We've regressed markedly in the last two hundred years. What could we possibly have to trade that would interest you?"

Lancer spread his arms wide and gestured at the contents of the room. "Your marvelous artworks, for one. The social elite of the galaxy vie with one another to find and display new, unusual pieces, and are willing to pay a great deal to indulge their tastes. In fact, the holofilm would be a good advertisement for your wares. I'm sure there are many things you take for granted that would be equally valuable."

He rubbed his hand across the morlawood table. "This table, for example. I assume it's handmade?" At Ketori's nod, Lancer added, "It would sell easily. The elite also appreciate unusual pets. Your pretty little moncats would bring a good price."

Pets! Thena had been fascinated by the man's enthusiasm and excellent sales technique, but now she felt compelled to intervene. "I'm afraid you don't understand. Moncats aren't pets. They're a necessary part of the oracular ritual and bond for life to one pythia. In any case, we don't choose them. They choose us."

"Pythia?" asked Lancer. "I'm not familiar with that word."

Ketori explained. "It comes from one of your ancient Earth legends. The shrine at Delphi was sacred to Apollo, the god of prophecy and patron of philosophy and the arts. To honor his killing of the monster python, his oracles were called pythias. Our ancestors were struck by the similarity, so they adopted their ways as our own."

Lancer raised an eyebrow. "Yes, the scout mentioned something about your . . . talents."

Thena bristled at the disbelief in his voice, but Ketori merely raised an eyebrow in return and replied calmly. "We've kept records since the first prophecy. I can assure you the existence of the prophetic talent is quite true and scientifically valid. In fact, I've devoted my life's work to determining the optimum combination of genes a pythia must possess to produce the highest accuracy rate. My daughter is living testimony of my achievements."

Thena shot Ketori an irritated glare. He had a habit of discussing her as if she wasn't there. He seemed to forget she was not only the Golden Pythia— she was a human being with thoughts and feelings of her own.

Lancer gave her an appreciative glance. "And an admirable one at that. I'm sorry for sounding so skeptical, but this talent doesn't exist anywhere else in the United Planets Republic. I'd like to learn more, so I can describe your talents accurately in the holofilm."

There went Thena's hope. If the prophetic talent didn't even exist anywhere else, he certainly couldn't help with her problem.

As Ketori appeared to contemplate the offer, Thena interrupted. "Father, are you seriously considering this? To let strangers who don't even believe in our prophecies come disrupt our society?"

Lancer answered her by addressing Ketori directly. "Under the rules of the Republic you control who comes and goes on your planet and what they may do once they're here."

Thena wasn't convinced. "It may be too late. Just the fact that two Terrans have visited Delphi has already put strange ideas into our people's heads and made them dissatisfied with their lives. Your mere presence sows dissension."

This time Lancer directed his remarks to her. "If the colony had landed where it had intended, your people would have the technology to make their lives much simpler," he said gently. "Can you honestly say that's wrong?"

"I am not—"

Ketori broke in. "That's enough, Thena. This is the Council's decision, not yours."

He was right, of course, but he could have found a more diplomatic way of wording his rebuke. Thena concentrated on controlling her irritation so Seri wouldn't broadcast Thena's feelings to the entire group.

She turned a serene face to Nevan. Would her Councilman back her against the Council Captain? Nevan gave her a bland smile that revealed nothing. Of course he wouldn't. She was stupid to even try.

The backing came, unexpectedly, from Lancer. "Though I don't agree with your daughter's assessment, she has a valid point." He darted a sidelong glance at Nevan. "And since other Council members may feel the same way, I'd like to get to know your planet and the people a little better."

Thena frowned. She hadn't expected support from that direction. The question was, *why* was he backing her? At times like this she wished she could read people's emotions as well as Seri's.

Lancer continued. "I won't go anywhere or film anything without your permission. I just want to see where we could best help you and, if you wish, assist you in finding good trade items. Of course, I'll need a guide to show me around and answer questions."

Lancer turned to Thena and smiled that devastating smile again. "Would you be my guide? That way you could be certain I won't corrupt any of your people, and I might even convince you there is some merit to what we have to offer."

Nevan interrupted. "I'm afraid that's out of the question."

Thena, who had opened her mouth to say essentially the same thing, was annoyed by Nevan's belated assumption of authority. "Oh? Why is that?"

Ketori turned a puzzled look on Nevan. "Yes, tell me. Why *is* it out of the question?"

"Her duties . . ."

"Nonsense. I'm well aware of my daughter's schedule. She'll be off pythia duty for the next two weeks. Any other duties you have assigned her can be done by someone else or delayed," Ketori said in a tone that would brook no argument. "Do you have any other objections?"

In the face of Nevan's thin-lipped silence, Ketori turned back to Lancer. "If you wish to know our people, you should live among us. Nevan will provide you with guest quarters and Thena will meet you tomorrow morning to show you our way of life. Is that suitable?"

"Very suitable, thank you. But I do need to visit my ship to retrieve some of my personal belongings."

"Nevan can assist you there as well. Come, Thena; let's leave them to it."

Thena followed her father out of the Council Chambers, but glanced back for one more look at the Terran. For a fleeting moment her gaze locked with his.

Thena's heart leapt into her throat. The look he gave her was of such scorching intensity; it left absolutely no doubt of his attraction to her. The way his gaze traveled over her body, lingering on her breasts, should have made her angry. Instead, she felt a warm feeling of pleasure and . . . gratification wash over her. It had been a long time since anyone had seen her as just a woman, and it felt good.

Thena recalled that look frequently over the evening and again the next morning as she lay in bed. But no matter how good it made her feel she didn't need some Terran coming along and ruining her life with a few provocative smiles—there were many far more suitable life-mate candidates on Delphi.

She needed someone who was familiar with her own world and its people, someone who understood and appreciated the very important role her life-mate would play in governing the planet. Someone like Nevan.

Thena grimaced at the thought. No, not Nevan.

But she *was* the Golden Pythia, not some village girl ripe for a flirtation. She'd just have to remember her position and discourage Lancer's attentions, hard as that might be.

Apollo take the man! He wasn't worth agonizing over. She rose from the bed and dressed, resolutely banishing all thoughts of his devastating smile from her mind.

Taking Seri up on her shoulder, Thena navigated the winding corridors toward the guest chambers and found Lancer's quarters. Since his drapes were still drawn it appeared he wasn't ready yet. She waited a few minutes, but he still didn't appear.

Thena was reluctant to enter a strange man's chamber alone—especially this man's—but she wanted to get started on the morning's tour. Making a quick decision, she turned to Seri and, concentrating hard, sent the moncat a mental picture of what she wanted her to do. Seri chittered her agreement and slipped through a small opening in the curtain.

The thick walls and heavy fabric prevented Thena from hearing what was going on in the chamber, so she stilled her thoughts and sought Seri's mind. *Anxiety . . . surprise . . . irritation.* Thena felt more than heard Seri's peevish scolding of Lancer and then heard his unrestrained laughter as he thrust aside the drapes and spotted Thena outside.

"Ah," he said, "I thought you must be here. Little Seri caught me by surprise and I'm afraid we came nose to, er, kneecap rather suddenly. Is it customary to use moncats to announce your presence?"

"No, it's customary to open your draperies when you are willing to receive visitors."

He gave her a disarming grin and moved the offending fabric aside, then gestured her into the living area.

"Sorry, I didn't know. Why didn't you just knock or something?"

Thena steeled herself against his charm. "Knock? On what? The stone walls? The fabric drapes?"

He chuckled. "Okay, you've got a point. I'll know better next time."

"Are you quite ready?"

He gave her a quizzical look. "Well . . . yes. Just let me get a couple of things."

Lancer entered the bedroom and picked up his equipment. Had he been too hasty in requesting Thena as a guide? His motives hadn't been exactly pure—he'd wanted to get to know her better and hadn't been able to resist needling the possessive Nevan. It was tough to like a guy who towered over him and looked like a marble statue of a Greek god—and acted just as warm.

Thena was far too warm and real to play Hera to Nevan's Zeus. Oh, she had the classically beautiful face of a Greek statue, but her voluptuous curves and rippling waves of honey-blond hair definitely gave her a more earthy aspect. At least she'd started out warm and friendly when he'd first met her. What had he done to turn her into this ice maiden who wore her dignity like a shield?

He returned to the living area and announced, "I'm ready."

Thena looked apprehensive. "What's that you're carrying?"

It was a reasonable question. After all, with their level of technology, she wouldn't be able to tell a stunner from a depilator.

Lancer hefted the object in his right hand. "This is a holocam. It records sound and movement like the holofilm you saw yesterday, but in very limited form."

"I see," said Thena, and hesitated. She pointed to the large bag slung over his shoulder. "And that?"

"It's a carryall. I keep extra tapes in it, different lenses, things like that."

She looked confused but said, "Very well. What would you like to see first?"

He stowed the holocam in the bag. "I'd like to see how you live, where you eat, work, play, and so on." His stomach rumbled and he looked at her plaintively. "Can we eat first?"

Damn. He'd made her blush. He didn't mean to sound censorious; he was just trying to amuse the girl.

Thena turned toward his bedroom and called sharply, "Seri!"

The moncat came running and, using the table as a springboard, leapt lightly to Thena's shoulder.

Good grief, she took that animal with her everywhere. Did she sleep with it too? And what did she do with it when she made love?

Lancer grinned. Having that curious, furry little face watching his technique would be enough to unman anyone. He wondered how the Delphian men managed.

Thena's face froze into an aloof mask. "I'm sorry for keeping you. Shall we go?"

The ice was back. Well, he'd just have to wait for the right time to heat things up and see if he could thaw her out a bit. He glanced once more at her luscious curves. Yep, it was definitely worth a try— it would give him something to look forward to.

Lancer followed Thena and Seri through the corridors and turned his attention to his surroundings, marveling at the colonists' adaptation to an alien environment. The cavern's native lightmoss had evidently been cultivated to provide illumination everywhere, and the colonists had taken ingenious advantage of the natural formations to construct the rooms and corridors; very few of the walls bore the telltale marks of a ship's digging lasers. And the air—Lancer sniffed appreciatively. How did they keep it so fresh? They must have hidden fans somewhere, keeping the air in constant circulation.

They passed several guest chambers and then turned down a branching corridor. Thena stopped in front of an opening to a dimly lit cavern, and Seri hopped to the floor and went inside.

Lancer peered in as well. "What's this used for?"

Thena raised her finger to her lips and said softly, "This is where the moncats eat. Our communal dining area is in the next room."

"I see," he said, equally as soft. "Why is the light so low?"

"They prefer it that way."

Lancer removed the holocam from his carryall and smiled at her. "Would they mind if I filmed them?"

"I guess not—just don't make too much noise."

Lancer flipped on the infrared and turned the holocam to record the scene. In the center of the room were two stone slabs. One was heaped with fruit and scraps of meat, and another was hollowed out and filled with water. He could see the food plainly, but no moncats, not even Seri.

"Where are they?"

Quietly, she said, "Look at the walls."

Now that she'd directed his attention, Lancer noticed small niches spaced intermittently around the room. About a third of them were occupied by moncats enjoying solitary meals.

"I thought they'd be more boisterous."

"Yes, they are rather rambunctious, aren't they? They love humans, but their desire for solitude when they eat and sleep is inherent to their species. To tell you the truth, this time apart is somewhat of a relief for both of us."

Well, that answered the sleeping question. And he'd finally gotten Thena to loosen up a little. He lowered the holocam and essayed a friendly smile, but that only caused her to withdraw again.

"Let's get our breakfast, shall we?" she said.

They entered the communal dining room next door, and Lancer gratefully recognized eggs, bread, and fruit among the assortment of food on the serving line. He filled his tray and followed Thena to a large table in the center, where they joined a man and a young woman already sitting there.

Thena introduced them. "Carina is one of our newer pythias, who just joined us here at Dodona. She'll be taking her tests soon, and Orgon, her Observer, is helping her get acclimated."

Carina gave him a sparkling smile, but Orgon just grunted and applied himself to his food. My, the men on this planet were a chummy lot. Thena's shield of ice was nothing compared to Orgon's permafrost. "Oh? What does an observer do?"

Carina, a pert charmer, peeked up at Lancer through dusky eyelashes. "Why, he observes his pythia's predictions and records them, of course. But that's boring. Earth must be *so* much more interesting. Do you think I'll ever have the chance to go there?"

Lancer smiled. "If my fellow Terrans ever get a good look at you, you'll be fighting them off in droves."

His instinctive gallantry backfired. Carina was delighted, but Thena didn't appear to be amused. He leaned close to Thena and added softly, "I, however, have already lost my heart to another Delphian."

Thena gave him a disdainful look and stared fixedly at her meal. He could almost feel the frost form. At this rate, he'd be needing his parka soon. He returned his attention to Carina.

"If you can tell the future, you should be able to tell *me* if you're going to visit Earth."

Carina giggled. "How can I? We're not in the querent caverns, and that question's too silly to waste a pythia's time. Besides, I'm not a full-fledged pythia yet. May I ask you some questions about Earth?"

"Sure." He might as well get some work done while he was at it and record their dress and mode of speech. "Do you mind if I film you while we talk?"

Carina looked confused and glanced at Thena for guidance. Thena nodded curtly, and Lancer focused the holocam on Carina.

"What do you want to know about Earth?" he asked.

"How do your pythias live?"

"We don't have pythias on Earth."

Carina's mouth fell open. "Why not? What happened to them?"

"We've never had them. Your prophetic ability hasn't been found on any other planet in the Republic. You're unique."

"But what do you do when a crime is committed?"

"Our criminal justice system has people who are trained to present evidence on both sides, and a decision is made based on the evidence."

"But without pythias to uncover the true facts in the case, you could punish the wrong person or let a guilty one go free."

"I'm afraid that does happen occasionally, but not as often as you'd think."

"And how do you identify the poor people who are incapable of living in society because they're unbalanced?" Carina persisted.

She made it sound so easy. He wished they did

have a foolproof way of spotting the nut cases—he'd run into some very strange characters on holofilm sets.

Bored with Carina's ingenuous questions, Lancer zoomed in on a more interesting sight—Thena's classic features. "We have doctors, healers who specialize in mental disorders."

Thena had been silent and unmoving during most of the conversation but she perked up at this statement. She leaned forward and opened her mouth as if to speak, then glanced at Orgon and apparently changed her mind.

How interesting, thought Lancer. *What she was going to say? And why did she change her mind about saying it?*

Orgon seemed to read Thena's glance differently. He turned to Carina and said, "I think you've bothered the man enough. Let's finish our meal so we can get on with your lessons."

Carina lowered her gaze obediently to her plate and they finished the rest of their meal in silence, then excused themselves.

Lancer didn't mind a bit. Now that they were gone, he was able to film the rest of the dining room. He panned the room slowly.

When he finished his sweep Thena tapped him on the shoulder. "Are you ready to visit the workrooms now?"

He lowered the holocam. "Sure; lead on."

Seri joined them at the door, and Thena led the way. "When our pythias have no criminal cases to resolve and no querents to attend, they spend their time in the workrooms, weaving clothing or tapestries, painting, throwing pottery, or performing various other artistic pursuits."

Maybe he wouldn't need his parka after all. The ice maiden appeared to be thawing, almost as if she'd suddenly found a reason to cultivate his company. "That's all, just artistic pursuits?"

"Yes, we exchange our oracular services and our goods with the villagers for food and necessities. It's a good trade," she added defensively. "We can't raise food in the caverns, and the villagers get the luxuries of life they don't have the time to produce. Aren't your mind doctors in the same situation?"

"We call them psychiatrists."

She tried the unfamiliar word on an inexperienced tongue. "Well, do these . . . psy . . . psychiatrists grow their own food?"

"No, you're right. They exchange services much as you do through a different bartering system—money." He began to explain the concept, but she interrupted him.

"Yes, yes, I learned about that in my history lessons. What exactly do these psychiatrists do?"

"Mainly, they listen while their patients talk." They approached the opening to a large cavern, and Lancer changed the subject. "Which workroom is this?"

Thena grasped his sleeve. "Please, it's important. I need to know more."

Lancer was surprised at her intensity. Before he could reply she glanced over his shoulder and released his sleeve abruptly. Backing away, she said, "Never mind, I . . . I . . . we'll talk later."

Lancer looked over his shoulder and raised a hand in greeting to Nevan. Now, why would such a seemingly normal, self-possessed young woman need to know about psychiatrists? And why didn't she want her Councilman to know about it?

Chapter Two

The next morning, Lancer still didn't have any answers. Nevan had stuck to them like polyglue the day before, and Thena seemed reluctant to pursue her question in her Councilman's presence.

Her other questions had been succinct and to the point, and Lancer had been impressed with the depth of knowledge Thena had shown about her world and her people. He had revised his opinion of her. She truly cared about the people of her world and worked to better their lot—she was no mere ornamental figurehead.

And that was another mystery. Thena seemed totally unaware of her voluptuous beauty and, strangely enough, so did everyone else. Were all men on this planet dead below the waist? Or did it have something to do with this talent of theirs? All in all, Thena was quite an enigma.

The enigma herself appeared at the open doorway of his quarters with the ever-present Seri on her right shoulder. Lancer felt his temperature rise. Thena's loveliness would put any holofilm star to shame.

Her honey-blond hair rippled in shining waves down the center of her back, caught up over her right ear in a morlawood comb carved in the shape of a flower. A beaten gold armlet resembling a Terran python wound sinuously up her left arm, disappearing into the split sleeve of a flowing white gown modeled on the ancient Greek chiton. The garment fell in graceful folds to her sandaled feet, embellished only by gold bands that edged the hem and sleeves and crisscrossed her full breasts, emphasizing her lush, enticing figure.

Lancer let a heavy sigh escape his lips. That dress should be declared illegal for the things it was doing to his testosterone level. The lady had intelligence, dignity, and drop-dead looks. It was a lethal combination.

He hesitated. She didn't *look* frosty today, but . . .

Thena smiled. "I see you remembered to open your draperies today. That's an auspicious start."

Good—no ice. He could leave his parka in his luggage. "Yes. I wasn't sure how Seri felt about playing fetch with dilatory Terrans, so I thought I'd save her the trouble."

Thena surprised him with a charming little giggle. Seri appeared equally as amazed. She opened her eyes wide, took a firm grasp on Thena's ear with her left paw, and reached down and gave Thena a gentle pat on the cheek with her right. Apparently satisfied the phenomenon wasn't dangerous, she resumed her position on Thena's shoulder and gave Lancer an unblinking stare.

Was that a surge of approval he felt? Nonsense. Next he'd start believing in prophecies.

"You're right," said Thena. "Seri's not used to running errands. She didn't mind, but she did let me know it was quite beneath her dignity to do so."

Ah, so that explained the giggle. "She let you know? How?"

"Moncats, being empathic, can send and receive emotional impressions from those they're bonded to. Seri is one of the best. I just visualize what I want her to do and she picks it up easily. That's how I got her to 'fetch' you yesterday."

Okay, he could buy that. Empathic animals weren't unknown in the Republic. It might even explain that sensation he'd had earlier. "And only . . . pythias have moncats?"

"Yes, by the moncats' choice. They won't bond with anyone else, though they can become very close to a pythia's family. In fact, that's one of the earliest indications of a young girl's talent—her ability to bond with a moncat."

"That's too bad. You'll have a lot of disappointed Republic citizens when they learn they can't have one of these pretty creatures."

Thena's expression became intent and she stepped closer to him and lowered her voice. "Do you think—"

"Thena, my dear," said Nevan, who had appeared

45

in the doorway behind her. "You're keeping our guest waiting. I'm sure he must be hungry. Shall we adjourn to the dining room?"

Annoyance flickered across her face, though she controlled it quickly. Hmm, curiouser and curiouser.

Turning to Lancer, she said, "We're dining this morning with Nevan and my father. Are you ready to go?"

Lancer agreed, and they joined Ketori in the dining room. Ketori nodded a greeting and gestured for them to take a seat. The Council Captain and his party seemed to merit special attention. Instead of going through the line, they were served with exotic fruits, a nutty-tasting bread, and a mild, pleasant cheese.

"Have you been seeing all you wanted?" Ketori asked Lancer.

"Yes, thank you. Your daughter is an excellent tour guide." Lancer paused. What had he said to make Nevan frown? "Yesterday, we visited the workrooms, the dining areas, the bathing areas, and some of the schoolrooms."

"Excellent," said Ketori. "What do you plan to show him today, Thena?"

"I thought perhaps he'd like to see the querent caverns."

Lancer didn't feel up to pretending a belief in their prophetic powers today. He swallowed a bite of fruit. "If you don't mind, I'd really like to visit the *Odyssey*, to see if I can find some clue as to why it landed here."

Ketori looked interested. "Yes, I think that can be arranged. I'd like to learn more of our origins myself."

"You don't know?" Lancer couldn't help but sound surprised.

"No, not really. History says our ancestors decided to renounce all ties with Earth once they landed here, to discourage people from counting on a rescue someday." Ketori smiled wryly. "They did too good a job; nothing but legends have been passed down to this generation."

"But the ship . . ."

Ketori shrugged. "After a few generations restrictions eased and attempts were made to try to get into the ship, but all efforts were frustrated by the loss of the technology. Finally the Council had to place the ship off-limits to everyone, to keep them from hurting themselves by trying to get into it. Can *you* get inside?"

"Yes, I have the plans of the ship from the original builders. I'm sure we'll be able to get in." Lancer turned to Thena. "Would you like to go too?"

Thena's eyes sparkled and she smiled broadly. She opened her mouth to answer but was interrupted by Nevan.

"That's hardly appropriate, now, is it?" he asked.

Thena looked surprised. "Not appropriate? What do you mean?"

Nevan's voice remained soft. "You aren't thinking. The trip will take at least three-quarters of a day, so it will be necessary to spend the night at the ship. You have your position to think of, and your reputation to uphold."

Thena slowly put down her fork and assumed an air of dignity. "You forget who I am. No one on Delphi would *dare* touch a pythia."

Nevan nodded. "That's true, but our guest is not from Delphi, and while *we* might trust him"— Nevan shot Lancer a private glance that said exactly the opposite— "the rest of our citizens might not be so understanding."

Thena turned to face Lancer. "What about your ship? It could make it to the *Odyssey* and back in one day, couldn't it?"

Lancer nodded. "Yes, but it's an interplanetary ship; it's not really designed for short hops."

"Why don't I go with you?" Nevan interposed smoothly. "Since I'm your Observer and your Councilman, no one could say *I* had anything but your best interests at heart."

Thena didn't seem very happy with Nevan's solution. "Yes, that's true, but I still don't think it's necessary."

Ketori frowned. "Nevan's right. You'll go only if he accompanies you."

Nevan turned to Lancer with a smirk. "Can you ride a horse?"

So that's why Nevan seemed to be supporting this trip all of a sudden—he wanted to make a fool of the greenhorn Terran. For the first time in his life Lancer blessed his upbringing as a rich man's son. He loved horses; at last all those horse shows and gymkhanas would come in handy.

"Yes, of course. A true gentleman has many skills

in his repertoire, including riding horses."

Lancer smiled to himself. He'd managed to strike the right note. Ketori and Thena looked pleased, and Nevan's smirk disappeared to be replaced by . . . what? Was that a flash of anger?

Thena stood up. "Good. Nevan, you can help get Lancer outfitted for the trip. I'll get the provisions and meet you at the stables in an hour."

Nevan agreed, and Lancer followed him out the door, resolving to make the most of the trip despite the surly Councilman's presence.

Thena waited impatiently at the stables for the men to show up. She had changed into soft buckskin breeches and a long-sleeved tunic and was eager to get started. She didn't often get to leave the Dodona caverns, so she was really looking forward to this trip.

Thena felt more optimistic than she had in months. Finally she had some hope, however slim, of finding someone who might be able to help her with her problem. She forced herself to control her excitement—it was making Seri jittery.

She heard voices coming, and Nevan and Lancer entered the stables, both dressed as serviceably as she. They filled the saddlebags with the provisions she'd brought, and Lancer gave his horse a meticulous inspection.

"Is something wrong?" she asked.

"No, I was just admiring this fellow. Your lighter gravity has made the basic Terran stock evolve into taller and leaner copies of their forebears."

The people on Delphi had probably changed, too, she realized, if Lancer's shorter height was any indication.

"Are you sure you can manage him?" Nevan asked in mock concern. "He's not too big for you, is he?"

Lancer just smiled and swung easily up onto the animal. Nevan and Thena mounted as well, and Seri moved from Thena's shoulder to the saddle horn in front of her.

They rode out of the caverns, and Thena was glad to see the day was mild and sunny. It appeared their trip would be comfortable and uneventful—if Nevan would just stop trying to needle Lancer.

They rode down the craggy, red-hued mountain toward the plains, and Thena drank in the rugged beauty of her world. The glossy green leaves and gray bark of the indigenous morla trees were a harmonious contrast against the red soil. The odd combination of the rich, spicy fragrance of the trees mingled with the wind-borne wildflower fragrances and the pungent aroma of her horse, making her feel closer to the land and at peace.

The only discordant notes were Seri's thoughts of boredom and the glaring reflection from the Terran's small ship in a nearby clearing.

As if it reminded him of the purpose of their trip, Lancer said, "Your ancestors were lucky to find such a habitable planet. Does your history give any clue at all as to why they landed here?"

"Not really. Our legends tell us the gods were angry with the blasphemous attempt to cross the heavens, so they forced the ship to land. Apollo took pity on them and guided them here in recompense for their suffering."

"You're right, that's not much help. Perhaps we'll learn more at the ship."

Thena rode closer to Lancer so they could talk more easily. She was concentrating so hard on how to phrase her all-important question, she didn't sense Seri's intentions. With a sudden leap, the moncat jumped from Thena's saddle to Lancer's shoulder.

Lancer jerked involuntarily on the reins. His horse reared and Seri lost her balance, grabbing Lancer's ears for support and ending up spread-eagled across his face.

Nevan rode closer. "Are you having some difficulty?" he asked smoothly.

Lancer gently detached Seri from her death-grip on his head and moved her to a more secure spot in front of him. Seri peered up at him anxiously and Thena felt the moncat's strange blend of apprehension and security.

The apprehension vanished when Lancer chuckled. "No, this little lady just caught me off guard. I'm not used to having company on a horse—or on my face, for that matter."

Thena laughed in relief. It was the second time he'd made her laugh, though she hadn't done so in months. It just added to the pleasure of her day. They shared a look of amusement and she couldn't help but giggle again. He'd looked so funny with Seri plastered across his face. Thank goodness he was such a good sport.

Nevan smiled too. Or was that a grimace?

"I'd be more than happy to take Seri up with me," Nevan said. "I'm more accustomed to my mount, and we wouldn't want you to have a mishap."

What was wrong with Nevan today? He didn't usually make so many sniping comments. And why was he offering to take Seri? He knew Seri didn't care for him.

Wait—if Nevan became absorbed in making friends with Seri, Thena would have some time alone with Lancer to learn more about Earth's psychiatrists. Nevan reached out for the moncat, and Thena mentally urged Seri to go to him. Unfortunately, Seri didn't cooperate. Pulling her small body to its full height, she aimed a short hiss at Nevan, then turned her back on him and curled up in front of Lancer and went to sleep.

Lancer grinned. "Sorry, old man. I think the little lady is quite comfortable where she is."

Thena had to agree, but couldn't help feeling a small stab of jealousy. Seri had never preferred anyone else's company to hers. It wasn't often moncats took to anyone other than a pythia's immediate family, and Seri was more particular than most. Yet she certainly seemed enamored of this Terran.

Nevan shot an irritated glance at Seri and drew closer to Thena and Lancer. It was obvious he planned to stick to them like morla sap for the rest of the trip, effectively preventing Thena from asking Lancer any further questions.

Thena ignored Nevan's silent, forbidding countenance and chatted with Lancer about trivial things. They discussed and filmed the scenery along the way, and she found herself sharing a growing camaraderie with him.

The ride was downhill most of the way, so Thena was relieved when they finally reached the level plains in late afternoon. She reined in her horse to take in the view, and the two men stopped beside her.

She had only seen it once before, on a school trip many years before. It was just as she remembered it. The colony ship was clearly visible two miles away, just beyond the outlines of an ancient settlement. The enormous vessel, shaped like a fat needle with many strange protuberances, stretched for half a mile. It appeared to be nestled in a mound of green vegetation, though the sun still reflected dazzlingly bright from its exposed surface.

Excitement mingled with a bit of awe filled her. Her ancestors had traveled through the unknown perils of space in that ship—traveled with their friends, family, possessions, livestock, and all of the paraphernalia necessary to support the colony. She wanted badly to see inside this piece of history. What was she waiting for?

Lancer gave her a roguish grin, then stood in his stirrups and whooped in sheer elation. Falling back into his seat, he kicked his mount into a gallop across the plains.

Thena laughed in delight. Poor forgotten Seri was clinging to his saddle for dear life—and if Thena didn't hurry, they'd beat her to the ship. She charged after him, matching his pace, and Nevan was forced to try and keep up.

Their wild ride finished abruptly at the ship. Seri had managed to stay with Lancer the whole way, but now that they had stopped, she gave full vent to her displeasure. Scolding Lancer stridently, she escaped to the security of Thena's shoulder.

Thena soothed the quivering moncat and took a closer look at the ship. What had appeared to be a green nest was actually the accumulated debris of two centuries that covered the base of the ship.

Thena's exultation turned to dismay. "How are we ever going to get inside?"

Lancer dismounted and removed some things from his saddlebags. "I've got some sketches of the ship on film. Let's take a look."

Thena and Nevan dismounted and Lancer activated his small holocam, projecting a likeness of the ship. He pointed to one spot on the image. "This is the passenger airlock. According to the plans, it should have a manual override." He squinted at the ship.

Taking swift strides to one section, Lancer compared it to the image. "This looks like the right spot. We'll have to dig out the opening. C'mon, Nevan, we've got some work to do."

To her surprise, Nevan had no objections. In fact, he looked as excited as Thena felt. They all put their backs into the job, and it took the rest of the afternoon to clear the area Lancer indicated. Seri helped by supervising the operation from a spot atop the mound, chittering away in what she obviously thought were sounds of encouragement.

When they finally reached the airlock door Seri abandoned her self-appointed post and came down to inspect it more closely. Thena took a break and swiped the moisture from her brow. She was hot and sweaty and covered in dirt. Not exactly the ideal Golden Pythia, but she didn't care. She was enjoying herself too much.

She watched as Lancer and Nevan worked together to remove the last of the debris. Both men had removed their shirts, baring their chests, and Thena was intrigued by the contrast between them.

To a stranger, Nevan would appear to be the pampered man of technology. Though he was taller than Lancer, Nevan now looked like a grubby schoolboy. Sweat, interspersed with smudges of dirt, gleamed on his hairless pink chest. Lancer, on the other hand . . .

Thena's gaze followed a rivulet of perspiration that ran from his forehead, down his neck, to lodge in the crisp dark curls on his tanned chest. Her gaze strayed lower down the muscled expanse to where the curls arrowed to an intriguing vee at his waistband.

Gorgeous—the man was utterly gorgeous in his primitive, bare-chested splendor. Thena dragged her gaze upward only to be caught by the full glory of his devastating smile. She caught her breath in a gasp, and a thrill shot through her body. She stared, transfixed.

Lancer's eyes clouded. He took a step toward her, but Nevan stepped between them and put an arm around Thena's shoulders.

"We finally got the door free," Nevan said. "Shall we open it up and see what's inside?"

Grateful to Nevan for bringing her back to her senses, Thena avoided Lancer's gaze and gave Nevan a bright smile. "Yes, please. I can't wait."

"The doors were made to be rust-resistant," said Lancer, "but not for two centuries. I brought something that might help."

He pulled a small flat metal canister out of his saddlebags and spurted an oily liquid on the outline of the door. Seri grimaced in distaste and retreated to a shelf above the airlock door.

Lancer dusted off his hands and grasped the wheel in the center. Supervised once more by the chittering moncat, Lancer strained to turn the wheel. His muscles rippled across his back with the effort, but the wheel wouldn't budge. He gave up, panting.

Wiping the sweat out of his eyes, he turned to Nevan. "Would you like to give it a try?"

"Me? I don't think . . ." Nevan shot a swift glance at Thena. "All right, let me try."

Nevan couldn't budge it either. "Maybe if we both tried it," he suggested. Lancer agreed, and they both grasped the wheel and pulled.

Bored by the seeming lack of progress, Seri began investigating the interesting protuberances around the door. Thena mentally warned her to be careful, but the moncat ignored her. Seri leaned out to investigate a particularly fascinating object, skidded on an oily patch, and fell.

Scrabbling madly for purchase, she clutched at the nearest handhold—a lever next to the door. Her grasp tightened and she hung, wide-eyed, by her forepaws. Thena sighed in relief—too soon. The lever creaked, then suddenly jerked downward. The door gave a loud, screeching groan and flew open, emitting a blast of foul-smelling air and depositing the surprised men on their rears. Squeaking in alarm, Seri hastily abandoned her precarious perch for the comfort of Thena's shoulder.

Lancer scrambled up and interposed his body between Thena and the door, then grabbed Nevan's arm and pulled him away. "Get back, man. That air could be dangerous. Can't you smell it?"

Thena wrinkled her nose. "How awful. What is it?"

"Probably just decomposing materials. Fiber, rubber, that sort of thing."

"Can we go in now?" she asked eagerly.

"I'm afraid not. That stale air has been in there for a long time. We need to let some fresh air circulate before we can enter."

Nevan tipped his head back and looked up at the sky. "He's right. It's going to be dark soon too. We should wait until morning, when we can see better."

Oh, great. Nevan sure picked a great time to finally agree with Lancer. "How did you get the door open, anyway?"

Lancer looked sheepish. "We didn't; Seri did. I

forgot about the air pressure. When Seri pulled on the lever, the pressure equalized, allowing the door to open."

Thena grinned. *Allowing* the door to open? From her point of view it had looked more like the door had been flung open. Lancer's look dared her to contradict him, and she decided to give the men the benefit of the doubt—and the credit. After all, they *had* done most of the work.

She changed the subject. "If I look as dirty and filthy as you two, I must need a bath. I'll take one at the spring."

Lancer quirked a grin at her, and Thena added quickly, "You two start camp, and when I get back you can bathe while I start dinner."

Thena didn't wait to hear their reply, but mounted her horse and headed for the stream. Much to her surprise, the men followed her instructions.

They ate a simple dinner, and everyone was so exhausted, they decided to make an early night of it. They made their beds in a triangle around the fire and settled in for the night. Rather than finding a secluded sleeping place as usual, Seri curled up next to Thena, needing comfort after her scare earlier that day. Thena soothed the moncat's soft fur and Seri quieted.

Thena's mind drifted to Lancer, sleeping just a few feet away. She found herself wondering what it would feel like to have such a man court her as a life-mate. The closest Nevan had ever come to passion was a chaste kiss on her forehead. Somehow she doubted Lancer would stop with her forehead.

How would it feel to have his lips pressed against hers, to be crushed against that magnificent chest?

Seri patted her face anxiously, and Thena sighed. She sent Seri a reassuring thought and eradicated the disturbing images from her mind. They both settled down to sleep.

The next thing she knew, it was morning, and she felt a soft caress on her face. *Seri must be anxious to get home.* Thena opened her eyes to reassure the moncat and saw Lancer bending over her with a tender smile, his hand gently cupping her cheek.

"Good morning, sleepyhead," he said softly. "It's time to get up."

Thena's heart pounded erratically. What a way to wake up! Lancer's face was so close. If she moved just a little . . .

Nevan lurched to his feet and groaned, breaking the mood. Lancer removed his hand from her face and stood up. Regret almost tore a similar groan from Thena.

"Let's get to it," Lancer said.

Too anxious to eat first, Thena crossed the short distance to the open door of the *Odyssey*, the men right behind her.

Now that she was free to enter, Thena felt oddly reluctant, uncertain of what she would find. Lancer took her elbow and helped her step in. He had brought a portable light, which he now played over the contents of the ship.

Nevan and Thena followed the glow of Lancer's light through the ship while Seri, uncomfortable in this alien environment, maintained a firm grip on

Thena from her perch on Thena's shoulder.

The ship had been stripped of many of its accoutrements, but Thena was baffled by what still remained. Nothing in her experience had prepared her for this, and she had difficulty comprehending it all.

Lancer's terse explanations were equally inexplicable: galley, hold, crew's quarters, communications, and hydroponics were just a few of the words she caught. She didn't understand any of them.

How could people live in such a bleak, uninviting place? Her ancestors had lived here, she reminded herself. The colonists had traveled from Earth in this ship, had eaten, slept, fought, and made love here. She couldn't imagine the determination and sheer courage it must have taken to travel through the stars. Would she be able to brave such hardships? She doubted it.

Up ahead of her, Lancer shouted in triumph. "Here's the bridge."

The "bridge" turned out to be the main operations center of the ship. Inside, Lancer handed the light to Thena and instructed her to shine it on a metal panel. "All of these old colony ships were made with a black box that recorded all of the instrument readings," he said. "If it's still here, it'll be able to tell us what happened to bring the ship down."

Thena watched him remove the panel and extract the "black box" from inside. "How can that tell us what happened?" she asked.

"Unfortunately, it can't right now. I'll have to take

it back to Earth to get the proper instruments to read it."

At the disappointed look on her face, he added, "The standard operating procedure was to leave the Captain's Log with the ship. If it's still intact, it may be able to tell us what happened."

Nevan shifted with impatience. "Where would we find this log?"

Their search turned it up in what Lancer called the Captain's Quarters. It was a hard, square object sealed in some strange material. "Log" was a strange name for it—it wasn't even made of wood.

Lancer grinned. "We're in luck. The *Odyssey*'s captain hermetically sealed the tape, so I should be able to play it on my scoutship and find out what happened." He glanced around. "It looks like the ship is pretty well stripped of anything useful. What do you say we return to Dodona and see what the log has to tell us?"

Thena agreed. She was totally overwhelmed by what she'd already seen and wanted to get back to more familiar surroundings. She needed time to think about this, to see if she could put it in perspective. Perhaps the log would help. Promising herself to return someday soon and explore some more, she helped the men clean up the campsite and headed back to Dodona.

They reached the Dodona stables at dusk, and Lancer eased himself wearily from the saddle. Thena and Nevan, both looking as tired and dirty as Lancer felt, dismounted beside him. Even Seri appeared to have lost her usual perkiness; she left the stables for parts unknown, presumably to take a much-deserved rest.

Lancer stretched. "I don't know about you two, but I'm beat. Shall we wait until tomorrow to listen to the log?"

Nevan nodded. "It's waited this long, it'll wait one more day." He turned to Thena. "I'm going to see what's happened in my absence, then take a long soak in the men's bath. Would you like an escort to your quarters?"

"No, I'll be along in a moment. I need to return the gear to the storeroom."

Nevan shrugged, tossed his reins to a waiting stablehand, and left. Lancer's mouth dropped open. The man was actually leaving Lancer alone with Thena, if you didn't count the two or three stablehands hanging around. Then again, Nevan probably figured Lancer was in no condition to be a threat at the moment.

He was right.

Lancer slung the saddlebags containing the log and the black box over his shoulder. At least he had accomplished half his mission. Unfortunately, he hadn't gotten very far on the other half—to determine the truth of the Delphians' claims of precognition. The second was even more important, since time was of the essence in averting interstellar war. Lancer needed to get the information back to Earth as soon as possible.

He saw Thena struggling with her saddlebags and

moved to assist her. "Here, let me help you with that. Where do you want them?"

She gave him a weary smile. "Thank you. I need to take them back to the storeroom. Just follow me."

Lancer enlisted the help of one of the young stablehands, and they followed Thena through the passageways of the cavern. The boy's respectful silence encouraged Lancer to converse with Thena. "I still haven't seen or heard any of your prophecies. Is there a chance I could see one tomorrow?"

"No, I'm afraid not. There are only three people allowed at the ceremony: the querent, the pythia, and her observer."

"Well, then, could I be the observer?"

She shook her head. "No, the observers are assigned by the Council, and it takes months of training to learn to conduct the necessary ceremonies and record the prophecies. Are you willing to spend that much time?"

Months? Just to watch somebody spout mumbo-jumbo and write it down? "Is that really necessary?"

"Yes, it is. The most important part of an observer's training is learning to be totally unobtrusive so he doesn't distract the pythia from concentrating on the querent's problem. That's why most pythias have observers they are familiar with: their life-mates, close relatives, or their councilmen."

They reached the storeroom and piled the equipment in one corner. The stableboy busied himself with sorting and shelving the equipment, and Thena collapsed onto a nearby trunk, stretching her legs.

"You, being a stranger to this planet, would be too much of a distraction. You see why it is out of the question?"

He didn't, but decided to humor her. "Okay. Since I obviously can't be the pythia, could I be the querent?"

She seemed surprised at his question. "Of course. Anyone may ask a question if they can pay the price."

"And what is the price?"

"It varies from person to person, depending on their ability to pay and which pythia they choose to give the reading. I really don't know what it would be. You'll have to ask Nevan. He sets the rates for the Dodona pythias."

Well, forget that idea. Lancer could just about guarantee Nevan would take him for an arm and a leg—and other body parts, if he could get away with it. It wasn't worth it just to get a simple question answered. "How do people know which pythia to ask for?"

"Each pythia is tested at menarche and given a rating corresponding to her accuracy."

"Like the tests Carina has to take?"

"Yes, exactly. The highest rank is gold, then silver, green, red, and blue. The higher the rank, the more accurate she is, and therefore, the higher her price."

And Thena was the Golden Pythia, so that probably made her services very expensive. "How do you find out which women are pythias and what their rank is?"

Thena yawned, but explained patiently. "Only pythias wear white chitons. The colored bands on the hems and sleeves indicate their rank."

So that was why she always wore white and gold. "I saw some people wearing two band colors. What does that mean?"

"Retired pythias wear their rank color bordered by black. That's the only other band color you'll see a woman wear. Men wear the colors of the pythias in their immediate family on their sash—the wider the band, the closer the relationship."

Lancer remembered seeing bands on Nevan's chiton. "So what do Nevan's mean?"

"The wide gold band is for his mother, and the thinner silver band is for his sister."

"I thought there was only one gold pythia—you."

"Actually, there could be many pythias entitled to wear the gold bands. But the one with the highest accuracy rating is given the title of the Golden Pythia. In this case, Nevan's mother was the Golden Pythia before she retired."

"I see. Do pythias always keep their same rank?"

Thena fidgeted. "Yes, most of the time."

"And the rest of the time?"

"There have been a few in our history who lost their ranking. . . ." Thena glanced at the stablehand and paused.

"Because their prophecies proved wrong?"

"Oh, no. The prophecies are never *wrong;* some just aren't as clear as others, or as complete."

"Never? How do you know?"

"Our observers keep very detailed records of the

prophecies and follow up to determine their accuracy." She gave him a searching look. "You don't believe me, do you?"

"It's not that I don't believe you," Lancer lied. He didn't want to spoil their budding rapport. "But if I'm going to do justice to your society on film, I need to know as much about it as possible."

Thena didn't look convinced, so Lancer changed the subject. "Do you have records of all the prophecies and their results?"

"Yes, we've kept records back to the first pythias. Why?"

"If I could take a look at your records, I might be able to use some of the actual prophecies to make the film more realistic. Is that possible?"

Thena rubbed her forehead. "Yes, I think that can be arranged, but can we talk about this later? I'm tired."

"Yes, of course." She was right. With his mind foggy with fatigue, now was not the time to ask probing questions. He reached out to help Thena to her feet, but she spurned the offer of his hand. Instead, she rose on her own, making a wide berth around him as she headed for the door.

The stablehand glared at Lancer, and Thena looked amused. Giving the boy a fond look, she said, "Thanks for your help, but you can go on back to the stables now." He departed, aiming another glare at Lancer.

"Come," Thena said. "I'll show you the way back to your quarters."

Lancer followed her, more than a little confused.

She hadn't seemed so standoffish this morning. Why had she recoiled from his touch now? He didn't normally have problems with attracting women. On the contrary, most women fell all over themselves to grab his attention once they learned of his money and influential connections. Thena, thank heavens, didn't seem to care about either of those things. That was one of the reasons he found her so attractive. In fact, he wanted to get to know her a lot better, to spend more time with her and discover the mysteries that lurked behind that classic face.

Then the idea struck him. It was perfect. If he could just get a pythia to Earth, his father could get a prophecy about the war firsthand and make his own determination about its validity. First, though, Lancer had to convince Thena to go.

"There are so many things about your society I need to know and will never be able to learn in the short time I have here. I need a consultant from Delphi to come to Earth with me to ensure I record all the details of your culture correctly for the holofilm. You'd be ideal. How about it?"

She looked puzzled. "Me? Come with you to Earth? Why don't you just make the film here?"

"Unfortunately, you don't have the power or technology I need here. I have to film it on Earth."

"My father would never let me go unless we had a chaperon."

Lancer grimaced. If he had to spend two weeks cooped up with Nevan in a scoutship, he'd probably end up spacing the bastard. Now, the same two weeks closeted with Thena had galaxies more appeal. "Sorry. My scoutship only holds two people, so a chaperon is out."

"Then I can't go."

"Damn it, why not?"

She stiffened. "You know why—it wouldn't be proper."

Lancer rolled his eyes, ignoring the warning signs in hers. "Oh, come on, Thena. No one really cares about that stuff anymore." Recalling her earlier probing questions, he wheedled, "I know a psychiatrist on Earth you might like to meet." Ah, he'd caught her interest there.

She paused, but shook her head, frowning. "No, I'm sorry. I'm sure I won't be allowed to go."

Damn. Ketori and Nevan had her browbeaten. "Are you going to let them dictate what you should and shouldn't do? I thought you were the Golden Pythia," he sneered.

"I am, but that doesn't mean I can just ignore the Council," she shot back. "Being Golden Pythia carries with it a certain responsibility—I listen to the advice of the Council, then make my own decisions." She drew herself up to her full height and glared at him. "And now that I think about it, I'm sure they're right—it wouldn't be proper for me to go."

Too tired to hide his irritation, Lancer bit out, "What are you afraid of? Losing your virtue?"

She recoiled as if he had slapped her.

"Don't worry about it—I assure you it would be safe with me."

Her gaze hardened and grew so cold, he could

almost feel icicles forming on his eyebrows. "Thanks so much for clearing that up for me," she snapped. "For the record, I am *not* afraid of you. I simply don't *want* to go. You'll just have to find someone else. Perhaps someone more . . . amenable?"

Before he could apologize, she whirled and stormed off down the passage.

Blast his insensitivity and unruly tongue! He hadn't meant to offend her. He'd been sneering at himself and his antiquated notions of propriety, not at her. How was he ever going to explain?

Chapter Three

Lancer left the men's mineral baths and headed toward his room. The long soak had helped his aches and pains. He would have stayed longer, but fielding questions about Earth and the colony ship from the other occupants of the bath had exhausted even his store of politeness.

Reaching his room, he laid down on the old-fashioned frame bed, propped his arms behind his head, and brooded over his earlier encounter with Thena. He'd really screwed that up. How could he make it up to her? The traditional wine and flowers routine? No, he had no idea how to go about getting them here.

Hmm. He'd brought some gifts with him—evidence of advanced technology to impress the natives. He ran through the list in his mind. What would please Thena?

Ah, the very thing. He got to his feet and began rummaging through his luggage. He found it—a wrist communicator. Not exactly a romantic gift, but the craftsmanship was superb. It resembled a chunky gold bangle bracelet, carved in an intricate depiction of Earth's solar system. Ten semiprecious stones served a dual purpose, representing the sun and planets as well as being the wristcom's function keys.

But why wait until morning? Why not give it to her now? He grinned. Yes, an excellent idea.

He located Thena's quarters easily from the directions the bath attendant had given him, and noticed her drapes weren't drawn. If he remembered correctly, that meant she was willing to receive visitors.

He hesitated outside her doorway, uncertain of the protocol involved. Should he call out, or just barge right in? He looked inside for a clue to her whereabouts.

The layout of her chambers looked very similar to his: laser-cut stone fashioned into several functional rooms. The area just beyond the doorway was obviously designed for entertaining guests. Soft pillows in muted earth tones lay scattered around a low wooden table. The walls were dotted with niches displaying books, pieces of decorative pottery, and delicate clay sculptures. The areas between the niches were hung with floral tapestries in the same hues, giving the walls a softer look. The overall impression was one of elegance and comfort. He liked it.

Thena stepped into the room and paused, looking startled to see him. She had bathed and changed into that form-fitting white and gold chiton again—the one that clung in all the right spots.

Didn't she realize what that damn gown did to a man's pulse rate—and his sanity? No woman had ever affected him with this intensity before, and he doubted she was even aware of it.

"I came to apologize," he said before she had a chance to order him out.

She lifted her chin defiantly and stared him straight in the eye. "Apologize? For what?"

He gave her a lazy smile and lounged against the doorway, playing with the bracelet in his fingers. Her glare dared him to repeat his earlier rudeness.

"For being such a boor," he said in soft tones. "When I said your virtue was safe with me, I didn't mean to imply you weren't desirable, because you certainly are."

His appreciative glance roamed over her lush curves and he entered the room, drawn inexorably closer to her.

A rosy blush stained her cheeks and she backed away, coming to an abrupt halt against the tapestry.

He glanced around, noting that Seri seemed to be wherever moncats disappeared to at night. Good—one less impediment to contend with.

He moved close enough to inhale her fresh scent. "I simply meant I was brought up to respect a lady, and I would never impose myself on you. See, I brought you a gift, in apology."

He held up the wristcom and watched as her face relaxed.

She reached out to stroke it with her forefinger. "It's beautiful," she said in a hushed voice.

He leaned closer. "It's more than just a bracelet," he explained. "It's a communicator—we call it a wristcom. If you press the sun, here, it activates nine different functions. Like this." He pressed the sun, then the Earth. "This one activates the homing device."

She withdrew her hand, and he realized the technology probably intimidated her. "I . . . I don't know," she said.

"Then again, if you never press the sun, it's only a bracelet." He turned it off, then gently captured her right hand and clasped the bracelet on her arm. Raising her hand to his lips, he kissed a small crescent-shaped scar on the inside of her wrist.

Looking deep into her eyes, he asked, "Am I forgiven?"

"Yes, I . . . yes. It's the most beautiful thing I've ever seen. How can I ever thank you?"

Her guileless blue eyes looked directly into his. He groaned. How could he resist an opening like that?

He couldn't.

"Like this," he murmured. He placed his left arm on the wall beside her head and slid his right hand gently behind her neck, burying it in the soft mass of her hair.

He paused, checking her reaction. She stared at

him, wide-eyed, lips slightly parted, unprotesting.

Good. Time to initiate phase one. Lancer dipped his head and lightly touched his lips to hers. She stood motionless. *Gently, gently,* he reminded himself. This was probably a new experience for her.

He caressed the nape of her neck and dropped soft kisses on her delectable lips. When he felt her first tentative response he deepened the kiss, and felt her arms circle his waist. Her innocence was a powerful aphrodisiac. Dizzy with triumph and desire, he prepared to move to phase two.

"Thena!" thundered Nevan from the doorway. "What in Apollo's name are you doing?"

Thena jerked herself from Lancer's embrace and blushed again. She covered her cheeks with her hands and stammered, "I . . . I . . ."

Lancer rescued her. Concealing his irritation, he turned to lean nonchalantly against the tapestry next to Thena and raised an eyebrow. "I should think that was obvious, Nev, old man. Have you never stolen a kiss from a pretty girl?"

Unfortunately, Lancer couldn't conceal the evidence of his desire as easily as his irritation.

Nevan looked murderous. He clenched his fists and strode menacingly toward Lancer, stopping inches from Lancer's amused face.

Strange. Even in anger, Nevan appeared to be in control. "How dare you trifle with our Golden Pythia!" he said through clenched teeth.

The mortification on Thena's face turned to anger. Lancer grinned. Nevan had really put his foot in it this time.

Thena stepped closer to Nevan, glaring at him. "Is that all you see me as?"

"What?" he snarled. "Stay out of this!"

Oh, she was mad now. Lancer just folded his arms and leaned back to enjoy the fireworks. Thena was finally defying this jerk and he wanted to enjoy every minute of it.

She leaned closer to Nevan's contorted face and, in a voice dripping with ice, said, "No. I want an answer. Is that all you see me as? Just the Golden Pythia?"

Lancer almost felt sorry for Nevan as anger warred with confusion on the oaf's face. "You *are* the Golden Pythia," said Nevan.

"Yes, but I'm also a woman, a woman with feelings and . . . and desires just like any other woman."

Lancer grinned, but she avoided his gaze. "You and Father treat me as an object, a thing to be put on display and used. Is it any wonder I respond to the first genuine human emotion directed at me?"

She was magnificent—her glorious breasts heaved and her eyes flashed as she dressed Nevan down. Damn. If Nevan hadn't been there, Lancer would have shown her just how magnificent *he* could be.

Lancer chuckled, and Nevan's gaze swung around to him, eyes narrowing to menacing slits. Obviously, Nevan knew he'd screwed up and was placing the blame squarely on Lancer's shoulders.

Ignoring Thena's question, Nevan spoke to Lancer. "I will find you a different guide. A *male* guide. That way you won't be tempted to ravish any of our pythias. Report to me in the morning," he said, pointedly indicating the doorway.

Lancer tensed. He didn't care for this turn of events at all. Fortunately, neither did Thena.

Her eyes blazed. "You will not! Father assigned me as his guide. You have no right to change the Council Captain's instructions. Try it, and I'll tell Father how rude you were to our Terran visitor. I don't think he'd appreciate that."

Thena had obviously struck a nerve, for Nevan clenched his fists once again and spat out, "Very well. Continue as his guide. But you'll be chaperoned from now on. Is that clear?"

"Fine!" snapped Thena, and pointed imperiously to the doorway. "Now get out of here, both of you."

Nevan glared at Lancer. "You first," he snapped.

Lancer grimaced. If he had to exit, he might as well make it a memorable one. Seizing Thena's outthrust hand, he brought it once more to his lips. "Until tomorrow, *shiya*."

He was rewarded with her surprised, tentative smile and a growl of disgust from Nevan. Playing it for all he was worth, Lancer grinned at her once more, blew her a kiss, and departed, whistling. All in all, he thought, it had been a very eventful, and very interesting, day.

Thena delayed reporting for her morning session with Lancer as long as possible. After the events of the previous evening she wasn't certain how to act around him.

She was . . . intrigued. And attracted. Yes, that exciting pull was definitely attraction. After all, he *was* a very attractive man, and he did know how to make a woman feel cherished.

Still, she probably shouldn't have let him kiss her. Maybe fatigue had left her receptive to his embrace and yielding in his arms.

No, be honest, she admonished herself. It wasn't fatigue—it was sheer curiosity, combined with a healthy dollop of desire. And why *shouldn't* she be able to kiss a man? Just because she was the Golden Pythia didn't mean she wasn't human. Stars! It wasn't like she was mating with the man; she just wanted to know what it was like to have someone treat her like a woman.

She recalled her embarrassment and chagrin when Nevan had interrupted them. That, combined with her anger at Nevan's presumption, had caused her to lose her temper. Apollo knew Nevan had no right to challenge her like that. He was her Observer and Councilman, not her father, and *certainly* not her life-mate.

But losing her temper around Nevan could be risky. As her Councilman, he could easily make her life miserable if he wanted to—like reporting the kiss to her father. Had he? She hadn't yet found the courage to venture forth and learn the answer to that question.

Seri finally became impatient with Thena's dithering and nudged her mentally.

Okay, Thena conceded. *I've been avoiding it long enough. We might as well get it over with.*

She picked up Seri, took a deep breath, and stepped out of her chambers, bracing herself for what would be out there.

Nothing.

Thena laughed at herself. What did she expect? That all of Dodona would be waiting outside her door to jeer at her? She kicked herself mentally and strode with more confidence to the dining area, dropping off Seri along the way.

Once there, she saw with relief that no one was staring at her—no one at all. So much for her fears. Nevan had been discreet, and she was grateful.

She spotted Lancer easily; he was sitting in the corner with Dendil. Thena filled her tray and joined them. Lancer was talking earnestly and gesturing with his long-fingered, sensitive hands. He flicked a glance at her wrist, where she wore his gift, and gave her a blinding smile.

Her heart turned over. She wished he would stop doing that. It could prove hazardous to her health.

Dendil bobbed his head at her and said, "Mornin', ma'am. The Councilman asked me to be your chaperon today."

Dendil was the Dodona butcher—a big man, with a barrel chest and huge, meaty arms. Nevan obviously thought he'd be more than a match for the slender, and much shorter, Lancer. Thena didn't mind, though. Dendil was a good man, and gentle for all of his bulk. It wasn't his fault she had to put up with a chaperon.

"Good morning to you, too, Dendil. I'm surprised the kitchens can spare you."

"Yes'm. They didn't much care for it, but I've got a cough, and they didn't want me around the food."

"I'm sorry you're not feeling well, but we're happy to have you," she said, refusing to look at Lancer. She wasn't going to give him the opportunity to embarrass her any more. As much as she would like to repeat their embrace, her duty to Dodona came first. She couldn't let it happen again.

Dendil nodded and discreetly edged his bulk between them. She needn't worry. Dendil would make sure nothing would happen.

Thena devoted herself to her breakfast, and the men continued their conversation. The butcher had a passion for history and was grilling Lancer on the origins of the colonists, their ancestors.

Thena chuckled inwardly. Nevan wouldn't be at all pleased. Lancer was charming their chaperon as easily as he had charmed everyone else on the planet—with the exception of Nevan, of course.

She waited for a pause in the conversation and interrupted. "A lot of Dendil's questions could probably be answered by the Captain's Log. When can we open it?"

"Nevan told us this morning that Ketori wants to wait until the entire Council is assembled," said Lancer.

Stars! That bunch of interfering old men would probably keep the whole thing to themselves as long as possible. She grimaced. "That's too bad. I was really looking forward to it."

Well, there was no sense brooding about it.

Ketori's word was law. She changed the subject. "Yesterday, you were asking how our prophecies work. Are you still interested in querying a pythia?"

Lancer grinned at her and raised an eyebrow. "Yes, but I don't think this is the right time to ask the Dodona Councilman for a price quote."

Thena blushed, Dendil frowned, and Lancer's smile grew wider. "If I did, would I be able to film it?" he asked.

Thena could just imagine her hidebound father's reaction to that. "No, Father would never allow it— nor would any pythia. It would be too distracting."

He frowned. "But I need to know exactly how the entire process looks and feels, to ensure I capture it accurately on film."

"That's easy enough. All of our prophecies are done in the querent caverns. You're welcome to film them while they're empty, and I can explain the procedure to you."

"Sounds good to me," said Lancer. He rose and gestured toward the exit. "Lead on, *shiya*. I am yours to command."

She ignored his dramatics and led the two men out of the dining area. *Shiya?* Lancer had called her that last night too. What did it mean? She was afraid to ask—there was no telling what the candid Terran would say, and she didn't want to give Dendil any tales to carry to Nevan.

Seri joined them in the corridor, and they headed toward the querent caverns. Once there, Thena escorted the men in. She immediately felt more confident. They were in her bailiwick now.

"The querent caverns aren't being used until this afternoon, so you can look around," she explained, her voice echoing and expanding in the austere, cavernous room.

Lancer cocked his head and grinned at her. Was everything a joke to him?

Thena assumed the dignity of generations of pythias. "This place is very sacred to us. Please conduct yourself accordingly."

Lancer looked at her with new respect, but Dendil appeared puzzled.

Am I overreacting? No, she decided. Dendil was probably just surprised at her hostility. Undoubtedly, Nevan had painted some lurid picture of Thena and Lancer going into a mating frenzy if they were left alone together.

"No problem," Lancer said. He looked around the large antechamber and pulled out his holocam. Peering through it, he said, "I'm going to need more light here. Denny, would you mind going over to the far corner to hold this light for me?"

Denny? Who but Lancer would dream of calling the butcher *Denny?* Even more surprisingly, *Denny* didn't seem to mind at all. In fact, he seemed pleased at the diminutive. Why did everyone fall all over themselves like silly little monkits to please the Terran?

Seri sensed the thought and shifted indignantly on Thena's shoulder, huffing in annoyance. Thena apologized mentally. Moncats, even their kits, probably had more sense. The big butcher was merely caught in Lancer's spell like everyone else.

Dendil hurried to do Lancer's bidding. When Lancer had the lights situated where he wanted them Thena said softly, "This is the antechamber. The altar against the far wall was constructed of morlawood by our best artisans and dedicated to Apollo."

Dendil moved the light closer to the altar so Lancer could film it. The reverent hush of the antechamber was broken only by the sound of Dendil's coughing.

Thena watched Lancer closely for any further signs of contempt. Nothing but awe showed on his face. "This is a work of art! What do these carvings represent?"

"It's the story of Apollo's defeat of the python at Delphi and the dedication of the original shrine on Earth," Thena explained.

Dendil stroked the altar in obvious respect and Thena realized he'd probably never seen the querent's chambers either. Few people had, unless they had the wherewithal to purchase a prophecy.

"What do you use it for?" Lancer asked.

"This is where the querent, the pythia, and her observer begin the ritual prayers."

"And what purpose do the prayers serve?"

What a strange question. Did prayers need a purpose? "It's very important for everyone involved in the ritual to clear their minds of mundane matters, to concentrate only on the querent's concern. Meditation allows them to do that. That's also why we keep the rest of the chamber unadorned, so there will be no distractions."

Lancer completed his filming of the altar and let the holocam slip from his shoulder as he, too, stroked the altar. "And once the desired state of mind is achieved, then what?"

She pointed to curtained doorways on either side of the altar. "The pythia and her moncat go to the right, the querent and the observer to the left. Shall we?"

She led him to the pythia's doorway, then paused, and communed mentally with Seri. Understanding this was not a normal augury, Seri left.

"Put out the light," she instructed Dendil. "That way you'll get the full effect."

She pushed aside the curtains and entered the next room. Dendil, consumed by a coughing fit, followed with Lancer close behind him.

The heady scent struck them, and Dendil's coughing fit stopped abruptly. The men gasped in wonder, and Thena tried to remember what it was like to see this familiar place for the first time.

The walls and ceiling were covered in masses of exotic white flowers. Each flower had five spiky white petals that shaded to deep purple at the center, providing a regal frame for the circlet of golden filaments.

Lightmoss wasn't needed here. The flowers provided their own illumination, casting an eerie violet glow over the room's occupants and emitting an intoxicating fragrance, redolent of lavender and musk, of hopes and dreams. Thena breathed in the familiar bouquet, savoring the sensations they engendered.

Dendil sank to his knees and stared around himself in awe. Lancer, too, appeared dumbstruck by the strength of the flowers.

Thena gave them a few moments to absorb the beauty of the scene, until she noticed their eyes begin to glaze over. "Dendil, please turn on the light."

The butcher moved slowly to comply. When the light snapped on the exquisite flowers closed up and ceased emitting their mind-drugging perfume. The exotic scene faded into ordinariness.

Lancer and Dendil blinked in the bright light.

"I had you turn on the light because the carolines induce a state of euphoria that can cloud the mind of those unfamiliar with them," explained Thena.

"Carolines?" repeated Lancer.

"Yes. Our legends say the flower was named after the first pythia."

Lancer looked doubtful. "Are they habit-forming?"

"Not at all; they merely help to cleanse the mind while the body is cleansed in the waters."

"Waters?" he echoed, and his gaze swung to the small stream, spanned by a narrow stone bridge, which ran through the middle of the room to the chamber beyond.

"The carolines also appear to be the primary catalyst for sending pythias into their prophetic trance," she explained.

"Oh? Then why aren't you in a trance now?"

"Because though they are the primary catalyst, another is required—the moncats. Their empathic abilities enhance and transform the effect of the flowers, enabling the pythias to enter the trance state. That's why I asked Seri to leave us."

"I see." He crossed the room to peer into the clear stream. "You bathe in here? I see it isn't very deep." He dipped his hand in it. "Why, it's warm."

"This stream is diverted from the main river near the bath's hot springs. Cold water might shock a pythia right out of her trance." She grinned at him. "Or so we keep telling them."

He smiled back at her, and Dendil's involuntary cough reminded her once more of the butcher's presence, as well as the reason for it. She pulled her gaze from Lancer's.

"What's on the left side, where the querent and observer go?" Lancer asked.

"Another room, just like this one. There, the observer assists the querent through the ritual and instructs him on how to phrase the question to get the best results. We keep them separate to ensure our pythias' privacy."

"And if the querent is female?"

"Then the observer performs his ablutions first, and the querent follows, assisted by a female attendant who can explain the ritual to her."

"Sounds like a good system," he said, shaking the water from his hand. "What's next?"

She crossed the small bridge and the men followed. "Beyond here are the querent chambers themselves, about ten in all."

She chose the nearest and motioned the two men inside. This room, too, was covered in carolines, though in much less profusion. Here, both the violet glow and the scent were diminished.

Thena pointed to two pillows in the center of the room. They were made of their best white fineweave cloth, shot through with purple threads, and placed on mats of morlawood bark. "The pythia and the querent sit there, facing each other; the pythia faces the doorway where her observer sits." She pointed to a smaller cushion half hidden by the drapes. "That way he won't distract the querent."

"Won't the observer distract the pythia?"

"No, the observer is a familiar presence, and by this time the pythia is deep in her trance."

"Is the observer in a trance too?"

"No, we acclimatize our observers to the flowers so they won't be affected by them, just as pythias are unaffected without their moncats."

"Then what?" he probed.

"Then the querent states the question, the pythia answers, and the observer records it."

"That's it?"

"Yes, that's it. Afterward, the observer escorts the querent out, gives him a copy of the prophecy, and calls the attendant to see to the pythia until she emerges from the trance."

Thena entered the corridor and gestured to the right. "This way." They left the querent caverns and entered the business section.

"This area looks familiar," said Lancer.

She was impressed at his astuteness. "Yes, you've

been here before. The room to the left is the Council Chamber, where you first showed us your film, and to the right are the administrative offices."

Lancer grinned wickedly. "Now that's clever. Catch them as soon as they come out and make 'em pay up."

Dendil smiled, but Thena ignored his levity. "The offices are here for the convenience of the Dodona Councilman and the Council Captain, who oversee all the pythias and the administrative details of running Dodona. It's not only convenient, but most appropriate to have them located near the querent chambers."

Lancer looked thoughtful. "May we go back in so I can film some more?" He gave her an engaging grin. "I was so fascinated by your explanation that I clean forgot."

"We normally don't enter from this side, but since the chambers aren't in use, I'm sure there will be no harm."

They walked back into the dimly lit corridor leading to the querent chambers, and Lancer handed Dendil the light. "Denny, could you take this to the end of the passageway?"

The butcher complied and Lancer began slowly scanning the cavern with his holocam.

Puzzled, Thena asked, "Why are you so interested in the corridor?"

He continued peering through the camera. "I want to be able to reproduce the set exactly, so I need to shoot this place from all angles," he said. Then in a softer voice, he added, "Besides, this is the first chance I've had to talk to you alone."

"Oh?" she asked, then chastised herself. Pretending not to understand him was a form of dishonesty, and she deplored that trait in anyone, especially herself. She *knew* why he wanted to get her alone.

"Do the flowers damage your mind?" he whispered.

Her mouth dropped open. Evidently she *didn't* know. That was definitely not what she'd expected.

"No," she whispered back. "Of course not!" How could he think such a thing? The carolines were a vital part of a pythia's talent, necessary for their existence.

Lancer continued filming the cavern. "Then why are you so interested in psychiatrists?"

"It's another reason entirely!" She kept her voice low so Dendil couldn't hear her.

"So why do you keep asking questions about them?"

The man was certainly persistent, but it would take too long to explain. With Dendil hovering nearby, she couldn't take the risk of the butcher overhearing their conversation. "I . . . I can't explain right now—but could you tell me a little more about them?"

"Like what?"

"Well, what do they do, exactly?"

Lancer considered for a moment. "They use a variety of techniques perfected over the centuries to help the mentally imbalanced reclaim their sanity, or help normal people deal with problems."

Thena sighed in relief. "There is a standard procedure, then?"

"No, it varies from person to person, depending on their problem."

"How long does it take?" She twisted her hands together in frustration. "To restore sanity, I mean."

"That varies too. In fact, some are never cured."

Thena's naturally optimistic outlook warred with despair. She wouldn't let him dash her hopes yet. "What if a person is not yet insane, but afraid they may be soon?"

"I'm not sure, but I think it's a lot easier then."

Thena's spirits lightened. There was hope.

Lancer pulled his gaze away from the holocam and gave her a grave look. "I don't know much about this, but I have a psychiatrist friend back home who could answer all your questions, if you're really interested."

Thena wasn't a demonstrative person, but she felt like hugging him in sheer exuberance. Dendil's cough reminded her of his presence, so she hugged herself instead and let her enthusiasm show in her whispered reply. "Yes, I am!"

"Okay, but you'll have to come with me to Earth. I doubt she'd come here—the expense would be too great."

Thena bit her lip, thinking. It sounded like a psychiatrist was just what she needed, but the trip to Earth might be difficult. The tough part would be convincing her father to let her go without explaining why, but she was desperate enough to try anything.

As soon as Lancer had stopped filming, Dendil started to look suspicious. Switching the light off, he strode toward them.

"I'll ask Father," she whispered hurriedly before Dendil could reach them. "But please, don't repeat this conversation to *anyone*. It's important—it could mean my life. Promise?"

Lancer's gaze searched her face, questions and concern showing in his eyes. "Yes, if it means that much to you, *shiya*, I promise."

Thena sighed in relief. Now the big hurdle was coming. How was she going to convince Ketori to let her go?

Thena hovered outside the Council Chamber where Ketori and Nevan were meeting. "Do you want to ask them now?" she whispered to Lancer, ignoring Dendil's presence.

"We might as well." He gave her a reassuring smile.

It didn't help. Taking a deep breath, she said, "All right, let's try it."

Thena paused in the open doorway and waited for the two men to notice her. Ketori glanced up and frowned, giving her a piercing look. "What is it?" he asked.

Uh oh, he sounded annoyed. They'd better come up with something good, to ensure their request wasn't doomed to failure before they even asked the question. At a loss for words, she turned to Lancer, mutely beseeching his help.

He came to her rescue. "I wanted to see you, sir,

to discuss your holofilm. May we come in?"

"Yes, please do," responded Ketori.

Thank heavens Lancer had taken the initiative. His charm might win the day where her pleas would surely fail.

Thena and Lancer entered the Council Chamber, leaving their chaperon outside. Lancer held the chair for her once again, and they seated themselves at the table. *I could really get to enjoy this*, Thena thought, then tried to be as quiet and unobtrusive as possible.

Lancer leaned forward and addressed Ketori. "Your society is very interesting, but so complex I'm afraid I won't be able to do it justice. To make the holofilm properly I need the advice and assistance of one of your pythias—someone who can give me additional insights on her talent and ensure I don't misrepresent your customs."

"Yes, we agreed to that already," said Ketori.

"Yes, sir, but the problem lies in the fact that I won't be able to do any of the actual holofilm production here. You simply don't have the power necessary to support the equipment needed for a film of the size I envision—I need my studio on Earth to do that. So, I'll need a pythia to go to Earth with me."

"I see." Ketori frowned, deep in thought.

Thena nudged Lancer with her foot. He gave her a half smile. "Since your daughter and I work so well together, I think she would be the perfect choice."

Thena held her breath. Her sanity could very well be riding on her father's decision.

"No," Ketori said, waving his hand in negation. "Not Thena. Perhaps Sola would do."

Thena's hopes faltered. He hadn't even *considered* it. Lancer raised an eyebrow at her and she answered his unspoken question. "Sola is a retired pythia."

"Retired?"

"Yes, once our pythias pass through the change of life, they are no longer able to prophesy."

"I see." Lancer turned back to Ketori. "I was hoping to have an active pythia join me, to help convince the Republic her talent is genuine. I'm afraid they wouldn't take your word for it—or mine either."

Thena grimaced. Of course they wouldn't take his word for it. He didn't believe it himself.

"I understand your concern," said Ketori, and he hesitated. "But Thena is our Golden Pythia. To most of our people, she *is* Delphi. How could I justify letting her go?"

Thena thought she saw Ketori weakening. "How long would it take?" she asked Lancer.

Lancer stroked his chin thoughtfully. "The trip takes two weeks each way. I'd need you another month or two to help me on the film and to give you a chance to convince the bureaucrats of your claims. Say . . . three months."

Thena looked expectantly at her father, who appeared uncertain. This time, Nevan frowned. "Dodona can't go that long without its Golden Pythia."

"Nonsense," said Thena. "You do most of the

work—I just prophesy. And with the price you put on my services, very few people can afford me. One of the other gold or silver pythias would be thrilled to take over for a while."

Nevan glared at Lancer. "As her Councilman and Observer, I couldn't possibly condone the trip unless I accompanied you."

Oh, no! Confined with Lancer and Nevan in a tiny ship for a whole month? No one would be left alive at journey's end! Thena searched her mind for a reason to refuse Nevan's presence on the trip.

Under cover of the table, Lancer patted her knee in a reassuring gesture. "Sorry, old man, not possible. My scout only has room and provisions for two people, and one of them obviously has to be me."

"In that case," said Ketori, "it's out of the question."

She'd been so close. "Why, Father? I don't *need* a chaperon. I have Seri. Moncats are enough protection for any pythia's virtue—I don't need anyone else."

Lancer looked startled, and she made a mental note to explain it to him later.

"Sir," Lancer interposed, "if you want to effect trade with the Republic, it's vital I bring back proof of your prophecy claims. Who better to represent you than the Golden Pythia? With her beauty and talent she'll wow them and have worlds falling all over themselves to do business with you. I don't think anyone else could do as well."

Thena admired his ploy. It was very plausible

and, more importantly, it looked like it might even have a chance of succeeding.

Ketori looked uncertain. "I'm not sure. . . ."

Lancer grinned. "Well, sir, what do you say we put the question to your Golden Pythia and let her prophecy decide it?"

Nevan matched Lancer's grin. "An excellent idea. Then no one can argue with the decision."

"Will you abide by the decision of the oracle?" Ketori asked Lancer.

"Yes, if you and Nevan agree to do the same."

"Of course," said Nevan with a smirk.

Ketori nodded decisively. "All right, we'll schedule the ritual for tomorrow."

Thena sat in confusion while Ketori, Nevan, and Lancer discussed the price of her prophecy. Why had Lancer asked for a prophecy when he didn't believe in them? And why had Nevan agreed so readily? Seeing Lancer and Nevan so easily in agreement was strange—and disturbing. There was something odd going on, and she didn't like it one bit.

Chapter Four

The next morning Lancer waited outside the querent caverns for the Delphians to show up, tapping his foot in impatience. He wanted to get this mumbo jumbo over with so he could return to Earth and start work on the holofilm.

Actually, things had worked out very nicely. He didn't know how the pythias had managed to keep everyone fooled, but he'd bet his next film's earnings the prophecies were bogus. The pythias probably made them up and couched them in such vague and ambiguous terms they could seldom be proven wrong.

And Thena was their best pythia, so a prophecy confirming her trip to Earth was a foregone conclusion. Not only would he return home with a successful mission under his belt; he'd have the added bonus of two whole weeks alone in a small scoutship with the lovely Golden Pythia!

The price wasn't bad either—with Ketori and Thena present, Nevan hadn't made off with any of Lancer's body parts. Instead, they had requested agricultural machinery, medical supplies, and communication devices. All were well within his power to grant.

Ah, there were Nevan and Thena now—and Seri, too, riding on Thena's shoulder. Lancer gave them a cocky grin. He could afford to be confident. He was positive of the outcome and Thena's ability to make the answer clear enough to convince even Nevan.

"Are you ready?" asked Nevan.

"More than ready," said Lancer.

"Then let's proceed." Nevan gestured him into the querent chamber, where a female attendant waited.

The chamber that had seemed so plain and ordinary in the bright light of yesterday now had an air of mystery and portent, the atmosphere laden with anticipation and unspoken desires.

It must be the way the dim lighting cast eerie shadows over the bare walls, thought Lancer. He'd have to remember this lighting trick for the film—it was very effective.

He glanced at Thena and found Seri glaring at him. Could she read *his* emotions too? Lancer throttled his cynicism and arranged his face in the proper respectful mien. This was a perfect opportunity to learn their ritual, and he couldn't blow it. What he needed was method acting—he needed to immerse himself in the part of the supplicant, to get in touch with the querent's emotions and feelings for the film.

He closed his eyes and concentrated. Slowly, he built the necessary persona and felt it take hold. When it was complete he opened his eyes to find the three Delphians and the moncat regarding him in silent approval.

The attendant took his arm in a gentle grip. "Are you ready?" she asked.

He nodded and she led him to the altar, instructing him to kneel. She stood behind him, and Thena and Nevan joined him on either side of the altar.

The attendant spoke in low and hypnotic tones. "Lancer Morgan, Terran, are you prepared to devote yourself to Apollo?"

Lancer, deep in his role now, felt a surge of undefined emotion: joy . . . fear . . . acceptance? "I am."

The hypnotic voice continued. "It is necessary to be in a state of grace, for only then will He respond to your question through the chosen one. Clear your mind of mundane concerns and repeat the supplication after me. Gracious Apollo, Guardian of Delphi and Patron God of Pythias, hear our plea. . . ."

Lancer repeated the words, though they barely registered on his conscious mind. Thena and Nevan murmured the prayers along with him and Lancer's thought processes slowed. He relaxed, going with the flow, slipping even deeper into the persona.

Lancer lost all sense of time, conscious only of

the murmured prayers and their slow infiltration of his senses. Eventually they ceased, leaving him feeling open and receptive.

He rose with the help of the attendant and followed Nevan into the next chamber. Once he entered the full fragrant force of the carolines immediately engulfed him.

Now was not the moment to question. Here, in their most holy place, he could surely trust Nevan to do him no harm. Lancer closed his mind to all doubts and opened himself to the ritual experience, breathing deeply of the mind-drugging fragrance. He felt the flowers work in swift order on his pliant mind, taking him deep into a trancelike state, yet enhancing his perceptions tenfold.

Dreamily, Lancer copied Nevan's actions, shedding his clothes and entering the small stream. He bathed in the spring, luxuriating in the warm, silky waters until Nevan touched him on one shoulder and silently guided him out to the other side. There, Lancer dried himself with slow, languid motions and donned the cool white querent's robe he found waiting for him. Progressing into the corridor beyond, he found Thena gliding out of the next chamber with Seri on her shoulder. Thena's eyes were half lidded, while Seri's were big and bright.

That bright, penetrating gaze bored into him, and a flash of excitement burst within him. Had it come from Seri, or from within himself?

He tore his gaze away when another attendant took his arm and escorted them to an oracle chamber. He sat where instructed while Nevan took up a position at the doorway and Thena settled into a graceful lotus position with Seri in front of her, both facing Lancer.

The silence of the room and the heavy perfume of the carolines seemed laden with suspense as he felt Thena summon her powers to focus on him and his question. Then, when he could endure it no longer, Seri fixed him with those bright eyes, and Thena intoned, "State your question."

The question emerged full-blown into his mind and tripped easily off his tongue. "Should the Golden Pythia come with me to Earth?"

Thena closed her eyes and threw her head back. Lancer's attention was pinned once more by Seri's brilliant eyes, unable to tear his gaze away.

Suddenly his senses were swept away into a spinning whirlpool that tugged him down, down, down—deep into the unknown. Terrified, Lancer flailed out mentally until he caught a warm, furry presence in his mind. Somehow recognizing it as Seri, he concentrated on grasping her in a firm grip and the spinning stabilized.

There was another being here. Unaware of, or indifferent to his presence, it was cold and efficient, full of purpose. She, for it had to be Thena, was completely focused on her target deep in his consciousness. She zeroed in on it with a single-minded precision, thrusting aside the whirling maelstrom in her path.

Lancer tightened his mental grip on Seri as she clung to Thena and they followed the Golden Pythia willy-nilly, down through the turbulence. When they reached the center of the vortex they broke through to the other side, where they found . . . nothing.

No, not nothing—just the absence of everything—everything but the three of them and the insistent Question, demanding an answer of the void.

After a timeless instant, Lancer felt the answer to his question burst into Thena's mind. She pulled them triumphantly from the abyss, clearly enunciating the response she had found there. "All paths lead to mankind's origin where Apollo's daughter shall fulfill a new cycle of destiny with Gaea's son."

Her . . . his . . . their last thought before they blacked out was that the oracle had confirmed the necessity of the trip.

Lancer waited silently with Ketori and Nevan in the Council Chamber for Thena to recover from her swoon. Having just recovered from the hypnotic effect of the flowers himself, Lancer had to admit they were powerful stuff. He was beginning to understand how the pythias could maintain their deception. An experience like that would make an instant believer out of almost anyone. It had all felt so . . . real.

Lancer grinned. At least he had gotten what he wanted. The prophecy said, *All paths lead to mankind's origin where Apollo's daughter shall fulfill a new cycle of destiny with Gaea's son*. Thena was obviously Apollo's daughter, and Lancer was the son of Gaea, the Greek Earth goddess. Lancer glanced at Nevan. He appeared remarkably composed and confident. Would he be gracious in defeat?

Thena arrived and Lancer rose, holding her chair for her. She seated herself confidently and he gave her a reassuring smile, then sat and turned to Ketori.

"It's highly irregular for a pythia to hear her own prophecy," said Ketori. "But since the answer concerns Thena, I'm allowing it this once. Nevan, would you please read the prophecy?"

Nevan complied. "All paths lead to mankind's origin, but Apollo's daughter shall not fulfill a new cycle of destiny with Gaea's son."

Seri hissed and Lancer leaped to his feet. "Now wait a *minute!* That's not how it went! The prophecy said Thena *would* go with me to Earth. Right, Thena?"

Thena just stared at him with a stunned expression on her face.

"I'm afraid you're under a misapprehension," said Nevan. "Our pythias do not remember their prophecies."

Now it was Lancer's turn to be shocked. By the look on Thena's face it was obvious she *did* remember. He regarded her with growing incredulity. "Is that true?"

Thena gave him a brief nod, then lowered her gaze to the table.

Like hell it was! She couldn't even meet his gaze. What was going on here?

"Nevertheless," Lancer insisted, "I heard the prophecy differently. Nevan recorded it wrong."

Nevan looked bland. "On the contrary," he said,

"you *heard* it wrong." He smiled. "Wishful thinking, perhaps? You *did* agree to abide by the oracle's decision."

Ketori frowned. "Yes, that must be it—wishful thinking." He turned to Lancer. "I know you're unaware of our customs, so I'll overlook the grievous insult you just gave Dodona's Councilman. Observers and Councilmen take binding oaths to uphold the sanctity of the pythia's oracle, and are incapable of the mere *contemplation* of falsely recording a prophecy. Indeed, he would have no reason to do so, since his status is tied to her accuracy as a pythia."

Damn, now I've got both Ketori and Thena upset. And Nevan, blast him, looked smug in his victory. What could Lancer possibly say or do that wouldn't make him look like a total boor?

Nothing.

He decided to concede as graciously as possible. "I'm certain I heard it correctly, but I can see I'm not going to convince you."

He heard the moncat hiss as she glared at Nevan, fur bristling. "Look at Seri," said Lancer. "Isn't it obvious she knows something is wrong?"

Nevan gave Thena a strange look. "What's obvious is that Seri is upset. Since moncats reflect their pythia's emotions, we can only conclude Thena is unhappy with the outcome of the prophecy, *not* that the prophecy itself is in error."

Ketori frowned repressively at Nevan and turned to address Lancer. "Though Thena will not accompany you, the prophecy did say someone should.

Would you mind waiting for the council meeting next week until we can decide who that should be?"

With an absentminded wave of his hand, Lancer said, "No, that's fine, just fine." At least it would give him time to corner Thena and find out what really happened.

"That's settled, then," said Ketori, and he stood up to end the meeting.

Lancer tried to catch Thena's attention, but Nevan hustled her out. She cast him a speaking glance over her shoulder that he was unable to interpret.

Damn. He'd have to find another way to figure out what was going on.

Making his way alone to his quarters, he thrust aside the drapes in anger. There, sitting on the guest table, was Seri, poking through the contents of his bag.

"And what are *you* doing here?" he asked. Irritation turned to amusement as he watched her assume a solemn but dignified expression, despite the fact that he'd caught her snooping. In mute answer, she tugged on his sleeve and held up a folded piece of paper. Lancer took it.

It was a note from Thena: "Meet me in the Council Chamber tomorrow two hours before the morning meal. I'll explain then."

Lancer tapped the note against the table. "Damn right you will," he muttered. "I intend to get to the bottom of this."

*   *   *

The next morning, Thena and Seri waited for Lancer in the Council Chamber. Lost in thought, Thena stroked the moncat's soft fur.

She had to tell Lancer about her problem and ask for his assistance. He was her only hope. If he couldn't help her, she had nowhere else to turn. She sighed. It would be a relief to finally confide in someone.

She heard the drapes swish aside and Seri purred, welcoming Lancer. He leaned casually against the open doorway with that lazy, devastating smile of his, eyes hooded sensually. "Hello, *shiya*," he said in a husky voice. "What can I do for you?"

It was a perfectly innocent question, but it sounded so . . . suggestive. Her heart beat faster, but she perversely ignored his question and asked one of her own. "*Shiya?* You've called me that before. What does it mean?"

"Mean? It doesn't really mean anything. Shiy is a planet where the women—the shiyan—are renowned as the most beautiful, sensuous women in the entire Republic. You remind me of them."

Thena could feel herself blushing. Sensuous? Her? Uncertain how to respond, she seized his arm and tugged him into the room. "Please, stay out of the doorway. I don't want anyone to know we're here."

Apparently taking her touch as an invitation, Lancer smoothly pinned her against the tapestried wall, lifted her chin with one finger, and lowered his face to hers. "I'm glad you found a way for us to be alone," he murmured.

She thrilled to the sensation of Lancer's lean form pressed close against hers. A seductive warmth spread from every spot where their bodies touched, making her feel dizzy and weak. It was like an overdose of carolines at close range—*very* close range. She couldn't think straight.

She needed all her wits about her for this discussion. With more than a little regret, she turned away and slipped from his embrace. Giving him her best no-nonsense look, she said, "I didn't come here for *that*."

"For *that*?" Lancer smiled knowingly and lounged back against the tapestry. "What do you mean, *that*?"

"You know quite well what I mean. Please, can we dispense with the pleasantries? I have something very important to discuss with you."

Lancer's grin faded and he became serious. "All right, we'll do it your way. What do you want to talk about—and why all the secrecy?"

They seated themselves across the table from each other and Thena took a deep breath. "What I'm about to tell you is very important to me. No one else knows, and I must ask you never to repeat it to *anyone*. Do you understand?"

Lancer covered her hand with his. "Yes, of course."

Thena sighed in relief. "Good. Now, yesterday, when Nevan read my prophecy, you said he lied—

that he had altered the prophecy. Well, you were right."

"Yes, I know."

"You don't understand. I don't just *think* you were right. I *know* you were right. You see, I remember my own prophecies."

"Good. Just tell Ketori and we can get on with our trip."

Thena leaned forward and spoke earnestly. "You don't understand. That's the one thing I *can't* tell him."

Lancer patted her hand. "It's okay; I really do understand."

"You do?"

"Yes. It's plain your female ancestors, shipwrecked on a strange world, concocted this elaborate deception to avoid reverting to the dependant plight of the preindustrial woman. What I can't figure out is how you have managed to keep the men in the dark for so long."

"In the dark?"

"Yes, how'd you get them to buy your whole story—lock, stock, and barrel?"

He *still* believed she was fabricating the prophecies. Thena had to convince him otherwise. "You experienced one of our prophecies last night. How can you say they aren't real?"

"Oh, I'm not saying the experience wasn't real. Those flowers would hypnotize anyone into believing *anything*. It's the prophecy bit I don't buy."

She decided to try a different tack. "For the sake of argument, will you humor me and behave as though you believed in them?"

Lancer hesitated, then nodded. "All right—for the sake of argument."

"Good. Now, most pythias can't remember their prophecies."

"But you can? Why?"

"No one knows why—only about one in a hundred pythias has this problem. Anyway, those few who do remember can't handle the emotional shock. Eventually, they've all descended into madness, including . . ."

Thena hesitated, finding it difficult to speak around the lump in her throat. Seri moved closer, offering wordless sympathy.

"Including?" Lancer prompted gently.

"Including . . . my mother."

"Your mother!"

"Yes, my mother. I do have one, you know." She didn't mean to be defensive, but he sounded so shocked.

Lancer looked puzzled. "Well, yes, I assumed you did, but I never heard anyone speak of her. I guess I thought . . . I don't know *what* I thought."

"It's not something we speak of very often. She . . . she was far more stable than most pythias who remembered their prophecies, and they thought she had escaped the curse." Thena sighed. "But she didn't."

"What happened?" asked Lancer softly.

"I was five years old. . . ." Thena remembered that day all too well. Rheta, her lighthearted mother, had gone into the querent chambers laughing and happy, but came out screaming, her face twisted in terror.

"One day Mother entered the ritual trance as usual, but somehow got locked into it and couldn't get out. She had violent seizures for hours until they were finally able to stop them. She survived the convulsions, but her moncat didn't."

Thena paused, stroking Seri and wondering how she would be able to exist without her moncat's love and unquestioning affection. "If you can call it surviving. Most of the time Mother is lucid, but the slightest thing sends her back into that hellish trap—especially anything that reminds her of the ritual, like the scent of carolines or the sight of a moncat. To keep from hurting others when she does go mad, she has locked herself away from the rest of the world."

And locked away with her was the only human love and affection Thena had ever known. After that day, her father had changed, as if by losing Rheta to madness he had lost his last vestige of human kindness. He'd turned inward and cold, single-mindedly devoting himself to his studies and to making Thena into his image of the perfect pythia.

"And you're afraid this will happen to you?" asked Lancer.

"I think Father is. That must be why he watches me so closely. He's so afraid I'll end up like my mother that I've had to hide the knowledge of my prophecies all my life. If he knew I remembered them, I wouldn't meet his image of the perfect pythia anymore. He'd probably remove me from office and lock me away too."

"Why don't you just ask the oracle how you can keep this from happening to you?"

"I can't ask the question of myself—someone else has to do it. I've been afraid to trust anyone else until now." Thena sighed. "And frankly I've been afraid of hearing the answer. But your prophecy yesterday told me the answer to what I seek is on Earth—the psychiatrists are the key."

"Okay, I see that, but what I don't understand is why Nevan is changing your prophecies."

"I don't either. I can't imagine what he'd gain by it."

"Has he changed any of your other prophecies?"

"I don't think so."

"Don't you know?"

"No, pythias don't normally get a copy of their prophecies—they're recorded and kept by the Councilmen."

"Don't you ever read them?"

"No, why should I? I know what they say."

"So, if you've never seen the transcriptions of your prophecies, you don't know if any of the rest are falsified either. Aren't you curious?"

Thena's eyes widened. "You're right. I don't. But I know how to find out!"

She stood and headed for the doorway. "Nevan's work area is just down the hall. No one should be around here for another couple of hours. That'll give us time to look."

Thena and Seri led Lancer into Nevan's area, past the worktable, over to the massive wooden cabinets against the right wall. The floor-to-ceiling cabinets were partitioned into a hundred small compartments, each about a foot square and containing stacks of paper.

"We keep all of the Dodona pythias' prophecies here," she explained.

"Are any of the first prophecies here—from the original pythias? I'd like to take a look at them, to see if I can use them for the film."

"Yes, they are. As a matter of fact, Dodona was the first Delphian Council, so the first prophecies should also be here—in the first cabinet in the top left compartment."

She waved vaguely at the cabinet in question, then busied herself looking for her own records.

"What if Nevan shows up?" asked Lancer.

"Oh, he won't. No one comes here this early. That's why I asked you to meet me here."

Lancer found what he wanted and carefully spread the thin ancient parchment sheets over the table. Thena smiled as Seri bent her small head next to his, for all the world as if she were reading along with him.

Thena pulled out her own set of papers and spread them out next to Lancer's. She glanced quickly through her prophecies, and spotted the first variation almost immediately. She riffled quickly through the rest and found another—and another— and yet still more. With each incriminating alteration she became more and more upset.

Thena stood staring down at the prophecies in disbelief, shocked to her core that a Councilman would do such a thing. Nevan—her Councilman, her *Observer,* had betrayed her. Oh, he was careful to do it subtly, changing only a word or two in every tenth prophecy or so, but when the results came back, her rating and professional reputation would suffer.

"Thena?" said Lancer, and he touched her arm. "Are you all right?"

"Yes. No . . . I don't know," she replied.

Seri scrambled to Thena's side and tugged insistently on her sleeve. Thena patted the moncat absently. "It's all right, Seri. I'm just a little upset right now."

Seri leaped to Thena's shoulder, clutched her ear, and frantically broadcasted mental distress. Thena forced herself to focus on the moncat's message. "Oh, no! Nevan's coming," she whispered.

"So?"

Thena gathered up the papers and shoved them hastily into the nearest compartment—she'd sort them out later. "I don't want him to know we're here, unchaperoned, going through his records. We must get out of here."

She tugged on his arm. Lancer resisted, looking stubborn.

"Please," she said, "This could ruin me!"

Thus appealed to, Lancer relented and stepped toward the curtain.

She heard voices coming from the corridor. "No time now! Here, behind the cabinets."

Thena backed into the dim corner where the lightmoss didn't reach and pulled Lancer in against her. There was just enough space between the cabinets and the back wall for the three of them, and with Lancer's dark garments facing out, they had a chance of remaining unobserved. Seri dropped to the floor and froze between their feet.

One of the men was Nevan. Who was the other one? Thena strained to hear.

"I told you not to come here anymore," hissed Nevan. "Quick, in here, before someone sees you."

Ah, the other man must be Nevan's father, Shogril. Ketori had banished him from Dodona for making trouble after his wife lost her position to Thena.

"I had to come—you haven't kept me informed on how things are going," said Shogril. "Besides, no one is liable to come here this early in the morning."

Thena exchanged a rueful smile with Lancer.

"I couldn't get away," said Nevan. "Thena isn't falling into line as we expected, and I had to stay to keep an eye on her."

"You idiot! If that fool woman isn't your life-mate soon, we'll never regain control over Dodona. Your sister should have been the Golden Pythia, not this upstart! You *must* redeem our family honor."

Thena clutched Lancer's lapels for support, stunned by Shogril's intense enmity.

"Don't worry," Nevan soothed his father. "I have another plan. I've been changing Thena's prophecies the past few months; only a few here and there, just enough to make her prediction rate go down. If she doesn't choose me as her life-mate soon, I'll step up the errors and she'll be deposed from her position by declining accuracy rates."

"You changed her prophecies?" There was grudging respect mixed with horror in Shogril's voice.

"Yes, I had to do something. Nothing else is working, and she's become uncontrollable since that Terran came along. I'm afraid she'll choose him as her life-mate, despite what's best for Delphi."

Startled, Thena looked at Lancer for his reaction to Nevan's statement. Thank goodness, Lancer didn't appear repulsed by the thought. Instead, he gave her a look full of sympathy and cradled her protectively against him.

Thena became all too aware of his body pressed close against hers in the narrow confines of their hiding place. She didn't dare move, for fear Nevan and Shogril would hear them and investigate—this would be *really* difficult to explain.

Thena succumbed to temptation and leaned into Lancer's welcome warmth. His heat stole slowly into her body, starting where his leg was insinuated between hers, rising to curl in the juncture of her thighs, then spreading delicate tendrils upward to envelop her breasts, making her nipples harden in response.

In some remote corner of her mind, Thena registered Nevan hustling Shogril out of the caverns. The rest was preoccupied with Lancer. His face was so close she could see the pulse in his neck, matching the frenzied beat of hers. He aroused sensations in her she had never felt before.

She wanted more. She wanted to be kissed.

Thena raised her lips in invitation and Lancer tightened his arms around her, claiming her mouth in a gentle kiss. The exquisite tenderness in that kiss made her light-headed. He treated her as if she were something precious—something priceless.

The sensation was as heady as the ritual carolines in the querent caverns, with a sensual component she had never experienced in that holy place. Seri's empathy amplified the emotion and dizzying waves of desire coursed through Thena.

She pressed herself harder against him and twined her arms behind his head, deepening the kiss. Lancer pulled back and looked at her with a question in his eyes.

Yes, she was certain she wanted this. In affirmation of her desire, Thena closed her eyes and sought his mouth with her own. This was dangerous, but it only added to the excitement.

Her mouth opened beneath his probing tongue and he initiated her still further into the mysteries of lovemaking. Lancer deepened the kiss and his breathing became ragged. Through the thin cloth of her chiton she felt his caressing fingers on her breast tease one taut nipple into tingling awareness. Thena moaned aloud in pleasure.

Her moan echoed in the silent workroom. Thena pulled back, alarmed. Dear gods, had they been overheard?

She listened. Nothing. Oh, yes, Nevan and Shogril had gone, but how long ago? She gave Lancer a questioning look.

He smiled tenderly and kissed her just under her

left ear. "They left ten minutes ago," he whispered into her neck, resuming his exploration of her body with his hands.

Thena froze. Ten minutes! Where had her mind gone? And his? Why hadn't he told her? Why hadn't *Seri?* Thena felt the heat rise into her face. Lancer must think she was a total wanton. Mortified, she pushed him away, back into the room.

Lancer looked surprised and more than a little wary. She gave him a rueful smile and pulled her dignity back around her. After all, she *had* started it. But much as she had enjoyed it, she had to get her mind back on the more important matters at hand. "I'm sorry; I didn't mean for that to happen. I'm afraid Seri's empathy inadvertently intensified our emotions—it shouldn't have happened."

Lancer reached out and stroked her cheek with the back of his hand. "Are you sorry it did, *shiya?*"

Thena's innate honesty forced her to say, "No, I'm not, but right now other things are more important. You heard what Nevan and his father said. What am I going to do?"

The mood was broken. Lancer dropped his hand and nodded. "Telling Ketori is out of the question?"

"Yes. I need more proof before he'd consent to putting it to a pythia's judgment—and I certainly can't tell him I remember my prophecies."

"Can't you get the querents to back you up?"

"No, they don't remember them either."

Lancer winced. "How could they forget that moment of blinding insight? I feel as if the prophecy was burned in my brain."

Thena stared at him. "You *saw* the prophecy? Others have *heard* them before, but no one's actually seen one. Are you quite sure?"

"Of course I'm sure. Seri dragged me along on your wild ride through my mind and I saw . . . no, I *experienced* the whole thing."

"I didn't feel you there." Thena had never heard of this happening before. She stared at the moncat, whose entire attention was concentrated on grooming her already immaculate tail. Thena tried to attract Seri's attention, but the moncat seemed suddenly deaf and blind. Puzzled, Thena turned back to Lancer. "That's strange. Moncats are supposed to protect querents from the experience, not drag them along."

This was just one more question added to the many already whirling around in her mind. She forced herself to focus on just one thing—Nevan's perfidy. From the conflicting maelstrom of emotions that had rocked her in the past hour—surprise, shock, desire, anger, and horror—one emotion emerged triumphant.

Anger.

Thena clenched her fists in impotent rage. "May Apollo damn Nevan to the nether hells! This trip to Earth is even more important now. I *have* to find a cure and come back so I can expose that bedamned spawn of a python for what he is."

Seeking a target for her anger, she snatched up a nearby paperweight and flung it with all her might against the wall. The polished stone ornament shattered, releasing her ire in a satisfying catharsis.

Lancer grinned. "Do you feel better now?"

Thena gathered her dignity about her once more. "Yes, I do, thank you." Her anger ebbed and she let her shoulders sag in disappointment. "But Father will never let me go."

Lancer gave her a roguish smile. "So why ask him?"

Why, indeed? Ketori would refuse, of course, but she had a right and a duty to follow her own prophecy. She *had* to go whether he permitted it or not.

She nodded. "You're right. I won't ask him; we'll just do it, the sooner the better."

"When can you be ready?"

Thena considered. All she needed was some clothing and her ritual items. "Tomorrow, at the same time we met this morning. I'll come for you when it's safe."

"Sounds good to me." Lancer pulled out the papers she had shoved into a compartment. "Could I borrow these? I'd like to take a closer look at the first prophecies."

"I don't know," she began, then stopped herself. Now, wait a minute: She was the Golden Pythia, and by Apollo, she had the *right* to authorize his use of the papers.

"Yes," she said decisively. "Take them."

Lancer grinned and Thena smiled back. She had just committed herself to leaving her planet—the first Delphian ever to do so. She should be terrified, but instead she felt strangely exhilarated. She was finally *doing* something about her problem.

Chapter Five

Lancer woke early the next morning, anxious to get going. The sooner he delivered Thena and her prophecies, bogus or not, back to Earth, the sooner he could dump this unwanted responsibility on someone else. Until then, there was no need to tell her *why* he wanted her on Earth. Talk of interstellar war might just spook her, and she'd be nervous enough as it was.

He packed his few things, including the Captain's Log and the black box from the colony ship, then dressed quickly and stationed himself by the door. He wanted to catch Thena right away so she didn't have to hover outside his doorway, but he didn't want to leave his drapes open in case anyone wondered why he was awake so early. Feeling a little foolish, he compromised by peering out through the concealing material.

Luckily, his skulking was short-lived. After about five minutes he spotted Thena and Seri coming down the hall. Thena wore a pack slung over her shoulder and carried a large rectangular clay pot covered with a close-fitting lid. The pot teetered precariously, and he thrust aside the drapes to take it from her.

Good Lord, why couldn't women travel anywhere without packing everything but the kitchen autochef? He hefted the heavy pot. "What's this? The ship isn't very big, you know. We can only bring essentials."

"That *is* an essential—it contains carolines."

He raised an eyebrow at her over the flowerpot. "Since when are flowers essential?"

She raised an eyebrow back at him. "Since they became a part of the oracular ritual. How can your psychiatrist friend help me if she doesn't understand the ritual?"

She had a point. "All right." He nodded to the moncat on Thena's shoulder. "But what about her?"

"Seri's a necessary part of the ritual too—I can't do without her."

Oh, wonderful. Just what he needed aboard ship—a frisky little beast who got her jollies from poking her nose into places where it didn't belong. And those mood-enhancing abilities of hers were gonna make it really tough to keep himself from taking advantage of Thena's innocence. He sighed. "All right. What other *essentials* have you got there?"

119

Thena showed him a small pack, about the size of his own carryall. "Just this—it has a few changes of clothing, some toiletries and jewelry, more ritual items." She bit her lip and frowned. "They aren't absolutely necessary, but I would like to have them."

He should have known sarcasm would be wasted on her. "I'm sorry, *shiya;* I'm just nervous and I'd like to get this wagon train moving with as few pack mules as possible."

She frowned her incomprehension, but he waved his hand in impatience. This was hardly the time for a discourse on film classics. "Never mind. If you take my holocam and the carryall, I can manage the" —*No, better not say it*— "flowers. Shall we go?"

"Yes, certainly. There'll be a sentry at the main cavern entrance, so we'll take another way out."

Thena led the way with Seri on her shoulder, and Lancer followed her through the winding passageways to an opening at the back of the caverns. They exited into the faint light of early dawn.

Lancer barely noticed the beauty around him as they trekked the quarter-mile to the clearing where he had landed his ship. All he could think about was the damn flowerpot, which became more awkward and heavy with each step he took.

Lancer heaved a sigh of relief when they reached the ship. Carefully placing the pot on the ground, he flexed his stiff fingers and punched the combination to the ship. The hatch opened upward with a screech and the ramp slid out. Thena jumped

120

and dropped one of the packs, but thankfully maintained her grip on his holocam. Seri flinched too, but soon regained her equilibrium and leaped onto the ramp and bounded up into the ship.

"Wait!" said Lancer, making a grab for Seri.

He missed. "Damn!"

He started up the short ramp after her. "Come on!" he yelled to Thena. "Don't let her touch anything!"

Thena reacted to the urgency in his voice and, hesitating only a moment, she followed him into the strange interior of the ship, broadcasting strong waves of caution to the moncat.

Lancer stopped abruptly in front of her, his broad shoulders blocking her view. She eased around him and found Seri standing wide-eyed in the middle of the scoutship, surveying her surroundings in awe.

"Please, make sure she doesn't touch anything," said Lancer. "Some of these instruments are extremely sensitive, and if she messes with them, it could delay our departure for hours while I recalibrate."

Thena chuckled at Seri's indignant look. "I'm afraid you've hurt her feelings. She's really very intelligent, you know. And she's afraid to touch anything anyway—the ship makes her nervous."

Thena could understand how Seri felt. The entire ship—the walls, floors, ceiling, and even the tables— was all made of cold, hard metal. It made *her* nervous too.

Lancer squatted down and spoke to the moncat. "I'm sorry, Seri; I didn't know. You do understand how important this is, don't you?"

Seri seemed pleased that Lancer had spoken directly to her. Everyone else treated the moncat like a pet, and a dumb one at that. Lancer had taken just the right approach to conciliate her. Seri solemnly patted his cheek with her paw and chittered softly.

Lancer slanted a grin up at Thena. "I take it that means I'm forgiven?"

Thena laughed. "Yes, I think so. I take it that means we can finish loading and get going?" she mocked.

Lancer gave Seri a quick rub between the ears, then stood up. "Yes, let's do it before someone notices we're gone. They'll know soon enough when they hear the ship take off."

He began loading their gear, strapping the flower-pot securely underneath one of the two bunk beds, and stowing the rest in compartments that folded out from the wall.

Thena just stood helplessly by, not knowing what to do. It seemed she could help best by staying out of the way, but even that was difficult to do in the cramped quarters of the scoutship. "I forget. How long is the trip to Earth?"

Lancer's reply came muffled from where he was stowing her bag inside one built-in compartment. "About two weeks."

"Oh, right. Two weeks," she echoed in a hollow voice. Thena suddenly realized what she was getting herself into, leaving her familiar surroundings to brave the dangers of space in a ship that was no bigger than the Dodona Council Chambers—and with a man she barely knew. Furthermore, a man to whom she was very attracted, and who had a hard time keeping his hands off her. There would be no running away on board this ship. Could she handle it?

Lancer finished stowing the gear and turned to look at her. "Don't look so stricken, *shiya;* everything will be all right. Please, trust me."

She bit her lip in uncertainty. It had all seemed so clear yesterday. Now she wasn't so sure this was such a good idea.

Lancer caressed her cheek. "If you can't trust me, trust yourself, your prophecy—and Seri. You said yourself that moncats make good chaperons."

Seri reinforced Lancer's words with a surge of confident approval. The moncat was an excellent judge of character—if Seri felt Lancer could be trusted, then Thena would go along with her.

Thena's sigh was heavy and decisive. "All right." Everything—her hopes, her dreams, and her mother's sanity—now depended on the Terran psychiatrist.

Lancer smiled again. "Good. Our gear's stowed away, so please sit here, in the copilot's chair, while I check out the console."

She and Seri made themselves comfortable in the padded chair while Lancer busied himself at the console in the chair next to theirs. He pushed a button, and the hatch closed with a screech. Thena jumped and Seri's tail tightened around her neck.

Lancer patted Thena's knee in reassurance. "Sorry

about that; I keep forgetting to oil it." He began flipping more switches and pushing more buttons, then glanced at her face. "So tell me, why *do* moncats make good chaperons?"

Lancer apparently thought talking would put her more at ease. Whatever his reason, Thena was glad to concentrate on his questions and avoid thinking about the strangeness around her.

"Because when they're angered or their pythia is threatened, they'll bite. Their bite is poisonous—it won't kill you, but it will make you very ill."

Lancer cast a sidelong look at her and raised an eyebrow. "Remind me not to get Seri angry at me."

He turned back to the console, then said, "We're about ready to take off." He stood up and crossed to her chair. "The takeoff can be pretty unnerving if you're not used to it. I'll need to strap you in."

Lancer reached behind her and pulled out a complicated arrangement of straps. "This harness will keep you safe. You'll need to wear it every time we take off and land, so it's important you learn how to do it yourself."

He began to strap the harness over her chest and cast a wary look at Seri. "She's not going to have a problem with this, is she?"

Despite her apprehension, Thena grinned. It was a little late to be worrying about that now. "She didn't bite you yesterday. Why are you worried now?"

"Because *then* I didn't know her bite was poisonous." He smiled, then showed Thena how to fit the harness snugly about her body, ensuring she could manage it herself.

Lancer gave Seri a speculative look, then rigged a net on the padded area of a bunk and coaxed her into it with Thena's help.

Strapping himself in, Lancer pushed more buttons and turned to grin at her. "Ready?"

Thena clutched the arms of her chair. Unable to speak, she closed her eyes and nodded.

"Okay," he said. "Here we go."

Lancer grinned at the death grip Thena still held on the chair. "You can open your eyes now, *shiya*. We're beyond the atmosphere and it's safe to unstrap."

She opened her eyes, looking a little pale. Lancer glanced back at the moncat and found Seri crouched wide-eyed on the bunk. He could almost feel the waves of fear and confusion emanating from the moncat and her mistress. He released Seri from the confining harness, and she scampered as fast as she could to the comfort of Thena's shoulder. Thena stroked Seri's bristling fur, and the tense atmosphere seemed to diminish rapidly.

How remarkable, he thought. Not many people could recover so quickly from such a jarring experience. In fact, not many people with her nontechnological background would even be gutsy enough to leave their planet and ride off into the unknown hazards of space on a small scoutship. True, she had compelling personal reasons for doing so, but he suspected she was making this trip just as much for altruistic motives—to help her world discover a cure for pythian insanity. His respect for her grew.

Thena fumbled with the harness. Lancer didn't offer to help, sensing she needed to do this for herself. She removed the harness and stood, albeit a little shakily, with Seri still clinging to her shoulder like a furry barnacle.

Lancer gave her a reassuring smile. "How are you feeling?"

Thena straightened and assumed the invisible mantle of the dignified Golden Pythia once more. "Fine, thank you. That was a . . . most unusual experience. Is it like that every time?"

"I'm afraid so. But you're in luck—the first time is the worst. It only gets better from now on."

Thena smiled. "It couldn't possibly be worse."

Lancer shrugged. Actually, he'd taken it easy on them. With no space traffic and carrying two greenhorn passengers, he'd deemed it wise to make the takeoff as smooth as possible.

Thena waved her hand at the control panel in a nervous gesture. "Shouldn't you be doing . . . something?"

"No, it's all automatic. I just set the course and leave the rest up to the ship's computer. It does the rest."

She bit her lip and gave the console an uncertain glance. "You trust it to do everything?"

"Well, not quite everything. We're heading for a transfer point—a sort of fold in space that will allow us to cut months off our time. When we reach it I'll need to pilot our way through it manually."

"What happens if you miss it?"

"Nothing, really. If we miss it, we'll just continue making course adjustments until we get it right—or until we run out of fuel."

Her eyes widened and Lancer grimaced. He'd better watch what he said or he'd find himself dealing with a hysterical woman—or even worse, a hysterical, poison-fanged moncat. He gave Seri a wary glance. "No need to worry. The odds against that happening are astronomical—the ship signals when we near a transfer point."

He pointed to an indicator on the upper right of the control panel. "You see this light?"

Thena nodded, and Lancer tapped the panel for emphasis. "When this turns red we are within twenty-four hours of the transfer point. If for some reason I don't notice the light, an alarm will sound twelve hours before we reach it and every hour on the hour until I take manual control or turn it off. You see how foolproof it is?" Of course, the system wouldn't do a damn bit of good if he were incapacitated, but it wasn't necessary to mention that.

Thena and Seri visibly relaxed. "Yes, thank you for explaining it to me. This is all so new, and I guess I'm just a little nervous."

Lancer resisted an impulse to take her into his arms and soothe away her fears. She was too vulnerable right now, and he couldn't bring himself to take advantage of an innocent. And despite her lush, provocative appearance and passionate response to his kisses, Thena was definitely an innocent.

Now, if *she* seduced *him,* all bets were off. *Maybe if I got the moncat on my side . . .* He smiled to himself. Not just to avoid being bitten, but to keep those mood-enhancing abilities on tap—just in case he needed them.

He rubbed Seri between the ears and she gave him an enigmatic look that was part amusement and part a strange wisdom that seemed to ask, "Just who do you think you're kidding?"

Lancer turned from that disturbing gaze to Thena. "Let me show you how everything operates. That way you won't be so nervous."

Moving aft of the cockpit, he pointed out the medical monitor and showed her how to fold the bunk beds up out of the way to reach the exercise mats underneath. Thena watched him closely, then copied his movements, not satisfied until she could operate the beds herself.

Leading her through the short passage, he gestured to the room at the left. "This is the bathroom." He demonstrated the flushing action of the chemical toilet, then pointed to the stall on the left. "That's the shower."

Thena peered at it, looking puzzled. "Shower?"

"I'll show you." Lancer gestured her into the tiny bathroom, then pressed the button to open the shower door. "There's no room for a bath. Instead, scoutships have sonic showers that use sound waves to cleanse the body." He demonstrated its operation.

Thena frowned. "It doesn't look as though it would get you very clean."

Lancer grinned. "It does, but it sure doesn't feel like it. Actually, I couldn't resist the luxury of adding hookups for a water shower as well. Unfortunately, water is very heavy, so we can't carry much on the ship. We have to ration it carefully."

Reaching across Thena in the cramped space to show her how the temperature controls worked, he accidentally brushed her breast with the back of his hand. She blushed, and he couldn't help noticing her nipples pucker under the thin white fabric of her chiton. Lancer cursed under his breath. He'd probably be spending lots of time taking showers this trip—cold showers.

Thena backed hurriedly out of the room. "What's on the other side?"

Lancer opened the other door and pointed at the two carrels inside. "This ship was designed for a two-man scout crew that travels for months at a time, stopping only to take on supplies. It can get very lonely, so most scoutships are equipped with entertainment consoles like these, where you can watch holofilms, listen to music, play games, read recorded books, or learn something new. It can be a great stress reducer." *Yeah, almost as good as cold showers.* He cleared his throat. "I'll, uh, show you how to use it later."

He closed the door and led her to the end of the passage, where storage cabinets and kitchen appliances curved in a semicircle around a dining table. "This is the kitchen. The appliances might be a little confusing, so I'll just show you how to use them when we need them, okay?"

Thena nodded. "Yes, that's fine. But, please, show me how to do everything so I won't be a burden to you."

It would probably be easier to do it than to teach her, but he could understand how she felt. "Okay, we'll trade."

"Trade? What do you mean?"

"We'll trade knowledge. You tell me more about your history and your world, and I'll tell you about mine. Is it a deal?"

She smiled, looking relieved. "Yes, it's a deal. Where shall we start?"

Thena had moved to the dining table and now stood backlit by the soft kitchen lights, the outline of her voluptuous figure clearly visible beneath the finely draped fabric of her chiton.

Lancer's mouth went dry. "Uh, do you have something else to wear? If you don't change into something less . . . enticing, I won't be responsible for my actions—or your virtue."

Thena blushed. She kept her head held high but averted her eyes. "Yes, yes, of course. Where can I change?"

Now why did she have to ask that? It summoned up a rosy picture of her naked form skimming out of the soft folds of the chiton, her innocent body inviting his touch. His hand tightened on the door handle.

Quickly, before he did something he would regret, Lancer grabbed her pack and shoved it and Thena into the entertainment room. The room was aptly named—he tried to block out the unbidden visions of the entertainment unfolding within.

If it was this bad now, what would it be like later, after he'd been subjected to her provocative presence for days on end? He groaned, and the moncat flashed him a look brimful of amusement. Lancer distracted himself with glaring at Seri until Thena emerged wearing breeches and a shirt made of buckskin. She still looked damn good, but he could deal with it now.

He breathed a sigh of relief. "How about breakfast? I didn't get a chance to eat, and I'm getting hungry."

Thena nodded. "That sounds good. Seri is hungry too. What do we do?"

Lancer showed her where the food was stored and explained the labeling system, then demonstrated the autochef. While he cleared out a cabinet and removed its door so Seri would have a comfortable place to eat and sleep, Thena fumbled with the unfamiliar technology, picking up the essentials quickly.

The food, too, was similar enough to what they normally ate that Thena and Seri had no problems with it. When they all finished eating, Thena gave the molded plastic plate a doubtful look. "How do we clean these?"

"Since space and water are at a premium, we recycle." Lancer showed her how to dispose of the waste in the compactor and use the sonic scrubber to clean the dishes and utensils. "Okay, now it's your turn to tell me about Delphi."

"Why don't we go up front where it's more comfortable?"

Lancer nodded and they walked the short distance back to the cockpit. He unlocked the chairs so they could swivel and tilt, and they seated themselves comfortably while Seri settled down in her new niche for a nap.

"Do you mind if I record this?" Lancer asked. "It would be like the holofilm you saw, but sound only. Is that all right?"

Thena bit her lip. "I—I guess so, so long as you promise not to let anyone on Delphi hear it."

"Okay, it's a deal." He reached over to the console to flip a switch.

"What do you want to know?"

Lancer leaned forward and looked straight into Thena's eyes. "Okay, convince me your prophecies are real. Tell me how they work."

She raised an eyebrow. Apparently she didn't care for his tone. "Well, Apollo—"

"Please, can you put it in terms I can understand?" *For heaven's sake, spare me the religious mumbo jumbo.*

She frowned. "I'll try, but I don't know your terms. Maybe the *Odyssey*'s log would have answers you'd understand."

Lancer nodded. "Good point. We'll check that out later, but for now I'd like to hear it in your own words. What does it feel like?"

She hesitated, then gave him a rueful smile. "I'm sorry—this is more difficult than I expected. I've been keeping it a secret for so many years."

He patted her hand reassuringly, then switched on the recorder. "It's okay; just take your time."

Thena took a few moments to compose her thoughts. "I really don't understand how it's done. All I know is, the ritual and Seri's empathic enhancement make me very susceptible to the carolines. When I breathe in that heady fragrance it's as if I . . . enter another world. No, that's not it."

She closed her eyes and wrinkled her brow, obviously searching hard for words to express the experience. "It's the same world, but on another level."

"You mean, like another plane of existence?"

"Yes! That's it—another plane. It's as if I'm outside myself, yet I can see myself and the querent and the observer. I can feel their thoughts . . . no, it's too confused for that. It's . . . a mixture of their hopes, their dreams, their past, their future, their potential, and their fears." Thena shuddered and opened her eyes. "Their fears . . ."

Lancer kept silent, not wanting to break her concentration.

She continued to stare, her eyes unfocused, her hands gesturing in an attempt to convey the experience. "Their fears, hopes, and dreams clutch at me, wanting release, expression. I fend them off until the oracle takes control—"

"Takes control? Just who—or what—is this oracle, anyway?"

"We're not sure, really. The theory is that we tap into the wisdom of the gods."

"Hmm. Sort of like a universal consciousness?"

Thena beamed. "Yes, that's it, exactly."

"Okay, what happens next?"

"Then, the querent asks the question, and it's as if a golden path opens up that leads straight to the answer. All I have to do is follow it to the end and reveal what I find there. Sometimes it's images of the querent's past or future, sometimes feelings, and sometimes I get nothing but the answer to the question. Then, once I reveal the querent's answer, I'm released back to the everyday world."

Thena sighed and focused her gaze on Lancer. "Did that make any sense to you?"

Strangely enough, it did. "Yes, I experienced something similar during your prophecy. I thought it was some sort of hallucination, but the sensations you describe sound very like what I witnessed."

Thena's eyes widened. "Yes, you did say you remembered it. That's very unusual—I would have said impossible. Are you *sure* it wasn't a hallucination?"

Lancer chuckled. "It seems neither of us believes the other. Why don't we try an experiment? Let's ask another question of the oracle and see if we can convince each other of our claims."

Thena shook her head. "We don't have an observer to record the prophecy."

"We don't need one. You remember your prophecies, don't you?"

"Yes, but . . ."

Lancer grimaced. She was so bound by convention, she might as well be tied up in red tape. "Okay, what if I use the ship's recorder as observer?"

To demonstrate, he rewound the recorder and played back their last few sentences.

Thena's eyes widened, then twinkled in unexpected humor. "Well, it will certainly be more accurate than Nevan. But it's not really the observer I'm worried about. I've been trained all my life not to ask frivolous questions of the oracle."

"What happens if you do?"

Thena thought back, trying to remember the tales she had learned as a novice. "Come to think of it, I don't think you *can* ask a frivolous question. I've heard stories of querents who intended to ask one question but ended by asking another, the one foremost in their hearts."

"Okay, I'll ask the oracle if I'll achieve my heart's desire."

"Yes, that would probably work," Thena conceded, giving Lancer a worried look. "But to do this properly, we need to duplicate the ritual as accurately as possible."

"Can't we just dispense with the trappings and go on to the main event?"

Thena squirmed in her chair. "Perhaps—if I knew which ritual elements are mere trappings and which are really necessary. If I leave one out, it might be the one absolutely crucial ingredient." At his doubtful look, she added, "At best, the ritual simply wouldn't work. At worst, it could send me into the madness I've been trying to avoid. I *must* control as much of it as possible."

Lancer put an arm about her shoulders and gave

135

her a quick hug. "Okay, *shiya*, we'll do it your way. What do you need?"

Thena sighed in relief at Lancer's understanding. "First, we need to meditate and cleanse ourselves to prepare for Apollo's blessing."

"Does it have to be done in that order? It would be easier to shower first, then meditate. That way we won't lose our concentration by traipsing off to the shower."

Thena bit her lip, considering. "I . . . I think that would be all right. The order shouldn't matter; it's the state of mind and body that are important."

Lancer rubbed his hands together. "Okay, what's next?"

"We need something to use as a querent chamber."

"What exactly do you need?"

"It has to be isolated. . . ."

Lancer grinned. "You can't get more isolated than space. What else?"

Thena began to catch Lancer's enthusiasm. "It must be dark and small enough so the carolines' fragrance can permeate it easily. Not too big, or the few carolines I brought won't be enough to put us into the proper receptive state. Oh, and we need two cushions to sit on."

Lancer glanced around. "This cabin looks like the best bet. It can be closed off from the rest of the ship, and the exercise mats can double as cushions."

"Good," Thena said, then frowned. She had almost forgotten one very important detail. "But there's still one problem—we don't have an attendant to remove us from the carolines' influence once the prophecy is over. We could be caught in their thrall forever, or until they die of lack of water. It's too risky. We can't do it."

Her shoulders slumped. It was too bad—she had been starting to look forward to Lancer's experiment.

Lancer turned to the control panel. "Hold on, don't give up yet—we can use the computer. How long does the whole thing take?"

"The entire ritual takes anywhere from an hour to an hour and a half. Why?"

"I'll just put the cabin lights on a timer. After an hour and forty-five minutes, the computer will automatically turn the lights on so the flowers will turn off. Will that do?"

Thena gave him an approving smile. "Yes, I think so." Technology was not only replacing the observer, but the attendant as well. She was impressed, yet still secure in the thought that a machine would never take *her* place.

But it *would* make the ritual very different from the traditional one. Would it even work? Well, if it didn't work here, it wouldn't work on Earth either, and the whole trip would be in vain. Thena sighed. It was risky, but if something went wrong and the madness claimed her, at least only one other person would be affected. She had to try.

They showered separately, and Thena changed back into her chiton while Lancer donned a querent's robe Thena had brought along for the purpose. Lancer dimmed the lights and set the timer, then turned on the recorder and crossed the room to the exercise mats. Placing the covered flowerpot within reach, he sat with Thena facing him, Seri perched in her ritual position on Thena's lap.

It was time.

Thena took a deep breath and sent a silent plea to Apollo to see them safely through this perilous experiment. Closing her eyes, she began speaking the familiar words of the ritual. "Gracious Apollo, Guardian of Delphi and Patron God of Pythias, hear our plea. . . ."

The ritual proceeded smoothly and Thena sank into it gratefully, feeling the tension and anxiety leave her body and a marvelous sensation of tranquility taking its place. When she sensed a similar serenity in Lancer, Thena opened her eyes and uncovered the carolines.

The flowers suffused the air of the cabin with their characteristic violet glow, and their heady fragrance threaded its way through the cabin, marking it with the unmistakable scent of the Delphian ritual. Thena watched Lancer's gaze fix hypnotically on the moncat, his pupils widening as he succumbed to the drugging perfume of the carolines.

Assured of his receptive state, she closed her eyes once more. A surge of dizziness washed over her as the moncat enhanced Thena's susceptibility to the flowers. Thena released her hold on the mundane world and let her consciousness flow into the deep

trance necessary for the prophecy, opening herself
fully to the experience.

Lancer's emotions began to swirl around her,
darting in and out like a swarm of angry bees eager
to plant their barbs. She identified the strongest
ones with the ease of long practice—curiosity mixed
with eagerness, a touch of fear, and a strong dollop
of desire. With an exercise of will, she held them
at bay until the sensations reached a fever pitch of
expectation.

All at once the oracle took control, and a myriad
of shifting paths opened before her. She caught
tantalizing glimpses of Lancer's past and potential
future before the oracle forced the ritual words
from her mouth: "State your question."

Thena felt Lancer's surge of confidence as he
asked, "Shall I achieve my heart's desire?"

The question solidified the paths Thena saw in
his unconscious, bathing one of them in a soft
golden light. Feeling the moncat nearby, Thena
hesitated for a moment, seeking Lancer's conscious
mind. She found him mentally clinging to Seri's
comforting presence, protected from the maelstrom
of emotions roiling about them. Confident Seri
would keep him safe as Lancer and the moncat
followed her through the void, Thena ignored the
temptation to explore other paths and zeroed in
on the golden one. She sped swiftly and surely
to her destination and burst into the void. As
she hung there, suspended for a timeless instant,
she was granted flashing images of Lancer from
his past.

Lancer, frowning sternly at a despairing young man standing before him.

Lancer, staring at news headlines with a look of horror.

Lancer, crying openly as a casket was lowered into the ground.

Lancer, resolutely handing a piece of paper to a reluctant older man.

The images paused, then another flashed before her, this one of an older Lancer.

Lancer, raising his hand in joyful greeting to the blurred figure of a woman, a crescent-shaped scar plainly visible on his wrist.

Thena almost gasped aloud, but before that blurred form could solidify, the oracle wrenched her back into the void with a blaze of light and gave her the answer. "To win love and happiness, Gaea's son must overcome the bonds of the past." So saying, the oracle released her into merciful oblivion.

Chapter Six

Thena roused gradually from her caroline-induced stupor and probed cautiously at the painful recesses of her mind. Satisfied when nothing pushed back, she opened her eyes to find herself lying on the exercise mat, nose-to-nose with Seri.

Seri gave her a little trill of encouragement, and Thena pushed herself to a sitting position, blinking foggily at the cabin lights. Evidently the timer had worked as Lancer promised. She carefully replaced the lid on the flowerpot and looked to see how he had fared.

Lancer groaned and sat up gingerly, holding his head. He opened one eye and peered at her with a rueful grin. "Those flowers sure pack a punch. Do you know of a good cure for a caroline hangover?"

She shook her head, wincing at the movement. "No, I guess we were just under their influence a little too long. The pain should fade soon."

"Yeah. Remind me next time to use a sound acti-vated timer, keyed to your voice."

Whatever that was. Thena nodded, not feeling up to discussions on obscure technological marvels at the moment.

Lancer coughed and slowly opened his other eye. "You're right. It's getting better. Do you feel like comparing notes on our experiment?"

Thena nodded again and Lancer started de-scribing the sensations he had experienced during the ritual. Thena's eyebrows rose. It was remark-ably similar to what she had observed, and, yes, she did recall sensing him there. He hadn't been hallucinating after all.

She touched his arm. "Wait, what did you see just after you asked the question?"

Lancer rubbed his forehead. "See? I couldn't see anything then—I could only feel the turbulence moving around us as Seri and I followed you to the eye of the storm."

"You didn't see the paths?" she persisted.

Lancer shook his head.

"What did you see after we broke into the void—the eye of the storm?"

"Flashbacks—from the worst time in my life." A pained look crossed his face; then it went still and closed. "I'd rather not discuss it."

"I'm afraid you must if you're to understand the prophecy. It said you must overcome the bonds of the past to win your heart's desire."

Lancer just gave her a stubborn glare, so Thena

decided to push a little more. "I trusted you enough to share my innermost secret. Can't you do the same?"

Lancer buried his face in his hands and heaved a heavy sigh. "Yes, *shiya*, I know you did—but this is something I prefer to forget."

He looked so forlorn, so unlike the confident Lancer she was accustomed to seeing. Thena longed to stroke the dark head bent before her, but refrained, uncertain how he would interpret the gesture—or what she really meant by it. "I'd like to help, but I can't if I don't understand. It might help to talk about it."

Lancer raised his head and gave her a halfhearted grin. "It won't, but you deserve an explanation." He ran his hand through his hair and stared unseeingly at the bunk behind her. "It happened when I was in school. The Morgans have always been in politics, so my father convinced me to run for class president, saying it would be good experience for my future career. I won, but I wasn't ready for the responsibility."

His mouth twisted into a grimace. "I discovered that the first time I had to exercise it. One of my classmates was caught cheating for the third time and asked for a trial of his peers. When the vote split I had to cast the deciding vote. It was the toughest decision of my life—and the worst. I voted to expel him."

Lancer emitted a heavy sigh. "He had many problems, and this was just the final straw—he couldn't handle it. He committed suicide and I tendered my resignation as class president."

Lancer cursed and slammed his hand against the wall. "I knew then that I lacked the family talent for leadership and no one would *ever* trust me with responsibility again!"

Thena's heart went out to the young Lancer who'd had to shoulder such an awful burden. She, better than anyone, knew what it was like to carry that kind of load. "You couldn't have known he'd react that way. And you were certainly not responsible for his actions. *He* was. Don't blame yourself for his death."

Lancer leaped to his feet and strode across the cabin to stare out at the stars, fists clenched. "No, you're wrong. I *am* responsible. If I hadn't voted to expel him, he would be alive today."

Even after all this time, that incident had an incredibly strong hold on him. Why couldn't he just let it go? "You don't know that! If he were that unstable, anything could have set him off and driven him to kill himself."

Lancer turned and gave her a steady look. "That may be, but it doesn't change the fact that it was *my* decision that pushed him over the edge."

It was obvious she wasn't going to convince him, so Thena changed the subject. "All right, try to remember that last image—it was in your future. What did it mean to you?" She held her breath in suspense, anxious to know how he interpreted it.

Lancer frowned. "I don't know; I didn't understand it. I guess it meant I'd achieve my heart's desire. Why? What did you see?"

"N-nothing." Thena stammered over the lie. She'd seen far more—the telltale crescent-shaped scar of a man who was life-mated to a pythia. But she couldn't bear to tell him that and watch his friendly, open gaze turn guarded and wary.

Besides, the image didn't specifically show *Thena* as his life-mate. And if it had, it would be worse. The life-mate of the Golden Pythia was slated to become the Council Captain, with responsibility for all of Delphi. How could she put that burden on him, especially now that she knew how much he abhorred it?

She couldn't.

This had to be the oracle's subtle way of telling her to stop dreaming and find a life-mate elsewhere. Thena sighed and changed the subject. Lancer was destined for someone else.

Lancer sat slumped in the pilot's chair, staring unseeingly at the console. He had escaped here, under the pretense of monitoring ship functions, to deal with the painful memories the prophecy had resurrected. Thena had left him to his introspection, tiptoeing around in an attempt not to disturb him. It only made it worse.

Damn it—this was no time to brood. He had to find some way to change this mood or they'd find themselves with a blue fog hanging over them for the rest of the trip.

Lancer sat up straight in sudden decision. The best cure for the moody blues was work. That was it— research. He needed to do more research on his

145

holofilm. He snapped his fingers in sudden remembrance. *"Shiya!"*

Thena and Seri popped their heads out of the kitchen and gave him identical inquiring looks, one four feet lower than the other.

Lancer grinned. He felt better already. "You mentioned earlier that you wanted to hear the *Odyssey's* Log. How about now?"

Thena brightened. "That's a wonderful idea."

Lancer dug the log out of storage. Carefully unwrapping the ancient artifact from its hermetic seal, he placed it in the reader.

Seri hopped up on one of his shoulders, and Thena came to peer over the other. "How does it work?"

Lancer pointed to a row of buttons and explained the basics of the tape player's operation. "Now, if you're looking for something specific, just type the word or date on the keyboard, press this red button, and it will take you to the next occurrence on the tape." He turned to look at her. "You can view the log as a written document like a book, or listen to it in the captain's voice, as he recorded it. Which would you prefer?"

Thena's eyes opened wide. "His voice, please. Father says we're descended from the captain. It would be wonderful to hear the voice of my ancestor."

Lancer rewound the tape to the beginning and pushed PLAY. Thena and Seri made themselves comfortable together in one chair, and he leaned back in the other.

The deep voice of a man spoke in authoritative tones.

February 18, 2142, Day 1. This is Captain Richard Spencer commanding the colony ship Odyssey, *outward bound for the fourth planet of the Canopus system. We have just left Earth's atmosphere, on the first thrust of our journey to what promises to be a challenging and prosperous new world. Five hundred men, women, and children are making this trip to escape the overpopulation, pollution, and restrictions of Earth and return to a simpler way of life.*

With this beginning, the log promised to be as long as the original journey. Lancer stopped the tape and turned to Thena. "Would you like to listen to the whole thing or just skip ahead to the point where they landed on Delphi? It may take a long time before we get to that point."

Thena looked puzzled. "I thought you said the trip was only two weeks."

"It is, for us. We didn't discover the transfer points until about fifty years ago, generations after the *Odyssey* left Earth." At her questioning look, he added, "Remember, the folds in space cut months, even years, off a trip."

Thena nodded. "I see. I'd still rather hear it all from the beginning."

"Good. It'll give me more background for the film."

Lancer started the tape again, and he and Thena leaned back in their chairs to listen to the mesmerizing tones of a man long since dead, detailing the history of a colony ship on its way to an exciting new life.

A few hours later they paused to get something to eat. Lancer and Thena ate quickly so they could return to the story unfolding in the cabin. Bored by the inactivity, Seri took off to her niche to sleep.

Lancer and Thena made themselves comfortable on the bunks and continued to listen to the tape well into the night. The litany of births, marriages, and deaths was surprisingly absorbing. So were the ancient trials and punishments resulting from the friction that arose naturally whenever there were large groups of people.

As Lancer and Thena vicariously shared the triumphs and disasters of the *Odyssey* and its crew through the chronicles of its chief officer, Lancer came to know and admire Captain Spencer. The captain's unflappable demeanor and fortitude in dealing with the chores of managing a large group of people while keeping the huge colony ship in good working order were amazing. He was the leader Lancer would never be.

Lancer's eyes began to droop as the captain, in his calm voice, described yet another infraction of ship's rules and the subsequent punishment of the offender. Lancer forced his eyes open and, as the tape paused, he noticed Thena's head nodding sleepily.

He slid off the bunk to turn the tape off for the night, but froze in mid-reach at the harried, frantic tones of the normally imperturbable captain.

Day 165. The unthinkable has happened. The ship passed through a strange singularity that threw us into unknown space, damaging the engines.

Lancer sat in the pilot's chair and looked toward Thena's bunk to see if she had heard. She had. She leaned forward with her eyes open wide, drinking in the captain's words. They both sat spellbound by the centuries-old drama unfolding before them.

There was a quick consultation of heated voices in the background and the captain's voice came on again.

I want to get this on record now in case we are unable to report later. The engineers tell me the primary drive is almost gone. Our momentum will continue to carry us forward forever, but we can no longer locate the Canopus system. Indeed, we couldn't reach it even if we could find it. If we are to survive, we must find a habitable planet nearby, one close enough to reach with the limited thruster power we still have. The probabilities are slight, but we must find one. We can't afford not to. I leave now to quiet the panic spreading throughout the ship. I will continue to provide updates on the crisis as they occur so that, even if we perish, this record of our tribulations may survive. Captain Spencer, signing off.

Lancer glanced at Thena. "My God, they passed through a transfer point, a hundred and fifty years before we learned how to navigate them safely."

Thena nodded, an expression of awe on her face, all thoughts of sleep apparently forgotten.

There was a brief blank spot on the tape; then the captain's voice resumed.

Day 174. It has been nine days since we passed through the singularity. The scientists have located a nearby system where there is a good likelihood of finding a habitable planet. We have just enough power to make it there, so we are changing course for the new system. It is our only hope.

The tape paused again, and the captain's voice came back on, sounding tired and weary.

Day 200. Twenty-six days after our decision to change course, it is my sad duty to report a mutiny. A group of misguided fundamentalists, believing we were courting God's wrath by swerving from the original course, overpowered and killed the scientists as they were working in the lab to save us. Much of the equipment was destroyed, including the communications gear we were counting on to reestablish contact with Earth. The mutineers' attempt to seize control

*of the bridge failed due to the quick action of
the crew on duty. Four officers were killed and
two badly wounded. Fourteen of the mutineers
died in the struggle and the remaining thirty-
seven have been incarcerated in the brig until
we decide what to do about them.*

Lancer sat as if riveted to his chair. Drama . . .
passion . . . angst. What a great story! Their unexpected passage through the transfer point and the
aborted mutiny explained why the colony never
made it to their planned destination—and why they
were never heard from again. He continued to listen
avidly, seeing the events unfold like a holofilm in his
imagination.

The captain's voice resumed, still fatigued, yet
overlaid with a note of suppressed elation.

*Day 219. It has been nineteen days since the
mutiny and all is quiet, with an air of desperate expectation throughout the ship. Two of the
junior technicians who escaped the bloodbath
repaired a drone to test the atmosphere of the
planets in this system. The surface of the fourth
planet appears to be suitable for habitation, so
we are going to take our chances and land there.
The ship will not rise again, so this is our only
hope for salvation. May God bless us and have
mercy on our souls.*

Lancer waited in strained anticipation for the
next chapter of the story, uncertain if there would

even be one. The pause lengthened; then the captain's voice came on once again, this time to the background of laughing celebration.

Day 221. We are down and the planet is beautiful. We found an excellent landing spot on the open plains in a temperate region. The air is fresh and the soil rich and fertile. Tonight we celebrate, and tomorrow we begin exploring our new world. As my last official act, I hereby decommission the Odyssey *and resign my position.* Mister *Spencer, signing off.*

Lancer turned off the tape and Thena jerked up with an inarticulate cry of protest. Lancer rubbed his eyes. "It's late. I'm sorry, *shiya,* but that's about all the excitement I can take for one day. What do you say we call it a day, get some sleep, and listen to it again tomorrow?"

Thena sagged back onto the chair and yawned. "All right. I guess I am a bit tired, after all. It's been a very long day." She gave him a dreamy smile. "But isn't Captain Spencer amazing? I'm proud to be descended from such a wonderful leader. I just wish I could be more like him. Don't you?"

Lancer grimaced. She sounded just like a starstruck holo-groupie. Perversely, he denied his admiration. "No, I pity the poor man." That wasn't a lie—he *did* pity him.

Thena's mouth dropped open. "Pity? For heaven's sake, why?"

"The lives and well-being of over five hundred

people were solely dependant on him and his judgment. It had to be a tough job—what if he'd made the wrong decision?"

"But he didn't. Besides, he had many advisers who gave him the benefit of their experience and shared the responsibility for the decisions. That's the way of all good leaders."

Lancer surged to his feet and chopped his hand, as if he could cut off her words. "Don't you see? No man should have so much control over other people's lives. There's too much possibility for error—too much room to screw up and . . . and too much temptation to feel like a god and abuse the power."

Thena stood up to face him and gave him a critical look. "Having an inept person as leader is still better than utter anarchy, and the inept and the corrupt will always eventually be deposed or taken down."

Lancer slammed his open palm against the console. "You know nothing about it!"

Thena's chin came up and her mouth firmed. "On the contrary, I have studied history and assisted in the governing of Delphi. I *do* know what I am talking about. If you weren't so afraid of command yourself, you'd realize it too."

Ah, a hit, a palpable hit, Lancer thought, still managing to retain his sense of humor despite her stinging accusation. She was only too right.

Unfortunately, the fear was a part of him, ingrained in his very personality. It wasn't rational, but it was there nonetheless. He allowed a heavy sigh to escape him. "Perhaps, *shiya*, but how unkind of you to say so."

Thena's face melted into confusion and distress. "I . . . I'm sorry; I didn't mean to . . ."

He should have felt remorse, but her criticism had cut too deep. "Yes, you did. And you were right. But I'm sorry; I don't want to discuss it right now. Let's get some sleep, okay?"

Thena nodded and they prepared for sleep in silence.

Intellectually, Lancer knew Thena was right, but deep down in his gut his instincts told him taking on responsibility would only lead to more soul-searing life-and-death decisions.

No, leadership wasn't for him.

Thena avoided the subject over the next several days as they settled into a routine of eating, sleeping, and listening to the log. Only the exigencies of politeness and the occasional cough from Lancer broke their self-imposed silence.

Lancer's ardent pursuit dwindled too. It was strange, but Thena missed his smoldering glances, even if they did disturb her equilibrium and tempt her to dalliance.

In fact, she was a bit miffed; his interest had certainly been short-lived. She didn't know whether to be relieved or insulted.

She did know she was bored. She filled the time by absorbing herself in the adventures of the colonists discovering their new world—her world. Thena eagerly awaited each new glimpse of the early days on her planet, hoping to learn the origins of their prophetic ability and perhaps even discover something that would help combat her eventual slide into insanity.

To her surprise, Captain Spencer continued the narration. He hadn't been allowed to resign his place as leader, having been overwhelmingly elected to the post of Council Captain by the colonists, who had recognized his outstanding leadership abilities.

He described the establishment of the first settlement near the ship and the heated debate, as yet unresolved, over the naming of their new planet. Some wanted to name it *Odyssey* after the ship, while others preferred *Blessing* to commemorate the miracle that had brought them to their hospitable new world. The business of building a new life and overseeing the colonists occupied most of Captain Spencer's time, and his accounts were spaced out less frequently.

Finally, after the fourth day of listening to the chronicles, Thena heard the captain mention the subject she had been waiting for. Stopping the tape, she went to get Lancer so he could hear it too.

She found him in the entertainment room, his dark head bent over the prophecies he had picked up from Nevan's office. He was making more of those interminable notes for the film that had kept him occupied over the last few days. Uncertain how to approach him, she stood at the door and cleared her throat.

Lancer's head came up, and he gave her a blank look.

He must be working too hard, she thought. *He looks terrible.*

He gave her a polite smile, his gaze devoid of interest or attraction. "Yes?"

Something twisted painfully in the region of Thena's heart. Where was the charming rogue she had started the trip with? She would have given a roomful of carolines to have him back again, even for a little while. "The tape . . . uh, Captain Spencer just mentioned an unusual discovery. I think it might be what we've been waiting for. Would you like to listen with me?"

Lancer shrugged, then coughed and rubbed his eyes. "Sure. I'll be right there."

He followed her into the cabin and sprawled out on his bunk while Thena rewound the tape to the beginning of the entry. Turning it on, she returned to her bunk to join Seri.

The captain's familiar voice resonated from the speakers.

Day 355. Something extraordinary has happened. Some of the youngsters, including my niece, Caroline, have been attempting to make pets of the local population of moncats. Two boys were a little rough and the moncats bit them, incapacitating them for weeks. We warned the rest, but, being a willful teenager, Caroline didn't listen.

Thena shared a meaningful glance with Lancer, neither of them missing the significance of the girl's name. Lancer shifted from his ungainly sprawl to lie on his stomach, propping his chin on his forearms to stare at the console as the captain resumed his story.

She continued to try to befriend one of the creatures and was bitten. Instead of incapacitating her, however, the bite merely gave her a mild fever for a few hours. Strangely enough, it seemed to bond Caroline and the moncat together in a relationship so close, they seem to be able to sense each other's emotions. What is even more remarkable is her discovery when she took the moncat and her friend, Alicia, on an exploration of the nearby caverns. There, they stumbled across a room filled with beautiful white flowers that seemed to exude a mind-drugging fragrance.

This was it. Thena rose from the bunk and moved to the copilot's chair, drawn inexorably closer to the fascinating voice detailing the origins of the first pythias. She stared into the tape player, hypnotized by its movement, as the captain's words continued.

Caroline succumbed to their influence quickly and went into a sort of trance. When Alicia asked what the flowers were doing in such an isolated cave, Caroline responded in a strange singsong voice, saying they and the moncats were to play a key role in the future of the colony.

Thena looked at Lancer, who nodded and whispered, "That was the first prophecy recorded."

Luckily, an adult happened on to the girls with a light. If he hadn't, they might still be caught in the flowers' thrall. He told us what happened, though the girls remember nothing of it. At first we shrugged it off as an odd occurrence, but more adolescent girls have been bitten and befriended by moncats, including Alicia. Strangely, the moncats haven't chosen any of the boys, much to their chagrin.

Seri huffed indignantly at the thought and Lancer grinned. Seri needn't worry; *he* hadn't planned on volunteering to get bitten.

To try and repeat Caroline's experience, Alicia returned to the caroline room, as everyone insists on calling it. She, too, entered a trancelike state and, upon being asked about the success of the colony, uttered a prediction that the settlement would be hit by a tornado. The prediction was uncannily accurate; a tornado did wreak havoc on the settlement on the date she specified. The damage would have been far more devastating if it hadn't been for her warning.

Thena sent Lancer a questioning glance. He

nodded at this second confirmation of the written prophecies he had been studying.

The prophecies have caught the imagination of the entire colony and, seeing the similarity to the Greek legend, everyone has been calling the planet Delphi, thus ending the dispute over its name. They also agreed to name the cave system for another famous Greek prophetic site, Dodona, and have even begun calling the young girls pythias to emulate the original oracles.

The captain paused and heaved a heavy sigh.

The young pythias are lionized out of all reason, and I fear for them. They are constantly importuned for predictions on crop failure, marriage advice, and other trivialities. Unfortunately, the advice is often so obscure, it is meaningless, and the querents blame the poor girls. I go now to meet with the Council to determine how to protect the pythias and how best to utilize this unusual new resource for the good of the entire planet.

Thena pushed the button to stop the tape and turned to face Lancer. "I'd like to stop here—it's too much to absorb. It explains so much, yet leaves so many more questions unanswered."

Lancer nodded and sat up. "Yes—I didn't understand that part about the moncats' bite. I thought you said it was always poisonous."

"It is—except on two occasions. One is when a girl becomes a pythia—"

Lancer raised his hand. "Wait. I don't think you mentioned that before. I need to know this for the film. How does it work?"

Thena bit her lip. "I don't know how it happened then, but now every candidate pythia is tested at the onset of her menses by leaving her alone in a moncats' grove."

"Grove? I thought they lived in caves."

Thena shook her head. "No, only those bonded to pythias live in the caves. They are naturally tree-dwelling animals and live out their lives there unless they select a pythia to bond with."

Lancer's gaze sharpened. "I see. Then what happens?"

"The young girl is left there overnight and the moncats wait until she is alone. Then, if she is lucky enough to become a pythia, one of them chooses her by biting her on the right wrist."

Lancer jumped down from the bunk and came toward her, lifting her right hand to inspect the crescent-shaped scar on her wrist. "So that's where this came from."

He caressed the scar with his thumb and Thena inhaled sharply at the surge of pleasure it sent winging along her nerves. Unfortunately, that intake of breath suffused her senses with his heady masculine aroma. The combination gave her an overwhelming desire to return his caress with a few of her own.

She jerked her hand back before she could

succumb to the impulse. He couldn't know how incredibly intimate that gesture was to her people.

Lancer shrugged and leaned back against the console, folding his arms across his chest. "How do you determine what band colors the new pythia will wear?"

Thena covered her trembling right hand with her left so he wouldn't see how his touch had affected her. She was grateful for the question. It was much easier to ignore his powerful physical presence if she concentrated on explaining her society. "All . . . all new pythias wear blue bands until they are tested. In their first ritual they are asked three standard questions. The accuracy and clarity of their responses determines their true rank, and they are given its colors then."

Lancer gave her a piercing look. "You said there were two times when a moncat's bite wasn't poisonous. What's the second?"

Thus pinned by his gaze, Thena couldn't evade the question. She could only hope he didn't understand the significance of the answer in relation to the vision in his prophecy. "When a pythia chooses a mate the moncat will bite her left wrist and his right wrist, but only if he is the right person for her. The mixing of their blood bonds them together for life."

Lancer looked down at her clasped hands. Before he could reach for her left hand and arouse more disturbing sensations, Thena turned it over to show her unscarred wrist.

"You are as yet unmated." His strange smile

showed a gratifying quickening of interest and . . . was that satisfaction?

Before she could decipher it, he turned it into a mocking grin. "They mate for life? What if one of them wants to play around with someone else?"

Thena frowned and leaned back in the chair, away from him. "The man may do so with impunity—isn't that always the way in society? Our history tells us Earth is no different."

Lancer gave her a mock bow. "Yes, the infamous double standard. Are you saying the woman may not?"

He hadn't yet recognized the significance of his own scar in the vision. Thena was glad to change the subject. "No, if she does, the moncat will reject her and she will lose her prophetic powers. Our legends are full of stories about what happened to unfaithful pythias or those who gave up their position for ungrateful lovers."

Lancer raised an eyebrow. "What—" He broke off to indulge in a bout of coughing.

Thena furrowed her brow. These coughing spells of his had been occurring far too often lately. When the fit subsided she asked, "How are you feeling? Are you ill?"

Lancer waved away the question. "No, no, I'm fine. Just a little under the weather. Ship air always makes my throat dry, and I probably picked up a cold or something. It's nothing to worry about. I'll be fine, really."

Thena gazed at him doubtfully and he straightened. "Would you like to see those prophecies Spencer mentioned on the tape?"

Thena nodded. She was willing to be sidetracked for now, but she vowed to keep a close eye on his health over the next few days.

Chapter Seven

Two days later, Thena was still bored. She discarded the book reader on the bunk next to her, slid one hand beneath her head on the pillow, and sighed. Terran history books were as dry and uninteresting as Delphi's.

Staring at the ceiling, she absently petted Seri, who responded with a comforting purr. Thena had never thought she'd miss the monotonous routine of the Golden Pythia, but at least it had kept her busy. On this tiny ship her only choices were reading, listening to the log, or watching the stars flow by.

She couldn't even use the entertainment room. Lancer had holed up there, skimming through prophecies, making notes, and generally absorbing himself in his silly holofilm to the exclusion of all else. Thena sighed again. She wanted some company—human company. Unfortunately, that meant Lancer, and he seemed to be avoiding her as much as possible. She was almost tempted to change back into the pythia robes he had found so alluring. Maybe then he'd pay her some attention.

Thena kicked herself mentally. Apollo take the man! He had figured all too prominently in her daydreams of late. Now that he seemed indifferent to her presence, she had perversely become infatuated with him. She'd never been man-crazy, never fixated on some handsome villager like the other pythias. Why did *this* man evoke such a response in her?

Thena's frustration was evidently strong enough to penetrate Seri's doze. The moncat stirred restlessly, then wiggled free to stare at Thena with an oddly intent look.

Thena sent her a questioning thought.

In answer Seri broadcast a strong emotion: deep affection and a soul-bonding closeness with overtones of physical desire.

Thena stroked the soft fur on Seri's head. "Yes, I love you too." But she was a little disturbed by the lust. Did Seri need a mate?

Thena pictured a male moncat sitting next to Seri, their tails entwined. *Is this what you need?*

Seri grimaced in an almost human show of impatience and repeated the surge of emotion. This time, however, she patted Thena's cheek, then scurried over to Lancer's bunk and patted the indentation left by his head on the pillow.

In response to Seri's expectant look, Thena put it

together. Love . . . Thena . . . Lancer?

No. It's not possible.

Is it? Thena gasped as the revelation struck. Seri was right—she *was* in love with Lancer. It was the only thing that would explain her moodiness lately—not to mention those titillating daydreams.

Thena's heart soared. She was in love. How wonderful!

Her heart plummeted. She was in love with Lancer. How awful.

No, not Lancer! she pleaded with the moncat, who had returned to Thena's side. Seri gave her a disgusted look, then closed her eyes as if to say Thena was on her own.

How could she have fallen in love with a man who couldn't see *her* beyond her body? A man who was irresponsible and afraid of command? A man who the oracle had told her was destined for someone else? A *Terran,* for heaven's sake?

Despair and elation warred within her, finally coming to a truce on rampant curiosity. She felt as if her love was emblazoned in golden light on her forehead. Could he see it? How would he react? Could she even be in his presence without giving it away? She had to know.

First, though, she had to get his attention. With the gods as her witness, she'd get him out of that carrel if she had to stand naked in the corridor. Well, maybe not naked, exactly, but she'd change back into the white chiton if she had to.

Perhaps it would be better to try the direct approach first.

Thena sat up abruptly, causing Seri to emit a hiss of protest before settling back down in the bedclothes. Thena gave her a small pat. Poor Seri must be bored too. Well, this was about to either generate a lot more excitement, or sink them even farther into the doldrums.

Sliding off the bunk, Thena strode the necessary few steps to the entertainment room. Lancer sat in the carrel as usual, but instead of being bent over in concentration, his shoulders were in an uncharacteristic slump, and he had his face covered with one hand.

Something was wrong.

She took a step forward, and his hand slid down his face as he looked up. His eyes and nose were red, and his lips looked dry and cracked.

So much for romance.

"You look awful," she blurted out.

Thena expected one of Lancer's flippant rejoinders at her blunt remark, but he just rubbed his eyes. "That's how I feel, too."

She moved closer, feeling her hitherto dormant protective instincts come to the fore. "Is there something I can do?"

"No, *shiya*, I just have the 'flu. Every time we think we stamp it out, a new strain develops. I'll just have to stick it out."

He looked so tired and forlorn, she couldn't resist reaching up to push back the dark curls that had fallen forward on his forehead.

Lancer jerked his head back. "No, don't."

Thena froze. She had her answer; he didn't care

167

for her. He wouldn't even let her touch him. She turned to leave before her face crumpled like the shreds of her self-esteem.

Lancer's chair grated against the floor as he got to his feet. "Please, wait."

Before turning to face him again she assumed the cool mask of the Golden Pythia, determined not to let him know how much his simple action had hurt.

He leaned on the desk with one hand and gestured helplessly with the other. "I didn't mean that the way it sounded. It's just that the 'flu is very contagious and I don't want you catching it too." Lancer ran a hand over his mouth. "I'm sorry; what did you want?"

That might be true, but it didn't quite explain the violence of his reaction. She gave him a nonchalant shrug. "Oh, nothing. I was just getting bored and I thought you might like a break too."

Seri hopped up on the desk next to Lancer, and he stroked the moncat's fur. He was taking so long to answer, Thena was tempted to tell him to forget it.

He finally gave her a grudging nod. "Okay, I could use a break. Besides, everything is going blurry anyway. What did you have in mind?"

His wary look was annoying. *What are you afraid of? That I'll tear your clothes off and ravish you so you'll be my life-mate forever?* Thena grimaced. She had a clear mental image of *that* happening. Seri gave her a startled look. Maybe the image was a bit *too* clear.

Thena shook her head to clear her thoughts. Lancer had asked what she wanted. "I . . . I just wanted to talk. I've read a lot about Earth and the political structure, but I don't know anything about the people. I'd like to know something about those I'm likely to meet."

Lancer nodded. "Good idea. Let's go in the other room where I can lie down. Maybe it'll help me feel better."

Thena congratulated herself on her fast thinking. This way she'd learn more about Lancer while relieving her boredom.

They went into the forward cabin and Lancer sprawled on the bunk, leaning on a pillow propped against the wall. Seri curled up beside him, and he absently petted her. "Okay, shoot. What do you want to know?"

Thena sat in the copilot's chair, where she could see the man and the moncat. Seri opened her eyes wide and broadcast thoughts full of an unspecified anxiety that Thena was finding difficult to interpret. Thena sent Seri a reassuring thought—she didn't really plan to ravish Lancer.

Seri's anxiety didn't abate. Not knowing how to help her, Thena turned her attention back to Lancer. "Who am I likely to meet on Earth?"

Lancer coughed. "Primarily my family. There's my father, Hudson, and my two older brothers, Alexander and Darian."

"And your mother?"

"She died." Lancer frowned slightly, as if remembering a wound that had long since healed.

"I'm sorry," she murmured. She always seemed to say the wrong things around him.

Lancer waved his hand in dismissal. "That's okay. It was a long time ago, when I was a teenager. In fact, just after I was elected class president." He gave her a wry look. "It was a wonderful year."

She was glad to find they had something in common. "I know what it's like to lose a mother's love at an early age. At least you had a large family to comfort you—I had only Father, and he's a very cold man."

Lancer's mouth twisted into a grimace. "My family was little comfort. My father and brothers are stoic lumps who have a hard time showing emotion. Mother was just the opposite." His lips curved into a smile, and his gaze focused beyond her, to a more pleasant past. "She was mercurial—vibrant and alive. I never figured out how she and my father ever got together. But she loved him, even though she hated the political life."

Lancer's gaze returned to Thena, his smile lingering. "It was obvious I took after her, though Father tried hard to mold us all in his image. He succeeded with Alexander and Darian, but my mother and I were kindred souls, supporting each other through the boring inanities of the Washington political scene."

Lancer's mother, his refuge and support, had died just when he needed her most. No wonder his classmate's suicide had left so many emotional scars on the young Lancer. Thena wanted to learn more about the man he had become. "What about your holofilms—they're very important to you, aren't they?"

He looked surprised. "Yes, of course. It's my work."

This was an integral part of Lancer's life, and Thena wanted to understand it thoroughly. She shook her head impatiently. "No, it's more than that. You must have some reason for choosing that work over others. What drew you to making holofilms?"

Lancer thought for a moment. "I suppose it was the lure of being involved in an exciting industry and making my mark somewhere—other than politics."

Thena persisted. "But what makes it so exciting to you? What specifically do you like about it?"

Lancer's face turned intent, and he gestured with his expressive hands. "I like handling all the myriad details that go into producing a holofilm—finding just the right director, actors, and story, and bringing them together—challenging them and myself to make the best possible product."

He paused, considering. "Most of my films are political satires. After people see one of them I want them to go away a little different. Amused, maybe, or a little smarter, or maybe even a little ticked off at the status quo. I want to touch as many peoples' lives as possible—maybe even change them for the better. That's important to me."

He shrugged and gave a self-deprecating smile. "I guess I'm just an idealist at heart."

Lancer had revealed more than he realized.

Though he fought the bonds of authority and claimed he was no leader, his words had just revealed him as a man who craved the perquisites of command. He obviously didn't realize it. "You know—"

Lancer bent over double in a coughing fit that went on for several minutes. Thena wanted to help but didn't know what to do.

Lancer looked exhausted from his efforts. "I'm sorry, *shiya*, but I don't feel like talking anymore." He pushed himself to a sitting position. "I think I'm going to take a warm shower and use up some of that water. That should make me feel better."

Thena regarded him anxiously. "Do you need some help?"

Lancer gave her a rakish grin, made pitiful by his haggard look. "I don't think that would be such a good idea. I may be sick, but I'm not dead."

Thena nodded and turned away, feeling warmth suffuse her face. She had been looking for some reassurance that he wasn't totally indifferent to her and had finally gotten it. Satisfied, she watched as he headed for the bathroom. She could handle her love for Lancer without giving herself away. She'd just proven it.

Now that she had some hope, however slim, that her feelings might be returned, she had to decide what to do. Where was a pythia when she needed one?

Half an hour later Thena emerged from her pleasant daydreams and realized Lancer had been in the shower a long time. Could something have happened to him? She wavered for a moment, unable to decide if she should go into the bathroom and check.

Yes, she should. After all, he *was* ill. She walked down the short hallway to press her ear to the door but couldn't hear a thing. Pressing her palms flat against the cool metal panel, she strained harder to detect a sound, any sound.

The door opened abruptly, and Thena lost her balance. She toppled toward Lancer, just barely catching herself on the doorjamb. Seemingly oblivious, he just swayed slightly and blinked at her in confusion.

He looked better. Much better. In fact, he looked positively wonderful. Clad in nothing but a white towel wrapped around his waist, with his hair wet and slicked back and his magnificent chest bared to her gaze, he looked good enough to model for a statue of Apollo.

She felt herself blush for the second time that day. "I was just—"

Lancer wasn't listening. His eyes rolled up and he sagged against her in a dead faint. In reflex, she caught him under his arms. His weight almost brought her to her knees, but she was able to prop him up between her body and the door.

Thena just stood there, stunned, as his dark, wet head pressed facedown against her breast and his cumbersome body sagged against hers. She shook him slightly. "Lancer." There was no response. "Lancer! Are you all right?"

What a dumb question. Of course he wasn't all right—he'd just passed out in her arms! She gave Seri a pleading look over her heavy burden. "Now what do I do?" she wailed.

Seri offered no help, so Thena quickly reviewed her options. If she put him down, she'd probably never be able to get him up again. She couldn't just let him lie in the corridor, and she *certainly* couldn't lift him onto a bunk.

The exercise mats!

Perfect. But first, she needed a better grip. Thena shifted her hold and spread her feet apart to balance his weight more evenly, inadvertently stepping on the trailing edge of the towel. The knot loosened and fell, leaving the towel hanging straight down from his slim hips.

She stared at the cloth in consternation. Should she fix it? No, she couldn't worry about that now.

Before he got any heavier, Thena lugged him backwards along the corridor, staggering in her haste. Halfway down the hall the towel lost its precarious purchase and fell to the floor, leaving her staring at Lancer's very attractive backside. Smooth and nicely rounded, a pale white against the rest of his tanned skin, it begged for her touch.

Thena stopped in mid-drag to gape, then resolutely turned her mind back to her task. If she wasn't careful, her face would turn permanently pink from all the blushing she was doing lately.

She reached the exercise mat and backed up over it. Afraid she might drop him if she shifted her grip, she eased down to squat on her heels, then rocked backward to sit flat on the mat. Keeping her eyes resolutely focused on the ceiling, she leaned back to lie down with Lancer in her arms.

Thank goodness that was over. She lay there for a moment to rest, her arms now relieved of her burden. Heaving a heavy sigh, Thena prepared to move out from under him when she caught Seri's quizzical look.

Thena shifted her gaze downward. To a casual observer, this would look very odd indeed. She was lying on the floor with a very naked Lancer sprawled on top of her, his head nestled between her breasts.

She allowed her gaze to linger a while longer, roaming over the interesting planes and curves of his lean physique. Their intimate near-embrace caused a warm flood of sensation to start in her loins and spread insidiously throughout her entire body. Thena reached out a tentative hand to stroke his shoulder, feeling the strength hidden beneath the velvet softness of his rich brown skin.

Seri coughed and Thena gave a guilty start, snatching her hand away. *What am I doing?* The man was gravely ill—he had just passed out in her arms—and all she could do was drool over his body. She directed her thoughts back to the problem at hand.

The first priority was to get out from beneath Lancer without disturbing him. Thena began sliding out backwards, then stopped abruptly. Seeing where that would bring his face in contact with next, she changed direction and slid out sideways instead.

Grabbing some bedclothes from Lancer's bunk, she regarded him thoughtfully. "What do you think, Seri? Male anatomy is different. He can't possibly be comfortable in that position. Should we turn him over?"

Thena met Seri's unblinking stare and sighed. "No, I guess not." Lancer wouldn't appreciate knowing he'd bared his all when he wasn't conscious to enjoy her reaction.

She covered him up with the blanket and slipped a pillow under his head. This "flu" seemed to have hit him hard, and she didn't know how to treat it. She hovered over his motionless form for a few moments, helplessly waiting for inspiration to strike. No such luck—her mind had gone totally blank.

Lancer stirred, and her heart leapt as he turned over and opened bleary eyes. "Medical monitor," he croaked. "Diagnosis . . . medicine."

That was right— he'd shown her the emergency medical station between the bunks earlier. She fumbled at the bright red cover, unlatching it to reveal a computer panel similar to the one on the tape player.

Thena pushed "start" and quickly read the directions.

List the patient's symptoms, it instructed.

Thena knelt down beside Lancer, who stared at her groggily. "What are your symptoms?"

"Thirsty . . . hot . . . cough . . . dizzy." He licked

his lips. "Tingling . . . all over. Tired." He closed his eyes and lay back, coughing.

She could help alleviate one of those symptoms anyway. Leaving Seri to watch anxiously over their patient, Thena hurried to the kitchen and filled a glass with water. She returned to kneel beside him, raising his shoulders so he could drink. Ever independent, Lancer shifted to one unsteady elbow and, grasping the glass in a shaky hand, downed half its contents. Apparently exhausted, he lay back down. "Thanks," he gasped.

Thena nodded, then hastened back to the medical station. She entered his symptoms, then sighed in relief when the computer signaled a match.

Display illness?

Thena pushed the "yes" button with unnecessary vigor and the description began scrolling down the screen.

Hana's Disease. Occurs only on the southern hemisphere of the colony planet Hana in female gortrab addicts experiencing menopause. Treatment:—

Thena punched "stop" in frustration. This wasn't Hana and Lancer wasn't a woman. Of course, she hadn't actually turned him over and checked, but she was certain of his gender even without the corroborating evidence.

She scanned the other buttons and pushed the one that said "next entry."

No additional matches found, flashed the computer screen.

It couldn't be! There had to be a match. Frantically, Thena typed Lancer's symptoms again. *Thirst, fever, vertigo, cough, tingling.*

Tingling? she paused. Those symptoms sounded familiar—just like Sharpe's Fever.

Sharpe's Fever? The butcher! Dendil must have given the fever to Lancer when he chaperoned them around Dodona.

Apollo save me from my own stupidity! This was a common ailment on Delphi—she should have recognized the symptoms long before now. But Lancer had been so sure he knew what was making him ill, she hadn't even considered it.

She knelt by Lancer's bedside again. "You've caught Sharpe's Fever from Dendil." He gave her a blank look and she patted his hand in reassurance. "Don't worry; I know how to cure it."

Lancer nodded and closed his eyes. She sighed in relief. Sharpe's Fever she could handle, and she had the cure at hand.

Thena opened the flowerpot and plucked a dormant caroline from her meager supply, taking it to the kitchen. She carefully crushed the flower petals and poured boiling water over them, allowing them to steep until the water turned a rich, dark purple. Straining the petals from the infusion, she added sweetener to disguise the bitter taste.

Returning to Lancer, she offered him the mug. "Here, drink this."

He took one sip and screwed his face into a grimace.

"Oh, come now," she said. "It's not that bad, and I added some honey to make it taste better."

"Too sweet," he muttered, but he drank down the rest of the brew.

Thena sat back, satisfied she had done all she could. His fever should break within the next 12 hours and his coughing ease. Then, in a day or two, he'd be almost back to normal.

Fourteen hours later his fever showed no signs of abating. She had kept him warm and liberally supplied with the infusion, but now she had an additional worry.

If the trip to Earth took two weeks, and the transfer point was halfway between, then that meant . . . the transfer point was coming up in three days! If Lancer wasn't conscious and at the helm then, there was a good possibility they wouldn't survive.

Thena shuddered. If the huge colony ship had been so severely damaged by its unexpected passage through the transfer point, she didn't want to think what would happen to this tiny craft.

Missing it altogether would be almost as bad. If they dallied in unknown space for too long, waiting for Lancer to recover, there was the distinct possibility they would run out of fuel and air.

She *had* to get him well enough to navigate the transfer point—and soon. Thena racked her brain, casting her mind back to her childhood lessons, wishing she'd paid more attention to the healer's lectures.

All right, the first thing she needed to do was find out why Lancer's case was so unique, so much worse than those she was used to.

Hmm, the only thing different was Lancer—he was Terran, not Delphian. No, that shouldn't matter; Delphians had evolved from Terran stock. But maybe . . . maybe the Delphians had grown more resistant to the disease over the centuries. If so, it was highly likely the colonists had experienced the same severe symptoms as Lancer, and . . . that meant Captain Spencer just might be able to shed some light on the problem.

Thena hurried to the console and sat on the edge of the copilot's seat. Putting the computer in search mode, she typed *Sharpe's Fever*.

The screen blinked, indicating a successful search, and forwarded to the relevant entry on the Captain's Log. Thena pushed "play," filling the cabin with Captain Spencer's familiar voice.

A week ago Charles Sharpe returned from a botanical specimen collecting trip with a virulent fever the doctors are unable to identify. They speculate the virus is native to Delphi and, afraid to let it spread unchecked throughout the rest of the colony, they have isolated Sharpe and three other victims until they can identify a cure.

Thena squirmed in the chair as the verbose captain went on to describe the fever's symptoms and the casualties it claimed. She needed the cure, not a recitation of the symptoms!

Finally the captain returned to the point.

Sharpe's Fever has claimed three lives, includ-
ing that of the man it was named for. If we don't
find a cure soon, I fear our fledgling colony will
be wiped out by disease.

No one Thena knew had ever *died* of Sharpe's
Fever. Dear Apollo, Lancer's case closely resembled those of the colonists. He could die of this.
Suddenly the impetus to cure him became more
urgent.

Desperate to find a cure, Dr. Crowley solicited
a prediction from one of the young prophetesses,
whom the colonists are calling pythias after the
Delphi legend. The pythia told the doctor to
make her patients comfortable in a caroline-
filled cavern and let a moncat bite each one.
Needless to say, this fired a raging debate in the
Council. With moncat bites poisonous to all but
their pythias, and with the vague, questionable
accuracy of the prophecies, some fear the cure is
worse than the disease. Others believe it cannot
make them worse than they already are.

Thena glanced at Seri. A moncat's bite? Maybe
that was why Seri was hovering over Lancer. Did
she realize she might have the means to heal him?

The majority of the Council voted to ignore the
prophecy, in hopes Dr. Crowley will find a cure
on her own.

Captain Spencer sounded depressed. Thena could sympathize with him; if the pythias had only been accepted immediately, she would have had her answer by now.

The captain's voice resumed.

An assistant medtech, also a pythia, took it upon herself to prove the efficacy of her fellow pythia's prophecy. Taking her ill young brother into a caroline bower, she had her moncat bite him. The results are not yet conclusive; there seems to be little change in his condition.

The tape paused and Thena waited anxiously to hear the next chapter. *"The cure works!"* came the jubilant voice of the captain.

It's slow, but it works. The moncats somehow manufacture an enzyme in their saliva that, when administered under the soporific influence of the flowers, becomes an antidote to the disease. It is most effective with women; the recovery period takes only a week. With men, it is longer, requiring a full week of comatose healing, then another week of recovery. All the doubters have been satisfied, and moncat bites are being administered to the patients as if they were the latest miracle drug.

Thena turned off the tape. Two weeks! The transfer point was coming up in *three days.* She buried her face in her hands, trying not to give in to useless tears. The dependable Captain Spencer had let her down.

Or had he?

Thena slowly raised her head. The computer had taken her to the first occurrence on the tape. Maybe there were more.

With shaking fingers, she typed *Sharpe's Fever* again. Clasping her hands together to steady them, she sent a prayer aloft to Apollo, entreating him and the captain not to let her down.

The computer screen flashed the discovery of another match and Thena crossed her fingers as it forwarded to the appropriate entry.

She pushed "play" and the captain's voice came on again.

Dr. Crowley has just about solved the problem. Synthesizing an antigen from the moncat's saliva and the carolines, she has come up with a fairly effective immunization for Sharpe's Fever.

This wouldn't help. Thena reached to turn off the tape, but was struck by the captain's amused voice as he continued.

In a bizarre footnote, we have learned of an even better cure. A young pythia's fiancé was stricken by the disease and, afraid he would not survive to wed her, she took him to her bower. The moncat bit both of them, and they mixed their blood together, consummating their love. The resulting combination of the two radically different enzymes served to speed the young man's healing. He recovered in a matter of two days rather than two weeks.

Thena punched the tape player's "off" button and danced around the small space of the cabin in pure exuberance. Raising her arms to the heavens, she cried, "Thank you, Apollo!" She smiled and patted the tape player. "And you, too, Captain. I'm sorry I doubted you."

The treatment worked fast—it would make Lancer well enough to take the ship through the transfer point. She sighed in relief. They would survive this trip. All she had to do was perform the life-mate ritual.

Thena's exhilaration died and her smile faded.

The life-mate ritual. Irrevocable. Final.

Her gaze turned to Lancer where he lay twisting in fever. Yes, she wanted him, and yes, she wanted him as a life-mate, but not like this. Not when it was being forced upon her, and especially not when it was being forced upon *him*.

Would the log have yet another cure? She had to find out. Seating herself at the console, Thena typed *Sharpe's Fever* once more. The machine whirred and clicked for what seemed like forever, then finally stopped and flashed its answer mockingly across the screen.

End of search.

Thena's heart sank. She had no choice. She had to perform the life-mate ritual. Their lives depended on it.

Chapter Eight

Lancer woke and immediately regretted it. His brain felt as though it had been pickled in rotgut and beaten to death with a sledgehammer. Nerve endings all over his body felt raw and exposed, and he was so dizzy, he couldn't focus properly. In short, he felt lousy.

Waking up had been a rotten idea. Closing his eyes, he drifted off to sleep again.

Some time later the heady scent of an exotic perfume filled his senses, and he felt the cool, welcome touch of a wet cloth on his fevered body. Opening his eyes just a fraction, he found a beautiful woman bending over him. With her flowing gown and the fuzzy violet-tinged halo surrounding her cloud of honey-blond hair, she had to be an angel—a dream angel.

Lancer smiled in approval. This was how angels ought to look: full-breasted yet ethereal. He peered behind her for her wings, but couldn't see them. She must have hidden them somehow.

He lay there, content to enjoy the sensations of the cool cloth on his face and shoulders. The cloth was removed, and she put a hand under his head to hold a glass of water to his lips. He drank greedily and her hand relaxed, lowering his head back to the bed.

The angel leaned closer and smoothed the hair from his forehead. "Lancer," she said softly. "You're very sick."

Ah, an angel of mercy. "Are you going to make me well?" he croaked.

She gave him a sad smile. "I know how, but it requires your willing cooperation."

Lancer tried to give her a vigorous nod, but his head felt so heavy he could barely move it. "Okay."

Caressing his cheek with a lingering softness, she said, "You don't understand. The only cure for your fever is a moncat's bite. And the only hope of getting you well enough in time to navigate the transfer point is by performing the life-mate ritual."

Lancer frowned, confused. He had heard what she said, but it didn't make any sense. He started to tell her so, but was distracted by the sight of another head sprouting from her right shoulder.

Narrowing his gaze to bring it into sharper focus, he realized the second head was definitely feline and attached to a body of its own. Good—he didn't think he could deal with a two-headed angel right now. He closed his eyes again. This dream was getting tiresome.

The angel shook his shoulder. "Lancer, I need your answer."

He opened his eyes and searched through his store of brilliant repartee. "Huh?" It was the best he could come up with on such short notice.

"*Do* you agree to the life-mate ritual?"

He blinked at her blearily, not understanding.

She heaved a sigh that drew attention to her magnificent breasts. "Will you make love to me?"

A slow smile spread across his face. "Hell, yes."

The angel blushed and turned to call the little creature by name. It sounded like "Sera." That made sense; it must be a seraph—only he thought seraphim had a human appearance, not feline.

The seraph descended from the angel's shoulder to sit beside Lancer and peer into his face. He *felt* it searching his mind and got the distinct feeling it was probing his soul as well. He didn't know how or why, but it was measuring him and his answer. Deep down inside, he felt the first stirring of a lasting contentment.

A flood of warm approval poured from the furry creature, so he was more than a bit surprised when it leaned down to bite him viciously on the wrist. Before he could cry out at the fleeting pain, the seraph bit the angel's wrist, then took off for parts unknown.

Unshakable in her aplomb, the angel grasped his hand in hers and placed their bleeding wounds together. "Repeat after me," she instructed. "Heavenly Apollo, witness this union. . . ."

He croaked the words after her, not understanding any of it. Was this some strange version of angelic foreplay?

Her words ceased, and she leaned forward to press her lips against his, still holding their wrists together. He returned the kiss weakly. Damn—he couldn't even kiss her properly. This dream was turning into a nightmare.

A bolt of fiery needles suddenly poured from the gash in his wrist, shooting through his bloodstream and bringing his body to tingling awareness. Lancer instantly felt 20 times better—and definitely able to perform.

His sight cleared, and in the way of dreams the vision before him segued into the alluring Golden Pythia, Thena. He felt another slow smile spread across his face. Things were looking up. A flesh-and-blood woman was better than an angel any day—even in a dream. Especially *this* dream woman.

Thena stayed kneeling by his bedside, giving him a tantalizing look compounded of hesitation and desire. It was irresistible. He curled his fingers around the back of her neck and buried them deep in the luxurious softness of her hair, bringing her lips down to his. She twined her arms around his neck and her mouth opened to his as he deepened the kiss, tasting her. God, her mouth was as sweet as the finest Shiyan liqueur—and just as intoxicating.

He pulled back to gaze at the perfection of her

face and found her eyes had darkened to a deep blue, brimming with passion and an unslaked desire. Wanting, needing to feel her against him, Lancer cast off his restraining covers and drew her down to lie beside him.

Thena looked down at him and inhaled sharply. The dream had made him obligingly naked, removing yet another impediment to their joining. He pulled her to him, pressing his burgeoning arousal against the softness of her flowing gown and the firm flesh of the woman beneath.

Thena lifted her face for another kiss and Lancer responded fervently, exploring the wonders of her body with caressing hands as he plumbed her mouth with his tongue. Her breasts peaked to taut attention under his ministrations, exciting a moan from her that merely fueled his desire.

Impatient with the barrier of her gown, he wished it away. When the dream didn't oblige, he helped her peel the silky fabric slowly off over her head. It was his turn to inhale in appreciation at the masterpiece revealed beneath. Each lush, ripe curve was a work of art. This was how a woman ought to look, not like those skinny, emaciated actresses he worked with.

"You're so beautiful," he whispered, and watched her turn pink clear down to her nipples as she gazed shyly at him. He pressed her back onto the bed and his hand gravitated like a magnet to one full breast, while his tongue circled the other in slow, intimate caresses.

Thena gasped in delight, encouraging him to explore further. Skimming his other hand down her slender waist, he passed over her full hips to dip lower into the hot, moist core of her femininity, glorying in her ardent response and the spicy scent of her arousal.

She moaned and arched her hips upward to meet him. He continued to torment her with teasing flicks of his tongue and intimate caresses until she begged him to stop. Showing no mercy, he delved deeper and faster until she was writhing in ecstasy. Clutching his shoulders, she tilted her head back in an inarticulate cry of pleasure as she came to a shuddering climax.

My God! Who would have thought the dignified Golden Pythia would be so passionate in bed?

Her excitement brought his own urgent need to aching awareness. Lancer dragged his mouth reluctantly from her breast, giving it one last caress with his tongue. He rose to kneel over her with a questioning look. Thena nodded with a dreamy, sated smile, and he entered her slowly, stopping when he broke through the barrier of her maidenhood. She stiffened momentarily, then wrapped her legs and arms around him and pulled him down into a deep, soul-satisfying kiss.

Lancer sent a brief prayer of thanks to the god of dreams, and slowly sheathed himself in her. Waves of unadulterated pleasure crashed over him—she felt like tight, hot silk. The need to possess her fully warred with the desire to take it slow for her sake, causing small shivers to race through his body and adding a certain spice to his desire.

Holding himself rigidly in check, he moved his

hips in long, slow strokes. Thena's eyes widened and she clutched him tighter, then matched his rhythm in a rite as old as humankind. Her uninhibited response shattered his control. Increasing his tempo until he felt the tremors in her body match his own, he felt the universe explode in a nova of brilliant stars as he arched above her.

Lancer remained in that position for one perfect moment, then relaxed to gaze tenderly down at his dream lover. Thoroughly sated, he gathered her in his arms and lay down beside her, falling once more into oblivion.

Thena gave him a tender kiss on the cheek and smoothed back the unruly lock of hair that had fallen onto his forehead. His arms loosened and she sat up, allowing herself to marvel at the tenderness and passion he had evoked in her.

Now that the life-mate ritual was completed, it would be best to leave him to his recovery. Thena slid carefully from the mat and stood. A chill touched her, reminding her of her surroundings and bringing her back to reality. Shivering, she covered Lancer with his blanket, then grabbed another one from her bunk and wrapped it around herself. Carefully closing the lid on the carolines, she turned the cabin lights up on low and returned to his side.

Huddled in her blanket, Thena stared lovingly at her life-mate, her lover. One corner of his mouth quirked mischievously as his features relaxed in sleep, giving him the endearing look of a little boy. She understood that smile—she couldn't help but wear one exactly like it as she reflected on the ritual they had just shared.

Thena had always yearned for the beauty of the ceremony, not realizing until now that the true bonding took place afterward. She felt a slight pang at missing the company of her friends and family on the most important day of her adult life, but nothing could overwhelm her delight at having become mated to such a remarkable man.

The ritual hadn't been at all what she expected—nor did it resemble any life-mate ceremony she'd ever attended. Tradition called for the declaration of their love in the sanctity of Apollo's shrine, followed by suspense over the moncat's affirmation or rejection of the prospective life-mate. If the moncat gave its approval—rarely withheld—it bit them and the lovers mingled their blood. They were then led away to retire to a secluded bower of carolines, where they consummated their union amid the exotic flowers.

Thena had always assumed the moncat's empathic enhancement, combined with the influence of the carolines, took the lovers to the height of cerebral affinity. Instead, this seemed to be the one time when the carolines had not affected either of them. Come to think of it, she didn't recall Seri enhancing her emotions either. Thena felt her face warm with a blush. She hadn't needed any enhancement.

That reminded her—where had Seri been during all of this? Thena tucked her blanket more securely around her shoulders and rose to walk the length of the tiny ship. She found the moncat fast asleep on the shelf Lancer had cleared for her.

Thena reached up to stroke the moncat's soft fur and Seri woke, blinking sleepily at her. Thena shared her feelings of sated lust and tender love with the moncat, curious to see her reaction.

Seri yawned and stretched, paws curled, then relaxed and closed her eyes with a smug smile on her furry little face.

Thena chuckled. So Seri was going to take credit for Thena's happiness, was she? Thena rubbed the moncat between the ears and broadcasted gratitude. After all, Seri *had* approved Lancer as Thena's life-mate.

If Lancer was awake, he'd surely want to pamper Thena. But since he wasn't, she'd have to indulge herself. She smiled secretly—she'd been wanting to try a water shower since the beginning of the trip, and now was the perfect time for one.

Retracing her steps to the bathroom, she dropped the blanket and stepped into the shower. Thena sighed in happiness as she luxuriated in the warm spray on the newly tender portions of her anatomy and daydreamed about the life she and Lancer would have together. Now everything would be perfect.

Lancer woke slowly but kept his eyes closed, unwilling to risk a repetition of his last disastrous waking. Gingerly taking inventory of his assorted parts, he realized he felt better—much better than he had in days.

The rotgut and sledgehammer were gone and his

throat was back to normal, without that irritating urge to cough. As he lay there reveling in the feeling of improved health, he felt Thena kneel beside his pad.

Opening his eyes the merest crack, he studied her surreptitiously from under his lashes. She was wearing that sexy white dress again, just as she had in the dream.

The dream! The memories came flooding back to him in a rush of pleasure. Too bad it had been just a dream, but he could imagine her shock if she learned of the fantasy he had lived out in the delirium of his fever.

He watched her face as she bent over him and pulled the blanket down to his waist, prudently keeping his major assets covered. As she began washing him with a warm wet cloth, he realized she was not at all shy with the close proximity to his body. In fact, she looked downright happy to be there.

Her touch recalled her passionate dream response, and he suppressed the memory ruthlessly, not wanting to raise her eyebrows—or the blanket—with his arousal.

Her swift, competent hands finished their cleansing of his chest and arms and worked their way down to his waist, smoothly drawing the blanket down to his feet. He lay there, stunned by her bold unveiling of his nudity, and even more so at her brazen, smiling appraisal of his full exposure.

She gave careful attention to cleaning the sensitive skin of his genitals, and he spontaneously came to full erection in her loving hands. Dear God, was this another dream? He spotted Seri sitting next to Thena, giving him an amused look. No, this wasn't a dream. Did that mean . . . ?

He glanced back down at Thena's continued cleansing of his already thoroughly clean shaft and his mouth dropped open. Plainly visible on her left wrist was the healing bite of a moncat. His gaze darted to his own wrist, where he found a similar mark. That was no dream—it was real!

He sat up suddenly, startling Thena into jerking backward. She lost her balance and sprawled on her rear.

Grabbing the blanket up around him to conceal the object of her attentions, Lancer tried to sort through the mish-mash of emotions churning through his belly.

Foremost was the throbbing excitement of his loins, brought to aching attention by her skilled hands. Following closely behind was shock and consternation, and other emotions he couldn't identify—not to mention feeling a little silly at his own show of prudery.

Thena smiled shyly at him, and he was glad to see she had the grace to blush. "Hello," she said softly. "Welcome back."

She moved to a kneeling position and reached toward his face, but he jerked back. "No!" He needed time to think about this, without the distraction of her erotic touch. He ignored the stricken look on her face, too wrapped up in sorting out his emotions to worry about hers.

"What—" he croaked, his unused voice cracking with the strain. Clearing his throat, he asked, "What happened?" He had to know. "Did we really make love?"

Thena nodded with a wary look on her face.

Lancer rubbed one hand over his face, careful not to lose his grip on the blanket, and gave her an apologetic look. "Oh, God, *shiya*, I'm so sorry. I was out of my head. I . . . I didn't know what I was doing. Can you ever forgive me?"

Several unidentifiable emotions chased across Thena's face as he waited for her answer. His heart sank as her expression finally congealed into a cold mask.

"Sorry?" she said. "What are you sorry for?"

Wasn't it obvious? He gestured helplessly. "For taking advantage of your innocence."

"But I *asked* you to make love to me." The mask didn't crack an inch.

Lancer was baffled. He'd been out of his head, hardly the figure of romance. "Why?"

"Don't you remember? We had to perform the life-mate ritual."

The realization hit Lancer with the force of a pile driver. That was what the churning in his gut was all about—it was reminding him that this woman had just blithely hog-tied him for life, committing him to a sentence of political expediency while he was too out of his gourd to protest.

Ha! That was what *she* thought!

"That was a dirty trick—catching me off guard while I was too sick to resist you."

"A dirty trick! I didn't hear—or see—any protests." She glanced pointedly at his midsection.

Still feeling foolish for clutching his blanket around him like a simpering virgin, Lancer lashed back. "No, but you knew I was out of my head. You can't possibly hold me to any promises I made while I was delirious. Just forget it happened."

Thena turned rigid with anger. "I can't. The ritual bonded me to you for life, or have you forgotten?"

Lancer hit the deck with his fist. "No, damn it, but I didn't agree to it—it's not binding."

"On the contrary, Lancer Morgan, you *did* agree to it. Seri never would have performed the ritual without your agreement, and your full acquiescence was plainly visible in your mind."

He vaguely remembered something of the sort, but shrugged it off as irrelevant. "But why then? Why couldn't you wait until I was fully conscious? Were you afraid I wouldn't agree?"

Thena struggled to her feet and balled her hands into fists on her hips. "No. I did it to save our lives. Check the Captain's Log—the life-mate ritual was the only solution. Otherwise we would have missed the transfer point or died passing through it. The alarm has been sounding for ten hours now."

"Yeah, right—" he began, only to be cut off by the klaxon warning of the imminent transfer point.

Forgetting his blanket, Lancer lurched to his feet and stumbled dizzily to the console. He slapped the shut-off switch, his only thought to stop the noise reverberating through his skull. Suddenly remembering his nakedness, he whirled to find

Thena gone and the moncat staring at him with a disgusted look on her face.

"Yeah, I know," he muttered. "I blew it."

Thena sat huddled in a corner of the entertainment room, where she had locked herself in after Lancer's cruel accusations.

Her anger gone, she curled around the ball of pain that had formed in her middle and rocked, desperately trying to keep from sobbing in humiliation at Lancer's utter rejection. She'd thought he loved her too, or would come to do so in time. Instead, he was angry. Why hadn't she heeded the oracle's warning that Lancer was not for her? Now she was paying the price. Dear Apollo, why did love have to be so painful?

She tucked her head into her knees and swallowed hard. How could she ever face him again?

The ship reeled and the ball of pain tightened even further. Soon she wouldn't have to worry about it anymore. They were nearing the transfer point, and they would surely be killed. Her efforts to save them had been in vain.

The ship rocked again, and she heard Lancer pounding on the door. "C'mon, Thena, open up!" he yelled.

Thena—he'd called her Thena. He'd never used her name before; he'd always called her *shiya*. Now even that small pleasure was denied her. She ignored him.

He pounded again. "You've got to strap in!"

Thena stayed huddled in her little ball. Better to

die than face Lancer and the mortification of his contempt.

The pounding stopped; then a heavy thud sounded and the door flew open as Lancer kicked it in. She didn't have time to react as he ran in, scooped her up, and ran back to the forward cabin. He dumped her in the copilot's chair and snapped, "Strap in—we're in for a hell of a ride. I cut it too close."

She did as he instructed, then belatedly remembered the moncat. Seri! Where was she? Thena looked frantically around the cabin and spotted the moncat crouched in her safety net on Thena's bunk, wide-eyed and broadcasting fear. Feeling guilty for forgetting the moncat while wrapped in her own misery, Thena concentrated on calming her own fears to soothe Seri.

The ship lurched, and Thena gripped the armrests tightly. "What's happening?" she shouted over the screaming engines.

"I took too long to get you up here," he yelled back. "There's a narrow groove we have to follow to ride out the storm; otherwise we'll be torn apart. I have to find it again!"

She changed her mind. She wanted to live.

Realizing they were in this predicament because of her, she kept her mouth shut so he could fight the chaos without distractions. Thena prayed to Apollo to spare them, her attention concentrated on the screen and the distorted, stretched-out streamers of starlight flowing past them.

This fight against the turbulence was strangely

familiar—a lot like riding a querent's golden path to the answer. A growing confidence replaced her panic. She had experience in this—she could help.

Closing her eyes, she sought mentally for their bond and found it on the periphery of her consciousness—a fine golden filament that connected her to Lancer. It was small, but it was enough to lend him her support.

Subtly, so as not to distract him, she drew upon her strength as a pythia and sent waves of confidence and reassurance along their connection. In the background she could feel Seri's panic recede as the moncat realized what Thena was doing.

Seri picked up the thread and reinforced it, slowly feeding Lancer with a subtle strengthening of his own steady nerves and quick reflexes. It worked—the bucking scoutship slipped into the groove and their ride smoothed as they rode out the rest of the transfer on the correct path.

The stars reverted to pinpoints of light, and Thena slipped out of the connection, now infinitesimally strengthened by their sharing of the ordeal. She released the breath she didn't realize she had been holding and suddenly remembered her humiliation. She fumbled at the seatbelt, anxious to escape, but Lancer was too quick.

He undid his harness and stood before her, his hand stilling her futile plucking at her own straps. "*Shiya*," he said softly.

Shame ignited in her stomach and Thena refused to look at him. Lancer knelt down and gently grasped her chin, bringing her reluctant gaze to his.

He looked remorseful. A tiny hope blossomed in the center of her pain.

Stroking her cheek with the back of his fingers, Lancer said, "*Shiya*, I'm sorry; I was wrong."

Thena gave him a questioning look, the churning in her stomach rendering her speechless.

He unbuckled her safety harness and drew her into his arms. "While you were in the entertainment room, I played back the last entry on the log." She stood unyielding, not yet ready to forgive the agony he'd caused her.

Stroking her hair, he said, "God, I'm such a jerk—I'm so sorry."

She relaxed a little, unable to resist this humble Lancer.

His arms tightened around her. "I understand. You had to perform the ritual in order to save our lives. How can I ever repay your sacrifice?"

Sacrifice? He didn't understand—she *loved* him. She opened her mouth to explain, but he stopped her with a finger on her lips. "Shh. It's okay."

Clasping both of her arms in a firm grip, he gave her a serious look. "I'll do anything to make it up to you—" her heart leapt into her throat— "anything but play Council Captain to your Golden Pythia."

Anything but the one thing she desired above all else. Her gaze dropped, along with her hopes.

He shook her slightly. "Okay, *shiya?*"

Her life-mate had just rejected her and everything she stood for. How could it be okay? Thena weighed and discarded various answers. None of them would work. Someone had to lose.

"*Shiya?*"

Thena sighed. She was bonded to Lancer, for life. If she wanted to be with him, she had to play by his rules. The alternative was to lose him forever. She couldn't face that now. Her love was too raw, too new.

She gave Lancer a falsely bright smile, though her heart was breaking. "Yes, it's okay."

May Apollo forgive my lie.

Chapter Nine

Thena absentmindedly prepared their dinner, marveling at how rapidly Lancer had regained his health since the life-mate ritual several days before. It was ironic—the very thing that ensured his health was the one thing driving them apart.

Oh, he was the soul of politeness—he merely did his best to pretend the ritual had never happened. But the more he tried to avoid her, the more his gaze seemed to linger on the rounded portions of her anatomy, driving him to seek cold showers with ever-increasing frequency.

Thena smiled to herself, enjoying the fact that he found her attractive. So far, she had resisted the temptation to play on his weakness by dressing seductively and playing the wanton. She wanted him to love her for herself, not for the fleeting pleasures of her body.

But, stars! It was difficult. He was her *life-mate*, and she wanted to learn more about the love between a man and a woman. Instead, she went along with his pretense that the ritual had never happened. She sighed. For now, it had to be enough just to be with him.

She called Lancer from the entertainment room and they sat down to eat. Lancer avoided meeting her gaze and tucked into his food as if he was starving.

After five minutes of silence Thena's resolve crumbled. *Enough of this walking on eggshells!* She slammed her mug down on the table. Lancer looked up in surprise.

Good—she had his attention now. "Lancer, won't you even speak to me?"

He swallowed and gestured with his fork, apprehension plainly visible in his eyes. "Sure. What d'you want to talk about?"

"I'm tired of this. Let's discuss it and get it out in the open."

He gave her a wary look. "Discuss what?"

It wasn't like Lancer to act coy. "We. Made. Love," she enunciated clearly. "I'm not ashamed of it. Are you?"

He looked startled. "No, of course not."

"Then why are you pretending it never happened?"

"I . . . I . . ." He floundered to a stop.

Thena sighed and let him off the hook. "Never mind; I understand. You're afraid if you admit to participating in the ritual, I'll hold you to the life-mate bonding and all the responsibility it entails. Am I right?"

"Yes, but—"

Thena pushed away from the table and rose. "Please, no explanations. I told you I understand."

Lancer looked relieved, and stood to face her, gesturing helplessly. "*Shiya* . . . "

Not wanting him to see the pain in her eyes, Thena turned her back on him, facing Seri in her niche. The moncat's compassionate gaze helped strengthen Thena for what she had to say. "I know. I know . . . and I don't care. As far as I'm concerned, you're my life-mate, with all that implies." She took a deep breath. "But I don't intend to hold you to a commitment you didn't ask for and don't want."

He kept silent, making it easier for her to continue. Thena turned around and faced him. "I . . . I'm going to need your friendship when we land on Earth. I just want to go back to the easy relationship we had a few days ago. Can't we do that?" Despite herself, a plaintive note crept into her voice.

Lancer's eyes mirrored the compassion in Seri's as he folded her in the comfort of his arms. "Yes, of course, *shiya*."

She relaxed in his embrace, needing the simple gesture of affection more than she'd suspected. Resting her head on his shoulder for a blissful instant, she allowed herself to enjoy this brief contact with the man she loved.

Lancer tilted her chin to look into her eyes and gave her the familiar, dear grin she had missed so much. "I'm sorry if I upset you, but it's so difficult to be near you without holding you, touching you."

Thena allowed a tremulous smile to cross her lips. "So stop trying."

Lancer tucked a curl behind her ear. "Ah, *shiya.*"

His head dipped lower and he captured her lips in an exquisitely tender kiss. A kiss that ended all too soon. Giving her one more gentle hug, he released her. Bereft, she stared at him in confusion.

He shoved his fingers through his hair. "I don't want to take advantage of your generosity. Let's just let things take their course and develop naturally, shall we?"

She nodded. It sounded good to her. Now that they had cleared the air, she felt much better. She even had a little hope that things might work out between them—someday. "All right then, let's finish dinner before it gets cold."

Lancer continued eating without tasting any of it, thankful for the concealing table. Thena was such an innocent; she had no idea how the mere touch of her body swelled his desire—not to mention his trousers. Hell, all he had to do was look at her to get hard. He couldn't understand it—he'd never been so obsessed with a woman before, especially after he'd already bedded her.

Tantalizing images flashed through his mind. Thena, standing shyly naked before him. Thena, abandoning her dignity to respond ardently to his intimate caresses. Thena, lovingly bathing his—

With a muttered exclamation, Lancer cut the thought off and rubbed his eyes, vainly trying to rid himself of the visions. He thought firmly about the coldness of space and the frigidity of Arctic, the ice world. It didn't help. Nothing helped lately.

"Lancer?" came Thena's tentative query.

He shook himself out of his reverie to look into the face that haunted his waking dreams. "Yes?"

"Why don't we finish the log? There's only one entry left and, while I hate to see it end, I can't help but think the captain still has something important to tell us."

Lancer nodded. "Okay, let's do that." Maybe that would help. He was willing to try anything right now.

They cleaned their dishes, then made their way to the forward cabin to settle in their accustomed chairs. Lancer turned the log on, filling the cabin with Captain Spencer's familiar voice.

We've been here fifteen years now and even the most optimistic of us have abandoned all hope of rescue. We lack the means to continue powering the ship for anything less than an emergency, even for something as small as this log. Consequently, this is my last entry.

Thena gave Lancer a sad smile. He knew how she felt. The captain had become so familiar to them, it seemed strange to be hearing from him for the last time.

For the benefit of any Terrans who may find this someday, I feel it necessary to explain the origins of our new society. Even now, most of the youngsters have all but forgotten Earth, caught up as they are in the mystique of this new culture. Having adopted the clothing, mannerisms, and the gods of ancient Greek Delphi, they've developed elaborate rituals around worship of Apollo and near-worship of the pythias. Hoping to come closer to their god, they have even eschewed everything technological—including the digging lasers that carved out their homes in the caverns and the very ship that brought them here.

Lancer glanced at Thena, who frowned at the sacrilegious sentiments her ancestor was spouting. Lancer reached up to turn off the tape, but she stopped him with a shake of her head.

Though I deplore the new society they're building, I cannot help but think they have come to terms with their straitened circumstances more easily than their elders. I am encouraging this fantasy, hoping it will see them through the difficult years ahead.

The captain sighed heavily, then continued.

Dr. Crowley has finally isolated the chemicals responsible for the pythia reaction, finding it is dependent on a combination of the caroline's narcotic fragrance, feminine hormones, and an unusual enzyme found in the moncat's saliva.

*She has developed a drug that temporarily mim-
ics the reaction, and tested it on a nonpythia
with remarkably successful prophecies.*

Lancer barely registered Thena's gasp as he
leaned forward to hear the rest of this new
development.

*The mere possibility of such a drug has the
younger generation up in arms. They are aghast
at the thought the pythia ability could come
from anyone but Apollo. To appease them, Dr.
Crowley agreed to destroy the formula, but hid
a batch of the drug in the ship against future
needs. Though it pains me to keep anything
from my people, I, too, shall keep this secret
in the event we may need it someday. For the
last time, Captain Spencer, signing off.*

Lancer turned off the tape and bounced out of
his chair. "What a terrific ending to the holofilm!
I can just see it—"

Thena rounded on him, eyes flashing, her magnificent bosom heaving. "No! You can't put this
on film!"

Taken aback by her vehemence, Lancer said,
"Why not?"

"If it became known that anyone could become
a pythia just by taking a simple potion, it would
destroy the basis of our entire society!"

He grasped her hands in his. "Yes, I know, but just
think for a moment. If we could spread this ability

throughout the Republic, we could save countless lives through avoidance of war, pre-warning of catastrophes—"

Thena tugged her hands from Lancer's grasp and spoke in a voice that dripped with ice. "At Delphi's expense?"

"It doesn't have to be that way, *shiya*. The Republic would ensure Delphi is taken care of."

"Are you sure about that?" Her tone was even frostier than before. "Can you speak for the Republic?"

"Well, no, but—"

"No! I came with you to find a cure for pythian insanity, not to help you ruin Delphi. Before I let you do that, I'll destroy all of the evidence and kill us both if I have to."

She stood there, rigidly defiant.

She means it, he realized. *This is very important to her.*

What were the implications of distributing the formula? Yes, it would do all that he said, and more. But in doing so, it would ruin Delphi—a unique society, the only one that had developed independent of Earth and the Republic's aid. It should be preserved, if only for that reason. But the benefits of that formula . . .

Lancer folded his arms. "Okay, *shiya*, I see your point. But I'd like to think about it for a while, to weigh the pros and cons. Perhaps we can find an answer we could both live with."

Thena nodded curtly. "Just be sure it doesn't hurt

Delphi." She stilled, the light of revelation in her eyes. "Why don't we get the answer from the oracle?"

"The oracle?

"Yes, why don't we ask it for a prophecy?"

Hell, those damn rituals had given him enough trouble already. He shook his head. "I don't think so."

"Why not? Don't you *want* to find an answer that will satisfy both of us?"

"Yes, of course," he temporized, searching for a suitable answer. "But . . . not at your expense. Who knows when the madness will hit you? It's better to wait until we find a cure."

She looked so uncertain and vulnerable, Lancer couldn't resist stroking the perfection of her face. "I don't want to lose you, *shiya*, not now."

Her expression softened and he drew her into his arms. He felt a bit of a cad for prevaricating—but only a little. Besides, he hadn't lied. He really *didn't* want to lose her.

He shied away from that thought. At least, not yet—not until he managed to find some way to get her out of his blood.

The next few days passed easily as Thena learned more about Earth and Terran customs. Lancer revealed a surprising knowledge of Republic politics, along with an old-fashioned patriotism, and the more Thena learned about him, the more her love and respect deepened.

It was only at times like this, as she lay alone

in bed, that she allowed herself to worry. Lancer's rejection of the Council Captainship and his willingness to consider jeopardizing Delphi's future still bothered her. She had avoided those subjects, unwilling to let anything spoil the easy relationship they'd worked hard to regain, but she'd still have to face those problems someday. Soon.

But not now. Thena sighed and turned over, hugging her pillow. For now, she needed some rest. She blanked her mind and drifted off into a light sleep, a sleep that turned into dreams—pleasant dreams of a prosperous Delphi and a loving Lancer as her life-mate.

Everything was perfect. Delphi had carved out an important niche in the Republic, her mother was cured of her madness, her father treated Thena with respect, and Lancer had taken his rightful position as Council Captain. Thena stood proudly next to him, and the entire Council acknowledged them as the best rulers Delphi had ever known. As she basked in the adulation of her people, Lancer gave her a loving smile and leaned down to whisper something in her ear.

WHOOOOP . . . WHOOOOP . . . WHOOOOP. The sound blasted from the speakers and bounced around the interior of the tiny ship, yanking Thena out of her dream.

She jerked up in bed, heart pounding with a nameless dread. Seri came running in from the other room and leapt up beside her, broadcasting panic. What was happening?

Lancer rolled out of his bunk and staggered

sleepily to the console to punch a button.

The awful sound stopped, and Thena clutched her blanket to her neck, her heartbeat subsiding to a more normal rhythm. "What . . . what is it?"

Lancer yawned hugely and scratched his bare chest. Thena wasn't so scared that she didn't appreciate the very attractive picture he made, clad only in a brief black undergarment that plainly revealed every contour of his male physique.

"No problem," he said. "Just Earth."

Thena averted her gaze, concentrating on reassuring the frightened moncat. "Earth?"

"Yeah, we just hit the outer planetary defenses—"

A stern male voice suddenly blared over the speakers, causing Thena to leap in alarm once more. "Scoutship, identify yourself."

His drowsiness apparently gone, Lancer pulled a lever and responded crisply, "Lancer Morgan of Earth, scoutship registry #XKT3569."

"Destination?" crackled the voice from the speaker.

"Dulles Spaceport."

"Cargo?"

"None."

"Passengers?"

"One."

"Name and planet of origin?"

Lancer halted at that question and swore under his breath. Turning to Thena, he said, "I forgot they'd ask that."

The speaker crackled to life again. "Passenger's name and planet of origin?" it persisted.

Lancer pressed the lever again. "Uh, that's classified."

They waited for a long beat as the voice on the other end apparently pondered his response. "State the classification authority."

Lancer grimaced. "Contact the Defense Minister for verification."

Another pause. "Verifying. Hold your current orbit until instructed otherwise."

"Affirmative," responded Lancer, and he slammed his hand onto the console. "Damn. I blew it again."

"What's wrong?" Thena managed to squeak out. What was going to happen to them?

Lancer shook his head. "Nothing." Evidently noting her frightened expression, he continued. "Really, it's nothing for you to worry about. I was supposed to keep your identity a secret, but I just blew it. Father will be royally ticked off—he didn't tell me how to handle entry to Earth, but I should have called for instructions while we were still out beyond the range of the defenses. If I hadn't been so besot—" His lips clamped shut as he cut the words off.

"I don't understand. It's still a secret. What's the problem?"

Lancer flicked another switch angrily. "The problem is, I just broadcast to anyone with a scanner that I have a passenger whose identity is classified. I compromised the integrity of the mission." He swiveled to face Thena. "Well, it's too late to worry about that now. It'll be hours before we get clearance. We might as well get some more sleep."

He rose and headed back to his bunk.

Thena trembled. Earth. They had finally arrived at their destination, the legendary origin of her ancestors. What awaited her there? The formerly alien surroundings of the scoutship seemed suddenly homey and familiar. "Sleep? How can you sleep now?"

The quaver in her voice must have betrayed her, for Lancer changed course to stand beside Thena's bunk and give her a penetrating look. She felt foolish, huddled against the wall with the blanket clutched fiercely in one hand and the moncat in the other.

Lancer didn't seem to notice. He just smiled and smoothed her hair out of her eyes. "Are you all right?" he asked softly.

Thena nodded, sternly willing her shaking to stop so it wouldn't betray her.

Lancer sat down on the bunk and gently pried the blanket from her fingers. He took Thena into his arms and rocked her back and forth, stroking her hair and making soothing sounds while Seri lay sandwiched between them, a shivering, furry lump. Thena clutched him as if her life depended on it, her shudders slowly subsiding as his comforting arms took away the fear.

Seri's fears eased along with Thena's until Thena felt the moncat became calm and aware of her surroundings—her very *close* surroundings. Suddenly scorning their solace, Seri pushed and shoved for freedom.

Lancer released Thena and they both stood to let

Seri scramble free. Seri shook herself briskly and gave Lancer a haughty, dignified look, then sauntered off back to her niche, tail and ears twitching.

Lancer chuckled, and gathered Thena back into the warmth of his comforting arms. He kissed her softly under one ear. "Feel better now?"

She nodded and leaned her head against his warm, bare chest, slowly becoming aware that all that separated them was the thin cloth of her night shift and his sinfully skimpy black briefs.

Those briefs were her undoing. She trailed her hand slowly down his muscled back, drawn irresistibly to the thin scrap of material at the base of his spine. She slid one thumb under the band and across the cleft of his buttocks, idly wondering if she could get another glimpse of what lay concealed in the black depths of the silky material.

Lancer inhaled sharply and grabbed her hand, pulling it away from his body. "You don't know what you're doing," he whispered.

Didn't she? She could feel the swell of his arousal press against her abdomen. It gave her a feeling of power, of control. Right now, things were moving so fast, she felt the need to be in control of something. Anything.

His protest wasn't very convincing. She freed her hand from his grasp and gently buried both hands in the dark mat of curls on his chest, kissing the hollow of his throat.

Lancer groaned. "I take it back," he whispered. "You *do* know what you're doing." He captured her

217

head in his hands and tilted her gaze up to his. "Are you sure you want this?"

Thena was never more sure of anything in her life. Their embrace had started out comforting but had changed quickly into something far more interesting. She couldn't stop now, not when the sight and feel of him had turned her insides warm and wet with longing.

In answer, she pressed her aching breasts against his chest and twined her arms around his neck. She kissed him, her lips parting to allow his tongue to explore her mouth. His probing was tentative at first, then grew bolder, until he was thrusting urgently and clutching her hips to hold her tight against the bulge thinly veiled by the black material. She smiled, glorying in the effect she had on him.

His hands slid up to remove her shift, but she stopped him with a murmured word. "No, let me."

Pulling away, Thena pushed Lancer down to lie flat on the bed while she stood facing him. Slowly she pulled her shift over her head, baring her body to her lover. She watched his pupils widen, thrilling at the way his gaze riveted to her hardening nipples, then moved lower to the gold curls at the apex of her thighs. She leaned down to tuck her fingers inside the top band of his briefs, and her breasts grazed the hair on his chest, sending tingles of anticipation winging through her body.

Lancer groaned and reached for her, but Thena forestalled him. "No, wait," she whispered, then gently tugged his briefs off and tossed them to the floor, freeing the prize within.

She straddled his thighs and gently wrapped her fingers around him. As he closed his eyes and moaned in pleasure, she stroked his velvet maleness, marveling at the way her slightest touch seemed to send him into ecstasy. Just thinking about it sent sweet waves of warmth rolling through her. Her caresses became faster and more urgent.

All at once Lancer flipped her over on her back, pinning her wrists to the bed. "I can't take any more without exploding," he muttered in a husky voice, and his mouth claimed her breast.

She relaxed, surrendering her control and her reason to his expert touch. His fingers moved slowly down between her thighs and delved deep inside her, rubbing, stroking, teasing, and bringing her trembling to the verge of ecstasy. He withdrew, holding back the moment, then renewed his ministrations to build the yearning ache even higher, higher, until she was aware of nothing in the universe but the feel of Lancer's fingers on her heated flesh. Finally she could take it no longer, and he took her over the edge to a shuddering release.

When the tremors ceased Thena opened her eyes to see the triumph in Lancer's gaze. She smiled. The least she could do was return the favor. She opened herself to him and guided him in, savoring his sharp intake of breath as he buried himself deep inside her. Lancer gripped her hips and began to move in long, slow strokes that swiftly turned to urgent thrusts.

She felt the tenuous thread of their bond grow even stronger in this affirmation of the life-mate ritual as, for a fleeting moment of true soul bonding, she actually felt everything he did, from inside his emotions. The wonder of being both lover and loved simultaneously shattered around her as she shared in his joyous release.

Thena tried to hold on to that sensation, but it eluded her, dissipating along with their passion as Lancer rolled to his side and gathered her in his arms. She let the feeling go, and basked in the wonder of their lovemaking as they fell asleep in each other's arms.

Hours later, the speaker stuttered to life again, waking Thena. This time, however, cradled as she was in Lancer's arms, it didn't frighten her.

"Scoutship XKT3569, this is Dulles Spaceport."

Lancer leapt out of bed, taking the warmth with him. She smiled as he answered the hail in the full glory of his nakedness. She didn't think she'd ever get tired of looking at him.

Unaware, or uncaring, of his nudity, he pushed a lever and spoke. "Go ahead, Dulles."

"You've been cleared to land. Please proceed directly to hangar thirty-two for decon in two hours."

Lancer frowned. "Decon? Why?"

"Those are your orders, signed by the Defense Minister himself. Will you comply?"

Lancer sighed. "Affirmative," he growled, and slapped the lever to the off position. He didn't sound too happy about it.

"What's wrong?"

He faced her with a rueful grin. "I'm sorry, *shiya*, but you'll have to go through decon." He raked his fingers through his hair. "Damn. I should've called Father before we hit the outer defenses and had him cut through the red tape. Now you have to go through *this*."

She still didn't understand what was bothering him. "What is it?" Just what were they going to do to her?

Lancer walked over to the bunk, and Thena watched in wistful regret as he slipped on his briefs, then his trousers.

"Decontamination," he explained as he pulled on a shirt and began to button it. "Since we're coming from an unknown planet, they need to cleanse us of all possible foreign organisms—so we don't infect Earth with any unusual diseases."

He paused in his buttoning to give her a rakish grin. "Come to think of it, that's not a bad idea. I'd hate to see you use your special brand of medicine to cure anyone *else* of Sharpe's Fever."

Thena blushed, suddenly self-conscious. Lancer came over to give her a brief kiss. "It won't be any fun—they'll strip you of everything you own, bombard it all with sterilizing sonic waves, then give *you* the same treatment, along with a disgusting concoction to drink."

It didn't sound pleasant. "But you'll be with me, won't you?"

He caressed her cheek. "No, I'm afraid not. There are separate facilities for men and women—and animals."

221

"Animals?" Her gaze darted to the back of the scoutship. "You mean Seri and I will be separated?" Thena's voice rose in panic. She couldn't handle it without at least one of them. And unless Thena was there to reassure her, Seri would undoubtedly bite anyone who tried to do those awful things to her. There'd be some awfully sick Terrans if they tried.

Lancer patted her hand. "Don't worry—I'll think of something. You won't be separated."

Thena sighed in relief. Lancer would take care of it.

He smiled. "And I'll be there when you come out, so make sure you don't leave without me, okay?"

She nodded solemnly. Once she was reunited with him nothing would be able to part them.

He finished buttoning his shirt and tucked it into his pants. "All right, then. You've got an hour and a half to shower, change clothes, and make yourself beautiful for the huddled masses of Earth."

"Masses?"

"Never mind, bad joke. You'll have to deal with far worse—my father and the Cabinet of Ministers."

That was a little more reassuring. She was capable of dealing with a few politicians—she did it all the time on Delphi. "All right." She wrapped the sheet around her and slid off the bunk. Lancer had the right idea. If she wore her Golden Pythia regalia, she'd feel more assured, more able to cope.

She showered quickly, brushed her hair until it gleamed, and dressed in her finest chiton. To give herself added confidence, she donned her most prized possessions: the polished morlawood comb and gold armlet she had received from her father upon achieving pythia status, and the bracelet Lancer had given her.

Now fully dressed, she entered the forward cabin for Lancer's inspection. He swiveled in his chair and gave her an appreciative whistle. "You're really going to wow them in that getup."

His gaze focused on her wrist, where she wore the bracelet above the healing moncat bite. Rising from the chair, he crossed the room to circle her wrist with his fingers. "I'd forgotten about this," he said. Lifting her arm, he touched several of the stones on the gold band.

Thena was puzzled by his actions. "What did you do?"

Lancer went to his bag and dug out another bracelet, far more utilitarian looking than hers, and placed it on his own arm, punching some more buttons. "I just keyed your wristcom to mine. Now if we get separated, all you have to do is press those two buttons and we'll be able to talk to each other. Go ahead; try it."

Thena followed his instructions and heard Lancer's wristcom beep. He touched it and said, "Say something."

Feeling slightly foolish, she ventured, "Hello?"

"No, you have to hold it close to your mouth, like this." He demonstrated. "Hello, Thena."

Thena looked at her wrist in surprise. She had actually heard Lancer's voice coming from there.

Bringing it to her mouth, she said, "Is this working?"

"Yes, it is," he replied, grinning.

"How do I stop it?" She heard her voice echo on his wrist.

"Just hit the same two buttons. And if I call you, you'll know by the beep. Just press them again and we'll be able to talk."

Thena smiled in relief. Knowing she would be able to talk to Lancer when he wasn't nearby was comforting. "Good."

He pointed out two other stones on her bracelet. "If you're ever in trouble, or feel scared and alone, just press these. It'll activate a homing device and notify me of your exact location so I can find you. Okay?"

Thena nodded. She didn't quite understand what a homing device was, but knowing Lancer would be able to find her if she needed him was enough.

Lancer gave her a quick, hard kiss and said, "Okay, let's strap in, get down there, and get it over with."

They secured Seri in her net, then strapped into the seats.

Lancer gave her a grin. "Hold on; we're going down, and it might be a little rough."

Thena nodded and watched as Lancer's competent hands flickered over the console and they began their descent toward Earth. For better or worse, they were on their way.

Chapter Ten

Once on the ground, Lancer unpenned Seri while Thena fumbled with the straps of her harness. Somehow, she managed to free herself despite her trembling and her odd feeling of heaviness.

Lancer helped her rise, then gave her a quick hug, searching her face with his penetrating gaze. "Don't worry; everything will be all right. Remember, if you need me, just call me on your wristcom, okay?"

Thena sternly reminded herself she was still the Golden Pythia, so there was no reason to be standing here shaking in her sandals. This was no different than visiting a strange village, and with her life-mate by her side, what could go wrong? She nodded.

Apparently satisfied with what he saw in her eyes, Lancer led her over to the door to the outside world.

Seri joined them, leaping to her accustomed perch on Thena's shoulder. The moncat reinforced and strengthened Thena's wavering confidence until she felt ready to cope with anything. Taking a deep breath, she nodded to Lancer.

He pressed some buttons on the console and came to stand next to her. "I've put a time delay on opening the hatch. There may be some people out there, and they might ask you questions, but don't answer any of them or we'll never get out of here, okay?"

Thena nodded again, not sure she could trust her voice to speak now anyway.

Lancer gave her another quick hug. "Great—let's get this over with."

The door, which he'd never gotten around to oiling, opened with a screech, making Thena jump and Seri's tail tighten around her neck.

The ramp slid out and two figures approached, dressed completely in white, even to boots, gloves, and strange transparent hoods covering their heads.

The larger figure turned to Lancer and said, "Mr. Morgan, we're the security decon team. Please come with me and instruct your passenger to accompany my partner."

Now that they were up close, Thena could see the larger figure was a man, while the smaller was a woman.

Lancer frowned. "Tell her yourself, Secdec. She speaks the same language we do."

The man glanced at her in surprise. "I'm sorry;

we didn't get that information at the briefing."

The other figure moved closer so Thena could see the woman's smile through her hood. "Never mind him; will you come with me so we can get this over with?" she asked, unknowingly echoing Lancer's early sentiment.

Thena smiled back and nodded. Seri's grip tightened, and Thena reached up to soothe the moncat.

The female secdec's eyes widened, and she turned to her partner. "We weren't briefed about that either. Call and have them send us an animal decon unit."

No—Lancer had said they wouldn't be separated. She turned pleading eyes to him, mutely begging him to remember his promise.

Lancer was quick to intervene. "Uh, no, you can't do that."

The man in white stopped in midcall on his wristcom. "Why not?"

"You'll have to decontaminate them together."

The man frowned. "That's against regulations."

"Nevertheless, that's what you'll have to do."

"Why?"

Lancer glanced at Thena and Seri. Aware of the undercurrents, but not the reason for them, Seri had wrapped her tail tightly around Thena's neck and had a firm grip on Thena's ear and hair with both paws.

A devilish twinkle was born in Lancer's eyes. "Do you have any idea what might happen if you try to separate a . . . a Thrix from her symbiotic Thring when they've been joined together at birth?"

The man looked doubtful. "No."

"Well, neither do I, but frankly" —Lancer slid an apprehensive sidelong look at Thena and lowered his voice.— "I'm afraid to try."

Lancer hadn't actually *lied* to the man. Thena had to admire Lancer's fast thinking—and his creativity. She had a sudden urge to giggle but suppressed it ruthlessly, schooling her face into what she hoped was the proper solemn mien for a Thrix and her Thring.

The man looked dubious and the woman backed off to await the outcome. Lancer pulled him over to one side, speaking just loud enough for Thena to hear. "For her safety—and yours—I'd suggest you decontaminate them together." Lancer ended with a meaningful look at the moncat and, in a spirit of mischief, Thena encouraged Seri to play along with a spitting hiss at the man in white.

Snapping the face of his wristcom shut, the secdec said, "Under the circumstances I think we can manage that. Especially if you insist it's necessary, Mr. Morgan."

"Oh, I do," said Lancer.

The woman stepped forward and beckoned to Thena, giving Seri a wary glance. "Now that they've cleared that up, we can get going. If you'll follow me?" She gestured down the hall.

Thena gave Lancer a grateful smile and followed the woman with a light heart. His machinations had put her in a good mood, and knowing he would be waiting at the other end would help her get through the coming ordeal.

The woman talked them through the nasty decon procedures, careful to let Thena handle Seri. Thena mentally apologized to the outraged moncat as she followed the secdec's instructions. Poor Seri was having a difficult time understanding why her pythia was doing such vile things to her.

An hour and a half later Thena was thoroughly worn out by her struggles with the recalcitrant moncat. But now, thank Apollo, the process was finally over.

The secdec, their tormentor, removed her gloves and hood. "Boy, is that a relief!" She shook out her short brown hair. "Okay, we're all done here. You're free to leave." She began to peel off the rest of her protective clothing.

Gladly! thought Thena, then hesitated. Which way should she go? There were three doors in the chamber. She had entered through one of them, so that narrowed it down to two—one on the left and one on the right. She shrugged and chose at random, striding with confidence out the door on the right.

Behind her, the woman cried out, "No, not that one!"

Thena tried to retreat back into the room, but it was too late. A horde of people descended upon her, forcing her back against the outside wall. They crowded close, pointing holocams and other metal objects at her, shouting questions one on top of the other.

"Who are you?"

"Where are you from?"

"What's that on your shoulder?"

Thena and Seri froze, stunned by the onslaught. One of the bolder men shoved a metal rod in her face. "What—" He broke off, swearing, when Seri hissed and clawed his offending hand, drawing blood.

Thena couldn't find it in her heart to chastise Seri—the idiot was lucky the moncat hadn't bitten him. Seri had suffered enough abuse for one day, and so had Thena. She drew herself up to her full height—a considerable advantage among these short Terrans—and gave them her best freezing glare. "That's quite enough—"

"I agree," said Lancer. He pushed his way through the jostling crowd to her side and put a comforting arm around her shoulders. "That's enough, folks. You'll all get your stories at the same time—when the Cabinet says it's okay, and not before."

"Who is she, Mr. Morgan? Your next ingenue?" shouted a jocular voice from the back of the crowd.

Lancer grinned. "Ah, you guessed it. What d'you think? Will she be a star?"

The men hooted and hollered, making Thena blush. She knew Lancer was trying to keep her identity concealed, but was it really necessary to embarrass her while he was at it?

"So why all the secrecy?" another voice yelled.

Lancer grinned wickedly and cocked an eyebrow at him. "If you had a chance to get her alone, wouldn't *you* take it?"

The crowd laughed and Lancer began edging Thena out of it, skillfully deploying his arsenal of charm and wit to field their questions. He steered her toward the edge of the building and urged her through the open door of a black metal vehicle, then turned to wave at the crowd with a parting jest.

Thena climbed into the plush interior and Lancer scooted in next to her, closing the door to shut out the noise of the crowd. They shared a sigh of relief at the blissful silence, then turned to face a dignified older man, who sat opposite them. The man spoke over his shoulder to a figure in the next compartment. "Take us home, Waller."

The vehicle rose about a foot and slid into motion. The older man gave Lancer a warm smile. "Welcome home, son. I'm glad to have you back, even if your entrance was, shall we say . . . a bit dramatic?"

Thena felt Lancer tense beside her. "Thanks, Pops." Lancer grinned when his father winced at the nickname. "I'm glad to be back—and I didn't plan that entrance; it just happened." He turned to Thena. "But we're forgetting our manners. Thena of Delphi, I'd like to introduce you to my father, Hudson Morgan."

Hudson held out his hand and Thena took it. His handshake was gentle but firm, and she was glad to see that his smile reached his twinkling eyes. "I'm very happy to meet you, my dear. I assume the small creature on your shoulder is what the scout called a moncat?"

Luckily, he didn't try to touch Seri, though the moncat had calmed down now that they had escaped the unruly mob. Thena smiled back at him. "Yes, Seri is a moncat, and we're happy to meet you, too."

Seri gave him a little trill of welcome and he laughed. "As soon as we get to a safe place, we can learn more about each other." Turning to Lancer, he said, "I had hoped to keep this quiet. What happened back there?"

Thena interrupted. "That was my fault—I went out the wrong door and those people had me surrounded before I could escape. I don't know how Lancer found me so fast."

Lancer shrugged. "Your secdec saw what was happening and came to get me. Why didn't you use your wristcom alarm?"

"They overwhelmed me so fast, I just forgot. Who were those people anyway?"

Lancer smiled. "Just some reporters who wanted a story for their news services. There was no harm done."

"On the contrary," said Hudson. "You may have just compromised your entire mission. Why didn't you contact me over the secure family channel so we could arrange for a more private landing?"

"Like Thena, I just forgot." Lancer's smile turned grim. "Don't worry; they didn't get anything."

She hated to see them squabble. Placing her hand on Lancer's forehead, Thena said, "How are you feeling? You don't want to overdo it."

Lancer gave her a look compounded equally of irritation and amusement, telling her he knew exactly what she was doing. "I'm just fi—"

"What's wrong with him?" interrupted Hudson

with obvious paternal concern.

Thena allowed her brow to crease into a worried frown. "I think he's all right now, but he's recovering from a virulent disease he contracted on Delphi. I'm afraid he hasn't been very well. No wonder he forgot."

Hudson gave Lancer a speculative look. "He does look a bit pale. How are you feeling, son?"

Lancer grimaced. "I'm just fine. The disease was nasty, but I heartily recommend the cure." He smirked at Thena, obviously trying to discomfit her.

It didn't work. She pretended to misunderstand him. "Yes, the infusion worked quite well." She looked around her. "Where are the carolines, anyway?"

Lancer patted her hand. "I left strict instructions for them to be kept sealed and delivered to Morgan House. We'll be staying with the family—it's more secure than my minuscule apartment, and far more comfortable."

Thena nodded and turned to look out the window as Lancer and Hudson caught up on what had happened since they'd last seen each other. She watched in awe as they passed other moving vehicles, huge buildings, and strange forms and shapes Thena couldn't put a name to. The tall buildings eventually gave way to smaller structures and increasing numbers of trees, grass, and shrubbery, the first she'd seen on this world.

After about an hour, the vehicle pulled up over a smooth driveway between two stone pillars. The stationary holo suspended above the entrance proclaimed it as Morgan House and Thena sighed in relief. They had finally reached their destination.

The vehicle wound up the driveway and came to a stop, settling down in front of an enormous building that looked as though it could house an entire cavern of pythias. "Is this where you live?" she asked in disbelief.

Hudson smiled. "Yes—it's a monster, but it's home."

How could he call such a huge thing home? Thena looked uncertainly at Lancer.

"Yes, the family ancestral home," he said with a mocking tone. "Where twelve generations of Morgans have lived and loved—and profited from the blood, sweat, and tears of lesser mortals."

Hudson gave him a censorious glance but didn't comment on Lancer's levity. "Come, let's go inside."

They entered through the exquisitely carved wooden doors, and the beauty and sumptuousness of the gold and white entrance hall took her breath away. It was far more elegant than any Council Chamber on Delphi, with colorful, exotic holographic images, delicate porcelain, and a rich gold carpet that felt as soft and springy underfoot as thick plains grass. What a setting for a Golden Pythia!

She looked around slowly, trying to drink it all in. This was where Lancer had grown up. Perhaps this place would help her to better understand him— and maybe even help her find a way to lay some of his ghosts to rest.

Lancer took her elbow and steered her toward the staircase. "What room have you given her?" he asked his father.

"The Rose Room."

Lancer smiled. "Good, then I'll take the other half of the suite."

Hudson looked as though he was going to object, but he merely smiled and said, "Of course. She'll want to be near someone familiar."

"Hello, Lancer, old boy," came a voice above them. "Glad to see you made it back safe and sound from your little pleasure trip."

They turned to watch as two men strolled down the stairs. The one who spoke wore a slightly mocking expression on his patrician features. He was tall and elegantly dressed—a perfect foil for his surroundings. The other was shorter and stockier, though still taller than Lancer. His dress was more subdued, and he wore a neutral expression that masked his feelings.

Lancer gave both of them a hearty, back-slapping hug. They returned his embrace, momentarily allowing their dignified facades to crack into welcoming smiles.

Stepping back, Lancer drew Thena forward. "Thena, I'd like you to meet my brothers. The lout who spoke so blightingly of his little brother is Alexander, and the silent one is Darian."

Thena murmured her greetings, and the two nodded graciously.

"So, brother," said Alexander with a teasing glint in his eye. "To what do we owe the honor of your guest's presence? Could it be you have decided to enter the marital lists at last?"

Lancer grimaced but wasn't given a chance to answer.

"That's enough, boys," said Hudson. "Come into the study and I'll explain everything." He motioned them through one of the doors.

The study was a cozy room decorated primarily with dark wood and leather in shades of brown and dark forest green, and dominated by a large wooden desk in the center of the room. There was no doubt in Thena's mind this was a wholly masculine sanctuary. It looked comfortable and familiar, but Thena knew from her reading that the display of rare natural fibers and wood products on Earth was possible only for the very rich.

Lancer's father gestured her to sit in one of the chairs facing the desk. She did so, and the chair moved beneath her. Startled, Thena recoiled. The way this thing molded to her form was practically indecent.

Lancer's brothers seemed to take their chairs' movement as a matter of course, so Thena ignored her discomfort, not wanting to appear gauche.

Lancer perched next to her on one arm of the chair and Seri took the other. Hudson sat on one corner of the desk and leaned forward. "First, I want to make sure this information won't leave this room." Upon receiving acquiescent nods from the two brothers, he said, "I sent Lancer on a secret mission." Hudson went on to describe the discovery of the lost colony planet, and Alexander and

Darian listened with an air of polite interest.

When Hudson came to a stop Alexander crossed his long legs in studied nonchalance. "So why all the secrecy?"

"The Cabinet of Ministers classified the information when they learned the Delphians had the gift of prophecy. I sent your brother to learn the truth of the matter."

Alexander arched an eyebrow at Lancer. "And what did you discover?"

Lancer crossed his arms and leaned back. "Based on my experiences, I'd have to say they do seem to have the ability to do something of the sort."

Something of the sort! Thena thought they'd resolved this long ago. She shot Lancer an annoyed look.

He continued. "Thena is Delphi's Golden Pythia—their top prophetess. On board ship we experimented with asking questions of the oracle and shared identical visions of my past that convinced me they somehow tap into the unconscious mind."

Lancer shrugged. "Whether they can really predict the future or merely tap into the other person's subconscious was difficult for me to tell. We'll have to do a lot more tests before we can determine the validity of their prophecies."

Thena forgave him—it was a reasonable explanation.

Darian frowned and spoke for the first time since Thena had met him. "Visions?"

Lancer stiffened and opened his mouth, but Hudson spoke first. "Lancer wouldn't make such a statement without good reason. He's right—we must keep an open mind."

The brothers looked surprised at their father's vehement defense of his youngest son—and so did Lancer. There were a lot of undercurrents here Thena didn't understand, but they might explain why Lancer didn't seem to have a great deal of familial feeling. She resolved to watch while Lancer did all the talking.

"And why is the Cabinet so interested?" Alexander asked.

Alexander never seemed to lose his look of amusement, though there seemed to be several layers of meaning to his simple question. Thena cautioned herself not to make the mistake of believing the man to be simple in any way. She suspected he was far more intelligent than his world-weary facade suggested.

Hudson answered, "If her talents prove to be genuine, we may be able to use them to find a way to solve our problem with the rebels."

Alexander's smile froze, and she could almost see the possibilities flickering through his mind. "I see," he said softly, and gave Thena a sweet smile. "Just how does it work?"

"That's what we're here to find out," Lancer reminded him. "But we do know it seems to be a combination of native Delphian flowers, the moncats, and the pythia's inherent ability. Prophesying takes a lot out of them, so their gifts command a high price." He gave Hudson a pointed look.

Darian inclined his head at Thena. "*Her* price?"

Apparently familiar with interpreting his brother's cryptic remarks, Lancer said, "In exchange for answering our question, she needs help with an occupational hazard. . . ."

Thena stiffened in shock. Was he about to reveal her secret?

Her sudden emotional surge caught Seri off guard. The moncat hissed, then leapt to her pythia's shoulder in instinctive protection, grabbing Thena's ear for balance. Thena winced.

"Let me guess," drawled Alexander. "Bruises and abrasions?"

Thena bristled and felt like hissing herself but relaxed when Lancer chuckled. Alexander had just been making a joke to smooth over a difficult situation. Seri apparently agreed, for she calmed quickly.

Lancer slanted Thena a questioning look and murmured, "What I tell them is up to you, but they meant it when they said nothing would ever leave this room."

Thena hesitated. Despite their apparent differences, she sensed a great deal of love and respect among the Morgan men—but did that make them trustworthy?

Thena kicked herself mentally. What was she afraid of, anyway? It was hardly likely they'd go rushing off to Delphi to whisper her secret in Ketori's ear. And with any luck she'd find a cure and return to tell him herself. If not, she couldn't go back anyway. Why *not* tell them? Thena nodded her permission.

Lancer rubbed his hands together. "The problem is, Thena remembers her prophecies. That's rather unusual on Delphi, and other pythias with the same ability have succumbed to madness, including Thena's own mother. Thena has come here in hopes a psychiatrist may be able to help her find a way to keep it from happening to her."

Alexander and Darian appeared thoughtful, and Hudson gave her a look full of compassion. "I had hoped to be given a demonstration, but if it's going to cause you distress . . ."

"Nonsense," Thena said with a smile. She *wanted* to prove herself. "It's not as if I'm in imminent danger. I'd be glad to show you how it works."

Lancer put a protective arm around her shoulders. "Yes, but not today. Thena's had a rough trip and an even worse greeting at the spaceport. Let's set it up for tomorrow—and see if we can get Juelle Shanard here too."

Someone else? How many people were going to be let in on this secret? She gave him a questioning look.

He squeezed her shoulder in reassurance. "Juelle is an old friend of mine. She's a psychiatrist as well as a trained observer and researcher."

Thena nodded. Good—Lancer was wasting no time in fulfilling his part of the bargain.

Hudson rose. "Excellent. Son, you make the arrangements our guest needs and we'll leave you both to get some rest before dinner."

Lancer helped Thena to rise out of the form-fitting chair, then escorted her out the door and up the stairs. "See, that wasn't so bad."

She grinned. "Who are you trying to convince, me or yourself?"

Lancer gave her a surprised look, then laughed. "Both, I guess."

He opened a door at the top of the stairs and ushered her in. The room was elegantly appointed in varying shades of rose accented with a soft green, and furnished in a beautiful light-colored wood. Seri jumped down to explore their new quarters and Thena exclaimed in delight.

Lancer smiled. "So you like it?"

"Oh, it's beautiful!"

"Here, let me show you the rest." He opened a door to the adjoining room. It was furnished in counterpoint to hers, with soft shades of green highlighted with rose. "This is my room, and this" —he opened another door next to the first "is the bathroom. It's the same as the one on board ship, only bigger."

Yes, and this one had a tub too. She could hardly wait to use it. Turning back to her bedroom, she spotted the caroline pot under the windows, its rough-hewn appearance looking exceedingly out of place amid all this elegance. "Oh, good, my things are here."

"Yes," came the gruff female voice behind them. "I unpacked them for you—and mighty few they are, too."

Thena turned to see a short, plump older woman standing behind them, glaring at Lancer with her hands placed firmly on her hips. "And just what were you about, boy, to let this poor lass leave her home with so little? Why, I thought I taught you better than that."

Lancer smiled and hugged the short woman. "You did, Maeve, you did. But we had to leave in such a hurry, there was no time to take more."

Maeve harrumphed and tried to look offended, though it was obvious she was pleased at Lancer's affectionate gesture. She pushed him away. "None of your lip now. What are you going to do about it?"

"I . . . I guess I'm going to buy her some more clothes."

Maeve gave him a look full of disbelief. "*You* are?"

Lancer looked uncomfortable, and Thena looked on in amusement as he kowtowed to this diminutive despot. "Well, actually, I'd planned to ask Juelle to help. You remember Dr. Shanard?"

"Yes, I remember. She'll do," Maeve said grudgingly. "She's got a good eye for color, that one."

Lancer sighed in relief, but Maeve didn't let him off the hook that easily. "Where are your manners, boy? Introduce us!"

Looking sheepish, Lancer did so. "Maeve, this is Thena. Thena, our housekeeper, Maeve."

Thena shook hands with the warmhearted woman, glad to see true welcome in her bright eyes.

"I'm pleased to see another woman in this great old barn of a house," Maeve said.

Seri abandoned her investigations to sit at Maeve's feet and look up at her curiously.

Maeve's eyebrows rose. "And who's this?"

Feeling comfortable around a Terran for the first time since she'd landed on this planet, Thena answered, "This is my moncat, Seri. Seri, say hello to Maeve."

Seri cocked her head and trilled a note of welcome to the housekeeper.

Apparently enchanted, Maeve leaned down to peer more closely at Seri. "A moncat, huh? Well, I'll be. Never seen one before. And polite, too, which is more than I can say for some of the humans who've stayed here." Straightening, she gave Lancer a piercing look. "Is it housebroken?"

Lancer choked. "Uh, *she* is quite sanitary, Maeve. Thena will take of that. You don't have to worry about Seri—all she needs is a private niche to eat and sleep in." He looked around. "The window seat should be fine."

Maeve gave a brisk nod and turned to Thena. "You just let me know what she likes to eat and I'll take care of it. And if you need anything, just ring for me. The boy will show you how." She left with a backward wave of her hand.

Thena glanced at Lancer. "The boy?"

He grinned. "She's been working here since before I was born. It's hard to convince her I've grown up."

"Well, you'd better do as she told you, then. Show me how to 'ring' her."

Lancer crossed the room to a small desk and pressed a button to swing out the computer console. "This is the house computer. It's similar to

243

the one on the ship." He showed her how to use it, then said, "You can also call outside the house. Just a moment while I call Juelle at work."

He glanced at her and hesitated. "No sense broadcasting your image over the net." He positioned a chair just to his left and patted the seat. "Here—now you'll be able to see whoever is on the screen, but they won't be able to see you."

Thena took the indicated seat and watched as Lancer's fingers moved swiftly over the computer keyboard. Soon, shifting colors appeared on the screen and a melodious voice said, "Ford Medical Center. Where may I direct your call?"

"Dr. Shanard, please. Lancer Morgan calling."

The colors faded and were replaced by the face of a lovely woman with a pointed chin, green eyes, and a sleek cap of short blond hair. With her small, fine features, she strongly resembled the illustrations of faerie creatures Thena had seen in some of her ancestor's books.

Lancer obviously knew this enchanting woman very well and had a great deal of affection for her. As they bantered back and forth, Thena felt a small stab of jealousy at their easy camaraderie.

Lancer laughed. "But that's not why I called you. I can't explain it over the 'com, but I have a special challenge for you—one that's right up your alley. Can you come to Morgan House tomorrow at eight o'clock to meet someone?"

The woman cocked her head, considering. "I don't know. My schedule—"

"You can work it out, I'm sure. Do come, Ju. I promise you won't regret it. This could prove to be the making of your career."

Juelle narrowed her eyes, her interest obviously caught. "It better be worth it, Lance—or I'll make *you* regret it."

He grinned. "What? You'll give my number to used computer salesmen again? I'm on to you now, you know."

She waved her hand dismissively. "Oh, that was when I was a mere child. I'm much older and wiser now, and my revenge a great deal more sophisticated. Just remember that, Mr. Morgan."

"Ah, Ju, I won't have to. You won't need to exercise that little brain of yours. Just be there, okay?"

"All right, I'll be there. Till tomorrow."

Lancer cut the connection, then crossed the room to lock the door and gather Thena into an embrace. "Now that Maeve's gone and Seri's sound asleep, I finally have you all to myself."

Thena melted willingly into his arms. She was content. Lancer might joke with Juelle, but Thena was the one he made love to.

He gave her a lazy, seductive smile. "Everything's all set for tomorrow." He kissed her eyelids, then her nose. "Dinner isn't for another three hours." Another soft kiss, this one on her lips. "Can you think of a good way to spend a few hours?"

Thena's heart turned over at the teasing glint in his eyes. "Mmmm, there's always reading." She kissed the corner of his well-shaped mouth.

He laughed softly and pressed her hips against

his so she could feel the full extent of his arousal. "Try again," he whispered.

"Sleeping?"

"Nope."

His caresses made her feel boneless and all quivery inside. "Mmmm, we could—" Feeling suddenly daring, she slipped the gown off her shoulder, baring her breasts to his view.

His eyes widened. "Bingo," he said softly, and leaned down to take one of them into his mouth.

Thena smiled down tenderly at her lover, fast asleep in her arms. His lovemaking had been wild and exciting, yet incredibly sweet as well. She ran her hand over the smooth skin of his shoulders, delighting in the way he felt. Now, thanks to this wonderful man and his psychiatrist friend, Thena was getting closer to realizing her dream of a cure for pythian insanity.

Her hand stilled. But her other dream—to have Lancer by her side forever—what of that? It seemed hopeless. He hadn't mentioned their budding relationship to his family, undoubtedly because of the onus that went with it.

Stars! When would he finally realize they belonged together? She projected a wave of love and longing so strong, it woke Seri with a start.

Lancer stirred, then gave her a sleepy smile. His arms tightened and he cuddled her to him. "Hrrmph," he said and nuzzled her neck. "Wazzat?"

Thena was struck speechless. Had he *felt* that? She tested their bond tentatively. Dear Apollo—it was twice as strong as before. How could that be?

Lancer moved his questing mouth down her throat to the swell of her breast, and she felt their link expand in response to his surge of desire.

She gasped. Could the stories be true? It was said that the Golden Pythia's bond with her life-mate grew stronger the closer they became, until it eventually became so strong nothing could part them.

It would certainly explain what was happening, but . . . did it work both ways? No, probably not—men never seemed as affected by the life-mate bond as their pythias. Did that mean she was doomed to become so attached to Lancer that she was unable to live without him, while he remained unaffected? She stiffened. What a horrible thought!

Lancer lifted his head. "What's wrong, *shiya?*"

"Nothing," she lied. Nothing that couldn't be fixed by ensuring their bond didn't grow any stronger. "It's almost time to go to dinner."

Lancer squinted at the clock. "Yeah, you're right." Giving her one last, lingering kiss, he rose slowly from the bed and raked her naked body with his gaze. "We'll continue this later."

Thena covered herself without answering. Where their lovemaking was concerned, there would be no "later."

Chapter Eleven

Thena breathed a sigh of relief when they reached the dinner table. Lancer's affectionate caresses and warm promissory kisses had been hard to resist on their way downstairs. It wasn't until they joined his family that he ceased his attentions and she finally had a reprieve from his determined onslaught on her libido.

How was she ever going to keep her resolution to hold him at arm's length? She couldn't spend all the time around his family—nor did she want to.

Thena put it out of her mind. For now, she'd relax and enjoy the respite. She glanced around the table. Hudson was seated at its head with Thena to his right, Lancer next to her, and Alexander and Darian opposite. The remaining expanse of gleaming wood was bare but for iridescent crystalline sculptures and lavish place settings.

Thena took it all in, awestruck at the beauty and formality of the Morgan family dinner table. She was glad Seri had stayed in the bedroom—she didn't want to imagine the frisky moncat loose amid all this breakable elegance.

She took another look around. Yes, it was beautiful, but a trifle cold and overpowering. How had Lancer turned out to be such a carefree spirit amid the oppressive grandeur?

While the men talked about their day, she surreptitiously examined the dinnerware. The porcelain was the most exquisite she had ever seen—delicate and translucent, and the crystal goblets sparkled in all colors of the rainbow, cunningly wrought into exotic free-form shapes.

The gold utensils were equally wondrous, and Thena fingered one curiously. It looked heavy, but felt light and airy in her hand. And, despite their fanciful shapes, she recognized counterparts to Delphi's more pedestrian forks, knives, and spoons. But why were there so many of them?

A uniformed maid served the soup, and Thena hesitated. Which spoon should she use?

Lancer must have noted her confusion, for he leaned over to whisper, "Just watch me and follow my lead."

Eager not to appear a backward savage, Thena selected the same type of spoon Lancer did and tasted her soup, savoring its creamy texture.

Hudson turned to her and said, "Thena, my dear, what do you think of Earth so far?"

Thena swallowed and considered her answer. "I'm

not quite sure yet; I've seen so little of it. My first
impression is that everything is so big and . . . I feel
rather strange, a little heavy."

Darian looked up. "Gravity."

"Gravity?" she echoed stupidly.

Alexander smiled. "What my lump of a brother
means is, Earth's gravitational pull must be greater
than Delphi's. You weigh more here, so you feel
heavier."

Thena nodded in comprehension. The concepts
were familiar, but somehow she had expected Earth
to be exactly like Delphi. "That must be why most
Terrans appear to be so short. Our gravity is lighter,
so we grow taller on Delphi."

Hudson entered the conversation again. "Exactly. How does your height compare to other
Delphians?"

"I'm about average for a woman. My father is
quite tall, however, taller even than most Delphians.
And your family?"

Hudson grinned ruefully. "On Earth, we're considered quite the giants."

Thena nodded. That confirmed her own observa-
tions. "Are the women in your family tall too?"

Hudson's mouth curved in a sad smile. "There
are no women in our family, not anymore."

Thena gave Alexander and Darian a curious look.
Unfamiliar with Terran bonding customs, she didn't
want to offend by asking the wrong question.

Lancer gratified her curiosity. "We have a marriage ritual. It's not much like your life-mate ritual,
but the results are the same—one man and one

woman bound together." He slid a glance at his brothers. "Darian has yet to take the marital plunge, and Alexander's marriage ended in divorce several years ago."

Thena didn't know how to respond. It had *ended*? How could such an important bonding be so . . . so temporary?

Apparently aware of her confusion, Hudson shot Lancer a censorious glance and changed the subject, turning back to Thena. "How did you persuade your family to let you come to Earth?"

Thena froze. Should she tell them the truth? She looked to Lancer for guidance.

He squeezed her knee reassuringly under cover of the table. "To be honest, we didn't ask them."

As Thena sat with her hands clenched in her lap, Lancer explained. "Thena's Observer is plotting to take over Delphi's Council by falsifying and discrediting her prophecies. She can't prove it without revealing her secret, so we have to find a cure for pythian insanity before we can return and confront him with his guilt."

Thena's heart soared. *We*—Lancer had said "we," and had said they'd be returning together. There was hope after all. The Morgan men made commiserating sounds and Thena relaxed, taking a bite of the delectable main course.

Alexander looked up from his plate. "Just what does this ritual entail?"

Lancer shot a questioning glance at Thena and she nodded. It would be easier for him to explain in terms they would be familiar with.

He described the role of each participant, then said, "The ritual takes place deep in the caverns. First, they use prayers to meditate and clear their minds, then they cleanse themselves in a special bathing chamber that is covered in exotic white and purple flowers that exude a mind-drugging fragrance. Once the flowers put everyone in the proper receptive state, they adjourn to the ritual chamber where the moncat's empathic ability takes the pythia into her trance. Then the querent asks the question and the pythia answers."

"That's it?" Hudson asked. "What happens after the question is answered?"

"Everyone passes out," Lancer said with a grin.

Hudson looked a little startled. Lancer added, "Not really—just the pythia and the querent. The observer and attendant help remove them from the influence of the flowers."

Hudson didn't look mollified. Thena took pity on him. "Don't worry. We've done this on Delphi for over two hundred years. We know what we're doing and no one has ever been hurt. You're in no danger. The worst you'll get is a slight headache."

Hudson nodded slowly. "It would be rather difficult to duplicate your ritual surroundings on such short notice. How much of it do you really need?"

All eyes turned to Thena. She shrugged. "I don't know. We've always done it this way."

"Let me phrase it a different way," Hudson said. "What do you think you'll need to give us a prophecy?"

All right, this was an area she felt confident in

and could discuss with expertise. "We've already learned the bathing isn't necessary, but I will need a private chamber, preferably free of distracting embellishments, with three cushions." She bit her lip and frowned in thought. "I have so few of the flowers—the carolines—with me, the room should be small. One of you will be the querent, while Lancer acts as observer."

Alexander quirked an amused eyebrow at Lancer, and Thena cursed her unruly tongue. As her life-mate, Lancer was the obvious choice for observer, but he had carefully omitted telling his family about *that* part of the trip. She wasn't surprised; it was just one more way he denied their bond.

Lancer turned to her with a peculiar apprehensive expression on his face. Unwilling to field questions from his family or betray Lancer's trust, she hastened to say, "Lancer is the only one who has attended the ritual, so he knows what to expect."

What she couldn't tell them was now that Lancer had gone through the life-mate ritual, he'd be less affected by the carolines' drugging perfume. Stars! She suddenly realized this would just strengthen their bond even more. "Or, we could just use a recorder, like we did on the ship."

"May we not all observe?" asked Alexander.

Thena shook her head. "No, it's not done."

"Perhaps this is one of those parts of the ritual you've been following without good reason," Alexander said gently. "Wouldn't the prophecy work without it?"

Thena hesitated. She really didn't know. "That's

possible, but you really wouldn't get much out of it by watching. You don't know what it's like until you participate in it yourself."

Alexander persisted. "Nevertheless, I would like to observe the process."

Thena balked. This just didn't *feel* right. "Since you're unaccustomed to the flowers, they would just overpower you. You wouldn't be able to observe anything anyway."

She turned to Lancer for corroboration and found him watching her with a smile of pride on his face. It was silly, but that little smile buoyed her spirits tremendously. He appeared pleased with her ability to hold her own with his forceful family.

It gave her the confidence to persevere in what she knew was right. "I'm afraid I must insist. Only three people may be present during the ritual: the querent, an observer, and myself. And Seri, of course."

Hudson sighed regretfully. "As you wish. I will be the querent."

Darian glanced at Hudson. "Studio," he said cryptically.

Alexander gave Darian a surprised look, and Hudson responded with a slow nod. "Yes, that might work." Turning to Thena, he said, "Lancer had a studio built in the house before he moved out. We still use it for political announcements and similar things. I believe the recording booth should meet your needs. It's small and as free of embellishment as you can get, and it's separated from the sound technicians by a glass wall. Everyone else could see and hear what's going on, but the carolines' scent won't penetrate. Would this be acceptable?"

Thena hesitated. She didn't want to appear unco-operative, but it still didn't feel right.

"Thena?" prompted Lancer. "What do you think?" He gave her an anxious look.

"I don't know—"

"What could go wrong?" asked Alexander with a persuasive smile. "Why don't we try it and see what happens?"

Lancer clasped her hand under the table. He was silent, leaving the decision up to her. She was grateful for his consideration, but unwilling to offend the hospitality of her hosts. How could it hurt? "All right," she said.

Alexander beamed at her and Hudson gave her a grateful smile. Even Darian deigned to give her a nod of approval.

Lancer squeezed her hand. "Are you sure?" She felt a wave of reassurance and concern along their bond.

She removed her hand from his under pretense of taking a sip of water. Maybe it *would* be better if she insisted on the recorder as observer. "Yes, I think it will be fine."

Thena avoided Lancer for the rest of the evening by resorting to the age-old headache excuse. Luckily, it worked. She made it through the night without engaging in any activity that would further strengthen their bond, and now that it was morning, everyone had resumed their seats in Hudson's study.

Thena perched on hers uneasily. She had been a little nervous to begin with, but the chair was making it worse. Every time she tried to fidget, the form-fitting furniture just shifted with her. It was far too obliging, and she made a mental note not to allow the contrary things on Delphi. Seri picked up her mood and started broadcasting edgy concern all over the place.

Lancer cast her a curious glance. "Are you all right?"

Thena nodded, though his easy reading of her emotions through their bond made her even more jittery. It just showed how strong their bond was becoming. "Yes, I just want to get this over with. When will your psychiatrist friend arrive?"

A melodious chime filled the air and Lancer grinned. "That's probably her now."

Thena heard a door open and a petite whirlwind of a woman breezed in, looking like nothing so much as a pixie. Thena stared in envy at the way the woman's scarlet jumpsuit hugged her lean, slender body, feeling gauche and awkward around this little sprite.

Lancer stood and opened his arms, grinning. "Ju!"

Juelle advanced, shaking her finger at him, the top of her head a good six inches below Lancer's chin. "Don't you 'Ju' me, Lancer Morgan. You'd better have a darn good reason for—"

Lancer swept her up in his arms and spun her around as lightly as if she were made of gossamer. Thena watched with envy. Lancer would never be able to do that with *her*. Should she be jealous?

Juelle laughed and shoved at Lancer's chest. "Put me down, you overgrown bully. You know I hate it when you do that."

Lancer complied, laughing. "Of course. That's why I do it."

Juelle punched him softly in the arm. He cradled it in mock anguish. "Ah, wounded to the quick."

The other three Morgan men stood, and Hudson strode to meet Juelle, holding out his hand. "Dr. Shanard, I'm happy to see you again."

She murmured a pleasantry, then hugged Alexander and Darian. Juelle was obviously well known in this household. Had Lancer brought her here often?

Lancer took Juelle by the elbow and steered her over to Thena's chair. "Ju, I'd like you to meet a very special person, Thena of Delphi. Thena, this is Dr. Juelle Shanard."

Thena rose to greet her, dismayed at how she towered over the petite psychiatrist. She felt huge and out of place.

Thena felt herself flush with embarrassment as Juelle's eyes widened. The Terran's gaze scanned her from head to foot, taking in the full details of Thena's Golden Pythia regalia.

"Good heavens," Juelle said. "You look like Hera, Queen of the Gods."

Thena warmed at once to the woman's friendly tone, stupidly blurting out the first thing that popped into her head. "And you look like Titania, Queen of the Fairies."

Everyone laughed and Thena blushed, embarrassed. "I-I'm sorry, Doctor. . . ."

Juelle patted her arm and leaned forward with a confidential air. "Just ignore them. I always do. And call me Juelle."

Thena smiled back. She didn't know if Lancer and this woman had been lovers in the past, and right now she didn't care. She liked Juelle and thought they could be friends. Thena introduced the psychiatrist to Seri as Hudson pulled up another chair.

Thena reseated herself and Lancer resumed his perch on the arm of her chair, absently playing with her hair. Juelle gave Thena an enquiring look.

Was Juelle jealous, or just curious? Thena had to know. She'd been avoiding Lancer's touch of late, but Juelle didn't need to know that. And besides, he was still *Thena's* life-mate.

Thena smiled languorously, letting the woman see her pleasure and acceptance of Lancer's simple act of affection. Understanding lit Juelle's gaze and her smile grew to match Thena's until they were grinning at each other like idiots. Thena relaxed. Juelle was obviously content with Thena and Lancer's relationship—there would be no opposition from that quarter.

Lancer caught their smirks and gave Thena a bemused look. "What—"

Juelle crossed her scarlet-clad legs and said, "Never mind, Lance. Girl stuff. You wouldn't understand."

Lancer grimaced and dropped the subject. "Okay,

Ju. Now that you're here, I can explain who and what Thena is."

Lancer told Thena's story once more and explained why she needed a psychiatrist's help. Juelle leaned forward, rapt in his storytelling, though she looked to Thena a few times for corroboration of his more outrageous statements.

When he finished Juelle sat back, looking stunned. "You're right. This *is* right up my alley." She slanted a mischievous glance at him. "I forgive you for making me change my schedule—and I'll cancel the male strippers I booked to attend your next staff meeting."

Lancer guffawed and the other men chuckled, but Thena ignored the byplay. "What do you mean, this is right up your alley?"

"You know I'm a psychiatrist?" At Thena's nod, Juelle explained. "I've been studying psionic abilities—powers of the mind—all my life. They're very rare, but when I do discover people with them, I usually find they need my help to understand and cope with their gifts."

"Juelle is far too modest," Lancer interjected. "Her research in this area is fast making her one of the leading psi authorities on Earth, if not in the Republic. You couldn't ask for better help."

"Lancer exaggerates," Juelle protested. "I'm becoming well known, but not because of my sterling research abilities. Most of my colleagues think I'm a crackpot for spending my time in this area." She shrugged, obviously indifferent.

This was wonderful. Lancer had indeed brought

Thena to the one person who could probably help her—and who was predisposed toward believing in her abilities. Thena could hardly restrain her eagerness. Oh, to be able to return in triumph to Delphi with a cure for pythian insanity! "Do you think you can help me?"

Juelle smiled. "I don't know, but I'm sure gonna try. Now, you said something about a demonstration, Lancer?"

Hudson nodded. "Yes, let's adjourn there now, shall we?" He led them to the recording studio in the basement, where the others politely left Thena, Lancer, and Seri alone in the sound booth to set the stage for the coming ritual.

Thena looked around the small room with a sinking feeling. The rustic clay flowerpot and the three soft white cushions in the middle of the floor looked as out of place as she felt. This room was so foreign with its high-tech metal and glass—even more alien than the scoutship had been out in the vastness of space. How could she perform the ritual here? It was all . . . *wrong*, somehow.

She stood staring blankly at the cushions as Seri fidgeted on her shoulder.

Lancer touched her other shoulder. "Are you okay?"

Thena gave him an anxious look. "I . . . I don't know. Something's wrong, but I don't know what it is."

He spoke softly, for her ears alone. "You don't have to do anything you don't want to, *shiya*. If it doesn't feel right, we'll just cancel it."

She glanced at the others in the room beyond, all obviously eager to witness the ceremony for themselves. She hated to disappoint them. Maybe it was just the strange surroundings that made her feel out of kilter, making her see problems where there were none.

She shook her head and gave Lancer a smile. "No, I'm okay. I'm sure it'll be all right. I'm just a little edgy."

He gave her a searching look. "If you're sure . . ."

Thena nodded her head more decisively. "Yes, I'm sure. Let's get on with it, shall we?"

"Okay. Do you want to use the recorder as observer, or would you like me to do it for you?"

Thena's heart warmed toward him. He must really be concerned about her if he volunteered to participate in another of the rituals he so disliked.

She'd been trying to avoid anything that would strengthen their bond and they'd already learned a human observer wasn't really necessary. But . . . she wanted him there. The strangeness of the room was disconcerting, and it just seemed important to have a human observer present this time.

Her unease won out over her unwillingness to strengthen their bond. "I think it would be best if you acted as observer."

Lancer squeezed her shoulder. "Sure; what should I do?" To his credit, he didn't look disappointed in her decision.

She picked up one pillow and placed it by the door, then turned to face Lancer. "This is where you'll sit to record the prophecy. There hasn't been time to train you as an observer, but I've worked with neophytes before. Just blank your mind of everything—make it receptive and open so it doesn't distract us. Can you do that?"

Lancer shrugged. "Sure. What else?"

"You'll need something to write with, to record the prophecy. And you'll need to close the carolines at the end of the ritual. Neither your father nor I will be able to at that point."

"And I will?" He sounded incredulous. "I wasn't exactly in control of my faculties during the last two rituals."

Thena lowered her voice. "You will be now. Seri won't be enhancing your susceptibility to the carolines, just mine. And the life-mate ritual gave you a certain immunity to their effect."

Lancer muttered something under his breath that sounded like, "At least it was good for something."

Unsure she heard him correctly, Thena stiffened. "I'm sorry; what was that?"

"Uh, never mind; it wasn't important. Now, how do you plan to duplicate the first part of the ritual, the antechamber and bathing in the stream?"

Thena glanced around uneasily. "We're going to have to do the prayers here and dispense with the bathing." It should be all right; they hadn't seemed to need it on the ship. "I'll begin the prayers, then open the carolines and ask your father for the question. We're about ready—would you explain it to him?"

Lancer gathered some writing supplies from the

other room and beckoned Hudson into the recording booth. "Okay, Dad, you'll sit here in front of Thena. It's important you're in the right frame of mind for the ritual, so just do what she tells you and blank your mind, leaving it open and receptive—like your meditation exercises. Can you do that?"

"Certainly."

"Good. Once you've both achieved the proper state, Thena will open the flowerpot and the carolines' scent will drug your mind. Just let go, and Thena will ask for your question." Lancer frowned. "The problem is, once under the influence of the carolines, most querents forget their intended question and ask how to achieve their heart's desire instead. I don't know of any way to get around that."

"No problem," Hudson said. "Ending this war *is* my heart's desire."

"Good, then let's do it." Lancer turned to Thena. "Are you ready?"

She was as ready as she'd ever be. She nodded.

Lancer turned to the others beyond the glass partition. "We're going to start now, so please turn off the light once we're seated. We need utter silence, okay?"

The others did as he asked and sat to watch the ritual unfold. Thena motioned for Lancer and Hudson to take their places, and Hudson bent awkwardly to take his seat on the pillow, his face frozen in a look of embarrassed dignity.

"He looks like he's been eating lemons with a

ramrod up his rear," Lancer muttered.

Thena frowned suppressively at Lancer's levity, but there was little heat behind it. She knew he was only trying to relieve the tension.

Unfortunately, it didn't work. The unaccustomed presence of the watchers in the room beyond distracted Thena, making it difficult to concentrate. To tune them out, she sat with her back to them. Her unease communicated itself to Seri, who took her position in Thena's lap with a few nervous twitches.

Thena calmed herself, then assessed her querent's state of mind. Her mouth quirked in a half smile. Lancer's description was right on target. Poor Hudson must be as uncomfortable as she was. The lights went off and she reached out to pat his hand. "Everything will be just fine. Close your eyes and relax."

He closed his eyes but remained stiff.

"Try to do better," she whispered, "or the ritual won't work properly. Don't worry; I do it all the time."

Concentrating on Hudson's nervousness had eased some of her own. They were in her area of expertise now.

Hudson took a few deep breaths and managed to relax a little.

Realizing it was probably as good as he was going to get, Thena said, "Repeat after me. Gracious Apollo, Guardian of Delphi and Patron God of Pythias, hear our plea. . . ."

Hudson obediently followed her instructions and

finally loosened up as the rhythm of the ritual washed over them.

Thena's tensions eased, and she let her worries drain away in the familiar, comforting words. When she reached the end of the prayers she said softly, "Now, open your eyes."

Hudson did so and Thena opened the hinged lid of the caroline pot. The flowers strained upward out of their confinement to light the room in a soft violet glow and tint the corners with purple shadows. Their familiar musky fragrance filled the air, marking the room as hers.

Hudson succumbed quickly to their lure, and the pupils of his eyes dilated in response. Confident he was now in the appropriate state of mind, Thena closed her eyes and let Seri enhance her susceptibility to the drugging scent, relaxing, giving herself totally to the ritual.

She achieved the necessary receptive state quickly and felt the oracle's presence as it took control and intoned, "State your question."

Hudson responded without hesitation. "How can we avert a war with the colonial rebels?"

The question now stated, the oracle cast Thena into the vortex of Hudson's mind. With the ease of long practice, she kept his fears and desires at bay as she searched for the golden path to the answer.

One suddenly appeared where she least expected it, off to the side. She hovered at the beginning of the blurred path, somehow feeling it wasn't right. Another appeared, then another, then two more.

Five paths where there should be one—what

should she do? Wavering in uncertainty, she waited too long to choose one. Her anchor to reality loosened and came adrift, leaving her stranded in the turmoil. The desires and fears redoubled their attack on her defenses, then became even more fierce as others joined them, buffeting her unmercifully.

Frantic, she tried to sort them out as senses and emotions became inextricably mixed. She tasted Hudson's salty fear of war . . . smelled Juelle's spicy eagerness . . . saw Alexander's red driving ambition . . . heard Darian's screaming for understanding . . . felt Lancer's prickly fear of commitment.

It was too much! The cacophony of sensory overload threatened to overwhelm her, and she redoubled her efforts to fight them off. Her exertions were to no avail, and she shuddered with the realization that she was losing the battle. Dear Apollo, was she finally going insane?

A surge of denial rocked her as Seri waded into the melee to add her bit to the struggle. Seri's heroic efforts appeared puny against the might of the emotional tempest, and the moncat yielded beneath the onslaught.

No—she couldn't let them have Seri too! Thena summoned all of her strength and shielded Seri with her mind, urgently seeking an escape—anywhere. The cacophony peaked to a screaming crescendo, and Thena felt her tenuous grip on sanity weakening.

She grabbed her head and cried out in wordless despair. *Apollo, help me! I can't take . . . it . . .*

any . . . more. Feeling her defenses start to crumble, Thena pushed Seri out of the link and prepared to brave the disintegration of her sanity alone.

Just before the madness could claim her, a barrier slammed down in her mind, yanking her back to reality. The sudden blissful cessation of tension was too much for her beleaguered senses. Thena surrendered her shield and fell into the welcoming embrace of unconsciousness, trusting her fate to Apollo's tender care.

Chapter Twelve

Lancer watched in horror as Thena and Seri stiffened, then toppled over. He reflexively jerked into movement, catching Thena before her head could hit the ground. Hudson, too, slid slowly to the floor, leaving Lancer kneeling beside three unconscious bodies.

His mind raced. What should he do? A doctor—he needed a doctor. Juelle!

Hearing someone fumbling at the door, Lancer quickly reached out with a free hand and closed the lid to the carolines. Three bodies were enough—he couldn't deal with any more.

He felt Thena's wrist for her pulse, relieved to find she had one. It was a little erratic, but it was there.

Juelle knelt beside him and felt Hudson's pulse, her face white. "What happened?"

Hudson groaned and opened his eyes. Darian switched on the lights and Hudson clamped his eyes shut, holding his head gingerly.

Lancer clutched Thena's still form anxiously. Hudson was moving. Why wasn't Thena? "Happened? I-I don't know. It didn't happen this way before."

Lancer should have heeded his doubts. He hadn't wanted to conduct the prophecy with Thena feeling so uneasy, but she'd seemed so sure everything would be just fine. Instead, it had gone terribly wrong.

Lancer forced his erratic thoughts to slow. He couldn't think. But one thing he did know—he had to get Thena out of this fear-filled room, to somewhere warm and familiar.

Juelle unclipped a portable medical monitor from her belt and ran it over the length of Thena's body. "She doesn't seem hurt, just unconscious."

Lancer tightened his arms around Thena in relief. "Can I move her?"

"I don't see why not. Let's get her someplace more comfortable."

That was all he needed to hear. Scooping Thena into his arms, he swept her out of the room and into the hall. He barely registered Juelle's retrieval of the unconscious moncat and his brothers' hurried opening of the doors in his path. All his attention was focused on the young woman in his arms.

Lancer bounded up the main staircase and into the bedroom, slowing only to lay Thena down on her bed. He released her from the shelter of his arms and stared down at her unconscious form. Her hair spilled across the pillow in honey-colored waves and his memory tortured him with visions of how she'd looked earlier, after they'd made love.

Then, Thena had been warm and passionate, her skin flushed from his lovemaking. Now, she just lay there, pale and unmoving. Straightening her limbs, he gently pushed the hair out of her eyes. Lancer was just beginning to learn how very special this woman was—she couldn't leave him now. He wouldn't let her. He clenched his fists in impotent frustration.

Juelle started to lay the unconscious form of the moncat on the window seat, but Lancer stopped her. "No—put Seri down next to Thena."

Juelle carefully placed the moncat by Thena's side, and Lancer asked anxiously, "Is Seri okay?"

Hudson staggered into the room and stared at Lancer in disbelief. "You're worried about the animal?"

Lancer whirled on him, glad to have a target for his frustration. "Damn right I am! The two of them are bonded together in ways none of us will ever understand. Thena's health may be closely tied to the moncat's, and I won't have it jeopardized by *anything* if I can help it!"

"None of us want that either, son," Hudson reassured him in a placating tone.

Juelle finished running the medical monitor over Seri and shook her head. "I don't know. The moncat's physiology is different from anything I've seen before." She glanced at Lancer. "She and Thena are both in the same state. If one is all right, they should both be."

Conversely, if one was on the brink of death, they both were. Lancer nodded, his fists clenching and unclenching as he stared down at Thena. Had he brought her here only to have her realize her worst nightmare—insanity? His gut spasmed in guilt as he relived the prophecy.

It had gone so smoothly at first. Thena had adapted remarkably well to the strange surroundings, and when the sense-altering fragrance of the carolines had filled the room Lancer had been relieved to find he could function rationally and even observe what was going on.

Everything had seemed normal until Hudson asked the question. Then Hudson's thoughts had begun to interweave with those of the others, coalescing into a powerful entity against the defenseless Golden Pythia. Lancer had frozen, not knowing what to do. He only knew he had to help her somehow. He'd tried to fight off the combined emotions of her foes—*his* friend and relatives—to no avail.

When Thena screamed he'd reached out instinctively with everything he had, trying desperately to shield her from her torment, but it hadn't been enough. Dear God, he'd been too late.

A rustling noise roused him from his reverie. Maeve hurried in behind Darian to take a blanket from the closet and cover Thena. The housekeeper clucked sympathetically, then glanced up at the people filling the bedroom. Placing her fists on her ample hips, she glared at them. "Out of here, now." She made a shooing motion. "Go on; get out of here. I'll watch the poor girl."

His father and brothers turned to the door, and Juelle touched Lancer's arm. "She's right, Lancer. We can't do anything now. Come on; let them rest."

Lancer didn't move, frozen in fear and guilt. There had to be something he could do.

Maeve touched his other arm. "That's right, boy. You go on. I'll let you and the doctor know if anything changes." Sympathy and concern sounded in her gruff voice.

Lancer sighed. Maeve was right. He couldn't do anything more to help Thena now, and he couldn't bear to see her this way. Nodding, he allowed Juelle to steer him out of the room and down the stairs to his father's study, where Hudson, Darian, and Alexander sat waiting for them.

Lancer collapsed into a chair and Juelle ran the monitor over his father. Hudson protested. "I'm perfectly all right, my dear. I was just a bit disoriented for a few moments—the flowers, you know."

Juelle nodded and clicked the monitor off. "Yes, I see that. I just wanted to compare your vital signs to Thena's."

The tension in the room eased, and Alexander and Darian seemed to relax. "Are there any parallels in their condition?" Alexander asked in a curious tone.

Damn them. Thena was lying near death upstairs and his family was acting as if she'd just skinned her knee. Lancer gritted his teeth in anger, but

272

Juelle's warning glance took him aback.

Was he overreacting again? Lancer took another look at their faces. Concern for Thena showed plainly. They weren't unfeeling; they just didn't understand how much danger Thena was in. How could they? They hadn't experienced the terror of that prophecy gone wrong.

"No," said Juelle. "No parallels. Just the lingering effects of the hypnotic fragrance."

Lancer looked up. "What about" —he forced himself to say it— "brain wave activity?"

Juelle perched on the arm of Lancer's chair and gave his shoulder a reassuring squeeze. "That's the first thing I checked. The monitors aren't sophisticated enough yet to diagnose mental disease, but they do a good job in showing where there are problems. Thena's scan doesn't show anything of that sort."

Lancer glanced up at her searchingly. He knew Juelle—she was leaving something out. "What *did* it show?"

Juelle shrugged. "Just a slight anomaly—it's probably nothing to worry about."

"Probably?" Lancer repeated, his voice rising. He didn't want to count on *probably*.

Juelle gave him a steady look. "Yes, probably. Since I didn't get a chance to get a reading on her before, I don't know what's normal for her and what isn't. The anomaly may be because of her psionic talent. I've seen similar readings on other psychics. Relax—I'm sure it's nothing. She'll be fine."

Lancer nodded and ran his fingers through his

hair. "I'm sorry, Ju. I'm just a little worried." He looked up and caught Alexander's knowing expression.

Afraid he had revealed too much of his growing fondness for Thena, Lancer resorted to sarcasm. "And you needn't smirk, big brother. Can't you understand the repercussions it would cause if the first Delphian to visit Earth were to be incapacitated for life? That'll really make them want to join the Republic!"

The smirk disappeared, but the amusement in Alexander's eyes remained. "Yes, of course," he said softly. "Never mind that the Delphian is a beautiful, desirable woman. And you, always so eager to do your political duty."

Juelle snorted in amusement and Lancer gave her a dirty look. She was supposed to be on *his* side.

Before Lancer could come up with a scathing reply, Hudson interrupted. "Never mind that. What happened? Did it work?"

All eyes turned to Lancer and he bristled. Why'd they ask him? He was no expert on Delphian prophecies, though Thena seemed to think he was after that meaningless life-mate ritual. Had Thena told them about it?

No, he reassured himself. Since Thena was out cold, it was natural they'd turn to Lancer. He *was* the only expert on Delphian prophecies present at the moment. He forced himself to relax and think calmly about the recent ritual. Maybe it would give him a clue to what had happened, how he could help her. "No, the prophecy didn't work—this time. Tell me, what did *you* experience?" he asked his father.

Hudson frowned. "I remember chanting a prayer with Thena, then nothing after she opened the flowers. Nothing until I woke with a splitting headache and saw you bending over us."

That made sense. Thena said querents didn't usually remember the experience. Lancer grimaced. Gee, why was *he* so lucky?

He turned to the others. "Anyone else?"

Juelle stirred on the arm of his chair. "We could see and hear everything that was going on, but the flowers didn't reach far enough to affect us." She gave him a strange look. "You must have sensed something wrong, though. You leaped to your feet *before* Thena screamed. Why?"

Damn Juelle and her training in observation. How could he explain the feelings and visions he had shared with Thena? Without experiencing it themselves, the others would be hard put to understand—or even believe—the sensations inherent in the prophetic ritual.

He wouldn't try. Avoiding her gaze, Lancer said, "I don't know—it just didn't feel right."

Darian nodded. "Different surroundings."

Alexander gave him a curious look. "You may be right."

The light dawned. Of course. "That's it!" Now how was he going to explain this without sounding incredibly flaky?

"Thena felt very uneasy about having so many

people watching her. Remember when I told you she appears to be able to delve into the unconscious mind?"

They all nodded, and Lancer continued. "Well, when there are only two other people in the room, she's probably able to ignore the observer and focus just on the querent. With so many others in the room who could see and hear what was going on, she was undoubtedly overwhelmed by so many minds to choose from and didn't know which to focus on. No wonder it didn't work."

Lancer frowned. "That's probably why the prophecies on Delphi are always done in a cavern with lots of rock between them and other people. We should have listened to Thena, and respected her fears." And damn Captain Spencer, too, for not mentioning this.

Hudson nodded. "Yes, but it can't be helped now. Dr. Shanard, how long do you think before she'll be well enough to try again?"

The unfeeling statement propelled Lancer to his feet. He leaned menacingly over the desk toward his father. "Try again? Not on your life—not till she's well."

Unperturbed, Hudson didn't budge an inch. He merely raised an eyebrow at Lancer's uncharacteristic vehemence. "Of course not. That's why I asked. Besides, that *is* why you brought her here, son. If her prophecies are as accurate as you say, the fate of the Republic may still rest on her answer."

Lancer backed off, realizing he was making a scene and causing Alexander no end of amusement.

Even Darian regarded Lancer with an air of faint surprise on his face. Maybe he *had* been overdoing it a little.

Lancer ran his hand through his hair. "Sorry," he mumbled. "It's been a rough trip."

Hudson's look of inquiry turned to concern. "I'd forgotten your illness. Are you feeling all right?"

Juelle turned to give Lancer a piercing look. He held up his hands. "I'm fine—really. I just need a little rest."

Juelle smiled at him. "Why don't you get some sleep, then? You can't help Thena in the state you're in, and we'll let you know if there's any change in her condition. I promise—no more prophesying until I'm satisfied she's well. And then only under strictly controlled conditions. Okay?"

Lancer nodded and grinned. Thena was going to be all right. She had to be. "Okay, you're the doctor."

Feeling distinctly as if his emotions were careening out of control, Lancer gratefully escaped from the room and the penetrating stares of his family. He needed time to figure out why Thena's collapse had hit him so hard, and how he was going to regain his mental equilibrium.

An hour later, Lancer lay on the bed in the room adjoining Thena's, staring unseeingly at the blank ceiling vid screen. He had it all worked out now.

He'd come to care for Thena—a little. There was nothing unusual in that; he'd cared for all the women he'd bedded in the past. His feelings for Thena only *seemed* stronger than any he'd experienced before. But it was only a temporary infatuation, an obsession with the way her cool beauty turned to warm passion when he touched her. The way she shed her dignity in his arms and responded with innocent abandon.

He sighed in regret. Eventually, that, too, would pall, and he would tire of her. He always had in the past. There was no reason to assume differently now.

The problem was Seri—and those damn flowers. True, they hadn't affected him as dramatically as they had before. Instead, they were far more insidious this time. They'd taken his mild affection and enhanced it out of all reason, making it appear he cared for Thena far more than he really did.

Lancer sighed in relief, glad he had figured it out. Now that he knew the cause, he'd be more careful when dealing with Seri and the flowers. He sat up, prepared to confront the smirking faces of his family with his realization, but stopped—an undefinable *something* pulled at him.

He stilled, puzzled. The feeling seemed to be emanating from Thena's room—a tugging that encouraged him to investigate. He tried ignoring it, but the sensation persisted, urging him to open the door to the adjoining room. Lancer gave in to the compulsion and got to his feet, only to have the door opened by Maeve.

"Thena?" he asked.

Maeve nodded. "She's stirring now. I thought you'd like to know."

"Good. Don't tell the others yet—give me a few moments alone with her."

Maeve smiled knowingly and Lancer grimaced. "Damn it, I just want to give her a chance to recover before they're on her like a pack of wolves. In fact, keep them out altogether. I'll call if I need anyone."

Maeve just gave him a look and edged out the door. Damn impertinent servants—just because they'd changed your diapers and bandaged your scrapes, they thought they *knew* you. Lancer scowled at the door Maeve closed behind her, then walked to Thena's bedside.

She looked better. Lying there with one hand across her eyes and the other curled protectively around the slumbering moncat, Thena looked more . . . alive.

"*Shiya?*" he said softly.

Thena's eyes flickered open and she gave him a wan smile. "Lancer."

Relief flooded through him. She was coherent and she knew his name. Thank God.

He sat gingerly on the bed next to her and took one of her soft hands in his. "How are you feeling?"

Thena's head felt like a blacksmith had been using it for an anvil, but she was exceedingly grateful to find she hadn't gone mad—at least not yet. She gave him a tremulous smile. "Not too bad. I-I'm sorry."

He stroked her hand. "You shouldn't be. You were right about not letting anyone else observe the prophecy. There were just too many minds bombarding you all at once. We should have

279

listened to you." He smiled at her. "Next time we will, I promise."

Thena smiled back. "It was terrible—too many paths, too many choices. I-I didn't know what to do. Neither did Seri. We were lost—until something saved us."

Seri stirred and woke beneath Thena's hand. The moncat's mind was reassuringly normal, but she confirmed Thena's puzzlement at their escape. Thena's eyes widened in sudden realization. "It was you! You saved us!"

Lancer looked startled. "Me? No, no, it couldn't have been." He grimaced. "I tried and failed. You must have done it yourself without realizing it."

Thena relived that blessed moment when the barrier had cut off the wailing, clamoring voices of her tormentors. A silent inquiry confirmed that neither she nor the moncat had possessed the strength to erect such a barrier, and that they had come very close to being overwhelmed and lost forever.

Yes, that wall had the definite feel of Lancer—solid and unyielding as bedrock when he wanted to be. "Maybe." She and Seri knew Lancer had been responsible, but if he didn't want to admit it, she'd go along with him.

She stored the memory carefully. To her knowledge, this had never happened before. Once she fulfilled her quest, she'd bring it before Delphi's Council, to see if this valuable ability could be encouraged and developed in other observers.

Lancer leaned down and kissed her on the forehead. "I think it took more out of you than you know. Why don't you get some more sleep? I'll be here if you need me."

Thena sighed and closed her eyes. Yes, sleep was what she needed. Warmed by the comforting presence of the two she loved most, Thena drifted off to sleep again.

When she woke the next morning she felt much better. Seri was nowhere in sight, having presumably gone to get her breakfast from the amenable housekeeper. Thena pushed herself to a sitting position on the bed and smiled down at Lancer, who had fallen asleep fully clothed beside her.

It was a bittersweet smile, full of the knowledge of their strengthening bond and his continued resistance to it. She searched for their link. Yes, it was as she'd thought. His rescue the day before had increased their intangible connection from the size of a golden filament to that of a thick thread.

It had been necessary, and it couldn't be revoked now. But if she wasn't careful, it would soon grow to the size and strength of the bond she shared with Seri. A pang of yearning stabbed through her, but Thena ruthlessly suppressed it. Removing herself from temptation, she slipped quietly from the bed to take a luxurious hot bath and soak away her aches and pains.

When she emerged from the bathroom wearing her buckskins Lancer was just waking. He peered at her sleepily. "You're up. How're you feeling?"

Apart from the pangs of unrequited love, she felt just fine. "Good—I'm back to normal. Shall we try

281

again today?" The sooner she got back to Delphi, the better.

He looked shocked. "Already? Maybe you could take it, but I couldn't. Let's wait at least one more day, okay?"

"All right, but I would like to start working with Juelle today. Would that be possible?"

"Sure, if that's what you want." Lancer looked like a disappointed little boy.

Thena repressed a smile. "What did *you* want to do?"

"Well, I was hoping you'd come to the studio with me. I want to show you where I work, how a holofilm is made, that sort of thing. C'mon," he wheedled. "We can take Juelle with us and you can leave if you get bored."

Thena smiled. He was irresistible like this, and it sounded harmless. Surely he couldn't make love to her in public. "I thought I wasn't supposed to be seen by anyone." She gestured down at her buckskins. "And I don't have any clothes that are appropriate for this world."

"I don't care what Father says; we can't keep you locked up in this house forever. If you go in Terran clothes without Seri, you won't attract any unwanted attention. Juelle can help." Lancer went to the communications console and requested to be put through to Juelle's office.

The psychiatrist came on the screen. "Morning, Lancer. How's our patient?" Her sharp gaze focused over his shoulder to where Thena was standing. "Good—up and about, I see. No ill effects?"

When Thena shook her head Juelle continued in a brisk, efficient tone. "I've turned over my patients to another doctor so I can concentrate on Thena's case. When can you get her here, Lancer?"

Lancer laughed. "Whoa, wait a minute. You two are in too much of a hurry. I wanted to take Thena to the studio and show her around first, okay?"

Juelle's eyes met Thena's over the screen and Thena smiled slightly, shrugging. They communicated wordlessly on the vagaries of the male psyche and decided to indulge him this once.

"Okay," said Juelle. "But not dressed like that, she's not."

Lancer turned to give Thena a bemused look. "Do you two have some sort of telepathy going on here or something?"

Thena smiled mysteriously. Yes, she had "some sort of telepathy" going on, but it wasn't with Juelle. They just understood each other—and Lancer—very well.

"Never mind that," said Juelle. "Just find her a cloak and bring her to Chez Chaz. They're very discreet. I'll meet you there in an hour and we'll find her something to wear that won't scream 'off-worlder' to everyone she meets, okay?"

"All right," said Thena. "We'll see you there." She cut the connection.

"Clothes," Lancer said with a baffled look. "Women everywhere are just the same, I guess."

She just smiled tolerantly and said, "Now, where is that cloak?"

Men didn't understand. Thena couldn't deal with

anyone on an equal level, especially strangers on a new world, until she felt confident she was dressed appropriately. Thank heavens Juelle understood, even if Lancer didn't.

Several hours later Thena had ordered enough outfits to keep her clothed for the foreseeable future, and had purchased one to wear away from the magical shop where there were so many choices and the salespeople were so very attentive.

At Juelle's urging she'd selected a form-fitting jumpsuit like the one Juelle had worn the day before. It was white, trimmed in gold, just like her pythia gown. But unlike her gown, the jumpsuit made her a little uncomfortable.

It hugged her curves and showed more bosom than she was accustomed to. The gold belt worked like magic to make her waist appear much smaller than it really was, and a salesgirl had painted her face with cosmetics, drawing Thena's hair back into a deceptively simple-looking style that made her appear even taller. Juelle and the others assured Thena she looked modern and Terran, but she just felt odd. What would Lancer think?

She entered the waiting room where Lancer sat slumped in a chair, listlessly thumbing through a magazine with a patient, long-suffering look on his face. Behind Thena, Juelle cleared her throat and Lancer looked up.

He stood slowly and inspected Thena with great care, his expression inscrutable. She wished she hadn't left Seri back at Morgan House. Maybe the moncat could have given her some clue to Lancer's feelings.

"Well?" prodded Juelle.

Lancer frowned. "I thought you were going to help her blend in. She stands out too much in this getup."

Thena's heart sank. She had hoped dressing like a Terran would make her more acceptable to Lancer, maybe even eventually reconcile him to being her life-mate. Instead, he seemed disappointed in her. She blinked back sudden tears and turned. "I-I'll change into something else."

Juelle blocked her path, arms akimbo. "You will not. Lancer, you big oaf, she can't help but stand out—she's gorgeous. You'll never be able to disguise that."

Thena stood with her back to Lancer, waiting for his reaction, not caring that her feelings showed on her face for Juelle to see.

"Damn it, I don't want strange men staring at her, ogling her like she was on display. She's supposed to keep a low profile. How are we gonna do that if I have to beat them off with a stick?" He sounded definitely perturbed.

Juelle winked, and Thena wiped away her tears. Maybe he was just jealous? She turned to face him again, and his gaze flew to her décolletage like a magnet.

He groaned and waved at the cleavage in question. "Can't you . . . cover that up somehow? It's distracting."

Juelle grinned wickedly. "That's the idea. If

285

we keep everyone's attention on her . . . assets, they won't notice her unfamiliarity with the Republic."

Lancer scowled, and Thena smiled at Juelle, silently thanking her for making her see Lancer's true feelings.

"Okay, okay," he said. "But it's too late today anyway. You took so long in there, I don't have time to show you around the studio. I still need to get some work done, though. Why don't you two go to Juelle's office and get started on helping Thena?"

"Chicken!" taunted Juelle.

Thena wasn't sure what barnyard fowls had to do with it, but Lancer reddened and Thena looked at Juelle with new respect. She had to find out how Juelle managed to reduce this charming rogue to a stammering little boy.

He grinned. "Okay, you caught me." He leaned forward and kissed Thena possessively. This was the first time he'd kissed her in front of anyone else, and Thena had come to believe he never would. She was so surprised, she forgot her good intentions and responded warmly.

Giving Juelle a challenging look, Lancer said, "I just don't think anyone could work at the studio with a distraction like her around—especially me." He gave Thena another lingering kiss and said for her ears alone, "But I still prefer you in your own gown—or in nothing at all."

It was Thena's turn to redden as Juelle looked on with a grin.

Releasing Thena, Lancer strode jauntily out of the shop. He waved, saying, "Take care of my girl, and I'll see you two at dinner."

His girl. Thena smiled. Maybe there was hope for them after all.

Chapter Thirteen

This room is truly hideous, Thena thought as she followed Juelle into the psychiatrist's spacious office. The big window overlooking the city made her dizzy, but the office made her downright nauseous.

The floors and walls were a soft shade of gray, but the furnishings were stark black and white in wild freeform shapes with touches of brilliantly coruscating metal. Bizarre forms hovered motionless in unexpected locations, then zoomed off at random intervals to spin recklessly about the room. Though they were obviously designed to avoid other objects and human occupants, Thena ducked as a gyrating needle of light skimmed by. How could anyone work in such a place?

Juelle closed the door behind her. "Awful, isn't it?"

Thena looked at her in surprise, and Juelle laughed. "It's the modern look. Most of my male clients expect me to have an office that looks like this, so I do. Strangely enough, it makes them more comfortable." She walked over to a door on the side wall and opened it. "This is my real office—where I see my special patients."

Thena followed her into the next room and immediately felt more at ease. Where the other was stark and ugly, this was soft and pretty. The same pale gray dominated the walls and floors, but the rest was done in a pleasing riot of pastel colors and cushiony fabrics, none intruding on the others, just soothing and pleasant. And the artwork, thank heavens, was stationary.

Thena breathed a sigh of relief. "This is much better."

Juelle smiled. "I thought you'd like it." She gestured to one of the two lounge chairs dominating the room. "Please, have a seat."

Thena cautiously sat down and felt the chair move beneath her. "I hate these things," she confessed, Juelle's open manner inviting her confidence. "The way they form to your body feels positively indecent." She was nervous enough without the distraction of bothersome furniture.

Juelle chuckled. "I don't like them either. Here, let me show you how to change the configuration and turn off the form-fitting option."

Following Juelle's directions, Thena adjusted the chair to her liking and sat gingerly, relieved when it didn't move beneath her.

Juelle sat in the opposite chair and leaned forward. "If you have no objections, I'd like to vidtape this session. No one but me will ever see it. Is that all right with you?"

Thena nodded, and Juelle flipped a lever on the machine beside her. "Now, before I can help you, I need to know more about how your ability works. Can you describe a typical prophetic session for me? Don't go into your feelings yet; just describe how it looks, the process."

Thena sighed in relief. This she could do. She described the ritual, and Juelle interrupted periodically to clarify a point or to ask a probing question.

Juelle finally nodded. "Okay, I think I understand the process itself. Let's concentrate now on your problem. Lancer said you were worried about the possibility of losing your sanity. Can you tell me about it?"

Thena tensed. She'd never told this to anyone but Lancer, and that had been difficult enough. She opened her mouth to speak, but nothing came out.

Tears blurred her vision and she trembled uncontrollably as lifelong suppression warred with her desire to share the torment. She couldn't get the words out. Looking up into Juelle's compassionate gaze, Thena gestured helplessly.

Juelle gave her a steady look. "It's all right to be afraid. Losing control is scary, but talking can help. Just take your time, and when you feel right tell me about it."

Juelle waited with admirable patience while Thena floundered for the right words. "I . . . I . . ."

Thena swallowed around the constriction in her throat, vexed by her body's betrayal. Juelle couldn't help until Thena told the psychiatrist her problem. Using techniques she'd polished around her perfection-seeking father, Thena took a deep breath and willed herself to be calm and rational, to *be* the Golden Pythia. It helped.

Clearing her throat, she said, "I'm scared. I've been scared most of my life—ever since I remembered my first prophecy."

Juelle nodded encouragingly, and then, as if those few words had opened the floodgates, it all came gushing out. How Thena's mother had gone insane from remembrance of her prophecies. How Rheta had been locked away and was still locked away to this day, refusing to see anyone for fear the madness would overtake her at unexpected times. How Thena had kept her own remembrance a secret from everyone, even her own father, for fear she would be locked away too. How Nevan would use this to take power and ruin her and her family if he ever found out.

Her story told, Thena's words finally trickled to a halt and she heaved a shuddering sigh of relief. She felt drained, but freer now that she had shared her fears. The trembling was gone, too, and with it, much of her anxiety.

Smiling tremulously, Thena said, "That's why I'm afraid I'll go mad. Do you think you can help me?"

Juelle turned the machine off. "I'll be honest with you; I don't know. There's still much we don't know about how the mind works—especially in those with psi abilities."

Thena nodded sadly, her eyes downcast. It was too much to hope that Juelle would have a magic cure-all.

"I'm not saying we can't, either," said Juelle. "We just need to learn more about it first. I'd like to run a series of tests, to challenge your prophetic ability and see exactly how it works. Once I understand it, perhaps we can discover why remembering this experience might cause a pythia to lose her hold on reality. How does that sound to you?"

Thena hesitated, remembering the botched, horrifying experience of the night before. "I'm not sure—"

"I'm here to help you solve your problem, not create another one. We'll conduct the tests under strictly controlled conditions and try to duplicate Delphi's surroundings as much as possible, varying them only when you feel comfortable with it." Juelle waited, giving Thena time to think about it.

"All right," Thena agreed, and remembered that she needed Juelle's cooperation on another matter. "But that's not all that's bothering me. After being on Earth and studying the Republic, it appears Delphi only has one thing of value to trade with you—our prophecies."

Juelle murmured a noncommittal answer, encouraging Thena to voice the rest of her concern. "In order for us to retain our monopoly, it's important we keep the means of our prophecies confidential, so others can't duplicate it. It's the only way we'll be able to survive as equals in your technologically advanced society."

Thena watched Juelle anxiously for her reaction. The psychiatrist nodded thoughtfully, and Thena pulled out the clincher. "So, I'd like you to keep the results a secret. Can you do that?"

Juelle smiled ruefully. "You realize that proving your psi ability would be the culmination of my lifelong dream, and you're asking me to give up publication?"

Thena nodded.

Juelle sighed. "All right— no publication. It's the results that count, not my colleagues' approval. But we may have to demonstrate it to the Cabinet in order to prove your ability to them."

Thena leaned forward and gazed earnestly into Juelle's eyes. "They don't need to know all of it. Not *how* it works, just proof it *does* work."

"That's not a problem; the doctor-patient relationship is confidential. But . . . it wouldn't apply to the observer. They might put pressure on Lancer to get that information. I assume you want him present during the tests?"

"No, not Lancer," Thena said quickly.

"No? I thought you two had a serious relationship. Was I mistaken?"

"No. Yes . . . sort of." Thena took a deep breath. This woman was a good listener, and Thena had to explain it to someone. She related the story behind the life-mate ritual and all it meant to her and to Lancer, unsurprised to learn Juelle was aware of the trauma of Lancer's youth and the reason for his subsequent shunning of responsibility. Thena twisted her lips in wry amusement. "So you see, I can't force him to accept a responsibility he doesn't want."

Juelle nodded. "Yes, but I've known Lancer for many years, and I've never seen him act like this around a woman before. I'd say he's well on his way to being in love with you. The propinquity of these tests could strengthen that. Isn't that what you want?"

Thena's heart leapt at Juelle's assertion, but she ruthlessly suppressed it. Juelle hadn't seen Lancer's reaction to their life-mating. If she had, she wouldn't be so sure of his feelings. "That's exactly what I *don't* want."

Juelle spread her hands in an attitude of puzzlement. "I don't understand."

"A bond is formed when two people life-mate and it becomes stronger the more it is employed in prophecies, rituals, lovemaking, and the like. The bond Lancer and I forged in the life-mate ritual has become too strong already—I *can't* do anything to strengthen it more."

"Why not?"

"Don't you see? If it becomes too strong, it'll overpower my judgment. I wouldn't be able to contemplate doing anything that would part me from Lancer." She shook her head sadly. "I couldn't leave him even to help my people on Delphi."

"What if Lancer returned to Delphi with you?"

That was merely wishful thinking, and Thena couldn't let herself indulge in it. "What if he doesn't? Would he be happy knowing I couldn't leave, couldn't *live* without him? He'd never forgive me for putting that kind of responsibility on his shoulders. No, I have a duty to my people, and I can't let them down."

Juelle frowned. "I don't think you're giving Lancer a chance."

"On the contrary, I'm giving him every chance. If he does love me, I want him to realize that himself and make his own decisions, without coloring it with my needs."

Juelle sighed. "Okay. I don't agree with your decision, but I'll do what you ask." Thankfully, she dropped the subject. "Now, back to the ritual. Don't you need to have three people present? Who'll be the third?"

"Well, on the ship we used the recorder as the observer."

"I thought you wanted to duplicate conditions on Delphi as much as possible."

Thena shrugged. "Maybe not. The observer is really only there to record the prophecy and be as unobtrusive as possible—a computer could do that just as well. And it can turn the lights on, too, so we don't need an attendant—we proved that on the ship."

"All right then, we'll try it with just the computer." Juelle glanced at her wristcom. "It's almost time for cocktails. Why don't we head on back to Morgan House?"

Thena agreed. The day had gone well, and she felt much better now that she had an ally, however unwilling, in her struggle against strengthening the life-mate bond.

Lancer idly twirled the delicate stem of his wine-glass, staring unseeingly into the ruby liquid as he leaned against the mantel in the salon. He ignored the inevitable political discussion that passed for cocktail conversation in the Morgan manse and waited for Thena and Juelle to join them.

The political prattle ceased, and Lancer glanced up to see Thena and Juelle making an entrance wearing identical white and gold jumpsuits. He grinned. They looked like nothing so much as storybook characters come to life. No matter how severely tailored the outfit, Juelle couldn't help but look like a pixie. And no matter what she wore, Thena looked like a Greek goddess come to life.

Lancer's grin faded. That jumpsuit! Though it revealed no more than her pythia gown, it made her look more . . . approachable, less aloof and dignified. By their appreciative looks, it was obvious his brothers agreed. It was just as Lancer had predicted—give any man an eyeful of Thena's charms and he was smitten for life.

Annoyed by their admiration, and irritated with himself for being irritated, Lancer strode forward to shield Thena from their view. Realizing at the last minute how foolish that would appear, he covered his lapse by bowing before Thena and Juelle and kissing their hands. "Good evening, ladies."

Juelle grinned at him, obviously not taken in

by his last-minute save, but Thena merely looked puzzled.

Hudson strode forward. "We're glad you could join us. Please, come in and have a seat."

They did so, and Thena conversed easily with the Morgan men, chatting about her day as Lancer looked on in silence. Despite her ignorance of Terran ways and her unfamiliarity with their customs, she was poised and confident.

Lancer scowled. Yes, too damn confident— almost like a typical Terran woman. She was becoming more and more independent now that they were off the ship. He wasn't sure he liked it. What would she need him for?

He turned his attention back to the conversation to hear Juelle tell Hudson about the tests she'd planned for Thena.

Lancer set his glass down on the mantel. "I'm afraid I can't make it tomorrow," he apologized. "I've got too much to do at the studio." He really was sorry. The studio was becoming a bit of a bore.

Thena cast her eyes down and Juelle spoke. "That's okay; we decided to use a recorder as the observer—the fewer minds assaulting Thena's the better, don't you think?"

Taken aback, Lancer glanced up to meet Thena's steady gaze. "Sure—if Thena agrees. Whatever you want is fine with me," he blustered.

He was right—Thena didn't need him and, apparently, she didn't want him either.

"When will she be able to prophesy again?" Hudson asked.

He certainly was persistent. "When Juelle says Thena's ready, and not before," Lancer snapped.

Hudson looked surprised at his son's vehemence. "But—"

"But, nothing! I don't want to risk a repeat of what happened yesterday."

"But we know what happened—"

"No," Lancer corrected. "We *think* we know what happened. We can't be sure until Juelle runs her tests."

Hudson nodded gravely. "Yes, son, I understand that. But what you don't understand is that time is getting short and the more we delay, the more we approach a crisis. We need a prophecy soon."

His father had a point, but he didn't have all the facts. "I do understand, but Juelle is right in insisting on tests first. How are you going to convince the Cabinet of Ministers to heed Thena's prophecy unless you have incontrovertible proof of her talents?"

Hudson looked thoughtful, so Lancer continued. "It's customary to pay for the prophecies too—and pay dearly. We've promised her payment in the form of psychiatric evaluation, and I intend to ensure she gets it before we start exploiting her."

Hudson held his hands out in a placating gesture. "No one intends to exploit Thena. It's just that our need is so urgent."

Okay, maybe he was being too harsh. "Her need is as urgent as yours. As I told you before, she can't go home until she finds a cure for the madness. And if you want to continue . . . er, exploring this resource, it would behoove you to show good faith to the Delphians by treating their Golden Pythia properly."

"All right—" Hudson began, only to be interrupted this time by Thena's quiet voice.

"Just a moment." Her gaze pierced Lancer. "You may be my Observer, but you are not my Councilman."

Her look reminded him that he had given up those rights when he'd repudiated the life-mate bonding. Lancer gritted his teeth but kept silent.

"I believe I should be the one to decide the urgency of this request," she said calmly. "Now, what is the problem?"

"It's the same one I mentioned in the ritual," Hudson said.

"Oh, yes. You asked about a war?"

Hudson looked at Lancer in surprise. "Didn't you tell her? I thought that's why she came."

All eyes were on him, questioning. He squirmed for a minute, then could delay no longer. "It never came up."

"It never came up?" Hudson queried incredulously. "Interstellar war is imminent, with billions of lives at stake, and it *never came up?* That's why I sent you on this mission in the first place!"

Damn. Lancer should've known he'd get no slack from that quarter. He risked a glance at Thena. Her face tightened in disbelief and the beginnings of anger.

He tried to defend himself. "We were too busy rescuing Thena at the time. Besides" —he nodded toward Thena— "I did what you wanted; I brought proof of their prophetic abilities."

Thena stood to confront him. "And once we were on the ship, why didn't you tell me then?"

Why? Because he'd been too damn afraid she'd think he was trying to exploit her. They hadn't been talking much on the trip either, and he hadn't wanted to jeopardize their budding relationship by complicating it with his father's needs. But how could he tell her that?

The others discreetly withdrew to another corner of the salon. No help there.

He shrugged. "I was sick, remember? I wasn't thinking too clearly then. Besides, I didn't want you to think we were just using you."

She employed one of his tricks, raising an incredulous eyebrow. "Really," she said flatly.

Her look was so frosty, he was surprised icicles hadn't started forming on his nose. Hell, he'd blown it again.

Before Lancer could redeem himself, Thena beckoned to the anxious patriarch and said with quiet dignity, "I'm afraid I agree with your son. I must put Delphi first, as you have all put your Republic first. Until you have proof my talents are valid, and until I learn to control my talent without going insane, there will be no prophecies."

Hudson bowed his head in acceptance of her decision, and Lancer grinned. Thena had cowed Hudson with her quiet dignity and self-possession. Not many people could say they'd faced down the Republic's Defense Minister and won.

Thena turned to glare at Lancer, and his grin faded. Uh-oh, now that she'd taken care of the Defense Minister, it looked like Lancer was next.

After two hours of freezing behavior that made him feel lucky he hadn't caught frostbite Lancer was glad dinner was finally over. Maybe now he could get Thena alone and work this out in the privacy of their suite. He grinned. Yeah, making up after a fight could be lots of fun.

As they left the table, Darian gave him a look full of sympathy and Alexander favored him with one of his enigmatic smiles, murmuring something too softly for Lancer to hear.

What? Me worry? Giving them a thumbs-up, Lancer grinned and followed Thena out of the room and up the stairs to their suite. As the door closed behind them, isolating them from the rest of the house, Lancer faced her rigid back and said tentatively, "*Shiya?*"

She rounded on him with eyes blazing, her emotions flaring so fiercely, Lancer could almost feel them. Her reaction was so violent, it woke Seri hissing from her sleep on the window seat.

"Don't call me that!" Thena spat out.

She was a lot angrier than he'd thought. The fury of her response was so surprising, all he could come up with was, "Huh?"

Thena stood stiffly, looking like an avenging goddess in her ire. "You *lied* to me. All the time you were calling me *shiya* and prattling on about your stupid holofilm, all you were really interested in were my prophecies, weren't you?" Seri watched, wide-eyed, but made no move to interfere.

"Now, wait—"

"It's what I should've expected from a Terran. You said you didn't want your father to exploit me, when that's exactly what *you* had planned all along."

She had it all wrong, and it was starting to tick him off. "I did not—"

"Oh, really? Then why didn't you tell me about it on the ship?"

"I wanted to help you. Okay, I admit it—my motives weren't totally altruistic, but I honestly wanted to help you. My father wanted me to learn the truth about your prophecies, so I figured I'd bring the prophecies to him. That way he could make his own decision—and help you at the same time. You know, kill two flyers with a single laser?"

He could sense she was starting to cool a little, and Seri's bristling fur began to subside. Less forcefully, Thena said, "That still doesn't explain why you didn't tell me."

This arguing was exhausting. Gesturing toward the two chairs by the window, he said, "Please, can we sit down and discuss this rationally?"

Thena gave him a penetrating look, then nodded coolly and took a seat in one of the chairs. "All right," she persisted. "Why didn't you tell me? It seems like a good cause. I would have been glad to help if you'd just given me a chance."

He spread his hands helplessly. "I don't know. I

guess I just figured Dad would take care of it—"

"Abdicating your responsibility again?"

She sure knew how to hit below the belt. "Yeah, if you say so. At that point, I was more interested in getting to know you, and in putting this holofilm together."

Thena's gaze was cool and assessing. She wasn't buying it.

"Damn it, I'm telling you the truth. Why don't you believe me?" His frustration didn't seem to be reaching her at all. She just sat there like a marble statue.

Finally she spoke, her voice low. "How can I? When you spoke so eloquently of how Dr. Crowley's magic formula could make pythias of anyone? How it could end suffering, avert catastrophes—even stop interstellar war, perhaps?"

Oh, God, she was right. He *had* said that. "That's not what I meant—"

"And where does Delphi figure into this? Were you planning on using me to ferret out the formula so you could destroy Delphi's one unique trade item? Eliminate the only thing that could make us equals in the eyes of the Republic instead of a poor supplicant?"

He frowned. "I promised I wouldn't reveal that without discussing it with you first. I meant it. I still mean it."

She inclined her head gravely, her eyes still measuring him.

"You do realize," he reminded her, "what one person could figure out, another will probably be able to duplicate. Your secret formula won't remain secret forever."

"Yes, I know that. But the only way they'll learn it is if we allow them to study our rituals. We won't. And if no one mentions the possible existence of the formula, we can keep the secret much longer."

"Look, I still think it could be worked out—we could find a way for Delphi to benefit even if the formula was released."

She frowned, and he grasped her unyielding hands in his, hurrying to finish. "But since you feel so strongly about it I promise—I won't mention it to a living soul."

"No?" She looked disbelieving.

He was sure as hell getting tired of having his honesty questioned. He had to convince her, beyond all shadow of a doubt, that he wasn't lying. But how?

He had it! He gazed steadily into her eyes. "No. I swear I won't mention it to anyone else. But if you don't believe me, put me on trial, the Delphi way."

"What?"

"You know—run one of your trial rituals and have the oracle look into my mind. That'll prove I'm telling the truth."

Thena pulled her hands from his. "No!"

"Why not? You're the one who told me no one could lie to the oracle in a trial. Let's do it."

Her gaze shied away from his and she began to stroke the moncat. "That isn't necessary. I believe you. If you're willing to subject yourself to the ritual, you must be sincere."

Finally she believed him! His triumph felt oddly flat. What was going on here? Her whole demeanor had changed as soon as he asked for a prophecy, almost as if she was afraid to have him in the ritual. His gut twisted in despair. Had he lost her trust as well?

Chapter Fourteen

Thena rose from the cushion in the isolated experiment room and stretched her back, marveling once more at how closely her surroundings resembled a Delphian pythia cavern. The small secluded room, deep in the basement of Juelle's office building, had been quickly transformed to Thena's specifications. The carolines had readily taken root, giving the room the look and feel of a real Delphian cavern. It almost, but not quite, fooled Thena into believing she was home.

Seri blinked in tired resignation and curled up on the abandoned cushion for a few moments of uninterrupted sleep. Poor Seri—Thena had been pushing all of them the past few days, anxious to find a cure so she could leave for Delphi as soon as possible. The strain of avoiding Lancer was a little easier thanks to Juelle's intervention, but it was by no means gone. Thena just wanted to get it over and done with.

"How many does this make?" she asked.

Juelle looked up from the corner where a jutting boulder hid the computer terminal. "This will be test number fifty-four."

Thena yawned. "It feels like a hundred and fifty-four."

"Yes, I know," Juelle said with a sympathetic smile. "But to ensure our tests are scientifically rigorous, we need to test all aspects of your ability. If everything goes right, we only have a few tests left." Her fingers played competently over the keyboard. "Let's see, we know the ability depends on a combination of the carolines, your empathic bond with Seri, and utter isolation. Take one of those three away, and it doesn't work."

Thena grimaced. "I could have told you that."

Juelle smiled back. "Yes, but we also learned the ritual prayers and cleansing parts of the rituals aren't really necessary for the prophecy. They just make it easier for the querent to be in the proper frame of mind."

"That's true. I didn't know that for sure until we tested it."

"And I'm not sure I should mention it, but I'm also fairly certain I now know what causes pythian insanity," Juelle said nonchalantly.

Her lethargy now gone, Thena's attention riveted on Juelle. "What is it?" she demanded.

"Since only those pythias who remember their

prophecies go insane, the insanity must have something to do with that memory."

"Yes, that makes sense."

"Now, the prophecy experience itself is not a pleasant one. You describe it as being attacked and buffeted by the emotions of the querent—terrible visions of the querent's worst fears, the basest of human urges and desires, right?"

"Yes," Thena said impatiently. She wished Juelle would just get to the point.

"Okay, so each time you prophesy, you're building more and more memories of these painful assaults." Juelle leaned forward, punctuating her words with empathic gestures of her slender hands. "And each time you add a little more horror to your view of the world—more atrocities, more depravity, more evil."

Thena shuddered. It was an all too accurate description. "But I can't let that stop me from prophesying."

"Right, that's the trap you fall into. The benefit of the prophecies so outweighs your qualms about the experience that you continue to prophesy. The evil builds slowly until one day it overwhelms you. You just can't take it anymore. Your world view collapses in the middle of a prophecy and your defenses shatter. You can't fight off the emotions of the querent anymore and they take over, feeding your innermost fears and those of all the querents who have gone before you. You go over the edge into insanity."

Stunned, Thena nodded. Not only did Juelle's

theory fit the facts; it had the remarkable ring of truth. "So why doesn't it happen to the other pythias?"

"Since they don't remember their prophecies, the horror never has a chance to build. For them, each time is a new experience."

Somehow, Thena knew Juelle had found the true cause of pythian insanity. "Yes—that's it! But how do we stop it?"

Juelle frowned. "I don't know yet—that's why I wasn't sure if I should mention it. I still think we should continue as we have been—learn everything about your ability first. Once we do, maybe we'll find the cure."

"All right. What do we do next?"

"Well, if you're going to market these skills to the rest of the Republic, we need to find a way for the querents to voice the question they really want to ask, instead of just their heart's desire."

Juelle was becoming frustrated by her inability to ask more than one question. Thena chuckled. "You mean you'd like to ask something other than how to attain definitive proof psi ability exists?"

The psychiatrist nodded ruefully. "Yes, but at least we know the oracle is consistent. It always gives me the same answer: 'Go to Apollo's Shrine.'"

"What question would you like to ask?"

Juelle rolled her eyes heavenward. "*Anything* else." She hesitated. "No, I'd rather ask something that can be proved or disproved quickly—like the newsvid headlines for the next day. That way we can also determine if you just tap into the person's subconscious mind, or if you really do have the power to foretell the future, even when neither party has knowledge of the subject or the outcome."

"All right. Let's get started. What's the next test?"

"Well, we know Seri can't vary the force of her empathic enhancement. It's either full throttle or none at all. So, I'd like to try changing the strength of the carolines by varying the light level. If I'm right, that should reduce their potency and I can ask the question I want."

Thena sighed and nudged Seri with her toe. "Let's get back to work."

Hours later, all three were exhausted but triumphant. Juelle grinned at Thena. "That's it! We know now exactly how much light is needed to allow the querents to ask whatever they want."

"Yes, and it has the added benefit of making it easier for me to recover from the trance—and for you to remember the prophecy before you hear it on the recording." Thena rubbed her aching forehead. "But so many prophecies take their toll. I don't think either Seri or I could do any more today. Do you have enough?"

"I think so. I recorded all of your prophecies on tomorrow's news with a time imprint, to prove they'd been made today. We'll check them tomorrow, to see how accurate they were." She bit her lip. "Unfortunately, most of them could be easily predicted by almost anyone who knows the news and keeps up with current events, which you could have gotten from my subconscious. All but the last one, that is—the drive failure and explosion of the starship. That'll be the clincher."

Thena shifted uncomfortably on her cushion. "We need to warn them—we can't let all those people die."

Juelle regarded her seriously. "You're right, but it would be hard to convince them without saying *why* we think it's going to explode. I can't do that without Hudson's approval and knowledge—your abilities are classified."

"Then let's ask *him* to do it—they'd have to take the Defense Minister seriously, wouldn't they?"

"I hope so. But you realize if they avert the catastrophe, it invalidates your prophecy?"

Did Juelle really think Thena would place her need for validation above the lives of innocent people? "Yes, but we have to save them if we can."

Juelle nodded in approval. "I thought you'd feel that way."

"Besides, the prophecies only predict what could happen if a particular course of action is taken. If someone changes their actions based on the prophecy, the outcome would naturally change."

Juelle didn't look convinced. "Perhaps—that remains to be seen. I guess tomorrow will be a good test." She stood up and turned off the computer. "Let's find Hudson so he can warn them."

Lancer stood at his accustomed place at the mantel as the Morgan men listened to Juelle explain why the two women had called them there. "With Thena's cooperation I've learned exactly how her ability works, and we recorded several predictions of tomorrow's newsvids headlines to check it against."

Hudson leaned forward eagerly. "How *does* it work?"

From his vantage point, Lancer saw Thena tense, but Juelle patted her knee reassuringly. "I'm sorry; I can't tell you that."

Hudson bristled. "Why not?"

Juelle gave Thena a sidelong glance, and Thena answered for her. "I asked her not to. It's important for Juelle to understand how my ability works so she can help me master it, but I don't want to reveal any more of Delphi's secrets to outsiders than I have to." She stared challengingly at Lancer, and all eyes turned to him.

Hell—he'd told her he wasn't going to reveal her precious secret formula. Didn't she trust him? Her glare didn't abate one iota.

Apparently not. Irritated by her lack of trust, he set out to prove her suspicious were unfounded. "She's right—Juelle's services are part of Thena's payment for her prophecies, not a government research project. You have no right to anything she doesn't choose to give you."

Hudson shrugged. "We can work that out later. Can you tell me if you have proof her predictions are valid?"

"We'll know tomorrow," Juelle said. "We have five predictions for the evening news headlines. Most of them are innocuous, but one could have catastrophic consequences." She tossed a disk on the low table between them. "If I read the predicition correctly, Starline will have a drive failure on their cruise takeoff tomorrow and explode, killing all aboard."

Alexander frowned and leaned forward, his normal indolence gone. "How? When?"

"The predictions aren't that clear. All we know is, it's going to make tomorrow evening's headlines."

Alexander shot to his feet. "If this is true, we need to warn them immediately. Did you?"

Juelle looked exasperated. "No. Who's going to believe a psychiatrist who calls to tell them one of her patients predicted an explosion? They'd probably lock both of us up."

Alexander opened his mouth again, but Lancer cut him off. "Juelle's right. They wouldn't believe her. It'd take someone on the order of a Minister to convince them the prediction wasn't a hoax— without telling them where it came from."

All eyes turned to Hudson. His brow furrowed as he looked at Juelle. "What do you gauge is the probability of this really happening?"

Alexander made an exasperated sound, and Thena's expression crumpled into resignation.

Suddenly angry at witnessing yet another insult to Thena's veracity, Lancer shoved his hands in his pockets to keep himself from breaking something— or someone. "Damn it, Dad, they wouldn't have brought it up if they didn't think it was true. Can't you just once take someone else's word and forget the dignity of your position? People's lives are at stake!"

313

Hudson rose to confront Lancer, his face set in stern lines. "You have no right to speak to me like that."

No right? Lancer clenched his fists and took a step forward, but Darian and Alexander moved to block him.

Placing a hand on his father's shoulder, Alexander said, "Lancer's right. It won't hurt to call and warn them to double-check their engines. If you like, I'll do it on your behalf. Starline's CEO is a friend of mine."

Darian nodded forcefully, and Lancer was so shocked by his brothers' support, he was momentarily speechless.

Hudson seemed equally surprised. Searching his sons' unyielding faces, he finally nodded. "All right, son, why don't you do that? If you need my confirmation, I'll be happy to provide it."

Alexander left to make the phone call, and Thena nodded approvingly at Lancer. He felt his chest swell with hope. Did this mean she was finally recovering from last night's little snit? Things hadn't been the same since she'd reverted to her ice sculpture imitation, and he was getting damn tired of it. He watched closely for signs of a thaw.

Thena broke the uncomfortable silence. "Thank you for letting us warn the people," she said quietly.

Lancer was proud of her—she didn't grovel or whine; she just continued in her inimitable fashion until those around her came to see things her way. She'd make a remarkable leader.

Thena continued. "This incident has made me realize I've been wrong to withhold my prophecies. If I can help avert your war and save lives, I would be selfish not to. It won't interfere with the research we're doing—I can do both."

Hudson brightened and gave Thena a grateful look. "Thank you, my dear. I would appreciate it."

Lancer was impressed. Not only had Thena handled his father gracefully; she'd managed to get what she wanted while making Hudson feel good about it. That was an art.

Hudson cleared his throat. "Would it be too presumptuous to ask when we can arrange it?"

Thena smiled graciously. "Not at all—we can arrange it as soon as it's convenient. Juelle has the pythia chamber set up, so we can do it whenever you want. Now, in fact."

Hudson stood again, apparently regaining his poise. "Now would be excellent." He looked up as Alexander came back in the room. "Ah, son. How was your warning taken?"

Alexander looked uncharacteristically serious. "He doesn't believe me, but he can't afford not to. He's having the engines checked."

"Good. Well, my dear," said Hudson as he faced Thena, "shall we go?"

"Yes, of course."

They all stood to follow her out the door, and Thena hesitated, obviously uncomfortable. "I'm sorry, but I'd prefer to have only the querent present—we don't want a repeat of last time. I need Juelle, too, to set up the equipment."

Alexander and Darian acceded quickly, returning to their seats. Thena stood stiffly between Hudson and Juelle. "*Only* the querent," she repeated firmly, staring at a point somewhere around Lancer's breastbone.

Why wouldn't she meet his eyes? "But I'm your Observer," he protested.

Juelle stepped between Lancer and Thena, as if to protect the Delphian woman. How ridiculous—Thena didn't need to be protected from him.

With a pugnacious thrust of her chin, Juelle placed her fists on her hips. "With the setup we've got now, we don't need an observer—the computer records the prophecy. Having other people present just makes it more difficult for Thena."

Thena didn't need him anymore. The realization hit him with the force of a sledgehammer. "But—"

Juelle leaned forward and, in a curt tone only he could hear, said, "Drop it."

Lancer knew Juelle well enough to know she meant it—for his own good. He shut his mouth and nodded grimly, turning back to join his brothers. He refused to watch as Thena walked away from him.

Two hours later Thena's rejection still rankled, and Lancer had come to the conclusion that they needed to talk. They hadn't made love since the night they arrived, and she'd been avoiding him ever since the prophecy went wrong. Hell, she said he'd saved her life. Why, then, had she been ignoring him, avoiding all contact with him? He definitely needed to clear the air.

Lancer heard the front door open and set aside

the script he'd been trying to read. Finally they were home.

He met the three of them in the foyer, searching their faces for a clue as to how it had gone. Hudson wore a peculiar expression Lancer couldn't interpret, and Thena and Seri looked tired. Only Juelle had a look he could fathom—she looked satisfied.

He addressed his question to her. "How'd it go?"

Juelle grinned. "Everything went fine, but I'm not sure your father cared for the answer he got."

That explained the strange expression on Hudson's face. "And what was that?"

Juelle glanced questioningly at Hudson, who nodded. "He asked the same question as before—how to avert the war without giving in to the colonists' demands for independent governing of their own planets."

Lancer nodded. That and the trade agreements were the colonists' sticking points. "But even I can see that would make the situation worse, not better, creating independent fiefdoms that would squabble among themselves and eventually result in utter anarchy."

It was Hudson's turn to nod, obviously surprised. "Exactly."

Good grief, I'm not a total idiot when it comes to politics. Some of the training had stuck. "So, what did the oracle say?"

Juelle cocked her head. "It said to give the colonists a seat on the Cabinet of Ministers. If he doesn't, the war will be long and bloody."

Lancer understood Hudson's concern. The Ministers were jealous of their power and wouldn't want to give any of it up. It would be difficult to convince them. "A Colonial Minister, huh? Not a bad idea, really. Do you think you can persuade them to do it?"

Hudson looked doubtful. "I don't know. I've got the two recordings of Miss—of Thena's prophecies to show them. I suppose it depends on how well her predictions pan out tomorrow—especially the starship disaster."

"Well," came Alexander's voice from behind him as he entered the room. "That's one worry you can put to rest." They all turned to face him, and he smiled languidly. "I just heard from Starline's CEO. They checked out the drive and found a faulty engine component the repair crew had missed on their overhaul. His engineers say if it hadn't been fixed, the ship would've exploded on takeoff, just as Thena predicted. She really *can* tell the future."

All eyes turned to Thena, and she smiled. "I'm glad I could help." Anyone else might have been excused for looking smug or triumphant. Thena merely looked relieved.

Alexander held up a disk. "I recorded our conversation, and the CEO agreed to testify to the Ministers any time you choose, without asking why. He's that grateful."

Hudson sighed in obvious relief. "Excellent. I'll call an emergency session for tomorrow so we can put the proposal to the Cabinet."

Alexander nodded, and the two men walked off to plan their strategy.

Lancer turned back to Thena with a small smile playing around his lips. "So how does it feel to have saved the known universe from the evil of interstellar war?" He couldn't prevent a little sarcasm from creeping in. That had been his job, not hers.

Thena's tired face froze into an expression of hurt, and Seri gave him a decidedly dirty look.

Hell. When would he learn to ensure his brain was engaged before he put his mouth in gear? There was nothing to do but apologize. "I'm sorry—"

"You've done enough for one night," interrupted Juelle.

Thena turned to go up the staircase to her room. "Wait," he cried. "I didn't mean—"

Juelle grabbed his arm. "Let her go."

He jerked his arm out of her hold and watched Thena ascend the stairs. She didn't look back once. "Why should I?" he snapped.

"She's tired. She's been through a lot today, and she needs some rest. She doesn't need you complicating things any more."

"Complicating things? What do you mean? You have no idea what—"

"Yes, I do." Juelle said.

Her habit of interrupting him was beginning to get on his nerves.

"Look," she said, "let's go to the dining room where no one will bother us. I need to explain some things to you."

Lancer followed her into the dining room and

closed the door. "All right; out with it."

Juelle faced him with a serious look that sat strangely upon her normally animated face. "Thena told me everything."

"Everything? Like what?"

"Like the life-mate ritual she went through to save your life. Like your refusal to take your rightful place as Council Captain. Like your plan to betray her world for the sake of a formula that probably doesn't even work." With each statement Juelle took another step forward until she was only a foot away from him.

Lancer felt his ears turn warm. "That's none of your business—it's strictly between the two of us."

"It *is* my business, because I care about her. I care about what happens to her and her world. You don't, or you wouldn't be acting like such a clod."

"That's not true," he protested hotly. "I do care. I-I just don't know what's gone wrong lately, why she's changed."

"Have you asked her?"

"That's what I was *going* to do when you stopped me!" he roared, losing his composure.

Juelle folded her arms and returned glare for glare. "Well, don't bother. *I'll* tell you." She shoved a slender finger into his chest. "Siddown."

Lancer sat. Anything to get the woman talking again so he could find out what was *wrong*. "Okay, I'm sitting. Now give."

Juelle sat opposite him and sighed. "This life-mate business means more to her than it does to you."

"I know that—"

She cut him off again with a sharp gesture. "No, you don't, so just be quiet until I finish."

Lancer pressed his lips together, biting back a retort. Would she get on with it?

Apparently satisfied with his silence, Juelle continued. "She didn't realize it herself. The life-mate bond is more than just a pretty way of saying you two have made love. In your case, the bond is a literal bond—a connection she can see and feel. A connection that grows stronger each time you complete a prophetic ritual together or make love."

A real bond? That was ridiculous.

He hesitated. Or was it? Hadn't he sensed something of the sort? Maybe that was why he was finding it so easy to read Seri's emotions lately.

Lancer nodded slowly. Compared to believing in Thena's ability to prophesy the future, accepting the existence of this bond was minor. "Okay, I can see such a thing might exist. But where's the problem?"

"It's tearing Thena apart. Each time the bond grows stronger, it makes it a little more difficult for her to contemplate leaving you."

Lancer scowled. "Why would she leave?"

"Once we find the cure for pythian insanity, she'll have to return to Delphi to her own people—with or without you. You know that."

Yes, Thena's pride and sense of duty wouldn't let her do anything else. It was one of the things he admired about her. "But I'd go with her."

"Think about it. How could you humiliate her in

front of her entire world? Either you go as her life-mate and Council Captain or you don't go at all."

"No!" The exclamation forced Lancer from his seat. "Damn it, I won't be browbeaten into taking on the responsibility for an entire world. I didn't ask for it and I don't want it."

"That's why Thena's avoiding you. She doesn't want to make the bond any stronger, so it won't be so difficult for her to return to Delphi without you. She knew you'd abdicate your responsibility." Juelle stood and walked toward the door. "I thought you were better than that. I guess I was wrong."

She said that exit line like she'd been watching too many old holofilms. Juelle closed the door behind her, and Lancer clenched his fists in impotent rage.

They were trying to force him into doing something he didn't want, but by damn, it wasn't going to work. He was going to stick to his lasers and make Thena come crawling to him. Either she took him as he was or she could forget it. He nodded decisively. Yes, it was the right thing to do.

So why did he feel as though someone had just wrenched a hole in the pit of his stomach?

Chapter Fifteen

Thena lay in bed, willing herself to sleep. The last two days had been exhausting. Ever since Juelle had sheepishly confessed her scolding of Lancer, Thena had felt relieved that the matter was now in the open. It made it easier to avoid Lancer without explaining why—he *knew* why. But it also made it more stressful when they did meet.

While Hudson and Alexander worked to convince the Cabinet of her power and Thena continued to work with Juelle, Lancer had locked himself away. He'd been working feverishly on Delphi's holofilm, emerging only to eat and sleep. He wouldn't have even done that if Maeve hadn't insisted.

Thena turned over to hug her pillow. Sometimes she wished Maeve hadn't bothered. Lancer didn't seem to be enjoying his work very much, and when he did emerge he emanated an almost palpable aura of hurt and confusion—directed right at Thena.

Stars! Didn't the man realize she was hurting too? She didn't want to leave him, but she had a duty and a responsibility to her people. If he couldn't understand it, that was his problem.

She heard a door open and turned to see Lancer enter through the adjoining room. He strode in, then checked when he saw her in bed. For a fleeting moment she thought she saw a look of naked yearning on his face; then it was gone, replaced by a cold, aloof mask.

He looked tired, disheveled, as if he'd worked all night in his clothes. Thena tried to remain indifferent, but she felt a yearning of her own—to forget Delphi, to stay on Earth forever with this man and care for him. Make love to him.

Her nipples tightened at the thought, and Thena drew the bedcovers up to her neck so the thin material of her shift wouldn't reveal her reaction.

Lancer didn't miss the protective movement. His lips twisted into a grimace and he slapped a disk down on the bedside table. "Here. I want you to read this."

Thena sat up, still clutching the covers to her chest. "What is it?"

Lancer folded his arms across his chest and glared. "It's the script."

"The script?"

"Yes, the script for the holofilm on Delphi. It's done. I want you to read it."

He sounded so angry about it. "Why?" she asked.

He made a grimace and shoved his fingers

through his hair. "Just read it, okay?"

It sounded very important to him. "All right, I'll read it now. I can't sleep anyway."

Lancer nodded tersely. "Good." He grabbed the disk and inserted it into her desk console. Punching the buttons quickly, he brought the printed contents up on the screen, then walked back to their adjoining door. "Let me know what you think," he said, and shut the door.

Well, that was certainly abrupt. She gave the console an apprehensive glance. What if she hated the script? If he portrayed Delphi in an unflattering light or mentioned the existence of the formula, she'd have to object—and that would put further strain on their already shaky relationship.

Thena sighed. She had to know. Reluctantly, she crossed the room, sat down at the console, and began to read.

Three hours later, she mulled over what she'd read. It wasn't bad. In fact, it was very good. But Lancer had revealed a great deal of himself in that script, whether he realized it or not.

Thena sighed. He was waiting for her reaction, so she might as well get it over with. She opened the adjoining door.

His room was dark and she stood in the opening, waiting for her eyes to adjust. Lancer, a shadowy shape in the darkness of the room, sat staring out the window.

"I read it," she said softly.

He didn't turn around. "And?"

"It's very good."

325

He turned to face her, then audibly sucked his breath in through his teeth. "Close the door!"

Thena suddenly realized how she must look with the light behind her shining through her thin shift and silhouetting every curve of her body. She shut the door hastily and stood with her back pressed to it, thanking the gods for the concealing blackness inside. She stood silently, her heart pounding as she let the cool darkness seduce her into calm.

Lancer stood and moved slowly toward her, stopping a couple of feet away, his face concealed in the shadows. "So," he said in a voice husky with fatigue. "You liked it?"

She could feel his warmth from where she stood. Dear Apollo, but the man was desirable. She felt her nipples pucker and harden with longing as she swayed toward him. "Yes, I liked it."

He took another step forward. "You aren't worried about me betraying your vision of Delphi?" he asked, fingering a curl that had fallen forward on her breast.

She swallowed hard. "No, you've captured our world wonderfully. And I do appreciate your not mentioning the formula."

Her eyes had adjusted enough that she could finally make out Lancer's expression. He continued to play with her hair, giving her a slow, sexy smile that made her insides melt.

He lowered his face to hers until it was only a kiss away. "Good," he murmured. "I hoped you'd be pleased."

She took a deep breath to shake off his

326

mesmerizing gaze. That was a mistake—it brought her chest into intimate contact with his hand. She gasped as his knuckles grazed the swollen peak of her breast.

He froze for an instant, then ran his thumb gently around the nub, as if to test it. "So," he said, moving closer, "do you trust me now not to reveal the formula?"

"Y-yes." Stars! She couldn't think—couldn't breathe. As he cupped her breast and moved his thumb in lazy circles around her nipple, she felt her body go languid with longing. A moist warmth enveloped her loins.

He molded his body against hers and kissed the sensitive spot on her neck. "And the people?" He clasped her buttocks in both hands and pressed her up against his arousal, moving in slow circles that drove her crazy with longing. "Do you trust me to portray them accurately?" he whispered, then gently bit her ear.

Her arms tightened around him involuntarily. It wouldn't hurt to let go this once—would it? His lips claimed hers in a devastating kiss that almost crumpled the last of her defenses. She struggled to regain the thread of their conversation. What had he asked?

Oh, yes, the people. Lancer trailed his lips down her neck to the valley between her breasts. Before he could distract her further, she struggled to answer. "Yes," she said, then paused to gasp when he suckled one breast through her night shift. "All but one," she managed to gasp out.

"Oh?" he asked, sounding uninterested as he moved to lavish attention on her other breast. "Who?"

Thena struggled to regain her composure. All her senses were concentrated on Lancer's hands and what he was doing with them. What had they been talking about?

Oh, yes, Lancer had done a wonderful job with all of the people. All but one, that is. "Captain Spencer," she whispered. Lancer hadn't caught the essence of the man at all.

As Lancer moved his hand down her ribs and across her stomach to pause at the band of her skimpy Terran panties, she remembered what had bothered her about the script. Lancer had portrayed Captain Spencer as a hollow, foolish man—a megalomaniac who didn't have the wits to realize how much responsibility he had over people's lives.

Thena grabbed Lancer's hand to keep his clever fingers from distracting her past the point of all rational thought.

He lifted his head. "What's wrong?" he asked softly.

In his portrayal of the captain, Lancer had unwittingly revealed his distaste of responsibility, proving once again how unwilling he was to be her life-mate. She had to stop this—now. She pushed him away quickly, before she could change her mind. "I-I can't."

As Lancer hit the wall in frustration, Thena slipped out of his embrace and back into her own room. Bereft of his touch, she huddled against the closed door and dashed the tears from her eyes.

She couldn't let this happen again. She had to finish her business here on Earth and return to Delphi as soon as possible—without Lancer. Any hope she'd cherished that he might join her had withered and died with that revealing script.

As Thena sat in the testing chamber waiting for Juelle and their next session, her mind wandered back over the events of the previous evening. She had been so close to giving in—so close to letting her heart rule her mind. So close to letting the pleasures of the flesh overshadow the welfare of her people.

For a fleeting moment Thena allowed herself to mourn her decision to refuse Lancer. But only for a moment; then her resolve hardened. She and Juelle had to find a cure right away and leave for Delphi, before Thena succumbed to temptation and forgot all about her people.

Seri stirred in Thena's lap, and Juelle breezed in with excitement animating her features. "Today's the day!" she said, and perched precariously on the computer console.

"The day for what?" After days of testing and grasping at straws, was her wish finally about to be realized? "You mean you've figured out the cure?"

Juelle laughed. "No, but *you*," she said, pointing a slender finger at Thena, "are going to give us the answer today."

As Thena frowned in puzzlement, Juelle added, "With a prophecy, of course."

Thena felt incredibly stupid. On Delphi she hadn't been able to ask the question of another pythia for fear of revealing her secret, and it was impossible to ask it of herself. But now, here, with Juelle's knowledge of the mind and Thena's prophecies, Juelle could ask the question that had been plaguing Thena for her whole life.

Thena began to tremble. Could it be so simple?

Seri looked up at her in concern, and Thena soothed the moncat. There was one way to find out. "You're right. Let's try it."

"Good. Now, how shall we word the question?"

That was the easy part. Thena had dreamed about it for years, playing with images of asking the oracle until she had worded the question just right—the question she'd dared not ask.

She instructed Juelle how to ask the question; then Juelle adjusted the cavern to the proper light level.

Thena prepared herself for the ritual, her excitement making it difficult for both her and Seri to calm down long enough to attain the proper state. Finally she tried the deep breathing exercises Juelle had taught her and felt herself slipping into the trance.

Continued exposure to Juelle's mind during the tests had made it easy for Thena to identify the mercurial, caring essence of the psychiatrist's consciousness. As Thena meshed comfortably with it, she felt the oracle take hold and said, "State your question."

Calmly, Juelle repeated the words Thena had

given her. "How may Thena cure Rheta and prevent pythian insanity from occurring in herself and others?"

Thena felt an odd thrill course through her at the voicing of her long-awaited question. The paths in Juelle's mind solidified immediately, the true path outlined in a golden light. The turbulence was a lot quieter than usual, almost as if the oracle had been waiting for Thena to ask this question and was impatient to give her the answer.

Without hesitation or resistance, Thena sped down the path to the void at the end. There, she hung suspended for a timeless instant of pure anticipation and suspense.

Finally images began to appear. Thena watched eagerly, but they flashed by so fast, she couldn't follow them. Frantically, she tried to slow them, to replay them, but they were unstoppable. All too soon the images ceased, and the oracle spoke the answer in her mind. "Take the Terran home."

Thena heard Juelle gasp; then Thena collapsed and the lights snapped on. She recovered quickly, trying to hide her disappointment. She hadn't been able to get a good glimpse of the pictures, and without them the answer was meaningless. What Terran? And whose home? Now she knew how the querents felt when they received obscure advice.

Juelle sat up gingerly, holding her head, but grinning despite her obvious headache. "We did it!"

Thena shook her head. "I got the answer, but I didn't understand it."

"But with the images it makes sense, doesn't it?"

Thena shrugged, trying to appear nonchalant despite her disappointment. "Probably, but they moved too fast—I couldn't see them properly."

Juelle's mouth dropped open. "But—but they were very clear."

"*You* saw them?" Was it possible? First, Lancer remembered his prophecies, and now Juelle saw and understood images the Golden Pythia didn't.

"Yes," Juelle babbled on, seemingly oblivious to Thena's shock. "Maybe the oracle knew I'd understand them and you wouldn't, so it showed them directly to me. What an experience! Is this what happens to you every time?"

"Juelle! What did you *see?*"

Juelle gave Thena a startled look. "Right. The pictures. Well, there's an old case study in paranormal twin research where they used drug therapy to assist a sane woman in buttressing the mind of her insane twin. It worked quite well, and they postulated the same technique would work on any two people so long as they are telepathic and extremely close."

"Close? What do you mean, close?"

"Well, the research showed strong indications that it would work with a married couple, or close relatives, or any two people who were telepathically linked."

"So how does that help Delphi?"

Juelle grinned. "The images showed me using the technique on an older woman with success. She looked a lot like you. Your mother, maybe?"

"Mother," Thena breathed. For the first time she felt able to think about her mother without an overwhelming sadness. Her spirit brightened until she felt light-headed with relief. She could cure her mother! "And the prevention?"

"It showed me teaching your Observer how to use the techniques to protect you during the ritual." Juelle's grin widened. "The Observer was Lancer."

For a heart-stopping moment Thena's spirit soared even higher. Lancer! She forced it down. No, it wasn't possible. Thena smiled wryly. "I'm afraid what you saw is a metaphor for all pythias and their observers. The oracle does that sometimes."

"But—"

"No, really. It must have shown Lancer and me since you're familiar with us. It doesn't mean he'll return to Delphi with us. In fact, I'm sure he won't. After reading his script last night I know he'll never join me on Delphi."

Thena hated to see Juelle's eager expression change to a frown. "Don't worry about that— nothing can change it. But we *can* make a difference on Delphi. We can cure my mother!"

Juelle's smile returned. "So, when shall we leave?"

"Right away," Thena decided. She needed to make the break soon.

"All right," said Juelle. "It'll take me a few days to arrange for someone else to take over my practice while I'm gone. During that time you can try and convince Lancer to go with you."

Thena nodded, though she had no intention of doing so. It would be an exercise in futility. His revealing portrait of Captain Spencer proved that.

Lancer lounged against the mantel, trying to conceal his impatience. Thena chatted with Alexander and Darian while they waited for Hudson to arrive. Lately it seemed the only time he saw Thena was at their evening get-togethers when she was surrounded by other people.

Except for last night. Last night had been frustrating as hell but, all in all, very encouraging. He didn't know what had caused Thena to run off like that, but there was no denying her response to him. He grinned as his loins tightened. No matter how much she pretended otherwise, her body betrayed exactly how much she wanted him.

"What's so amusing, little brother?" asked Alexander.

"Oh, nothing. Private joke." Feeling himself harden in remembrance of her response, Lancer abandoned his place at the mantel and sat down to conceal his arousal from the others.

Seri looked up in mild amusement, then lightly leaped down from Thena's shoulder to come over and curl up in Lancer's lap.

Thena looked startled and Lancer grinned, scratching Seri behind her ears. Maybe there was something to this bond after all. In fact, why not test it?

As the conversation eddied around him, Lancer

closed his eyes and concentrated hard. What would the bond feel like? He groped mentally until he thought he could feel a tenuous something, just barely within his perception. It might just be his imagination, but he decided to try it, focusing the full force of his desire along that imagined thread. He opened his eyes to gauge the result.

Thena gasped in astonishment, then glared at him. Great; it did work! Flushed with success, he sent another wave of desire and longing along the thin band. Seri stirred, then suddenly kicked for freedom, using his lap as a springboard. The resulting explosion of pain in Lancer's groin brought an abrupt termination to his experiment—and his desire.

Lancer glared at the traitorous moncat. Seri just twitched her tail and strode calmly over to lie next to Thena. Both of them seemed to find it difficult to hide their amusement at Lancer's predicament.

Luckily for them, Hudson chose that moment to arrive. "I'm so glad you're all here. I have good news."

He seated himself and continued. "It seems your prophecy will be vindicated, my dear. The Cabinet was impressed with the accuracy of your predictions—especially the Starline disaster you averted—and is looking very favorably on adding a seat for the colonies. We've approached their leader, who seems disposed toward accepting this compromise, and our scouts report the war preparations have ceased."

Amid everyone's congratulations, Lancer discovered an opportunity to further Thena's goals. "Terrific! Now that you've convinced them of her talent, you can announce Delphi's discovery and bring them into the Republic."

Thena brightened, but everyone else looked distinctly underwhelmed.

Hudson frowned. "I'm not sure that's such a good idea."

Lancer rose to his feet, Seri's hasty departure from his lap having taken care of any concealment needs he might have felt. "Why not?" he challenged.

"The announcement of the Delphians' prophetic abilities could still be catastrophic. The Cabinet wants to study the potential consequences thoroughly and come up with a plan to prevent the use of their abilities for nefarious purposes. Until then, they will not release the information."

"But what about the Delphians? Are you going to doom them to an imprisoned existence on their planet and refuse them access to the rest of the Republic?" Lancer saw his father's hesitation and continued to press his advantage. "Will you deny them the right to trade their primary export—their prophecies—with anyone they choose? Restraint of trade and independence are what you're battling about with the rebels now. Do you want another recurrence of interstellar war in the future?"

"Now, son, I know it looks bad, but we truly have their best interests at heart. We don't want them to be exploited any more than you do."

Lancer glanced at Thena. She looked troubled,

but Seri sent a wave of encouragement across their connection, giving him the confidence he needed to pursue the matter.

Lancer deliberately calmed himself and made his voice more reasonable. "They've dealt with these problems for over two hundred years. Don't you think they're the most qualified to judge how best to use them and keep others from exploiting them? They have a built-in advantage—their own prophecies."

Hudson still looked unconvinced.

Thena rose to stand next to Lancer and face Hudson. "Lancer is correct. We should be the ones to make these decisions, not the Republic. However, I do understand your concern. How can we resolve this?"

"Send an ambassador to Delphi," the phlegmatic Darian suggested.

Lancer paused in thought. It was wise to pay attention to Darian's occasional enigmatic utterings. He might appear stupid, but he was far from it.

"Yes, I see." Lancer turned to Hudson. "An ambassador could work out the details to the satisfaction of both parties. Once they reach an acceptable solution, you can announce Delphi's existence."

Hudson nodded thoughtfully. "That may work. What do you think, my dear?"

"Yes, I think it would," Thena said.

Lancer grinned. "And I know the perfect person for the job."

Thena stared at him incredulously, her mouth widening in a brilliant smile.

Lancer turned to face his brothers. "Alexander. You've got firsthand experience with politics and Delphi's prophecies. You'd be perfect." And he'd also keep an eye on Thena for Lancer, maybe even persuade her to return to Earth once her mission was complete.

Alexander lifted one eyebrow. "Thena? What do you think? Would this be acceptable to your people?"

Lancer turned back to Thena, surprised to see her face closed and set. She studiously ignored Lancer's gaze. "Yes, that would be just fine," she said in a flat tone.

"It's been a long time since we needed an ambassador," Hudson said. "But there is a precedent for what you suggest. I'll present it to the Ministers tomorrow, but it's up to them who shall be appointed—if anyone is appointed at all."

Maeve entered and announced dinner. Hudson stood and gestured toward the door. "Let's eat, shall we?"

Thena followed Hudson out the door, and Seri paused to give Lancer a disgusted look.

Lancer's stride faltered. He'd just brought both sides to an agreement with a smooth finesse any politician should envy. What had he done wrong?

Chapter Sixteen

The next morning Thena sat in her room and brooded. Juelle had taken the day off, and Lancer had left for his studio, leaving Thena and Seri alone with nothing to do but think.

It was just as well. Though her every action had been aimed at returning to Delphi, Thena knew in her heart she still hadn't made the final decision: go or stay? She'd been putting it off, knowing that once the decision was implemented, it was irrevocable. Final.

Thena stroked the purring moncat. "What should I do, Seri?"

The moncat looked up at her in concern but offered no answer, only wordless sympathy. No matter what decision Thena made, she knew Seri would always be there for her.

But Lancer wouldn't. What would it be like to

return to Delphi without him?

She spoke her thoughts aloud, hoping it would help her find the answer. "If I return to Delphi, I can cure Mother and expose Nevan's scheme."

Seri hissed at the mention of the Councilman's name. Thena soothed her. "I know, I know. I want to see Nevan brought to justice, too. But if I return without Lancer, I'll have no one to share the rest of my life with. No one to share the joys and responsibilities of Delphi's leadership. No one to love and to be loved by. No one to make love to. . . ."

And if she went, she could never return to Earth and Lancer. She'd abdicated her responsibility as the Golden Pythia once, for a very good reason. To do so again would be unthinkable—and unforgivable. But staying on Delphi without her life-mate meant facing certain humiliation. She couldn't pretend the ritual had never happened—the scar on her wrist proclaimed her status to all and sundry.

Thena sighed. All in all, it was a bleak picture. Seri patted her pythia's face, and Thena smiled half-heartedly, trying to reassure the moncat that everything would be all right. It didn't work. Thena couldn't even convince herself.

If only Lancer would join her in governing Delphi, everything would be perfect. For a brief moment Thena allowed herself to imagine what it would be like.

Lancer didn't realize it, but he was a born leader. Thena had overheard some of his calls to his studio and had learned how much his people respected him. He was an excellent motivator, and he treated everyone, down to the lowliest clerk, with respect and an unforced affection that made people adore him. He treated every problem, no matter how minor, as the important thing it was to the person who brought it up.

Yes, Lancer was a born leader. He'd be good for Delphi—and for her. Anguish filled her. Why couldn't he see it?

Thena remonstrated with herself. There was no sense lamenting over something she could never change. The dilemma was still the same: go or stay?

A thrill shot through her at the thought of staying on Earth—staying and exploring her deepening relationship with Lancer. No man had ever made her feel the way he did—desired, cherished, and just a little wanton. Every time he touched her, she felt a surge of love and desire that she doubted would ever wane. He was everything she wanted in a life-mate: caring, loving, and with a sense of humor that kept her on her toes. She could live until she was a hundred and never tire of him.

But could *he* say the same? If she stayed, would their bond strengthen beyond her capability to resist it, only to find that he had tired of her in a year or two? Thena wanted badly to stay, so badly she almost convinced herself he would never abandon her.

Why *couldn't* she have the best of both worlds? It *was* feasible—Juelle didn't need Thena's help to cure Rheta, or to implement the necessary preventive measures to ensure no other pythia ever got caught in the insanity trap again.

But what about exposing Nevan? Could Juelle do that too? No, Thena decided reluctantly. She couldn't. Thena would either have to do that herself or let Nevan's perfidy go unpunished. Ketori and the rest of the Council would never take a Terran's word over Nevan's without Thena there to back it up.

And if Thena was being totally honest, she'd have to admit they'd never let Juelle cure Rheta either—not without Thena there to vouch for her.

Go or stay?

She could go to Delphi, cure her mother, expose Nevan, and lose Lancer forever. Or, she could stay on Earth and share her life with Lancer, but doom her mother to continued agony and let Nevan go unpunished. Put that way, Thena had no choice; she had to go.

Sadness filled her at the inevitable decision, yet there was a certain measure of relief that the decision was finally made and she could get on with implementing it. Seri gave her a questioning look, and Thena stroked the moncat's soft fur again before setting her on the floor. At least she would still have Seri.

Thena rose and strode decisively to the bedroom comm unit. Now that she had made her decision, she'd waste no time in putting it into action.

She punched up Juelle's call number and found the psychiatrist at home. Wasting no time in pleasantries, Thena said, "Juelle, I've decided to return home immediately—now, if possible. Can you help me?"

Juelle quirked an eyebrow. "Isn't this a little sudden?"

"No, not really. I've done what I came here for. With your help, I've found a way to control pythian insanity, and I've given the Ministers what they wanted. There's nothing left here for me."

"What about Lancer?"

Seri jumped up onto Thena's lap and shifted nervously, trying to get Thena's attention. Thena ignored her. "What about him?"

"C'mon, this is Juelle—your friend *and* your psychiatrist. You can't hide your feelings from me. He's your life-mate and you love him. How can you leave?"

"How can I not?" Thena replied softly. "My mother's need is more important right now, and besides, Lancer doesn't feel the same way about me—or Delphi."

"How—"

"No," Thena said, cutting Juelle off. "I'm convinced he'll never take his rightful position as Council Captain on Delphi. It's best for me to leave immediately, before our bond becomes too strong."

"When are you going to break the news to him?"

Seri tugged at her sleeve, and Thena pushed her away. "I'm not going to tell him."

Thena had succeeded in shocking the psychiatrist. "You're not going to tell him?" Juelle repeated in an incredulous voice. "Why not?"

"Because he'd just try to talk me out of it, and neither of us needs that sort of pain. It's best to make a clean break—no tears, no recriminations."

Juelle shook her head. "I really think you're making a mistake. You're not giving Lancer a chance."

"I've given him every chance. Besides, he'll know where to find me." Not that he ever would. A more stubborn man she had yet to meet.

"All right," said Juelle. "It's your life."

Seri renewed her tugging, this time on Thena's hair. Thena absentmindedly fended her off, and Seri settled herself in Thena's lap with a huff of annoyance. "So you'll help me?"

"Yes, I'll help you, though I may lose Lancer's friendship over this." Juelle held up her hand. "And before you ask, yes, I'll even go with you to Delphi. Since we started the tests, I've been slowly turning my practice over to others. I just used it to finance my telepathic research anyway. Delphi is the opportunity I've been looking for."

"Good. When can we leave?"

Juelle paused in thought. "My family has a small ship we can use. Give me some time to arrange for the provisions and meet me in, say, four hours at my office. Is that soon enough?"

"Yes," said Thena. The sooner, the better. "And thanks, Juelle. I really appreciate all you've done for me."

Juelle grinned. "Good—remember that when I need some favors on Delphi to conduct my research."

Thena smiled back. "Don't worry; I will."

They said their good-byes, and Thena tipped the

moncat's chin up with her finger. "Now, what in the world is wrong with you?"

Seri gave her an exasperated look and glanced pointedly behind Thena at the door.

Thena turned and her heart sank. Maeve stood there, arms folded uncompromisingly across her ample chest. How much had the house-keeper heard? Judging from Seri's reaction—and Maeve's—it seemed she'd heard everything.

Maeve advanced into the room. "So you were going to just take off, with nary a word to any-one?"

The housekeeper had been a friend—Thena owed her the truth. "Yes. If you heard that, you probably also heard my reasons."

"You're the best thing to happen to my boy since his mother died. He needs you. You can't leave him." Beneath her gruff exterior, Maeve looked genuinely distressed.

"My mother needs me more," explained Thena gently. "Right now I'm her only hope for release from an intolerable mental prison. And you're wrong about Lancer—he doesn't need me at all. He has you and the rest of his family. Why, in the short time I've been here, I've seen his relationship with his father and brothers improve tremendously."

Maeve thrust her pugnacious chin into the air. "Yes, all thanks to you. You bring out the best in him, make them realize how talented my boy is. He needs you. We all do."

Thena shook her head. "Not anymore. Besides, needing isn't enough. He doesn't love me."

"Are you sure about that?" Maeve challenged. "He's been hovering over you like a hen with one chick. I've never seen him do that before with any woman."

"Yes, I'm sure. He had his chance to prove it last night. Instead of volunteering to be Delphi's ambassador, he nominated Alexander for the post. Is that the act of a man in love?"

Maeve looked doubtful. "Then what was this life-mate business you mentioned?"

Patiently, Thena explained the life-mate ritual and the reason for it. "Lancer refuses to accept the bond, but I have no choice. It's a part of me."

"I agree with the doctor—you're making a big mistake. Can't you stay just a little longer, give him more of a chance?"

Thena was beginning to weary of this argument. "No, it's out of the question. If I stay any longer, the bond may grow so strong, I'll never be able to leave. I've got to help my mother. You can see that, can't you?"

Maeve nodded reluctantly. "I see your point, but the Morgans are the only family I've got, and I hate to see any of them hurt."

Thena regarded her steadily. "Maeve, I need to ask you to keep this quiet. Please, it'll be easier on both Lancer and me if I just go. Otherwise, he might talk me into staying, and I'll never be able to cure my mother. She's *my* family. I couldn't live with myself if I didn't do everything in my power to help her. Could you?"

Maeve shook her head and sighed. "I guess not.

Will you at least write him a note? I promise he won't get it until you're gone."

Thena hugged the short woman. "All right, I'll do that much. And thank you, Maeve. This means a lot to me."

Maeve returned the hug, then sniffed and searched in one of her capacious pockets for a handkerchief to dab at her eyes. "Okay, but as soon as you're gone, I'm gonna give that boy what for, for not living up to his responsibilities. You mark my words—he'll follow you."

Thena smiled at the housekeeper but kept her thoughts to herself. Maeve was being overly optimistic. Thena's heart wanted to believe, but her head told her Lancer would never follow her.

Lancer closeted himself in his studio office and locked the door. He wanted to be alone, away from the bustle of studio production. He sighed wearily. Lately the entire holofilm business had begun to pall on him.

At first he'd loved the excitement. Starting with nothing but an idea, then using his wits and persuasion to find just the right people to pull it all together and come up with an end product he could be proud of was a thrill.

But somehow, lately, the whole thing seemed so shallow—the excitement forced and the people grasping and snide. Why hadn't he seen it before? When had he changed?

Delphi. It was Delphi that had done it—and Thena. Seeing the lost colony world and learning about their trials and tribulations as they tried to forge a new life for themselves on an unknown planet had been eye-opening. The real-life struggle for survival had touched something in him, made him want to go out and do something noble and uplifting.

He had to chuckle. Nobility wasn't exactly his strong suit, and he couldn't think of anything sufficiently awe-inspiring that wouldn't involve a great deal of inconvenience or make him look foolish.

Lancer sighed. The best he could do was to produce this holofilm about Delphi and try to portray what had touched him so much about the colonists. That is, if the Cabinet of Ministers ever declassified it so he could start work on it.

Yes, that was the thing to do. He'd portray them as the noble people they were. It was so unlike his usual biting political satires and exposés that it would probably kill his career, but he had to make the film this way.

Thena was right. Lancer hadn't done justice to Captain Spencer. Keeping in the tradition of his past successes, Lancer's script had lampooned the colony ship captain, making him out to be something he wasn't.

The truth was, Lancer envied Captain Spencer. The heroic commander was what Lancer had always wanted to be and had never been able to achieve. And Thena had been so enamored of the man that Lancer had wanted to belittle him in her eyes—a dumb thing to do.

This time he'd write the script the way it should

be written, to accurately portray the captain and the rest of the courageous men and women of the *Odyssey*, who had risked everything to create a better life for their children. It would be Lancer's gift to Thena, to prove . . . what?

The thought caught him by surprise. Just what did he want to prove to her? And why?

The realization hit him with the force of a megaton pile driver. He loved her. He was *in* love with her. Lancer Morgan, perennial playboy, had finally met his match. He'd been kayoed by a curvy blond from a backward planet—and had gone down for the count.

All right, now that he was flat on the mat, what did he do next? His first inclination was to get up and get his sparring partner in a clinch she'd never escape.

No, no, wrong approach. His original thought had been the correct one. He'd rewrite the script to show Captain Spencer in his true colors and prove to Thena how much her opinion meant to him.

He felt his enthusiasm build. Then, once she was convinced, he'd take the plunge and ask her to marry him in a Terran ceremony. They'd visit Delphi to cure her mother; then they'd return to Earth to take up their new life together. Once the Delphi holofilm was over, they'd decide what to do with the rest of their lives.

Lancer grinned. It was a good plan—and he couldn't wait to broach it to Thena. But first he'd have to rewrite the script.

Five hours later the deed was done, and Lancer

was satisfied. It was good—damn good. Possibly the best he'd ever written, though he doubted the critics would agree with him. So what? There was only one opinion he cared about right now—Thena's.

Whistling a catchy tune under his breath, Lancer headed home to give her the news.

He opened the door of Morgan House and bounded up the stairs toward their suite, taking the steps two at a time. Seeing Thena's door ajar, he went in, only to find her room empty. Puzzled, he came back out to the hallway and spotted Maeve heading toward him. "Where's Thena?" he asked.

Maeve frowned. "Gone."

"I can see that. Gone where? I thought she had the day off."

"Gone for good. She left for her home two hours ago." Maeve handed him a folded piece of paper. "Here. She left you a note."

Lancer automatically took the missive, his senses reeling in astonishment. Gone home? How could she have left without him? He eyed the message still clutched in his hand. Maybe it had some answers. He opened it.

Juelle and I have discovered a cure for pythian insanity, and I must return home to try and cure my mother. I'm sorry to leave without saying good-bye, but it's for the best. What we have between us could never work out. Thena.

He crumpled the paper in his fist. No! She couldn't have left—not just when he realized how much he loved her. Not when he was just going to ask her to *marry* him, for God's sake. Her timing was lousy.

He found himself growing angry. Yes, damn lousy. Why couldn't she have stayed to talk about this instead of running off? It was the coward's way out. He shoved the note in his pocket. "Well, if she thinks I'm going to follow her to Delphi, she's wrong. Dead wrong."

"Then you're a fool," Maeve said.

Lancer glanced at her in surprise. He must have spoken his thoughts aloud. "Huh?"

"You're a fool if you don't follow her. You love her, don't you?"

How did she know? "Yes, but—"

"No buts, boy." Maeve shook her finger in a familiar scolding gesture. "You've done that girl wrong and you need to make it right."

"I've done *her* wrong? She's the one who walked out on me!"

"Yes, and we both know why, don't we?"

Lancer shook his head. "I guess she doesn't love me as much as you think, or she would've stayed."

Maeve's mouth tightened into a grim line. "Boy, I raised you better than that. Be honest with yourself. She does love you. That's not why she left. She left because you don't love her enough to face up to your responsibilities."

Hell. Did Thena have to tell everyone about that

silly ritual? "Now wait a minute; you know nothing about it."

Maeve advanced on him, a finger shaking in admonition. "I know enough to know you performed a ceremony that was sacred to her and you refuse to acknowledge that commitment."

"I can't." Maeve should know that. She'd been around when the suicide happened. She knew what it had done to him. "You know why."

She snorted. "Because you're afraid to take on responsibility? Lord love a duck, but God didn't give you the sense he gave a doughnut. What d'you think you've been doing these past ten years? Babying those film folk, making decisions for them, paying their livelihood? What is that if not responsibility?"

Lancer stood there, stunned. She had a point.

Maeve reached into the pocket of her apron and pulled out a piece of paper, which she pressed into his hand. "Here's another note. Maybe this will knock some sense into you." She shook her head and stomped off down the stairs.

Lancer walked back into his room and sank into the chair at the window.

Was it possible? Was he over the trauma of his youth? He relived the memory, probing cautiously at it like a tongue at a sore tooth. Yes, it was painful, but he could live with it. The agony had faded, leaving only the realization that, ultimately, it had been his classmate's choice to take his own life.

It wasn't Lancer's fault the boy had committed

suicide, or that he had cheated to begin with. The boy had made his own decision on what to do with his life—as Lancer now had to decide what to do with his.

Paper crackled in his clenched fist. Oh, yes: the other note. He opened it, wondering if Thena had relented and left him another message.

No such luck. It was from Juelle, short and succinct: *You're a fool.*

Yeah, well, it seemed to be the consensus of opinion. He crumpled the note and threw it into the bedroom disintegrator.

They were right. He'd been a fool, but he'd be one no longer. He was going after Thena and he was going to do whatever it took to get her back—even find some way around this Council Captain mess that would satisfy both of them.

Now that he thought about it, shunning responsibility had become a habit, one he'd finally outgrown. He'd be willing to help the Council, so long as he didn't have the ultimate responsibility for governing Delphi—what did he know about their world? But they needed someone to watch out for their interests, to ensure the Republic didn't take advantage of them. And he was just the person to do it—if Thena would have him.

Lancer made plans swiftly. He'd leave the holofilm business to one of his subordinates, who'd been itching to take over. Once that was done he could take the scoutship and—

"Son?" came Hudson's voice from the doorway.

Lancer's head came up. "Yes?"

Hudson entered, looking uncomfortable. "I'm sorry . . . I heard Thena left. I know how much you cared for her." He shrugged. "Well, I just wanted you to know I'm sorry."

Had everyone known how he felt about Thena except Lancer himself? Lancer was annoyed for a moment; then his irritation dissolved in wonder.

Hudson, his stiff poker of a father, had just expressed concern for Lancer's feelings. Lancer couldn't ever remember that happening before. Unexpected warmth and gratitude flooded him, and he stood to give his father an awkward hug. "Thanks, Dad. That means a lot to me."

Hudson returned his embrace, his eyes suspiciously moist.

Lancer grinned. "But she's not going to get away with it, you know."

"She's not?"

"Nope. I'm gonna follow her to Delphi and hunt her down until she agrees to be my wife, even if I have to stay there forever. Do you have any objections?" he challenged.

"Of course not. She's a wonderful person, and I'm sure she'd make an excellent wife."

"Yes, I know, but I don't know if she'll have me. I've been a jerk and an idiot. It took Juelle and Maeve to make me see it, but I'll make it up to Thena—if she'll let me."

Hudson smiled ruefully. "Oh, I'm sure she will. You received the entire charm and charisma quota for the whole Morgan family—enough to convince anyone of anything. It's one reason I tried so hard to convince you to enter politics. You're a born diplomat, a leader people enjoy following."

For a moment Lancer was speechless. "You never told me that before."

Hudson shrugged. "I just wanted you to be happy. And you appeared to enjoy making your holofilms."

"And now that I'm entering the Morgan family business you can finally be proud of me too."

Hudson gave him a peculiar look. "I've always been proud of you."

Lancer merely looked incredulous.

"Yes, always. It took a lot of courage and skill to learn the holofilm business from the ground up, and you made a success of it despite the odds and your detractors."

Lancer's mouth dropped open in disbelief, and Hudson grinned. "You wouldn't be so surprised if you'd heard me bragging to my colleagues about my son, the famous holofilm producer. Just ask Alexander and Darian—they're tired of hearing it."

So that explained the jealousy he'd sensed from his brothers. Lancer had never understood it before. "I thought . . . I thought . . ."

"I know." Hudson's voice softened. "I've never been demonstrative, but I just thought you ought to know, before you leave forever and it's too late."

Lancer caught his father up in a crushing hug, unable to put into words the sheer relief he felt—not to mention the weight suddenly lifted from his shoulders after a lifetime of pain and misunderstanding.

Hudson returned the hug forcefully. "And Thena seems to have brought out the best in you. I've never been more proud of you than when you stood up for her. Now go after her, son. All I ask is that you return for a visit a time or two—especially if you ever give me grandchildren."

"Okay, Dad, I'll do that. And I promise, I'll keep in touch." Suddenly buoyant and feeling on top of the world, Lancer left for Delphi and Thena.

Chapter Seventeen

Thena squirmed in her seat as excitement and apprehension filled her. After two weeks of traveling in Juelle's luxurious pleasure craft they were finally approaching Delphi. Quickly, Thena used the craft's viewer to locate and focus in on the small clearing where Lancer had landed his scoutship and pointed it out to Juelle. "Land there."

The ship landed smoothly, and they released themselves from the protective webbing. Juelle rose and stretched. "Okay, now what?"

This was the moment Thena had been waiting for. Was she ready for it? She took a deep breath. There was one way to find out. "Well, I need to contact my father, but I left Delphi secretly, without explanation or farewell. I'm not sure he'll give me a chance to explain."

Pam McCutcheon

A sudden thought made her shudder. Had she already been replaced as Golden Pythia? Dear Apollo, let it not be so.

"So what's your plan?"

Thena had had plenty of time to think about it on the trip. "By leaving, I thwarted Nevan's plans. He's probably started on another scheme to regain power on the Council, but I have no way of knowing what it is. I have to find some way to talk to Ketori before Nevan finds out I'm here."

"Is that a problem?"

"Yes. I can't go myself—everyone knows who I am. The first person who spots me will undoubtedly spread the news of the Golden Pythia's return throughout Dodona like wildfire."

"What if I go?" Juelle suggested.

"No, that won't work. You're obviously not of this planet, and Terrans won't be very popular here since one took off with Delphi's Golden Pythia a couple of months ago. If Nevan finds you before Ketori does, there's no telling what he'd do. No, the best thing to do is send Seri with a note to my father."

"Won't she be recognized?"

"One moncat pretty much looks like another. Only those who know a pythia very well are able to distinguish her moncat from the rest."

"So, Ketori and Nevan both know Seri." Juelle paused. "But what if Nevan is with Ketori when she gives him the note?"

Thena bit her lip, considering. She hadn't thought about that. "That's a good point. I'll just have Seri

358

put it in Father's private message box. She can do that easily—she's done it before. Let's see; it's late afternoon now, so he's probably out on Council business. He'll check his messages just after dinner, so I'll ask him to meet us in the stable storeroom at midnight."

Juelle frowned. "How can you be so sure he'll read it then?"

Thena smiled wryly. "Oh, Father's schedule is very precise and predictable—he seldom wavers from it. He'll check it then; take my word for it."

"Will we be able to get to the storeroom unobserved?"

"That's the easy part—we'll go in the back way, by the stables. No one will be there at midnight. If they are, we'll worry about it then."

Juelle shrugged. "Okay, you're the boss."

Thena scribbled the note to Ketori.

Father, I have returned to Delphi and need to speak to you privately on a matter of great urgency. Please meet me in the stable storeroom at midnight. Come alone and tell no one else of my presence. I will explain everything then. Thena.

Thena folded the note and hunkered down to stare Seri in the eyes. Slowly, carefully, she projected an image of what she wanted the moncat to do. Seri had carried messages for her before, but this was a little different. This time Thena wanted to ensure the moncat delivered the message without being seen—especially by Nevan.

Seri twitched impatiently and broadcast irritation, letting Thena know she was no silly little monkit—she knew exactly what to do. As for Nevan, Seri hissed at the mere mention of his name. Thena didn't have to worry. Seri would avoid him like the plague.

Thena smiled at the moncat's indignation and handed her the note, instructing her to meet them at the storeroom only if she failed in her mission. Seri had been so patient about their trip to Earth, she deserved some time off to eat, sleep, and visit with other moncats in familiar surroundings.

Juelle opened the door and the moncat scampered out, intent on her errand.

The familiar scent of Delphi's woods filled the cabin through the open door, making Thena long to leave the ship. No matter how luxurious, the cramped surroundings had begun to pall after a couple of weeks. She was eager to set foot on her native soil again.

Juelle stood beside her and drank in the peaceful woodland scene. "It's beautiful," she breathed, then grinned at Thena. "What are we waiting for? Let's leave this tin can and get some fresh air."

Thena nodded slowly, her mind working. "Yes, that's a good idea. If anyone saw us land, they'll be coming to investigate. Let's take some food and hide in the woods until darkness falls so we can enter the stables without being seen."

"Fine by me," Juelle said cheerfully.

Thena glanced at her wristcom, then stood and brushed off her buckskin trousers. "It's almost midnight. We'd better get going."

Juelle helped pack up their cold camp, which was easy to clean up since they hadn't been willing to risk a fire. "You're sure this is the right thing to do? I didn't bring any weapons with me."

"Yes, I'm sure. No matter how angry he is, Ketori would never hurt his own daughter."

"It's not your father I'm worried about. It's your Councilman."

Thena sighed. "If something had gone wrong, Seri would let me know."

"But what if she's been captured or hurt?"

"Then I'd know that too—our bond is strong enough that I would know instantly if something like that happened."

Juelle shook her head. "It still doesn't seem right. I'd feel a whole lot better if I had a weapon."

"That's not a good idea. If you want to petition the Council for permission to research our abilities, it's best to start off on a good foot. That means no weapons."

Juelle shrugged. "Okay, you're the boss. But let's set our wristcom homing devices. That way if we get separated, we can find each other later."

"All right," Thena agreed. It was a sensible precaution. They set their wristcoms, buried all traces of their camp, and headed toward the Dodona caverns.

As they emerged stealthily into the dead blackness

of the rear entrance, Thena wondered what her people would think if they could see their Golden Pythia sneaking in the back way. With what she had learned on Earth, she should have returned in triumph. Instead, she was skulking around like a common thief.

Nevan had much to answer for. If it weren't for his plan to overthrow Ketori, she wouldn't be reduced to this. Thena forced her irritation down. Soon enough, she'd see Ketori and convince him to take the case to trial by pythia and get rid of Nevan once and for all.

She and Juelle crept along the unused corridors with the help of Juelle's flashlight until they intersected one that was illuminated by lightmoss.

Thena paused and motioned for Juelle to turn off the light. She froze, listening for activity in the corridor beyond. Hearing nothing but silence and the beating of her own heart, she glanced at her wristcom. The storeroom was very close, and they still had a half hour left before their appointed meeting time with Ketori.

It would be better to arrive early and hide in the depths of the storeroom than to remain in the corridor and risk being seen. Thena motioned for Juelle to follow her.

A hundred yards farther, they were at their destination. Thena breathed a sigh of relief. They'd made it. She pushed aside the draperies and entered, Juelle close behind her.

Suddenly a hand clamped over her mouth, and her right arm was twisted up behind her back.

Her heart leapt into her throat and she struggled instinctively, to no avail. Her captor twisted her arm cruelly and gripped her face so hard, she could feel bruises forming. Thena stopped struggling. It was no use. He was too strong for her.

Juelle! What was happening to her friend? Thena's captor forced her around to face the center of the room. There, Juelle was in combat with another man. Juelle's struggles were more effective than Thena's. The petite Terran scored a knee in the man's groin and he bent over in agony, driven to his knees. Juelle was free!

No, too late. Another man emerged from the shadows and struck the psychiatrist on the head with a rock. She crumpled to the floor and lay still.

Thena's eyes widened in shock when she recognized the rock-wielder as Nevan and the man at his feet as his father, Shogril. Who, then, was holding Thena? Surely not Ketori? He wouldn't betray his own daughter, would he?

Nevan knelt to feel Juelle's pulse, then stepped gingerly over her still form to touch Shogril's shoulder. "Father, are you all right?"

Shogril's head came up, and he nodded, grimacing. "Who was that hellcat, anyway?" he growled, still clutching his groin.

"I don't know, but I'll find out." Nevan strode purposefully toward Thena. Glancing at the man holding her captive, he said, "Orgon, let her talk."

Thena almost went limp with relief. It was Orgon,

not Ketori who held her captive. Orgon removed his hand from her mouth, but his relentless grip on her arm didn't ease one iota.

"You whorespawn!" she spat at Nevan. "What have you done to her?"

Nevan shrugged. "She's alive; she'll just have a rather nasty headache when she wakes." His eyes narrowed. "Who is she?"

Thena ignored him.

"Answer me, Thena, or you'll regret it." His voice was casual, as though he were accustomed to making threats every day.

Thena's lips thinned in contempt. He wouldn't dare hurt her—not the Golden Pythia.

Nevan sighed, then casually reached out and slapped her, hard. The blow rocked her head to the side. "I asked you," he repeated, "who is she?"

"None of your damned business!"

Nevan held his hand up as if to hit her again. She winced but continued to glare steadily at him. He looked thoughtful, then dropped his hand and turned to Shogril, who stood over Juelle with a knife. Nevan waved negligently at the Terran. "Kill her."

Shogril grinned and kneeled down to Juelle's side.

"No!" Thena shouted.

Nevan's lips curled into a smile that was more of a sneer. "Wait," he instructed Shogril, then turned back to Thena. "Are you going to tell me who she is?"

Dear Apollo, the man was mad with power. She'd thought she knew him, but she didn't. Had she ever? This man was as cold and calculating as a sandsnake. He probably *would* kill Juelle if Thena didn't cooperate. "Juelle—her name is Juelle Shanard. She brought me here from Earth." She didn't mention Juelle's profession or her reason for being here. There was no telling how Nevan would take it—it was liable to get them all killed.

Nevan smiled. "A Terran, eh? Good, then no one will miss her."

Panic rose within her. She couldn't let him kill Juelle! "No, please, you can't. The Terrans know she's here—and if she doesn't return or contact them soon, they'll come looking for her."

"So? I don't want to have anything to do with them or their Republic anyway."

Thena's mind worked frantically, trying to find a rationale that would convince him. "It won't work—they'll come anyway and hound you until they find her. They have weapons—huge weapons, big enough to destroy an entire cave city at the push of a button. And they'll use them if you harm her. Do you want that?"

Nevan frowned, and Thena pressed the point home. "It won't do you any good to regain power if there's nothing left of Delphi."

Nevan's eyes narrowed. "You have a point. But tell me, how did you know of our plan to regain power?"

Thena kept silent, cursing her unwary tongue.

Orgon twisted her arm tighter, and Nevan glared at her. "Tell me everything you know or I'll make her *wish* she was dead."

"All right," Thena conceded. "But first tell this sandsnake to let go of me."

Nevan hesitated.

"What's the matter?" Thena jeered. "Afraid of a mere woman against three men?"

Nevan's face darkened with anger, but he held his emotions in check. "Let her go."

Orgon did as he was told and released Thena's arm. She stretched the sore shoulder and cradled her right arm in her left.

Just then a small, furry tornado swept into the room, spitting and hissing. Seri! Thena had forgotten Seri would sense her distress. Fangs bared, the enraged moncat advanced on Nevan, the closest target of her rage.

Nevan stepped back, startled, and Shogril took a tighter grip on the unconscious Terran.

"No!" screamed Thena. Seri mustn't bite Nevan—one bite would lay him low, but it would take a couple of days for Seri's venom to regenerate. That would leave Shogril and Orgon very much in the action—and leave Juelle, Thena, and Seri at risk of being killed by the angry conspirators.

Seri paused at her pythia's frantic command and waited. She crouched with her tail twitching, never taking her eyes off Nevan. A growl rose from her throat.

Nevan pointed at the moncat. "Stop her or you'll all die."

Thena communicated the urgency of the situation to Seri, who had a hard time understanding it in her rage. Finally the moncat reluctantly relinquished her offensive position and moved to her pythia's side. Orgon quickly moved out of range of the moncat's teeth and claws, and Thena picked her up.

She winced when Seri scrambled to her sore shoulder, but she soothed the moncat's bristling fur. Seri had accepted her pythia's decision for now, but a low rumbling growl told Thena the moncat didn't like it.

Once Seri was safely ensconced on Thena's shoulder, Nevan relaxed and resumed his confident stance. "Now tell me, what do you know of our plan?"

"I overheard you and Shogril talking about it the day before I left."

"And?"

"You said if I refused you as life-mate, you'd get the Council Captainship another way—by discrediting me and becoming life-mated to another pythia."

Nevan and Orgon shared a significant glance.

Thena gasped as understanding of their plan clicked into place. "Carina! You plan to groom *Carina* to replace me? That nitwit? She's just a child."

Nevan smiled. "Yes, she's a nitwit, but a very pliable one. She'll make a perfect life-mate for the Council Captain, don't you think?"

"But she's no Golden Pythia. Why, she'll be lucky

to be awarded the lowest blue when she takes her tests!"

Nevan and Orgon merely smiled, and Thena's heart sank. And who would be in charge of Carina's tests? These two smirking oathbreakers, that was who—Carina's Observer and her Councilman. She whirled on Orgon. "How can you be a party to this? Once Nevan achieves his objective he'll dispose of you too."

"Nice try," Nevan said, "but it won't work. Orgon is my first cousin. He, too, will benefit by our family being back in power."

She had to find some way to stop him. Clutching at straws, Thena said, "Father will never let you get away with it—he must know Carina is a ninny."

"As you reminded me, she was my second choice. I would much prefer to become your life-mate. It would be neater all around. But I hardly think Seri will give her consent now."

Seri snarled, and Thena reached up to soothe the moncat.

Nevan's breath hissed between his teeth. He jerked forward, reaching for her hand. Seri growled warningly, and he stopped. Pointing shakily at Thena's left hand, he said, "Where did you get that?"

Thena glanced at the healing crescent scar of the moncat bite on her wrist. "I . . . I . . ."

"You're already life-mated to someone else. Who?" His eyes widened in incredulity. "That bedamned Lancer Morgan," he spat out. "You became life-mated to a *Terran?*"

Thena's chin lifted. "Yes, and he's a better man than you'll ever be."

"Where is he?" Nevan shouted.

Thena couldn't help it; her face crumpled in humiliation.

Nevan's anger cooled visibly. "He's not here, is he?" He laughed. "You took a Terran as a life-mate and he deserted you within a month!"

Thena bristled. "It wasn't like that!"

"No?" he jeered. "Then why isn't he here by your side to claim the Council Captainship?"

Thena knew she couldn't lie convincingly, so she remained silent.

"Tell me!"

Shogril held his knife to Juelle's throat and grinned at her. "Do as my son says, whore, or your friend here won't live to see another day."

Thena might as well tell them—the story was sure to get out eventually anyway. "He hates anything to with politics and responsibility, so he's refused the obligations imposed by the life-mate ritual."

Nevan paced, obviously thinking about this new turn of events and trying to work it into his plans. "That fits—he seemed interested in nothing but his own pleasure." He turned to face her. "You're sure he'll never come here?"

Thena grimaced. "I'm positive. You can ask Juelle when she regains consciousness. He wanted me as his—" Thena swallowed. This was even more humiliating, but it had to be said. "As his . . . lover, but nothing more. I left without his knowledge—

Pam McCutcheon

his pride will never permit him to follow me."

Nevan searched her face with a hard gaze. Apparently satisfied she was telling the truth, he nodded. "That changes things."

Shogril removed the knife from Juelle's throat and stood. "How?"

Nevan pointed at Thena. "She has the life-mate mark, but no mate. Now all I need to do is fake my own mark with a knife and tell Ketori we were mated secretly. He'll believe me; he has no reason not to." He paused, then grinned nastily. "We'll say she was afraid Ketori wouldn't welcome his disobedient daughter after she came crawling back from the horrible Terrans, so she confessed her love for me and asked for my protection."

"You'll never get away with it," Thena said.

"Oh, I think we will." Nevan gave her another of those sneering smiles. "Because you are going to confirm it—or your loved ones will die. First the Terran woman, then your mother, your father, and Seri. Do I make myself clear?"

Thena gasped. His gaze was as hard as the rock around them. He meant what he said. "You would commit murder?" Her voice emerged as a disbelieving squeak.

"Believe it. To regain the honor of my family, I would do anything."

Honor? Hardly. Power was more like it. But Nevan obviously meant what he said.

"Make it easy on yourself," he suggested. "Agree to this small deception and your loved ones will live."

370

If she didn't, she knew she and Juelle wouldn't survive the hour. Thena nodded reluctantly. She'd agree to Nevan's deception for now, but only until she found a way out of this mess.

"I'm glad you're being sensible," said Nevan. He took out a knife and made a crescent-shaped cut on his wrist. He looked at Thena. "Now you. Hold out your hand."

"Why? I've already got a life-mate scar."

"Yes, but it's healed, and we want to make sure they match, don't we?" He gestured with his knife toward Orgon. "Hold her."

Carefully avoiding the moncat, Orgon captured Thena's wrist in a viselike grip and held it steady while Nevan carefully opened her almost-healed scar. He compared his against hers, apparently satisfied. "Now we've got to get you looking like a pythia again before Ketori sees you in the morning."

Thena could feel her face swelling and knew she'd be black and blue by morning. She pointed to her face. "And how are you going to explain this?"

"Ah, so sad. Your trip down to Delphi was a little rough and you got banged around a little. And your poor pilot was so badly hurt, we had to send her to the House of Healing."

Apollo take the man—he had an answer for everything.

Juelle moaned and sat up, holding her head. Thank Apollo, she was alive. Shogril forced the Terran to her feet, and he and Orgon each took one of her arms. Apparently they were determined not to let her get the upper hand—or knee—again.

Juelle blinked. "Wass happenin'?" She glanced at Thena, and the shrewdness in the Terran's eyes belied her slurred speech. It appeared Juelle had been feigning unconsciousness, at least part of the time. How much had she heard?

Nevan scowled. "Never mind. Thena has just agreed to become my life-mate, and we're going to see her father in the morning. Until then, we'll give you a place to sleep off your headache. Be a good little girl, and you and Thena will come out of this alive and well."

He nodded to Orgon and Shogril, and they dragged a limp Juelle out of the cavern.

"Where are you taking her?" Thena demanded.

"Where no one will find her. Don't worry; I meant what I said. If you both do as I say, neither of you will come to harm."

Thena felt Seri stiffen and bunch her leg muscles. Now that Thena and Seri were alone with Nevan, the moncat obviously felt more confident. Thena grabbed her and broadcast a strong negative. If anything happened to Nevan, Thena had no doubt Shogril would avenge himself first on Juelle, then on Thena's family.

The moncat calmed once more, and Thena reinforced her warning, mentally picturing the disaster that Seri's attack would occasion. Seri broadcast irritable acquiescence and shook off her pythia's restraining hand, then paused to groom herself, as if she hadn't had murderous thoughts only a moment before.

Thena relaxed, and so did Nevan.

"Good," he said. "I'm glad to see you're being sensible. Come, I'll set up an extra cot in my chambers so we can get some sleep before our meeting with the Council in the morning."

"The Council! Are they still here?"

"Yes, we're still debating the Republic's offer. The others have been vacillating up to now, but you're going to change all that."

"Me?" she echoed in disbelief. She wasn't allowed to attend the Council sessions without an express invitation.

"Yes, you. I think it's appropriate the Council hear how badly the Terrans treated you, don't you?"

"But they didn't—"

Nevan gripped her wrist painfully. "That's what you're going to tell them, aren't you?"

Thena winced. Nevan never missed a trick to turn things to his advantage. "All right," she muttered.

"I want your word," he said. "Your word as the Golden Pythia that you won't try anything foolish."

She had no choice. "You have my word," she muttered, and then asked the question that been bothering her: "How did you know I was here, anyway?"

He shrugged. "Ketori isn't very forthcoming about his work. If I'm to be Council Captain, I need to know what's going on. I read his mail."

Of course. How could she have been so stupid? She'd thought the Council Captain's private mail was sacrosanct. She should have known that wouldn't stop Nevan.

Pam McCutcheon

What would? As she followed him through the corridors, she took mental inventory of her assets. Nevan had taken her friend, leaving her with nothing but her wits and Seri—and the wristcom. It would have to be enough.

Nevan paused to open the drapes to his chambers and gesture her inside. She complied, then halted when he gripped her shoulder.

"Wait," he said, his gaze narrowing on her wristcom. "What's that?"

Chapter Eighteen

Lancer landed on Delphi a couple of hours before dawn, Dodona time. His repeated hailing of Juelle's ship brought no response, not even when he landed next to it and pounded on the hatch. She and Thena must have left for Dodona already.

Damn Thena! It was just like a woman to go haring off as soon as she landed. She should have waited.

He'd only been half a day behind them all the way—just long enough to gather provisions and go. He'd wanted to be there when Thena denounced Nevan to Ketori, to add his support and let her know how much he loved her. But he wanted to do it privately, not in front of an audience.

Lancer returned to his ship and decided to head for Dodona despite the early hour—he couldn't wait a moment longer. He threw a few essentials into a small pack—flashlight, stunner, food, and water—and left the ship.

Remembering the route he and Thena had taken out of the caverns, Lancer retraced their steps. It would be the fastest way in. He made his way quickly through the woods and into the half-concealed cave entrance. Shining his light down on the loosely packed dirt floor of the corridor inside, he saw footprints leading away.

Thena had said this entrance was seldom used, so these footprints should take him back to where he and Thena had exited from the main caverns. Or, if Thena and Juelle had come this way, it would lead him to them. Either way, he couldn't lose.

He followed the footprints until they stopped at the smooth, packed floor of a main Dodona corridor, where lightmoss lined the walls. He turned off his light and thought back, remembering. They had exited near the stables, so the stables should be . . . there, off to his right. That meant the sleeping chambers were off to his left. At least he thought they were—all these corridors looked alike.

Making a sudden decision, he turned left. He came to a branching corridor and took another left. Luckily, he encountered no one during his travels. He hadn't really expected to; most people should be abed at this hour. It was just as well. He didn't know what he'd do if he did meet someone. Belay that; he knew exactly what he'd do—ask directions.

Lancer came to another branching corridor and decided to go right this time, or he'd end up walking in circles. It was the right decision. He smelled the sulfur of the baths before he saw them, and recognized the wooden bench piled high with clean towels. Now he knew where he was.

Quickly, he made his way to Thena's room. Her drapes were drawn, but he didn't let it stop him. He smiled. He'd surprise her in bed and make his declaration quickly, then get on with loving her.

Softly, he padded through the empty outer chamber to the doorway of the bedchamber. He drew the curtains aside and frowned. Her bed was empty.

He glanced around. It didn't look as though anyone had been here for quite a while. The bed was made and everything was as neat as she'd left it over two months ago, with a thin layer of dust over her belongings.

Now what? How could he find her in these immense caverns? He didn't even know where to look next. If only he had some way to locate her. . . .

The wristcom! Lancer berated himself. If she still had her wristcom, he could call her and find out exactly where she was.

He raised the instrument, then paused. What if she wasn't alone? What if Nevan was with her? Lancer didn't want to communicate his presence to that slime-worm just yet. No, he'd much rather do it in person. Communicating his fist to Nevan's nose would be much more satisfying.

Lancer had a better idea. If Thena hadn't turned off her homing device, he'd be able to locate her that way. Quickly, he punched the appropriate buttons. Hallelujah! There was a signal. It was faint, but it was there.

He followed it, but the directions were difficult to understand. They only showed him where she was in relation to him, not how to get there through the winding corridors.

A frustrating hour later he was deep in the bowels of the Dodona caverns. The lightmoss didn't reach back here, so he had to use his flashlight to find his way. The homing signal began getting stronger, then finally flashed bright green. He was now within fifty feet of his objective. What on Earth—or rather, what on Delphi—was she doing way back here?

He turned, playing his light over the entrance to a small cavern.

"Nevan, is that you?" came a deep voice from inside the darkened chamber.

Lancer froze. He didn't recognize the voice, but if the man thought he was Nevan, he must be up to no good. Lancer scrabbled in his pack and pulled out the stunner.

A man appeared in the doorway and said, "Why— you!"

Lancer stunned him, recognizing the Observer who had eaten breakfast with them one morning. Another man appeared, and Lancer stunned him too.

He waited, but no one else emerged. "Thena?"

"Lancer, is that you?" came the reply, but it wasn't Thena's voice.

Juelle stepped out of the cavern, looking pale and disheveled. "It *is* you. Thank God!"

She leaped over the motionless bodies of her former captors to give Lancer a back-breaking hug.

He grinned. "Whoa, that's my shooting arm. Any more of those bastards nearby?"

"No, there were only two of them guarding me, but Nevan—"

"Where's Thena?" Lancer interrupted, looking around for his life-mate.

"She's not here—"

"But her wristcom is here."

"Yes, I know." Juelle's words tumbled out quickly. "That's what I was trying to tell you. Nevan took away her wristcom—he hates anything to do with Earth. I lost contact with Thena, but the last I heard Nevan was going to force her to claim him as her life-mate."

"Like hell he is! That's my job."

Juelle looked at him in surprise. "Well, it's about time."

Lancer frowned. "Yeah, I know, but forget the lecture and tell me where she is. Now!"

"Nevan is going to present her to the Council as his life-mate first thing this morning so they can acknowledge him as Council Captain right away. You'd better get there quick. According to these guys" —she glared down at her former captors— "it'll start at any time."

And he knew exactly where they'd be—the Council Chambers. Quickly, Lancer checked his weapon. There was almost a full charge on it. "Here." He thrust it at Juelle. "You take this and watch these guys. I'll come back for you later."

She grabbed his arm. "Wait—let me go with you."

"No, these two will only be out for a couple of hours. Someone has to make sure they don't escape, and I want someone here in case Nevan returns before I find him."

Juelle gestured with the stunner. "But won't you need this? Nevan—"

"Hell, I won't need a weapon to take care of that son of a bitch. I'll wring his neck with my bare hands."

Juelle nodded. "Okay, but be careful."

He grabbed the flashlight and took off running, hearing Juelle call after him, "And don't forget to come back for me!"

Thena was in trouble. Nevan had her. Fear for her safety sped Lancer's feet as he sprinted down the corridor. Fear turned to rage at the thought of what Nevan must have done to Thena to convince her to lie to the Council.

Lancer's hands clenched into fists, and he had the urgent desire to smash something. Anything—but preferably Nevan's pretty face. By the time Lancer got through with him he wouldn't be so pretty anymore.

All the corridors looked alike, and Lancer soon became lost. Nothing looked familiar, but he had to get to Thena soon! How? Damn. Nevan had removed his only link to her—the wristcom.

Lancer stopped short. No, it *wasn't* his only link to her. There was still their bond.

He stood still, searching for the thread that connected him to Thena, but his heart was beating so loud, he couldn't distinguish anything else. He calmed himself, willing his pulse to subside, and soon caught the trailing edge of the tenuous bond.

He focused tightly on it and it strengthened, until he could distinguish a golden thread with his mind's eye. It stretched off back down the corridor the way he had come. Shutting off the flashlight so he could see it better, he followed it until he came to a branching intersection. There, the golden thread ran into and through a wall.

Frustrated, Lancer pounded on the rock. This was no better than following the homing device. Each second he was delayed put Thena in more danger. Now what?

He had to go right or left. He took a step to the right and sensed the bond weaken. His hopes rising, he turned to the left and felt it intensify. Yes! This would work.

He strode off to the left and followed his lifeline to Thena until he reached the main corridors. Now that he knew where he was his stride quickened to a run.

He saw more and more activity in the hallways as people began to move about their daily chores. A few protested his running, but Lancer didn't stop to explain, continuing undaunted toward his objective.

Finally he came to a halt outside the Council Chambers, where a burly guard stood and barred his way with a pike.

Lancer stopped, gasping for breath. "Is the . . . Council . . . inside?" he asked.

The guard frowned. "Yes, the Council is in session."

Lancer put his hand on the wall to steady himself. "Is . . . Nevan?"

"I just told you, the Council is in session. All Councilmen are inside."

"Good. I need . . . to go in." Lancer felt his heartbeat return somewhat to normal as he recovered from the run. Thank God he stayed in shape.

"No one enters without the Council's permission."

Lancer leaned forward confidentially and whispered, "But I don't need permission." The guard leaned forward to catch his words, and Lancer continued, "I have this."

He drove his fist into the guard's stomach. The burly man bent over in pain, and Lancer chopped the back of his neck. The guard went down for the count, and Lancer smiled. He'd needed that. Too bad it wasn't Nevan.

Lancer shoved his hair out of his eyes and thrust aside the curtains to the Council Chamber.

Inside he saw Ketori and three seated men facing Nevan. The oily snake charmer was standing possessively next to Thena and declaiming, "—have completed the life-mate ritual. I am your new Council Captain."

Thena looked sad but resolute. The side of her face turned toward him was purpled and bruised. Had Nevan dared hit her? A cold rage filled Lancer. "Like hell you are."

All eyes turned toward him, but Lancer only had

eyes for Thena. His heart skipped a beat when he saw the clear joy reflected in hers. Even Seri seemed happy to see him. Lancer stepped into the room, determined to bring Nevan to account.

One of the unknown men stood up. "Explain yourself!"

Lancer gave him a bow. "I'd be glad to. Thena can't be life-mated to Nevan because she is life-mated to me."

The man gasped. "Are you claiming to be our Council Captain?"

Ah, hell. It looked like he wasn't going to be able to do this in private after all. Lancer made a sudden decision as his gaze locked with Thena's. "If that's what it takes to stay beside your Golden Pythia, then yes, I'll be your Council Captain."

Thena's gaze became even more joyful, and Lancer felt her elation amplified through the moncat on her shoulder. He grinned at her.

One Councilman looked bewildered. "Who *are* you?"

Nevan sneered. "Just a Terran trying to push his way into our government. I told you, they'll stop at nothing to take control of Delphi."

Lancer took a menacing step forward but stopped when Ketori raised his hand. "Wait. I want to know what you mean. Can you prove your claim?"

Lancer raised his wrist to show them the scar. "Here's your proof. That's where Seri bit me to initiate the life-mate ritual."

The Councilman examined the healing scar. "It looks genuine," he said doubtfully. "Nevan?"

Nevan silently raised his wrist, so all could clearly see his crescent-shaped wound, still bloody. He grabbed Thena's wrist and raised it, showing them all that it, too, was bloody—not healed like Lancer's.

Rage shot through Lancer. "Impossible—he faked that bite. He had to."

"Nonsense," scoffed Nevan. "You're the fraud. Admit it."

Lancer shook his head. "How would I, a Terran, know how to fake a moncat bite authentically? And how would I have known to do it weeks ago so it is healed by now?"

The other Councilmen began to look uncertain, but Nevan's sneer didn't abate. "Yes, you're a Terran, with all your magic technology. Technology can do anything—you told us that yourself. Even fake a healed moncat bite."

Ketori stepped between them. "Enough of this. Thena? Who is your true life-mate?"

Thena looked down at the floor and shook her head, refusing to answer.

What the hell was wrong with her? Why wouldn't she acknowledge him? Had he come all this way only to have her reject him? No, the joy he'd seen in her face was too telling.

Lancer straightened his shoulders. "I demand a trial—a prophecy to prove which of us is telling the truth."

Nevan laughed. "That's fine with me. And, as the accused, I reserve the right to name my own pythia. I name Carina."

Carina? A sudden memory of the pythia and her

Observer flashed through Lancer's mind. That's where he'd seen Juelle's captor before—he was Carina's Observer. Nevan must hope to pull another one of his false prophecies. Well, he'd have a hard time doing it with *that* guy. Lancer felt a little uneasy. Did Nevan have other observers in his pocket too?

As Lancer hesitated, he suddenly felt a sharp instrument in his back. He didn't need to glance back to know the guard, now undoubtedly mad as hell, was on the other end of the weapon now prodding him. Lancer froze.

"You want me to take care of him, sir?" the guard asked.

Ketori shook his head. "That won't be necessary. Please, remove your weapon, but stand by in case we should need you."

Lancer glanced back to see the guard glare at him but drop the pike anyway. Lancer felt his shoulders relax in relief.

Nevan grinned. "When shall we set the trial?"

"Carina is not yet a full-fledged pythia, and we can't wait until she takes her tests," Ketori said. "We need to resolve this now, and there's one very simple way to do it." He beckoned to Thena. "Come here, dear."

Thena went to stand by her father, and he whispered in her ear. Thena lost her dejected look and gave Ketori a beaming smile, then placed Seri on the table and stared deep into her eyes.

While Thena communed with Seri, Ketori continued. "Both men claim to be her life-mate. Either one or both is lying, and there's one way to find out.

Her true mate is immune to a moncat's bite, but the impostor is not. Seri will bite each of them in turn, and the one who doesn't succumb to the poison is her true mate."

Thena rose, her instructions complete, and Seri glanced at Nevan with a distinct gleam in her eye. The moncat leapt for him. He turned white, batting her away in midair. "No!" he screamed, and lunged for the door.

Lancer leaping into motion, catching Seri before she hit the wall, then tossing her to Thena. He whirled for the door, but the guard was there before him.

Damn! He was too late. Between the pikeman and the other Councilmen, Nevan was held fast.

Lancer glared at Nevan and took a menacing step forward. The coward turned even whiter than before and tore away from his captors.

The opportunity was too good to pass up. Lancer hauled off and let the bastard have it—a round-house punch full in the face. Nevan's head snapped back and he crumpled to the floor. Wouldn't you know it—the wimp had a glass jaw.

Two of the Councilmen moved to grab Lancer's arms, but he shook his head. "That won't be necessary, boys. I feel much better now."

The Councilmen backed off. Ketori glared coldly at Nevan, who was lying on the floor of the cavern, nursing his jaw. "Why? Why did you do it?"

Nevan, his nose bloodied, just snarled and struggled to his feet. The guard took a tighter grip on him, apparently glad to be taking his annoyance out on *someone*.

Thena spoke. "He and Shogril have been planning to take over the Council. When I learned of their schemes he forced me to pretend to be his life-mate."

"Forced you?" Lancer frowned menacingly. "How?"

"He threatened to kill Juelle and—Stars! Juelle! She's—"

"She's okay," Lancer cut her off. "I found her and stunned Nevan's two accomplices. She's standing guard over them now."

An expression of palpable relief flooded Thena's face as she stroked the groggy moncat, who was slowly coming to. "Thank Apollo."

"Who are his accomplices?" Ketori asked.

"Shogril and Orgon were holding Juelle," Thena replied. "I don't know if he has any more."

Ketori's face turned icy. "Well, Councilmen? Do you need to hear any more? I propose we conduct a trial immediately. Since Carina's Observer seems to be one of Nevan's accomplices, *we'll* choose the pythia. Your decision?"

The Councilmen returned a resounding "Yea!" and Ketori nodded crisply. "Then this Council meeting is adjourned." He waved at the guard. "Take him away."

The other men exited, leaving Lancer alone with Ketori and Thena.

Ketori's face crumpled and he took his daughter in his arms. "Oh, my dear, I thought I had lost you too."

Thena looked as though she had been poleaxed.

Ketori hugged her tight and Lancer, seeing the suspicion of moisture gleaming in her father's eyes, began to feel a distinct sense of déjà vu.

"I thought you didn't care," Thena whispered.

Ketori smoothed her hair and smiled down at her. "You're my daughter. I've always cared. It's just that, after Rheta . . . after your mother . . ." He swallowed. "Well, I just didn't dare get too close to anyone. Why did you leave without telling me?"

Thena glanced at Lancer and he smiled encouragingly at her. It was finally time for her to admit her secret. She needed to get this out in the open and there was no better time than now.

Thena pushed away from Ketori and looked him in the eye. "I had to leave because I found out about Nevan's plan to discredit me."

"Discredit you? How?"

"He was falsifying my prophecies. I found out because I . . . I remember them, too, just like Mother."

Ketori's eyes widened. "You do? Finally! I thought I'd failed."

Thena looked as puzzled as Lancer felt. "What do you mean?"

"What do you think I've been searching for over the past thirty years?"

"You've been studying genetics, but how—"

"You know I've been trying to find the optimum combination of genes a pythia must possess?"

Thena nodded, and he continued. "Well, I hoped I'd found it in you. I pursued Rheta as a life-mate because my calculations showed the stability of my line crossed with the power and strength of hers should produce a pythia who was strong and would never succumb to the insanity. It was just luck that we also fell in love. When you never showed any sign of remembering your prophecies I thought I'd failed. I've been looking for another such pairing ever since." He captured her head in his hands. "You've shown no sign of the madness?"

Thena shook her head and grinned at him. "No, and now I never will. I went to Earth to bring back one of their psychiatrists—a healer of the mind. The oracle says Juelle can help us prevent the madness, and maybe even cure Mother."

Ketori's face lit with a joy that was painful to see. "Where is this healer? I must see her!"

Lancer swore. "I forgot—I promised Juelle I'd send someone after her. She's stuck in an abandoned cavern guarding those two goons. You'll need some more men to take care of them." Quickly, Lancer gave Ketori his wristcom, with instructions on how to find her. "And be sure to tell her I sent you, or you're liable to end up stunned too."

Ketori nodded and clasped Lancer's hand. "I will. And you—I'm entrusting my daughter to you. I hope you're worthy."

"I'll certainly try to be," Lancer promised solemnly.

Ketori nodded and left to find Juelle. Seri, obviously recovered from her ordeal at Nevan's hand, scampered out after Ketori. Lancer turned to face Thena.

Alone at last.

389

He grinned and took a step toward her, but she backed away, holding out a hand to ward him off. "Did you mean it?"

"Mean what?" He continued to advance until she backed into a tapestried wall and could go no farther.

She gave him a wary glance. "Did you mean it when you said you'd be my life-mate . . . and Council Captain?"

Her uncertainty cut like a knife in his gut. He reached out and cupped her poor bruised cheek in his hand. "Yes, *shiya*," he said softly. "I meant every word."

He longed to claim her lips with his, but first he had to chase away the doubt in her eyes. He stroked her cheek with his thumb. "Remember what your prophecy said? 'To win love and happiness, Gaea's son must overcome the bonds of the past.'"

At Thena's nod, Lancer continued. "Maeve helped me see that I've been responsible for people all along—the past no longer bothers me. And your other prophecy: 'Apollo's daughter shall fulfill a new cycle of destiny with Gaea's son.' How can I fight destiny? Being Council Captain alongside you will be a pleasure and an honor."

"But what about your work? How can you give that up?"

He shrugged. "It no longer interests me, except for telling Delphi's story—the real story, heroic Captain Spencer and all. If I really feel the urge, I'll just build a studio at Dodona. Besides, I've got my work cut out for me here. Together, we'll convince the

Council to let Juelle cure your mother, and to install recording devices in all of the pythia chambers, so no one else will be able to falsify prophecies the way Nevan did."

"It sounds wonderful. But your family—what will they think?"

"I already told them I wasn't going to live my life without you. They're thrilled at having you in the family."

The guarded look faded from her eyes. "But what—"

Lancer silenced her with his finger on her lips. "Shh, it's not important. Nothing is important except that I love you."

Her eyes and lips widened into a gorgeous, heart-stopping smile. "You do?" she asked, wonder replacing the doubt in her eyes.

"Yes, *shiya*, I do. And you?"

She flung her arms around him. "Oh, Lancer, I've loved you for ages!"

That was all he wanted to hear. He pressed her delectable body against his and brought his lips to hers in a soul-searing kiss that spoke eloquently of promise and commitment.

Thena broke the contact with a sigh and laid her head against his shoulder. "Feel that?" she asked.

"What?" he murmured against her hair.

"Our bond."

He felt a slight tugging at the periphery of his awareness. "Yes, I feel it. It's how I found you."

"You can never lie about your emotions across the bond, you know."

Pam McCutcheon

"Oh?" He kissed the sensitive spot on her neck.

A surge of desire flowed across the bond from Thena—straight to his libido. She grinned. "Did you feel that too?"

He pressed her harder against his arousal. "Yes, you little witch, I did."

She giggled, then turned serious. "I'm sorry I didn't acknowledge you as my life-mate when Father asked. Nevan held Juelle captive, and I didn't know you'd already freed her. Can you forgive me?"

A wave of love and pride passed over Lancer. This woman was a treasure. He'd treated her badly, and yet she begged *his* forgiveness. He opened his mouth to tell her so, but changed his mind. Better yet, he'd show her. He sent his emotions winging along their bond.

Thena's eyes widened. "You *do* love me," she whispered.

"Yes," he said. "Forever. Now, come here, life-mate. We've got some catching up to do."

He leaned down to claim her lips in a kiss, and felt a sudden sharp jolt of satisfaction, as if from a distance.

Thena froze and turned pensive.

"What was that?" he asked.

Her face relaxed. "That was Seri."

"And?"

Thena's eyes widened and she giggled. "She bit Nevan."

Futuristic Romance
Nancy Cane

"Nancy Cane sparks your imagination and melts your heart!"
—**Marilyn Campbell, author of *Stardust Dreams***

Circle Of Light. When a daring stranger whisks attorney Sarina Bretton to worlds—and desires—she's never imagined possible, she is tempted to boldly explore new realms with Teir Reylock. Besieged by enemies, and bedeviled by her love for Teir, Sarina vows that before a vapor cannon puts her asunder she will surrender to the seasoned warrior and his promise of throbbing ecstasy.

__51949-6 $4.99 US/$5.99 CAN

Moonlight Rhapsody. Like the sirens of old, Ilyssa can cast a spell with her voice, but she will lose the powers forever if she succumbs to a lover's touch. Forced to use her gift for merciless enemies, she will do anything to be free. Yet does she dare trust Lord Rolf Cam'brii to help her when his mere presence arouses her beyond reason and threatens to leave her defenseless?

__51987-9 $4.99 US/$5.99 CAN

TIMESWEPT ROMANCE
TIME REMEMBERED
Elizabeth Crane
Bestselling Author of *Reflections in Time*

A voodoo doll and an ancient spell whisk thoroughly modern Jody Farnell from a decaying antebellum mansion to the Old South and a true Southern gentleman who shows her the magic of love.

_0-505-51904-6 $4.99 US/$5.99 CAN

FUTURISTIC ROMANCE
A DISTANT STAR
Anne Avery

Jerrel is enchanted by the courageous messenger who saves his life. But he cannot permit anyone to turn him from the mission that has brought him to the distant world—not even the proud and passionate woman who offers him a love capable of bridging the stars.

_0-505-51905-4 $4.99 US/$5.99 CAN

TIMESWEPT ROMANCE
A TIME TO LOVE AGAIN
Flora Speer
Bestselling Author of *Viking Passion*

While updating her computer files, India Baldwin accidentally backdates herself to the time of Charlemagne—and into the arms of a rugged warrior. Although there is no way a modern-day career woman can adjust to life in the barbaric eighth century, a passionate night of Theuderic's masterful caresses leaves India wondering if she'll ever want to return to the twentieth century.

_0-505-51900-3 $4.99 US/$5.99 CAN

FUTURISTIC ROMANCE
HEART OF THE WOLF
Saranne Dawson
Bestselling Author of *The Enchanted Land*

Long has Jocelyn heard of Daken's people and their magical power to assume the shape of wolves. If the legends prove true, the Kassid will be all the help the young princess needs to preserve her empire—unless Daken has designs on her kingdom as well as her love.

_0-505-51901-1 $4.99 US/$5.99 CAN